HARBOUR VIEWS

Philip Chatting

Book Guild Publishing
Sussex, England

First published in Great Britain in 2014 by
The Book Guild Ltd
The Werks
45 Church Road
Hove, BN3 2BE

Typesetting in Sabon by
Nat-Type, Cheshire

Printed in Great Britain by
CPI Group (UK) Ltd, Croydon, CR0 4YY

A catalogue record for this book is available from
The British Library.

ISBN 978 1 909716 25 4

To Hong Kong, thou art the dragon of Cities all.

1

Dear Colleagues,
I write to you today with a heart made heavy by the death of our beloved Chairman, Mr Jakob B. Odergaard.

Mr Odergaard, or JBO as he was called by those of us who had been with the company since its early days, died at home last night of an unexpected heart attack. The tragic loss of our founder leaves us devastated and our thoughts and condolences go out to his loved ones and to his wife and daughter, who, alas, were not able to be with him at the very end.

The organisation we serve became a market leader in the production and distribution of cost-effective modular furniture largely as a result of JBO's inspiration and none will underestimate the power of his vision or our determination to follow in his footsteps.

His strengths, free of all controversy, will be the cornerstone of Odergaard Holdings' continued growth. Where mistakes and poor judgements have been made, I assure you, they will be amended.

Throughout the years your hard work and loyalty have been exemplary, and each of you can rest assured I will give you a company where such qualities always have their place. In support of that goal we will, over the course of the next week, hold a series of get-togethers to meet and express our allegiance to the future and JBO's succession. Declarations for those who wish can be placed on personal records.

Our tireless leader's example in and outside work, even on the day of his untimely demise, leaves us humbled, but, while recognising the baton has fallen from his grasp, you can be certain of its continued safety.

I count on each of you as you must count on me.

Yours very sincerely,

Claude C. Halt

Chief Financial Officer and Board Member

Odergaard Holdings Limited

2

When Jakob Odergaard arrived in Hong Kong almost thirty years ago, he came with two closely related ambitions; first, he would become inordinately rich and then, with more money at his command than anyone could reasonably spend, he would live as he chose and without worrying how much offence that caused. Wealth was to be his first-class ticket and unrestrained freedom his destination.

Because Hong Kong gave scant attention to activities other than making money and none at all to the means by which it was made, there was no better city in which to pursue a financial dream. Local convention, so strict at one level and so slack at another, had the capacity to face in two directions by encouraging the struggle for legitimate prosperity on one side and in permitting the production of unimaginable quantities of dirty laundry – which by unspoken agreement was devoid of visible stain – on the other. With interests thus well established, newcomers like Jakob Odergaard were left to splash and dabble in whatever mucky waters they found congenial. While ambitious men laboured and private laxities were ignored, the unscrupulous of all complexions plotted course unhindered and he created Odergaard Holdings; 'Holdings' not because the corporation owned any others, but because he, in pre-public days at least, held the lot.

JBO's sudden death at only fifty-eight caught everyone off-guard. The hole he left at Odergaard's could not be plugged by an itinerant executive of comparable stripe, because there simply wasn't such a person. The founder had been the company, the beating heart, without whom most, although not quite all, were unable to imagine the existence of Odergaard Holdings or anything else bearing his indispensable and reassuring name.

For many old hands, with personal well-being so closely mirroring that of the company to which they had given long years of service and in whose ordinary stock entrusted much of their modest fortunes, the realisation that a beacon had gone out was overwhelming. Only a catastrophic collapse of the share price, or a competitor's takeover and summary dismissal to make way for another owner's trusted nominee, could have affected them more profoundly.

But alone among the timeservers the thin and evasive Claude Halt held his nerve and sought to steady the undirected ship, which, until that very day, had been so reassuringly navigated by a sea-wise captain.

While all but one in the executive suite reeled in confusion, less exalted parts of the organisation tittle-tattled. Along the corridors, in stairwells and around congested cubicles, gossipy employees huddled to dissect the blunt but ambiguous news before moving away to empty burgeoning in-trays.

In the shipping department, where casual drivers and temporary clerks with scant emotional attachment elbowed between stacked cartons of modular furniture and piles of pre-printed stationery, the conversation had, for the Odergaard faithful, a puzzling tone.

'What I'd like to know is 'oo is taking over now he's gawn and 'ow can you die of anything while sitting in an armchair watchin' telly?' Anil Patel asked without expectation of an answer.

'No any rudeness, please,' protested Johnny Lau, the transport supervisor, who, like Claude Halt, was a company servant tested by the storms of twenty-eight years in the long private and short public forms of Odergaard Holdings.

So integral to the enterprise's workings had he been in the early days that office myths surrounding corporate life recounted how, 'In the beginning, there was JBO, Johnny Lau and Claude Halt; JBO did the thinking, Johnny made the goods move and Claude banked the cash.' If any of them, or at any rate someone like them, had not been on board at the time, the business would never have prospered.

The doggedness and mechanical predictability shown by Johnny and his sort were exactly the qualities the founder favoured in his hirelings. But, if that was true, why had he put up with a different set of standards from his accountant, who was just a little bit too sharp to find permanent contentment in creatively juggling the books and avoiding tax?

'Everyone knows there's a lot more goin' on than what's seen on the company website. I mean, just ask yourself,' Anil went on. 'Did I tell you the story when ...?'

'Enough; do not disrespect. We are all looked after.'

'Only speaking as I feel and in case you hadn't noticed, in some places family and loved ones are often the same thing.'

'Must keep to yourself unpleasant thinking.'

For a man of Johnny's persuasion, where clues to one's thoughts were deemed a weakness, he was getting unusually demonstrative.

'Suit yourself; ain't no skin off of my nose.'

Being of limited sophistication Anil treated the exchange with Johnny Lau and every other conversation in exactly the same way. He made no distinction over others' sensibilities and gave no allowance for preferences not his own. If he had fallen into unlikely dialogue with a nun, he would have regaled her in exactly the same coarse banter learned on the streets and around the billiard tables of his late school years and nowadays heaped chummily on an earthy drinking fraternity.

Despite, or because of, his name's implications, Anil was a London youth more familiar with the public houses and kebab shops of South Wimbledon than with the gleaming towers of a newly prosperous East Asia. On liberation from the straitjacket of compulsory education and responding to the prods of an undefined whim, he packed a rucksack and, in opposition to more industrious parents, set off on an unplanned exploration and through the many casual jobs required to support an ill-defined adventure. On his mother's parting suggestion that he 'settle down' and look for 'steady work', he shrugged his shoulders and chewed the end of a ball-point pen before writing, in a ringed note-pad borrowed from his father's sub-post office and general provisions shop, the names of several cities suggested by his younger sister.

Only the possibility of Hong Kong claimed Anil's grasshopper wits for more than a few months, a fact the caustic sibling put down to his recollection of seeing the name on the underside of cheap porcelain sold in the family retail outlet off Wimbledon's high street. While her remark may have been an exaggeration, Anil would certainly have been hard pressed to say whether Hong Kong was a town or a country. To him, the precise status, or indeed geographical location, of any place on earth were matters of staggering irrelevance.

But once unpacked and familiar with his new surroundings, he began to feel at home and settled at a natural level, like undissolved impurities hanging near the bottom of a water glass, where the pointless enquiry of 'Why this town?' never arose.

The loading bays at Odergaard's warehouse and the bars along what had once been the Wanchai waterfront were not so different from the places of occasional employment and more frequent amusement he once frequented in the undefined but easily recognisable space between London's inner city and outer suburbs.

But on the day of Jakob Odergaard's death Anil's off-the-cuff comments touched a subject none in the organisation's higher ranks ever saw fit to mention. Among this supposedly staunch band there was a consensus such delicate personal issues did not exist, or, if they did, they were matters of purely private election. In other parts of the company and city, however, where reputations counted for nothing, Anil's views were shared in the loudest of bar-room conversations.

'Mine's a lager, what'll you 'ave then?' enquired Isidor Nash when he and the junior messenger met later at The Cat's Meow club on Lockhart Road.

'That's not much of a sun downer; think I'll do a 7 and 7. Get myself in the right mood for tonight. Hey! Stevie,' he called across the bar to another member of the international diaspora, 'can we get some service over here then, eh?'

'Why, what's happ'nin'?' asked Isidor.

'Well, weekend started just 'bout an hour ago. Thought I'd do a couple of bevies in here, get a shampoo and a shave and then try my luck at the Inn on the Park; lots of unattached tourist ladies over there looking for excitement before they go home. Don't want them disappointed now, do we?'

'Is that what you learned from old Jakob B and his cheesy mates then?'

'Nah! Worked that one out for myself, didn't I? Those blokes don't fish in my sort of pond; they prefer higher-class tarts.'

'How would you know? Aih! This beer don't have no bubbles. There mixin' in the slops again.'

'Look, trust me on this one, 'cos I know,' Anil replied with a confidential and educated nod.

Untenured employees with nothing in their minds but the snail-like approach of day's end were never lulled by official Jakob B. Odergaard pronouncements for the simple reason that carefully spun marketing statements recounting high achievement hardly penetrated to the deepest parts of the organisation and, besides, drivers and messengers, whose business was to connect communicators, had other, some would say more reliable, sources of information. During meandering journeys through city streets and up and down company floors they enjoyed a migrating bird's licence of flexible routing to predetermined destinations.

Anil's principal contact at Odergaard's, other than Johnny

Lau, was the office administrator, Carol Tung. In Mrs Tung, life's unremarkable and frequent disappointments had contorted into unforgiving peevishness. Her once uncomplicated but humourless personality had over the passage of time soured into the bitterest of dispositions.

On the transport floor, where she was occasionally obliged to seek out the busy supervisor, her passage provoked sniggers from the partially dressed and extensively tattooed loaders. These visits were an abomination for her, because, under the hum of packing machinery, she was sure she detected the repetition of an old story relating how her long-suffering husband had abbreviated his time with her in a capitalised, but perfunctory, text message.

None but she knew the real truth of the episode, but there was no doubt that when her feelings were touched the hurt erupted symptomatically, like blisters on a diseased body, in her application of ever sterner discipline on junior workers and in compressed lips resembling the shape and size of a large coat button.

But, in spite of Mrs Tung's many dyspeptic interventions to turn the sow's ear of idle youth into the silk purse of hard-working and efficient staff, Anil's work was not entirely objectionable and, as his income exceeded his costs, he was content to just amble along without strain, imagination or desiring anything better. In contrast to the office administrator, continuous labour was conceptually alien to his view of how life should be enjoyed and sounded rather like one of those commitments in the same league as marriage. If he knew anything at all, it was that obligations of any serious duration were simply untenable. Eight hours of more or less honest daily work was the extent of what he would willingly surrender before fleeing to favoured haunts and the promise of yet more inconsequential and mindless revelry.

3

The balmy interval separating winter's gloom from summer's humidity arrived late and brought only the shortest of respites to harsh weather. The disappearance of quilted coats and wet noses from the streets should, after long cold months, have warmed the city's heart, but, perversely, contentment among the multitude remained mired in daily occupation.

At Odergaard's, where – to return to a point earlier in our tale – JBO's iron hand still gripped the tiller, his devotees, secure in their voyage, went rodent-like about their master's business. In spite of the sun, a sense of inevitability pervaded the air and even people like Anil, who hadn't a trace of amniotic empathy in his constitution for the officer on the bridge, felt its constant presence.

'Time to switch modes,' he declared cheerfully as he lined up at the automatic clock to punch out his Friday exit.

'Hey! Wanted … by upstairs,' Johnny Lau called out from somewhere in the darkening warehouse.

'Who … you mean me … now?' Anil's jaw dropped. 'But I'm off already.'

'Suggest to think again.'

In the administrator's office, to where Anil had been peremptorily summoned and, after his arrival, given scant attention, Mrs Tung's busy fingers struggled to complete half a dozen consuming but unimportant tasks. A pile of papers was crossly sorted, stapled and stacked into neat, matching bundles, while she contrived ignorance of the messenger's presence. Dismayed by the late call and annoyed by the administrator's shallow activity, Anil fiddled with the ordered heaps covering her desk and took up a round object with the words 'Fully Furnished by Odergaard Holdings' cut deeply into its sides.

'Don't touch,' Carol Tung scolded, snatching back the company give-away on whose inanimate behalf she had been compelled to intercede.

'So, what's it for then, aih?' Anil enquired.

'To hold down paper and if don't mind ...'

Her admonition was interrupted by a telephone ring.

'Bit old fashioned, 'en it? I thought everything was on computers these days, although your desk ain't movin' with the times, you know. I had a mate once who took his pending file home once a month and burned ...'

Carol Tung banged the paperweight down and, with the telephone pressed tightly to her ear, spoke with the rhythm of an agitated pigeon pecking seeds.

'Yes, Mrs Chou ... messenger found ... arrangements in hand ... any particular time ... for delivery?'

The question was followed by a lengthy silence, before other words took off.

'Of course ... making sure ... straight away.' Each phrase, offered in appreciation of evident urgency, floated in the air as if through no fault of its own it had become orphaned from the rest of Mrs Tung's scattered utterances.

Free of her telephone she resumed rummaging across the invisible surface of her desk. From the centre of what Anil viewed as a fire hazard he extracted a photograph suggesting that, contrary to warehouse rumours, some form of life awaited the office administrator outside.

'What's this?' he enquired, holding up the head-and-forelegs picture of a dog with long stiff whiskers.

'Put back,' she demanded.

'Looks like a rat; one of them lapdogs, is he then, aih?'

'He's a schnauzer, if know what that means, and trained to bite.'

For an unrelievedly austere woman the resort to rough sarcasm demolished at a stroke the conceived view that she was a woman of only one dimension.

'Oh! La-di-da, we are prickly today,' Anil retorted as Mrs Tung continued her abortive search.

'Lookin' for these then, are you?' he asked and unhooked a keyring from the rim of a container holding several pens, letter openers and other miscellaneous and necessary office paraphernalia.

'What? ... Yes ... where find? ... Now ... take van and pick up floral display ordered by Mrs Chou from Baby Loon's Hanging Garden and deliver to Harbour Hotel, room 2018 before six.'

'Ah-ah! So the old man's got a promise for tonight again, 'as he?'

'Just do as told.'

'Aw right, keep your shirt on. Any name I'm supposed to be deliverin' to, or message you want sendin' round? Could make one up extempore if you like ... How about ... "Dear Doughnut ... looking forward to licking your glazed rings sometime soon" ... Aah, ha!'

'Uhh! You too repulsive. Why Mr Lau hire you, huh?'

''Cos I do a good job and they wanted someone to make that straight face of yours crack. Am I right, or am I right? But you ain't givin' me much time, you know.'

On the weak foundation of half a year in Hong Kong and a notionally international background Anil had built his world-view. Rudimentary education, social milieu and the endless stories heard of the similarities between his grandfather's Kampala barbershop and the Wimbledon sub-post office and general provisions store, which were said to conduct business along identical lines, left him ill equipped to pinpoint cultural distinctions. His younger and far brighter sister, who provided a geographical focus for his travels, constantly teased him by asking, with as much seriousness as she was able, where on the map Uganda and other countries remoter to the family heritage lay. He understood no more than that there was a loose connection between the sari his grandmother wore until her death and a place – or was it a concept? – called India. The one advantage his origins bestowed on him, in which he took great pride, was a dusky and handsome face with deep-brown eyes verging on black that pulled in more girls than the range of his conversation, or the generosity of his nature, deserved. In all other respects he was an uninformed working-class lad with no serious aspiration or application owning a tormenting sister who progressed to university and a promising medical career, while he hopped from job to job and place to place until eventually finding himself washed up, as it were, on the shores and into the bars and bordellos of Hong Kong's meaner districts.

But the administrator, the taut and precise Carol Tung, was an entirely different kettle of fish, who conducted, in a deliberate and irrational way, a personal mission against loose 'Western' ways, and Anil Patel, whatever his face might proclaim, was, in her opinion, as Western as a public drunk who lacked the slightest vestige of discipline or responsibility. The transport supervisor's decision to employ him in a temporary emergency that rapidly became permanent was for her a source of constant exasperation.

In light traffic Baby Loon's flower shop was hardly fifteen minutes from the Odergaard warehouse, but this afternoon, with eager crowds descending on Happy Valley's race course, the journey took triple that time. At the entrance to Hennessy Road three lanes of converging vehicles shoved into one and tides of pedestrians streamed across the road between a cluster of bus stops and the track's revolving turnstiles.

Regardless of priority, or laws of the road, a silver saloon and its female driver probed uninvited into the traffic from an unsignposted alleyway immediately in front of Anil's labouring delivery van.

In the Orient there are no rights-of-way, and among the

thrusting congestion of Hong Kong's byways the extraterrestrial notion was especially beside the point. Unoccupied square inches were not that way for long and, on a crowded speck of an island, were soon conceded to those who moved fastest.

'What's the old bat doin'?' Anil wondered out loud.

A noisy blast from a horn somewhere at his rear went unnoticed, but, feeling he had a part to play in clearing the way, Anil leant across the van's bench seat and wound down a kerbside window. In the hubbub of exhaust fumes and rushing feet he heard the noisy clatter of jack hammers excavating a distant strip of the jam-packed road.

'Gawd almighty! What a madhouse. Oi! You there; yeah you!' he called out. The woman swivelled away from his confrontational gaze and looked steadfastly in the direction of her intended travel.

With irritation overpowering customary insouciance Anil flung open the van's door and stepped into the street. The woman, fearing a disagreeable encounter, adjusted her spectacles with one hand and pulled upright on the saloon's steering wheel with the other to better assess her predicament and chances of escape. As if her nervous shuffling had released a blockage, vehicles around her began sliding slowly forward and the much relieved, but still deadpan, saloon driver glided away towards the banging cacophony further along the crowded thoroughfare. Behind Anil's van, the massed ranks of dammed-up vehicles so far denied access to the growing exodus exploded into choruses of honking impatience.

Extricated from the deafening roar, but with time running short, Anil skipped the customary banter with the girls at Baby Loon's, which, for a number of months, had been the springboard to several pleasant evenings with Anna Talaba and her friends. Later, after disposing of today's pressing priority, he would restore the relationship with a quick and cheerful phone call and still have stories to tell capable of bringing Isidor near to weeping enviously into the faded froth on his lager.

Outside the Harbour Hotel a parking attendant nodded. He had seen similar deliveries in the past by the Odergaard logo-splashed vehicle.

'Watch the van, will yer? Only be gone a few secs,' Anil called as he tugged his baseball cap low and hurried into the hotel lobby with the flower arrangement held stiffly in front.

Above the reception counter five clocks showed the time in cities spread across the globe. The middle one, with Hong Kong written underneath, read five fifty-five.

'Bloody hell; just in under the wire.'

The concierge had once seen the brash young driver escorting a Chinese girl and decided then that Anil was not someone he should be well disposed towards. There were boundaries after all and, while international residents were welcome to integrate as they wished, people other than bar girls whose business it was, should, he felt, be more discerning.

'Yes; what can do?' the concierge enquired.

'For room 2018; to be delivered right away.'

'Name of occupant?'

'I don't know for cryin' out loud! Look this isn't the first time. I'm from Odergaard's, you remember?'

'Please, we have security. Must check.'

'OK, OK, but make it snappy.'

While the official consulted his records, Anil paced anxiously to and fro and gawped about. He was not a greatly curious person and what the world got up to in its spare moments was none of his concern.

The hustle and bustle of the lobby was nothing compared to a few yarns and a laugh over a beer, or a couple of hours with a friendly girl, and the hotel's diverse patronage failed to stir his slightest imagination, although he did stop to wonder for an instant whether the doorman, dressed in green overcoat and similarly coloured felt top hat, felt in any way ridiculous.

Through massive glass doors, embellished with gold-coloured

fittings, he could see the lights and familiar streets of nearby Wanchai and wondered how close his mates would be to their favourite watering hole.

Several oversized automobiles drew in from the backdrop of tumbled buildings and adjoining garden to disgorge the city's rich and infamous and well-heeled visitors. Welcomers of various ranks effused and porters, unloading custom-made luggage, ushered guests toward the comfort and indulgence for which they were evidently paying a great deal. Anil looked around without excitement and from behind parting teeth and trembling lips he struggled to suppress a yawn.

A woman of about thirty, dressed in a fur-collared coat dotted with glittery pieces, like old-fashioned sequins, stepped through the outer doors to the accompaniment of much ceremonial bowing. She turned to neither right nor left and, enjoying some manifest but inexact entitlement, sailed purposefully past the reception desk towards a waiting lift. A trolley carrying four red, differently sized suitcases followed in her wake. Even a man as disinterested as Anil could scarcely miss ostentation when it paraded under his nose.

The red suitcases drew up temporarily beneath the centre clock, which now showed the time to be exactly six in the afternoon.

'Christ, that must be JBO's bit of stuff,' Anil said out loud. 'Aih! Have you got the name sorted yet?'

The concierge, who still had his head immersed in whatever he was examining, said nothing.

'Well, stuff you,' Anil remonstrated, before snatching up the floral display and running towards the elevators.

'Hey! Must not ...'

Whatever was forbidden was lost in the drone of a busy lobby and the urgency of a messenger in fear of discontinued employment.

Standing at the woman's left side and in the light halo of her scent he could not help but observe, 'Hmm! Not a bad looker really, but if old JBO can't get a floozy out of the top drawer, who can?'

On a single chime a door opened and Anil stepped forward behind the assiduously attended woman.

'Please take next lift,' breathed a hotel escort.

'But I've got an urgent delivery.'

'In case you missed my meaning ... I said next lift,' the burly figure repeated some three inches from Anil's slightly perspiring neck.

'Right, got it, mate.'

With understanding clarified, Odergaard's messenger stood back and watched the doors close. An overhead indicator recorded the lift's unstopping ascent through nineteen floors to a destination at the twentieth 'club' level signalled by a blinking pink light.

Anil pushed through the next open door and backed into a corner. The thought had not previously occurred to him, but he began to appreciate how far removed the haunts of the frivolously affluent were from those parts of the planet where he and other members of the partying poor spent their time. Money may have been in short supply at the lower end of the spectrum, but at least it was spent by blokes looking you in the eye. Here, in this pampered cabin, where air changed every thirty seconds, passengers gazed determinedly ahead and focused their slightly upturned faces on a middle distance untouched by humankind. He hadn't previously realised that highfalutin dislike for the throng extended to rejecting the tainted air it breathed.

'How about I fart a real whopper and get their attention? That should make their eyes water. Ha!' Anil's shoulders shook at his private joke.

At the twentieth floor the doors slid gently apart and he and another man stepped onto richly piled carpet and into the perfume of lilies radiating a welcome from an overflowing bowl. At both ends of the lift lobby room directions were displayed on glinting brass plates. Anil checked the numbers and turned right.

The man who had arrived at the same time was apparently familiar with the floor layout and walked purposefully ahead. From behind he looked tall and, for a man of his years, quite straight and slender. Thick, snow-white hair, curling over an open-necked collar in a slightly old-fashioned but still imposing way, added impressions of nature-given substance.

'I bet he doesn't buy his togs at Stitch-Up Tailors in Tshim Tsa Tsui.'

The elegant figure stopped at a door on the even-numbered side and raised his hand to knock. Following at some distance, Anil counted off the rooms until suddenly realising the visitor was standing outside room 2018.

'Fucking hell! It's him and he can't wait to get his leg over. She's only been in there a minute and he's ready to jump on her before she's got her coat off,' he thought and, quite forgetting his own predilections, added, 'What a scumbag!'

Gaunt white knuckles, with a hint of shadowy blue veins, tapped firmly beneath the embossed room number. A far-off female voice called gently, 'Who is it?'

'Jakob, darling.'

With head down, as if worried by a trailing shoelace, Anil walked straight past the visitor until coming to an abrupt halt at a fire door. Above him a green neon sign read 'Exit' and illustrated a stick figure making a hurried descent down a flight of stairs.

'P'raps I should be off as well.'

Escape, however, was easier to think about than accomplish, being caught, as he later described to Isidor Nash, between a chore and a randy old man.

Behind him a door clicked into place.

Was that the trill of giggles trembling along the passageway, or had the hitherto flawless lift developed a need for unscheduled lubrication?

The bars would already be open and his pals at The Cat's Meow well into the evening's first or even second round of drinks by now, while he was still stuck in indecision and nursing the consequences of his boss's love affair.

'What a stoopid situation! Should have left them at the desk and had them sent up. I'm goin' to look a right dick now.'

So what should he do? Dump the flowers in front of room 2018 and run off as fast as he could, or make up for the delay with a person-to-person delivery and hope not to be recognised by 'The Man'?

Both options held risks, but getting rid of the flowers and escaping the Harbour Hotel without prompting a serious disruption to his uncomplicated life was as much as Anil wanted. A messenger's job was not exactly exciting, but it did provide regular if small funding and that, he reminded himself, was not to be scoffed at. The sudden withdrawal of vital props would be just too annoying and bring with it the major distraction of looking for a new job when he should be concentrating on those matters most delighting him. A short delay in the instructed six o'clock delivery and a face-to-face presentation, he decided, was the least dangerous way out of what had turned into an annoyingly tricky assignment.

Anil breathed his chest back to the position from where it had recently subsided and retraced his steps back along the corridor. His tapering index figure, which would not have been out of place stroking a sitar's strings, hovered reluctantly at shoulder level.

Without entirely drowning out the indefinable fluttering emanating from the opposite side of the door, the near-summer air-conditioning's low hum should have soothed the corridor's length and breadth into a comfortable embrace, but instead it chilled Anil right down to his procrastinating marrow.

'Well, here goes,' he muttered and prodded the bell push. The mysterious interior noises stopped in the abruptly cascading notes. A shadow passed behind the viewing bull's-eye and the bedroom door jerked open with more than necessary force.

'What ... is it?' hissed Jakob B. Odergaard, his voice dropping away on the last syllables as if an outrageous assault was held in check only by utmost determination.

'That,' thought Anil, before he peered up from beneath a dense thatch of jet-black hair and the greasy peak of his favoured cap, 'sounded just like Mrs Tung in an off-mood; maybe a bit gruffer, but otherwise just the same.'

But the feared recognition did not occur and in its absence the beginnings of a smile tugged the corners of Anil's mouth. He should have realised JBO was no more familiar with the names and faces of employees in the deepest recesses of his organisation than those belonging to the Mongolian ladies lacrosse team. Obviously, there were parts of the universe not worth an important man's notice and management at that remote level of obscurity was best delegated to characters like Johnny Lau, Mrs Tung and others of their ilk.

For unclear reasons Carol Tung continued to intrude into Anil's thoughts and he wondered why she had been neither disturbed by Mrs Chou's request nor intrigued by the identity of the guest to whom flowers were being sent. Was her indifference forced to enable the blurring of the line between corporate and personal demands, or was her real opinion that a man as exalted as JBO lay beyond anyone's disapproval? Since the man was so powerful surely he was free to do as he wished and no one, especially timeserving wage-earners who owed him their loyalty, had a right to condemn?

'Just look at him,' Anil thought. 'His curls ain't half as tidy as when he went in and that knot in his tie looks like it's been strangled by someone swinging on it. Bet if I peek round the rear, his shirt-tail 'll be hanging out. Cor! What a prick.'

Being at ease was Anil's normal state, but tolerance had never got the Chairman anywhere and when the figure at the doorway offered no immediate response, JBO's combustible tendency, especially after the intrusive interruption to whatever had occupied him, became instantly magnified.

'Look, if you haven't got anything to say, I suggest you bugger off.'

'Oh! ... hum ... sorry ... delivery here for this room ... from Baby Loon.'

'Where? So seeing how late you are, I suppose you've walked all the way from Mesopotamia?' JBO snatched the arrangement from Anil.

'Huh! ... Pardon?'

'Don't hang around for a tip – you don't deserve one – and if you're not on your way right now I'll have you thrown out.'

The door banged into place.

'Some people,' Anil decided, 'really can't help being arseholes, and if poking them one on the snout wasn't an option the next best thing was to see the humour and get on with whatever made you feel OK.'

Imprecise images of a fearful row in early childhood swam to the surface of his idling mind.

There had been an altercation between his father and a male customer, yes, that was it. The man wore suede shoes and dragged behind him an old bulldog that lay spread-eagled and dribbling on the sub-post office's vinyl floor tiles. The customer's soft, brushed shoes had impressed Anil almost as much as the animal's contented lethargy and he began to realise satisfaction had origins quite unconnected with the sort of drudgery his father felt bound to deliver day after repetitive day.

The confrontation had not been an argument in a conventional sense, but more a one-way stream of invective heaped on the head of an unsympathetic listener. The cause had been an oversized package, which the customer insisted on mailing that very afternoon despite the lateness of the hour. The offending article had stuck in the sub-post office's window grill and, following a great deal of ineffective pulling and pushing, had degenerated from a firm box shape into a sponge-like sphere. Being of an impassive disposition, Anil's father absorbed the gratuitous protest without comment and his blank and unresponsive gaze inflamed the customer to fits of near apoplexy. At the time, Anil had been much impressed by his parent's utter disregard and imperturbability in the face of incoherent rage and downright manic behaviour.

Threads of hair in Anil's long black mane stirred in the slammed door's gust, and below them his shoulders rose and fell.

4

Never had Mrs Chou been so roundly criticised or so deeply humiliated. The smart was doubly painful because, in her opinion, it should have troubled an altogether different conscience. When Jakob Odergaard delivered instructions, whether to do with company business or not, she was at pains to act promptly. Anything else, she knew, was an unforgivable failure of duty to a superior. Other calls on her time, including the weasely and almost daily requests for information from that detestable Claude Halt, were put to the back of the queue, while she attended to matters of first importance. Today she could have protested innocence, but, given Mr Odergaard's habitual frame of mind, that would not have been an especially wise thing to do, because, of course, the speed and efficiency of her reaction was not the issue.

Retaining a well-paid job in what was, for all its public gloss, essentially one man's company was always a balancing act, and getting caught between Mr Odergaard's famously inconsiderate insistence on results and the shortcomings of people delegated to make them happen often left her exposed, like a hermit crab deprived of its shell. To explain everything reasonable had been done might, if pressed over-zealously, tip her off the delicate tightrope on which she continually swayed, into the free-for-all of an unpredictable employment market.

The real culprit was undoubtedly the office manager, about whom Mrs Chou always had the gravest misgivings. Not that Carol Tung was lazy, or slow, but she did have a habit of claiming credit when something went well and contriving disengagement when it went badly.

Mrs Chou wondered whether summoning the offender to pass on the recent rebuke was a justifiable next step. But, as face-to-face conflict was behaviour of last resort even while choked with injustice, she paused rather uselessly, to consider whether someone higher up could deliver a reprimand on her behalf. The realisation that she lacked sufficient influence to make that occur drove her customarily grey ears to near scarlet until, without actually making a decision, she snatched up the telephone to make Carol Tung pay for her ineptitude.

'Mrs Tung speaking.'

Without conscious preparation Mrs Chou had little to guide her apart from spitting rage and a towering feeling of unfairness.

'You were supposed to make the delivery to the Harbour Hotel before six o'clock. Can't you follow a simple instruction?'

'Mrs Chou? Are you querying pick-up from Baby Loon's?'

'Of course I am! It's the only job I've given you all week, or are you telling me there are other requests you've performed as badly?'

'Oh! ... But I'm sure if transport log is checked you'll find driver was dispatched immediately after your call. If you like, copies can be sent ...'

'I don't care about the log; I don't care about the driver. The fact is the flower arrangement didn't arrive until after the time I gave you for the guest's arrival. Do you understand what I'm saying?'

'Perhaps vehicle needed fuel. Can check if –'

For the second time Carol Tung was cut short in mid-sentence.

'It doesn't matter if the van was as dry as a parrot's throat,' snapped Mrs Chou, whose tertiary education had been obtained at the London School of Economics. 'Your job is to make prompt delivery; nothing less will do!'

'Messengers are supervised by transport department, but, as you mention they would be more accountable if –'

'Don't say any more; I can't stand it!'

Rather than being pacified by the chance to let off steam, Mrs Chou was on the verge of irreparable self-inflicted harm. If only the office manager would accept a portion of the blame, the defeat implicit in withdrawal would have been avoided and the modest satisfaction of partial victory claimed. But, as there was no solution to stupidity, the most that could be achieved was to leave Carol Tung something to think about during her long homeward commute.

'Mr Odergaard will hear of your incompetence tomorrow,' she fumed and banged down the receiver before anything further could be said.

Jakob Odergaard's self-awarded freedom to fulminate was coupled with an absolute disregard for who precisely bore the blame for anything, but, while indifference to exact culpability was unlimited, it did nothing to moderate his mood. He remained, in other words, hopping mad that a calculated manoeuvre had not gone according to plan and his raging annoyance compelled him to mug someone, anyone, everyone, to register in the loudest possible terms his considerable displeasure.

Like the Harbour Hotel room-service waiter who had received a tongue-lashing that very morning after conveying cold pancakes to room 2018, Mrs Chou had simply been in the wrong place at a fateful juncture. In these circumstances her verbal drubbing was entirely unexceptional. If Claude Halt had somehow popped up in the office entrance as JBO trooped in, he too might have had his ears assailed with the sort of abuse later piled on the founder's unfortunate assistant. Seniority at Odergaard Holdings gave no one a right to protection from the great helmsman's indiscriminate indignation.

In the grand scheme of Jakob Odergaard's philandering, the flower delivery's delay was one small event that might well, even after the knock-about in front of room 2018, have quickly passed into history and Anil's collection of personal anecdote. But, as it happened, JBO's initial irritation set the tone for the rest of his unusually unsatisfactory outing.

While not in his athletic prime or capable of a woodland buck rabbit's performance, Jakob Odergaard should still have had the wherewithal to make loose habits worthwhile. Alas, last night that had not been the case and at three o'clock in the morning he roused from patchy, middle-aged sleep to find his guest reading a book to take her mind off her disappointments.

Inevitably, his failure tumbled down through the office pecking order, first on to Mrs Chou's blameless shoulders and then, by proxy, over the twisting and ducking head of Carol Tung who, if she had wielded the power of retribution and dismissal over the lowest level of transport staff she craved, would almost certainly have meted out the punishment their many inadequacies rightfully deserved.

But as that ultimate sanction was not hers to inflict she could do no more than admonish the transport supervisor and nurse her grievance, just as Mrs Chou had intended, all the way back to the fortieth-floor apartment she occupied in the crowded dormitory suburbs surrounding Shatin. On the dismal journey home only the knowledge that the timely delivery of the flowers had been frustrated gave her perverse and mean-spirited nature the slightest secret contentment.

Although Carol Tung shared her residence with a sixteen-year-old son and an Indonesian domestic helper, she effectively lived alone. Her husband was a factory manager in a distant part of inland China who up to recently had come home infrequently to settle his bills and pore thoughtfully over bank statements that failed to excite him as much as his long exile warranted. In the years leading up to his now-total absence he had taken to dyeing his hair glossy black to retain the lustre that had once stirred even Carol Tung's deformed capacity for erotic love. For a while, after taking up the posting, he returned to the family apartment every weekend, but as time passed the intervals between visits got longer and longer until they stopped altogether and he and his wife were left sharing nothing other than ownership of a few stocks and shares and the obligation, which he carried in his heart and she on her back, to launch an apparently neglectful son into something approaching adulthood.

If the meagre financial support once provided by Cheung Man Kit to his wife and son had indicated anything, other than that the China appointment was not a great money-spinner, it was the possibility his income stretched over a wider domestic commitment than just the Shatin family. When the frequent home visits were no longer an expectation and lengthened without word, before stopping altogether, into two and three weeks and beyond, Carol Tung began to suspect all was not as it should be. On those increasingly rare occasions when Man Kit returned, and slept throughout the weekend, she searched his pockets for clues to infidelity. But, finding none, she eventually grew weary and lost interest in the principle of exclusivity or whether Man Kit came home or not.

The long dreary elevator ride up the exterior of the building rose through views of distant railway tracks and nearby laundry lines; so many laundry lines that washing clothes could have been a civic obsession. At the upper levels, openings appeared between the claustrophobically clustered towers to reveal glimpses of yet more high-rise blocks in further-off industrial Kowloon and, in these less grimy days, further away still in serried ranks on the other side of a faraway harbour.

Two lights showed in the Cheung apartment: one in the tiny kitchen, where the domestic helper, who spoke thousands of words of unpunctuated English at every opportunity, would be preparing the evening meal, and the second, which did not please Mrs Tung at all, as a flickering white light on the ceiling of the living area. Her son would be taking advantage of her late return and breaking the strict no-television-on-weekdays rule.

Before her key turned fully in the lock a pet schnauzer scraped and yelped at the door in a manner only a person who had nothing else to love would find pleasing.

'There, there,' she said soothingly, 'missed me, did you?'

before barking at the top of the juvenile head appearing above the back of a sofa, 'And what you doing?'

'Watching TV,' the head replied without turning, or giving away anything that was not already patently obvious.

'Turn it off this instant and show me your homework.'

'I haven't got any tonight and Budi says dinner's ready.'

'I've told you what happens when you are disobedient, haven't I? If nothing is set, you should practise violin. Go and get father's belt.'

'Again, Mama? Must we?'

His parent's implacable glare left no doubt and with the resignation born of long experience the boy dragged away to his mother's dingy bedroom.

'Hurry; not got all night.'

The trouble, in Carol Tung's opinion, was that the boy had an incorrigibly idle streak inherited from his father, which was not made any better by the domestic helper's failure to appreciate the first thing about regulation. And, besides, wasn't he old enough to know why hard work was necessary?

She shook off her outdoor shoes for the pet dog to worry and carry away to a secret location, where he nuzzled into his owner's familiar and unwholesome scents, and slid into a pair of cheap pink slippers bearing the imprint of ten crossed toes.

'Where are you?' she called out to her son.

The boy returned with a thick brown belt and an expression of total weariness.

'I wish Dad was here,' he said, blinking several times at his pitiless mother.

'Well, he's not and not likely to be, so let's get on, shall we?'

To the accompaniment of a tired sigh he tucked a frayed school shirt into his trousers and bent across the sofa's arm. His mother took off her glasses, folded the ear pieces flat, before placing them carefully on a bookshelf holding one much-thumbed paperback, unremarkably titled *Ten Paths to Prosperity*, and a plaster model of a flatulent but smiling

Chinese Buddha. She wound the belt round her hand and studied her son's unflinching bottom. A damp stain covered almost the entire left cheek.

'What's that?' she demanded, dabbing at the mark with her left hand and sniffing her fingers.

The liquid had a sweet smell, but not one she instantly recognised.

'Coke.'

'What do you mean "Coke"? Where come from?'

'I spilled some and it got on my seat.'

'Where? No such thing in house.'

From the muffled noise in the cushions the boy's clicked tongue sounded a bigger reproach than the one intended.

'I got it outside.'

'Don't play games with me now. Where have you been to, the arcade?'

Carol Tung beat her son at least twice a week. She believed her responsibility as a parent was to amend deviation whenever and wherever it occurred. On most occasions she delivered the chastisement without emotion, but tonight the baldness of his admission goaded her to a level of furious punishment exceeding her customary three or four lashes. At the fifth stripe the boy, assuming the ritual over, stood up shakily, but not at all crushed.

'Not yet!' Mrs Tung ground out the words through clenched teeth. 'Not finished with you by long way.'

Mystified by his mother's excesses, but determined to concede nothing, he subsided with superficial acquiescence across the sofa's arm and bit his lip.

Bang ... bang ... bang ... bang ... The din rattled overhead light fittings and brought the schnauzer yapping from its hiding place.

'Is that you, M'am,' a voice called from the kitchen.

Exhausted by her efforts and suddenly discomforted by a blister on her thumb, Mrs Tung reeled back from her labour.

'No dinner until you understand your mistakes,' she hurled at her son as he limped silently and painfully away to the bathroom.

If order was to be maintained in a turbulent world, there was no alternative but to administer the sternest correctives. Families needed strong parents and nations deserved unflinching governments. All of society cried out for direction. Young people, who did not understand the difference between right and wrong, or what was best for them, required a stern hand to save them from themselves. Man Kit may have reneged on his family contract, but his wife had no intention of repeating the failure by allowing their son to slide into delinquency's abyss.

With the belt still gripped tightly in her hand, Carol Tung stalked purposefully to the kitchen. The open room was so small there was no space for either a conventional oven or more than one normally sized person at a time. Conversations of any confidentiality were impossible and instructions had to be delivered from the living area. Not that the mistress of the house had any wish tonight to huddle in secret debate with her employee. No, indeed, her mood was so far gone she did not care who heard, or whether a few plates got broken.

'What happening to my son?'

If anyone knew the answer to that question, it was surely Mrs Tung, and to seek an answer from elsewhere appeared a deliberate obstinacy.

'Came home moments before and put his bag away ... Here I am preparing dinner and not watching out for him ... but I knew he was back ... because the dog rushed about all wild, not like when you come in when it patters around and whimpers so.'

Why Man Kit had insisted on Indonesian help was beyond comprehension. None of them spoke English without endless elaboration and, of course, Cantonese was non-existent. Half the time Mrs Tung wanted to put fingers in her ears and run from the blather that turned a simple statement into a folk story. And what did any of them know about good Chinese food?

They all had to be taught the most elementary steps as if they had been living in a forest all their years.

'Is this how you like it?' Budiwati enquired, thrusting a spluttering wok at Mrs Tung's face.

In rural Sumatra, where the cook had her upbringing, placid water buffalo, with sentinel egrets perched upon their backs, were driven through the sloshy paddy fields and wallows by children of five or six with cries of 'hut, hut' and strokes from thin bamboo canes across their massive rumps. But inside each docile browser lurked a fearsome temper capable of uprooting fences and scattering dogs, chickens and farm hands from the paths of wildly flailing hooves.

Budiwati had seen as much when village waifs dressed in T-shirts and nothing besides endlessly teased her father's animal by throwing smooth round pebbles picked up from the nearby streams. Heavy breathing and widening nostrils should have warned the boys to stop, but the suddenly plunging beast chased them in as many directions as there were homes to fly to.

If her starting eye was any indicator, a water buffalo lurked in Mrs Tung's unknowable interior. The wok was hastily withdrawn and, while hoping for the best yet fearing the worst, Budiwati smiled her South Sea smile and flashed two rows of gleaming white teeth.

Bucolic charm, however, failed to loosen her employer's tight grip on the sturdy belt, or allow the resuscitation of stillborn generosity.

'Detest your cooking and hate your silliness,' she stormed and raised a shaking arm over her head.

Budiwati, who had experienced her employer's outbursts many times before, dropped the almost-ready dinner onto the gas ring with a clang and ducked beneath the flurry of blows raining down on her bare head and shoulders.

'Teach you ... to behave ... in my house ... how to look after ... my son and ...'

Each strained phrase was followed by a strike and in the heat of the ensuing mêlée the wok tipped over and toppled sizzling bok choy and chopped pork onto the cold kitchen tiles. Finding an unanticipated opening in the confusion, the pet schnauzer threaded between struggling legs and set about completing the demolition of its owner's late evening meal.

With the kitchen entrance blocked by Mrs Tung's body and no other escape available, the unfortunate Budiwati took her beating with a few gasps and the resignation only the humble and dependent can muster. Her employer – knowing possessions, including a much-prized sewing machine, had been sold and debts incurred with a 'handling' agent for the privilege of working in Hong Kong – had the girl under her coldest thumb. Power conferred by another's frailty was an aphrodisiac too seductive to resist.

'Speak to you ... in the morning ... go to room.'

Mrs Tung had quite forgotten there was no room of any real description to go to and that at night, after the rest of the household had gone to sleep and work was finished, Budiwati rolled out a compressed foam mattress in the narrow space between sink and gas-ring stand to snatch at the few fragments of peace and rest allowed her.

But the domestic helper, accustomed to the manifestations of seething passion and knowing her presence was more likely to fan flames of immoderation than calm them, retreated to a small toilet behind the kitchen and squatted on the lid where she was in the habit of performing her morning ablutions, writing letters to her family and worshipping her gods.

Satisfied that the smooth running of her household had been re-established and, in spite of nagging hunger, only temporarily assuaged by a dry cracker and cup of bitter green tea, Mrs Tung prepared to take the relaxation she believed the rigours of a more than usually arduous day had earned.

Behind her the dog snuffled at her heels; it had missed the daily dinner ritual of curling up on a ready, if not warm, lap and accepting the choicest pieces from dishes overhead.

Tonight, in the absence of her regular meal, Mrs Tung went straight to the cramped bathroom and began putting up her hair and flooding the small porcelain bath. She discarded her clothes one by one onto a soiled towel mat, in spite of the proximity of a wicker laundry basket, and the schnauzer, circling the sweat-stained garments, inserted his eager nose and snorted in relish. The one reusable article, a crumpled skirt, was thrown across a disconnected heating rail weeping condensation.

She liked her bath water hot and deep and thick with soft suds rising to her chin, even if the tub's restricted space forced her to lie with shins pressed hard against the green-corroded taps, and tonight enjoyed whisking at the water with the one hand not still clinging to her disappeared husband's thick leather belt.

Outside the bathroom the house was in darkness. Her son had gone to bed and Budiwati was doing whatever chastised servants do when left alone. Wreaths of steam sucked past her as she climbed from the bath and pulled back the door, first an inch and then far enough to slip sideways into the living room. The schnauzer watched his mistress from under twitching, bristly eyebrows and snuffled down deeper into damp, seedy warmth.

By the time Mrs Tung returned and pressed the lock back into place the suds had settled lower and steaming patches of water threw back the glow of an overhead strip light. She stepped over her supine pet and leaned forward to prop a photograph between the spotted taps and moist wall. The unframed picture was damaged around the edges as if frequent handling had caused it undue wear and tear.

With a tiny sigh stretching her pursed lips Mrs Tung slid gratefully back into the hot water. Her ecstatic descent delayed for the briefest of seconds as the torn blister on her thumb came into sharp, stinging contact with soapy water. But, once past the minor shock, she immersed her whole body, with the exception of a gently perspiring head and suddenly chilling knees, in eddying caresses. Abandoning herself to luxury she looked up into the direct gaze of a young Jakob B. Odergaard staring back at her from his frozen pose by the damaged copper taps.

The photograph had been taken years ago when the company had a mere ten employees and operated out of a backstreet basement in Sheung Wan. That was a time so far removed no one now remembered it with any accuracy, or could pull back the obscuring veil of nostalgia hiding both ordinary and ugly events. Even the founder's naked greed and licence could not be separated today from the single-minded determination that passed unquestioned all those years ago. His virtues, if there had been any, were left in the dust of ambition and a lavishly accelerating limousine. But still Mrs Tung recalled her first days at Odergaard's as if they contained the touch of a sun god.

She didn't know who took the picture, but did remember the occasion. There had been a celebration, although its purpose, too, had faded from recollection. A hired junk had taken the entire ten staff to an outlying island. They anchored near a sandy beach and, between diving from the boat's roof, ate and drank the whole day through. For those accustomed only to the society of their inner circle, the outing was a revelation. Unfamiliar freedom and spontaneity left them all a little drunk, even before touching the liberal quantities of New World wine.

JBO had noticed her. As she turned on her back to swim to the shore he was leaning on the rail, smiling and waving to her. Odergaard's was her first job and after that dazzling day she never thought of going anywhere else. But, while he flirted with every young woman who crossed his path and as quickly forgot them, she lost her heart and never got over the pain.

Unlike those paid to provide the service, company messengers could spot a motive with lightning speed and their crude assessment and thoughtless happy-hour hilarity was rarely wide of the mark. Without knowing its name they had read the torture that turned the office administrator's blood to bile.

In Mrs Tung's bath-time imagination Jakob Odergaard was

noticing her again. But, tonight, instead of the slight protection of a gaily coloured and clinging swimsuit, she wore nothing at all. Pulling on the sides of the cramped bath, she drew her torso above the water until his strong gaze seemed to stroke her most private parts. Even an unexercised body grown slack from motherhood and office work can feel a little firmer under a steady and intimate stare.

With closed eyes she sank back into the lather-covered warmth and reached down to her toes before slowly tracing her hands up over ankles and calves and then, going ever slower, along her inner thighs until, until … 'Aaah!' … she breathed into the shivering foam. Speeding up again, her outstretched fingertips circled over the loose abdomen once, twice, three times and then on across her suddenly stiffer breast to neck, chin and rosebud-tight mouth, stopping, and, descending, she retraced an identical route to the very tips of her trembling toes. Carol Tung's light hands repeated the entire journey, back and forth, again and again, until at the last, while still below her wrinkled stomach, they stopped, and her eyes opened wide and locked on to the gaze of Jacob Odergaard smiling back at her from his position against the wall. A thin sob, as if emitted by a nocturnal rodent caught in the smothering embrace of an owl, squeezed between her frigid lips. The sudden stifled shudder slapped minute wavelets against her newly flushed face.

Spent by the effort she lay back with hair falling from the temporary knot on top of her head. The suddenly anxious schnauzer sat up and lent its trembling snout and whiskers on the tub's rim. Mrs Tung fondled the animal's ears. This and that one other were her two best friends, who gave life meaning, and without whom she would be completely lost.

The door knob suddenly rattled and a warbling voice called.

'Are you all right, Ma'm? I thought I heard a scream.'

'Uhh! Not now, stupid girl. Thought I said go to bed?'

'You said,' Budiwati corrected, 'go to my room, but I don't have no room … not that it matters to me, Ma'm, because – did I tell you? – I was brought up with six brothers and four sisters and we all slept alongside each other and Mum and Dad and Granddad, too ... but the strangest thing was how the children kept coming when we were all so close together and no one heard a thing ... it still kept raining babies and besides ...'

'You did tell me, over and over ...' Mrs Tung yelled through the thickness of a jerry-built door, 'Don't need you; do you hear? Go to bed ... instantly.'

'Oh! ... Yes, OK then, M'am ... if you think ...'

'Yes, I do think. Go ... now.'

'And will it be congee for breakfast? I forgot to ask, but as it's Wednesday and all and ...'

'Yes, congee; enough, enough ... end all this.'

'Hey! I've just seen wet patches out here ... I'll just tidy them up and go.'

'Please ... please ... not another word.'

A duster whisked around the base of the bathroom door and footsteps slapped away towards the kitchen. Carol Tung reminded herself that the subject of bare feet in the house was another issue needing urgent attention. Hadn't she spoken about this several times already? But Budiwati evidently still thought herself to be a farmer's daughter in a rural village and not the employee of a middle-class family in a progressive country.

Quickly towelling herself down, Mrs Tung smoothed the creased skirt over an arm and left, undisturbed behind her, both the clothes on the floor and the water in the bath. There was, after all, no point in hiring expensive help and doing menial chores oneself.

In the quiet of her bedroom she placed the unframed photograph on the pillow next to her and, on a daring impulse to sleep naked, crept between the sheets. A faint odour of camphor rose from the grey bed linen and the wooden chest at the foot of her bed. With the evening's activities compressed into a small, hard knot in her consciousness she patted the covers beside her and the schnauzer sprang up and burrowed a hollow near the luke warmth of Mrs Tung's unexercised and unappealing body.

5

'You have a nine o'clock appointment with a representative from the Arts Association and a three o'clock with the bank's investment manager. Tomorrow, Saturday, there is dinner with your daughter, Sigrid, and her family. I have put the correspondence for this morning's meeting in the folder marked 'Arts' and for the afternoon meeting in the one marked ...'

'"Investments"?'

'... "Private investments" actually ... to distinguish it from corporate matters.'

By the side of JBO's rosewood desk Mrs Chou was all cold efficiency.

'What does the Arts Association want? Doesn't sound like something I'd find interesting.'

'It's in the material and ...'

'Did I ask where to look, or did I say what do they want?'

Mrs Chou's face was impassive, but she paused before completing her sentence.

'... to talk through a second round of sponsorship covering next year's events.'

'That's a financial matter. Why doesn't Claude deal with it?'

'The representative especially asked to meet you and ...'

'I don't care what the representative especially asked for; I have other things to do with my time.'

'Mr Halt, I understand, is not in his office today.'

'Well, damnit, schedule a meeting when he is ... And what might Claude be up to on a day as fine as this one?'

'I don't keep Mr Halt's diary, but there will be an explanation.'

'Of course there will and you know how to make a phone call, don't you? And while you are about it make arrangements for someone to pick up Mrs Odergaard on Saturday afternoon. My job doesn't include ferrying people about.'

'Yes, Sir; will that be all?

'Unless I need you, in which case you'll find out.'

If Mrs Chou had allowed her feelings full expression, she would have stamped from the room. But, as a subordinate, she knew claiming justice in an autocracy was foolish. Her task was to perform, not to feel or contest, and anything else was not just futile; it was wrong-headed. The least of JBO's employees knew of the parallel narratives in Odergaard's success story, including the one recounting how many careers had ended at the drop of an inconsiderate hat. She had no wish to become the latest chapter in an already lengthy saga.

On later enquiry with the woman who vacuumed carpets and dispensed green tea and unofficial news up and down the executive floor, Mrs Chou confirmed Claude Halt had taken an unannounced day off. But instead of interrupting the evidently very busy Mr Odergaard with the results of her investigation she committed details to an email message, even while sitting just a few feet and a cough away from his intimidating desk.

Arrangements for Mrs Odergaard's Saturday evening collection took her a little longer, while the merits of a direct request to Johnny Lau, the transport supervisor, were considered as an alternative to going through the tiresome and obscure practice – cemented in place by ancient office politics and never questioned since – of coordination though Carol Tung's department. Side-stepping the despicable office administrator would certainly have soothed personal resentment and might, more legitimately, have reduced the frequent errors plaguing simple operational activity. But perpetuating, or even heightening, recent discord was not, she decided, the best solution to her profound sense of annoyance.

The late-Saturday errand fell to Anil Patel and this second

unwelcome intrusion into his free time left him considerably put out.

'But that's the weekend and after Friday night the most important time I have,' he whined.

'So what want me to do?' the tetchy Mrs Tung asked with heavily disguised delight. 'Mrs Odergaard expects you at six thirty. After taking her and Mr Odergaard to destination, wait until wishing to return. And this time must not, I repeat, must not dawdle.'

'I didn't dawdle before; just did what I was told when I was told. Horse race meetings are not something I can change.'

For days the rebuke received from the hands, or more specifically, the tongue of the Chairman's apparatchik rankled in Carol Tung's distempered mind. But, while fretting over the unfairness, just as Mrs Chou had over the one inflicted on her, she too was persuaded a continued cat-fight, so close to Jakob Odergaard, would sooner or later reach his ears and undermine the reputation she incorrectly believed he had of her. Anything was better than that JBO should have doubts about either her competence or devotion.

In lieu of antagonising Mrs Chou further, she decided that penalising the messenger, whose slackness had caused the unfortunate dressing-down in the first place, would give her almost as much satisfaction and, coupled with shifting the blame, enable a renewed assault on the lamentable standards demonstrated by Odergaard's junior employees and young people in general.

Realising Anil's idle time was more important to him than the rewards of conscientious work, her glee over its summary forfeiture, in so far as she was capable of such a frivolous sensation, could not be restrained.

'Here, what needs to be done is done regardless of convenience. And, if not working, what instead? Get drunk, like all you people do on Saturday?'

The coat button over Mrs Tung's pointed chin took on a

distended shape, bringing her face close to the smile once experienced on the long-ago junk ride.

But for Anil, cheated out of half his weekend by Mr and Mrs Odergaard's inconsiderate needs, the imposition riled.

'Why,' he wondered, while already knowing the answer, 'were their stoopid jaunts any more important than mine?'

Waking at close to three o'clock on Saturday afternoon, after stretching the previous night as far as it would go into the following day, he was left with a troubling hangover and barely enough time to bathe, eat a bowl of cornflakes, collect the car from the warehouse and drive up the hill to Jardine's Lookout and the unhurrying Mrs Odergaard.

Arriving slightly earlier than his instructions strictly demanded, he parked some way from the daunting three-storey residence with two wheels on the quiet street's pavement and two in a spotlessly clean gutter. To placate his disappointment and fuddled wits, he wired music into his cranium from a shirt-pocket device and ran throbbing eyes over the hushed neighbourhood.

These snooty avenues, he thought, were too neat and very different from the parts of town he knew best, where narrow lanes and high-rise apartments housed indolent vagrants like himself, in the cheek-by-jowl company of three-generation families, who hadn't the least notion of what space was needed to swing a cat.

If Anil was attached to anything as impersonal as a location, he did enjoy the conflicting smells and noises of bustle and neglect a hundred feet below his sparsely furnished bed-sit, where all-night shops, often left in the care of the proprietor's youngest family member, stocked nails, dried fish, cellphones, drain plungers, bubble wrap, saucepans, deer antlers, guavas, condoms, screwdrivers and dried medicinal mushrooms.

Up here, far from congestion and clamour, the high walls and iron gates let in only the infrequent murmurings of a nearby limousine and, from the tangled hills, the intermittent calls of birds.

When the minute hand of the illuminated dashboard clock ticked on to six-thirty, Anil nudged forward into the already open entrance.

'They're expectin' me,' he observed.

A white-suited gatekeeper blocked the saloon's path. Were the gloves and stiff Chinese collar pressed tightly into the small, circular ears really necessary now that winter was done?

The guard took out a note-pad and circled authoritatively to examine and punctiliously record the registration number, which he already knew by heart, and other information necessary to his fastidious mind. Satisfied with his documentation he indicated a space and, with the hand not already occupied with his jotter, described elaborate circles as if to suggest the demands of parallel parking required more than the usual level of intelligence possessed by those employed to conduct such manoeuvres.

'Wait there,' he commanded.

When someone was in charge, supporting players like Anil were not required to think and no one, least of all the gatekeeper, expected to explain how long the wait could be. So, the messenger, knowing a summons would arrive in the fullness of time closed delicate eyes beneath the rim of his baseball cap and settled back into the base-enhanced thump of this week's bestselling music.

At seven o'clock, when late afternoon had already passed into night, he twisted sideways and looked across the empty forecourt.

'Gonna be late again; bet that'll mean more ear-bending from the old she-dragon. My life just ain't in my hands no more.'

Another hour dragged by before Dagmar Odergaard stepped unannounced into the yard. Two agitated attendants ran ahead and through the glare of arch lights cleared from her path whatever imaginary obstacles impeded her brisk steps.

'Ma'm,' a solicitous voice intoned, as its owner drew open the door behind Anil's head.

Struggling upright from a liverish doze tasting of Friday night's last round of drinks, the driver looked in his rear-view mirror. Mrs Odergaard was adjusting a cashmere shawl over her pale shoulders and looked up to meet his reflected stare.

'Turn off that noise,' she said abruptly.

He saw her lips move, but could not be sure what was said. Extracting an earpiece and flipping the cap up off his forehead, he asked,

'Sorry, what ...?'

'Your music, if that's what you call it, is enough to deafen a mule; turn it off.'

'Oh! Sure,' he replied, grappling with the gadget in his shirt.

For a steady driver the journey to the warehouse and its overhead office would take less than twenty minutes. Anil, acutely aware he was transporting eggshells, made no attempt to shave seconds from that estimate.

When the limousine reversed into an empty loading bay, Jakob Odergaard, having been alerted by Mrs Chou's pre-emptive scouting, emerged from a side door and strode grimly across the concrete deck.

'Will anyone care we are two hours late?' he enquired harshly.

'More importantly, will we care if they do?' Dagmar replied.

Nothing more followed. The conversation had run its course.

Not wishing to intrude, still less risk detection for a second time in almost as many days, Anil reached out and shoved down the rear-view mirror. The chests of his two passengers were just visible at either end of three feet of yawning space.

'Not,' he thought, 'what you'd call super friendly.'

He turned up his collar and screwed back into the bench seat. From this adjusted angle he could see two chins pointing firmly in opposite directions as if their owners were brooding on matters that had nothing to do with the misted harbour on one side or steep green hills on the other, or, for that matter, the family experience waiting at destination's end.

'Turn on some music, will you?' Jakob Odergaard called out.

'Oh ... but ... I thought ...?'

Startled by the contradictory request but still hoping to avoid conversation, Anil heaved out of the rich upholstery and, against his wish, encountered two steely blue eyes glaring back from the mirror. 'Oh, my Christ, he's going to spot me.'

'I suggest you pull yourself together, or we'll be in a ditch.'

'Right, yes ... OK.' Anil flustered and prodded hopefully at the sound system's remote control, while steering with a reasserted grip around the winding lanes. A pot-pourri of shrills, scratches and wails ended at what could have been a string backing from an old *Tom and Jerry* cartoon.

'That'll do,' he thought with some relief and turned the volume down to the merest whisper.

Behind him the Odergaards resumed their reveries, which, for all the desolation of the occasion and despite Bach's and Haydn's intervention, lay at opposite ends of a thousand miles of empty desert sand.

'Just keep my nose down and get this over with,' Anil mouthed at the tumble of hillside falling away into Central's skyscraper Legoland. 'Funny old place Hong Kong – sometimes cool and classy in a Johnny-come-lately sort of way and sometimes as rough as old boots.'

Far from the glinting towers, in the hutch-like tenements and furthermost reaches of Mong Kok and Quarry Bay, the coarser throngs rubbed shoulders with Anil's kind and speculated how 'Lookout' residents higher up the slopes lived their lives.

Further off still and away from hierarchies of wealth and possession, of haves and have-nots, lay Sai Kung, where Jakob and Dagmar Odergaard's daughter, Sigrid, lived with her husband, Eric. She, like other residents of the area, never looked for a place on the social ladder and drifted through the days with whatever came along and, lacking the urge to compete, fell into a half-world where long-term foreigners with no other place to go found their niche.

By any standard Sai Kung was a backwater to a city living on the rise and fall of stock indices and property values, where sandaled women and men in unbuttoned tunics and dark glasses lounged around roadside cafés and marine inlets. Some maps of Hong Kong omitted the peninsular altogether, as if the low-rise huddle and semi-rural community had no clear connection, either physical or philosophical, with the 'special administrative region's' impatient and acquisitive soul.

Neither Jakob nor Dagmar Odergaard enjoyed Sai Kung; it smacked too much of inconsequentiality and opting-out and lacked the essential financial truth on which was founded all they were.

Their daughter and her husband, Eric Manley, were, by the older Odergaards' standards, a disappointing couple. His age and earlier marriage had once been tedious. Real displeasure, however, was saved for his and Sigrid's purposelessness and incessant dabbling in whatever sparked their separate interests, later compounded by dotty notions of meat-free diets and irregular income that were somehow seen as wholesome and morally uplifting.

Where Sigrid's half-baked world-view, or enthusiasm for an older man already in possession of a grown son, had come from her parents could not for one minute imagine. Not that they seriously cared, although both agreed she was a source of eternal regret. Only the worn joke – that she had come into their lives accidentally after being abandoned on their doorstep by hippies influenced by a waning moon and cannabis – formed anything approaching a mutual expression of opinion.

Destructive humour and bad-tempered jousting kept the Odergaards in a kind of balance. Enmity that tore other marriages apart was the meat and drink of their association.

The vehicle drew up in a narrow lane more used to the rattles of infrequently oiled bicycles than sleek saloons. Without a word Dagmar stepped out and strode determinedly towards the untidy entrance of a squat house standing on the perimeter of human settlement with its back to the ragged hillside. Jakob held behind just long enough to give instructions for their later collection and journey home.

'Wait there. I don't want to search for you when we're done.'

'Yes, Sir, I'll be right over by ...'

'Stop wittering, for Christ's sake; just be where I want you.'

Broken flower pots of drooping poinsettias and the white, peeling door at the top of a short, uneven slope framed Dagmar's irritable and arm-folded figure.

'Wouldn't you think they'd leave the door open?'

'I don't spend energy thinking about such matters.'

'I suppose we have to press the button and speak into that thing.' Dagmar indicated a tarnished intercom with bird spottings on its upper rim.

'What are we doing here?'

'She's your daughter as much as mine.'

'I'd almost forgotten.'

The speaker crackled and an unknown female voice asked, 'Who is it?'

'Your guests,' Jakob replied, inclining stiffly towards the sound of the enquiry.

A lock sprang free with a loud snap and Dagmar pushed her way into the shadowy interior smelling of Indian incense and last week's cooking. A short, round South-East Asian woman with a very broad face hurried forward.

'They're on the roof. I'll show you up. This way please, Madam, Sir.'

The home help wiped her hands in the ballooning folds of her skirt and retreated to a spiral staircase running from the middle of the untidy living area to a circular patch of dim light in the ceiling overhead. Her heavy hips appeared far too wide to squeeze between the narrow flight's handrail and central column, but, having passed that way many times before, they adjusted and in a practised, sideways slant jumped rhythmically up through ten vertical feet. Dagmar, exuding inconvenience, followed with Jakob's sharp, pencil-erect figure close behind.

On the rooftop and beyond a clutter of plastic furniture and gardening paraphernalia a scattering of people holding drinks hung about in desultory conversation.

'M'am?' the domestic called across the disorder.

A woman in her mid-thirties with bare feet and a long, loose sarong detached herself from an elderly couple.

'Well, this is a fine time to turn up. We'd almost given up on you.'

'Don't be tart, dear,' her mother replied. 'We've been busy; you know how it is.'

'I haven't the foggiest. But, as they've asked to meet you, you should come and talk to Eric's parents before they die of hunger.'

For reasons other than consideration of her mother's expensive clothing, Sigrid Odergaard led her parents on a circuitous route round, rather than through, the roof's gardening jumble towards the small band of visitors squeezed into the only space not occupied by piles of abandoned odds and ends.

Before releasing her parents and while still short of the gathering, Sigrid felt compelled to offer advice.

'Look, I know this sort of event pains you beyond belief, but as a courtesy to Eric's folks, who've asked to meet you, I'd like you to be on your best behaviour. That means no arguments, no bad temper and no putting people down. Is that too much to ask?'

'My dear, I had no idea our manners were unsuitable. Jakob, were you aware we didn't meet our offspring's expectations?'

'There,' Sigrid said with exasperation, 'you see how crabby that is and you've hardly got in the door?'

'We haven't come to spoil your night, so introduce us and let's get on with it,' Jakob interjected.

Unconvinced her request had been heard, Sigrid tapped her naked foot. Was this going to be another of those occasions when she had to constantly apologise for her unruly parents whose money had helped them forget they once knew better?

Returning to the couple with whom she had been talking, Sigrid touched the elderly man's elbow.

'Here they are then. Feliciano and Yessenia Mantageras, please meet my parents, Jakob and Dagmar, who apologise for keeping everyone waiting.'

'Huh? Manta-what?' Jakob asked sourly.

'Enrico's parents; from Spain, just this week. This, my wife, Yessenia.' A creased palm at the end of a starched shirt cuff swept gently to one side.

'And who's Enrico?'

'My son, your daughter's husband ... no?'

'Don't be dense, Dad; it doesn't entertain anyone. This is Feliciano, Eric's father.'

Dagmar's gaze drifted off to the Chinese family graves high up on the hillside and Jakob fiddled with something in his pocket.

The failure to connect yawned cavernously until Jakob's eyes met Sigrid's.

'Could do with a drink,' he said.

'... And what would you like?' she asked.

'Cognac maybe?'

'We've wine; white and red and soft drinks. Maybe there's some whisky lying about somewhere.'

'In that case red; Bordeaux would do.'

'It's South African.'

'Oh, so ... South African ... I guess.'

'Everyone getting to know each other?'

A man, twenty or so years older than Sigrid, edged into the group. His thickly framed glasses and almost concave upper body suggested a contemplative cleric rather than the weak-lunged and tobacco-stained waster better known to his friends.

'We don't entertain much like this, so tonight's a bit hit and miss.' Eric's greasy ponytail swung heavily with each turn of his awkward head.

On the circle of faces only the Mantageras' indulgent smiles broke uniformly blank expressions.

Enrico had abandoned his Spanish roots soon after arrival in Hong Kong in an act of expediency made to accommodate what he perceived to be the half-anglicised surroundings. The more accessible Eric Manley wanted to avoid repetitive explanations, particularly during hunts for the sort of haphazard employment he preferred.

Dagmar opened a small, shiny handbag and took out a packet of cigarettes. The unlit tube, grasped firmly between her crimson-painted lips, pointed accusingly at Jakob.

'Uuuh!' she exclaimed.

'Something wrong, Mother?'

'Not in the slightest. I can't remember when I last had an evening to compare.'

'The food will be up soon. Why don't we make our way across?'

Against his inclination Eric tried hard to play the affable dinner host and indicated an assembly of plastic table and chairs in the middle of the roof's assorted debris, which at some stage in the last few minutes had been laid with cutlery and glasses. There was not a complete set of anything and where consistent patterns ran out oddments had been culled from a miscellany of other household employments.

A tiny bat searching for insects dodged low over the rooftop and a paper serviette fluttered limply onto the grime of the old house's weathered floor.

Fearing his suggestion had gone unheard, Eric placed a languid arm across his father's shoulders and a hand on his mother's sleeve. 'Come on,' he mumbled and chivvied them closer towards the absent meal.

'Now,' he said, standing at the head of the table next to a seat with legs strangely contorted by a combination of fierce summer days and cold winter nights, 'let's see ... Sigrid, at the far end please; Mama and Papa either side of her. And then,' he added with a short between-the-teeth laugh, as if embarrassed by a joke only he understood, '... how about Mum and Dad Odergaard on either side of me? Son Vernon? You and Jintana in the middle, opposite each other.' He wagged a hand over the tablecloth in conclusion of a tiresome but necessary announcement.

Warm air spiralled round the rooftop, stirring torn edges in a heap of old newspapers, and in the lane below a dog barked.

'My boy,' Eric called desperately to Vernon, as if suffocated by the atmosphere's leaden weight. 'Pass round the wine, will you? I'm sure the women must be getting thirsty.'

Taking two bottles from the table, one in each hand, Vernon stood up and pushed his chair back with a tooth-numbing screech. Along the linen-cloth of Hindu design, oddly sized glasses jangled. Not certain what to do next, he turned to Yessenia Mantageras as the least intimidating option.

While Vernon trundled mechanically round the seated visitors, Eric's defective social antennae began questioning the table's arrangement. To draw incompatible ends together, he and Sigrid should have sat in the middle, where he'd put Vernon and the lad's Thai girlfriend. Pimply faced love, he guessed, was fine up to a point, but it was unlikely to bridge the chasm between gentility and thrusting greed.

'Man, how dumb can you get?'

Nearing the halfway point of a second circumnavigation and having dealt with the women, Vernon pulled up at his father's side.

'You'll have to take white; it's all that's left.'

'Don't worry, there's a cart-load downstairs, although it may be warm,' and then turning to Dagmar in a feeble shot at chumminess: 'We're set for a wild night if you're up for it. Sai Kung's supermarket does a lot of specials for the party types round here. So we get ours by the case.'

The suggestion that she might be interested in similar bargain hunting left Dagmar icily unmoved and she responded to her host's comment with looks chiselled from the granite of a northern fiord.

'And they deliver at no extra cost,' Eric went on, as if none but the mentally deranged could avoid such temptation.

Realising his small talk had fallen flat, Eric leaned back on his creaking picnic chair and tugged at the sleeve of his son's shirt in the rough way only male intimates recognise as affectionate.

'Look, I need help. Your stepmother and I have to be in the middle. We must all move round. Do you think Jintana can cope between these two?' He jerked his scalp backwards intending to indicate the Odergaards without being explicit.

'But, Dad, I want to be near her!'

'Young love has all eternity; take a couple of hours out for your old man. Huh?'

'Oh ... OK.'

'Thanks; you're a top guy.'

Swivelling back towards his guests, Eric opened his mouth, but, in the interval he took to collect his thoughts, Jakob butted in.

'So you were adopted, is that it?' he stated, as if the question was beyond dispute.

At the other end of the table Jakob's crude contention killed stone dead a budding conversation on the prevalence of rooftop horticulture in Asia.

'I thought we had an agreement,' Sigrid pleaded.

'Just like to know who I'm dealing with, unless I'm hurting someone's feelings. In which case, forget it.'

Only in his early years had Jakob allowed people around him comfort. Putting them on edge, he discovered later, gave distinct advantages and satisfied the heartlessness never far below the surface.

'Wow! That's weird,' Eric replied. 'Why should you think that?'

'Always thought my daughter's husband was Manley, but your parents are something else. Couldn't catch what, but seems contradictory.'

'Oh; is that all? No mystery there, of course, and,' he continued, not conceding anything to Jakob's bullying, 'Sigrid can explain when you've got time.'

Eric Manley was out of his depth in polite society, but when pushed into a pub brawl he could handle himself relatively effectively.

Denied the easy brow-beating he expected, Jakob drank back the remains of his wine and put his empty glass down with a bump.

'As a suggestion,' Eric offered, 'let's shuffle the pack and change a few places. Please pick up your drinks. Sigrid into the middle and, Jintana, please come round here to where I'm sitting. Vernon, over there on Sigrid's end.'

'Look, Dad,' Vernon murmured after some second thoughts. 'Putting her next to him is not going to help much. In this family you have to be let in gently.'

'Most women can look after themselves; believe me. And if you make the mistake of thinking they can't, you're in for some rude shocks, my lad. Trust me.'

Diners, like zombies in graveyard fog, stood up and circled the rooftop in time to nameless clanking sounds issuing from the bowels of the building.

Breathless from the rigours of the kitchen and her ascent, the overweight and sweating home help emerged from the stairwell carrying a triple-decked contraption built for just this type of entertainment. Each deck held two or three white-rimmed soup bowls, which, surprisingly, had lost none of their liberal contents in the laborious climb. Without distributing the plates, which were left standing in their transport device, Ligaya disappeared back into the vent and returned almost instantly with a large basket of steaming bread rolls, which she placed between Sigrid and Eric Manley.

'How did you come back so quickly?' asked Vernon, who felt more at home with humble servants than stuck-up grand-parents.

'Had it by the steps waiting for me, so I don't have to walk all the way back to the kitchen,' she confided.

'What does that tell us?' Eric enquired, in a renewed shot at self-sustaining conversation.

'I'm sure I wouldn't know, Sir,' she replied, as if the question had been addressed solely to her.

Feliciano looked blankly at his son and Yessenia nodded encouragingly as if to say the universe waited for enlightenment only he possessed.

'Why, that people should be left alone to do what they do best.'

No one bothered to support the contention, or undermine it with a 'so', and Eric's observation died like the sound of snowflakes falling into an ice field's crevasse.

Dagmar peered into the plate of orange potage lying before her. 'This is?' she enquired.

'Home-made pumpkin soup, M'am, and those green specks, fresh parsley brought this morning in the market.'

'Then we are dining at the Oscarshall and shall sleep content tonight.'

No one had ever effectively softened Dagmar's intemperance and, because her cutting tongue was beyond anyone's influence, the question of why Jakob sought periodic relief in a multitude of beds not his own was assumed to need no answering.

And tonight's captive audience unwilling to protest took the cowardly way out and sat and suffered the buffeting squalls abjectly.

The home help looked anxiously at Sigrid, hoping the feeling of disapproval would be made to go away.

'Don't worry, Ligaya; there's no need to think about things that make no sense.

Mother's and daughter's eyes met in freezing ill-will.

From childhood until the end of her teenage years, when nothing new was left to uncover, Sigrid had slowly and painfully learned how different her mother's conduct was from that of other people.

One particularly appalling incident typical of those excesses occurred when, as a child, she was still young enough to unconditionally love her parent and cling affectionately to the long and shapely legs. But that and other distant events, even while purged from present conscious thought, had shaped her adult's mind more surely than anything gleaned from an ultimately futile education in a succession of expensive schools.

The girl's favoured, but untrained, pet cat had soiled her mother's bedroom rug and Dagmar, in her fury, had caught the animal by its neck and beaten it half to death. The distraught girl had thrown herself between the brutal hands and whimpering victim, but, instead of tempering her wrathful parent, succeeded only in driving her to greater heights of ferocity, which ended up spotting the surrounding walls and furniture with pathetic feline blood.

In her infancy Sigrid was tormented by ugly nightmares of crows contesting the spoils of her pet's discarded corpse. Later, as the memories faded and she grew out of childish idolatry into loathing of her mother's emotional incontinence, she emerged a damaged woman, struggling into sunlight like grass through layers of farmyard muck.

Poor easy-going Eric hadn't had a clue what he was getting into and now his other-world parents had dropped into the maelstrom without the least idea of how hideous these people were. How would anyone who had never encountered ungoverned selfishness before know how to respond?

The aging Mantageras were not by anyone's definition uneducated, but what they knew was of a different time and place, where politeness and polished gentility, so at odds with the raw and carping ways of the Odergaards, were the mechanisms by which people lived. The worst they had known was war and that, too, had its honour, but here among those with everything there was not that small redemption.

Feliciano Mantageras had been born into the dying days of Spain's civil war to a colonel of the royalist right and a daughter of a landed family impoverished by the turmoil sweeping the land. Yessenia, the seventh of her parent's ten children, was born a few years later and baptised in the great cathedral at Cadiz. Her father's family had owned vast wine-producing estates stretching along the dry, brown hills of Andalucía's western shoreline, but they, too, suffered the costs of political affinity's shifting fortunes. Even Franco's eventual triumph, while maintaining some continuity and appearance of old ways, failed miserably to restore position and wealth consumed by the inferno.

Feliciano and Yessenia met in the fifties at a ball held in honour of the 'coming-out' of a minor royal. They had been the youngest people present and almost inevitably thought of themselves as having much in common. The short-haired and straight-backed guests around them were fast becoming ghosts of a lost and forgotten army.

Events like the ball remained part of the social calendar throughout the Generalissimo's rule, but, while Feliciano and Yessenia enjoyed the frequent opportunities to meet and look to the future, the shabby old order resisted the ticking clock, until it was blown from a bored public's interest into the corners of a changed nation.

Around the table diners studied the bowls of stiff, warm liquid. From his corner position Jakob tipped forward to secure a bread roll, which he broke, or more exactly crushed, without the use of a second hand.

'Shall someone say grace?' Yessenia enquired tremulously.

'Thhhhh!' Her son sucked air through his uneven brown teeth. 'Maybe that would not be a natural step.'

'And why not? I'm sure the young lady has someone to thank, just like the rest of us,' she nodded in the direction of Jintana, as if an Asian face somehow precluded the possibility of Christian values. Vernon's girlfriend smiled back with the brilliance of orchids under a morning shower. 'There, you see.'

Not at all convinced there was more than his mother's support for the ceremony, Eric examined surrounding faces for clues. Not many, but some would have the manners not to protest, but whether the bellicose Odergaards could be relied on not to make a big deal out of a small custom was another matter altogether.

'I suppose ... something generic might pass?' he suggested hopefully.

But, if Eric expected agreement to coalesce around his proposal, Dagmar quickly demolished the possibility by flinging across the pumpkin soup an uncompromising view: 'I thought superstition was grown out of – like diapers?'

'Well, in that case,' Eric's face flushed, 'private reflection will have to do.'

The elderly Mantageras turned closed eyes towards their shrunken laps, but whether out of shock or supplication it was impossible to tell. In the prickly delay that failed to sooth anyone's anxiety, faint, elegant Spanish glided along the table like olive oil over warm plates.

With hindsight, and even if it meant disappointing his parents, Eric should not have invited the Odergaards. They hadn't the capacity to take pleasure in kinship, even the remote sort brought about by marriage.

'So you're Manley then and not something else?' Jakob wouldn't let his question dangle.

Would an explanation appease or encourage this antagonism? Eric was not at all sure. 'When I first came to Hong Kong, Enrico Mantageras sounded clumsy, a bit of an oddity. Calling myself Eric Manley just made life simpler and stopped people going on about where I came from and how I got here.'

'Really? How would that help? Never had any problem with my name.'

'Our situations are different. I don't own anything and have to work alongside people, often asking for help. Blending in is useful, especially when long hair gives headmasters the feeling you're inescapably aberrant.'

'I'd have thought a trim and a regular job were better options. But, your call, not mine.'

'Thanks for the observation, but as you can see the call's been made.'

One man had sought invisibility through relabeling and without rejecting his homeland, while the other, on the instant of boarding his flight from Oslo and without a scrap of feeling for either his new or fast-receding country, kept his name and brandished it about as if it was a cudgel.

The manner in which they had set out as young men said as much about them as all their subsequent history. In his hurry to seek a fortune Jakob had taken a jet plane, while Enrico ambled onto the highway without the slightest idea of what lay beyond the next hill's rise. On arrival in Hong Kong and after journeys of enormously different lengths, one tackled his objective with the narrow ferocity that was his hallmark and the other tumbled accidentally, and after several false starts, into casual teaching, where he spent most of his time sharing the experiences of an aimless and rambling adventure, rather than providing access to the kind of knowledge required by school examiners.

There was probably not much more than five years between them, but sometimes Eric was not at all sure to which generation he belonged, especially when in the older man's presence and while married to his daughter.

The nagging sense of being left behind was nothing new and had probably started years ago when he habitually avoided joining the gangs of competitive neighbourhood boys running wild in the open spaces behind Feliciano's and Yessenia's dilapidated apartment block on the fringes of Madrid's southern suburbs.

Home, with its down-at-heel, yet high-minded, values common to the time and his family's class, had been superficially adequate, but, while Church, family and the privacy of his room were comfortable pegs on which to hang the weeks and months, they had signally failed to equip him for the rigours of a testing world.

Eric's poor student record hardly seemed the basis for a career in instruction, even one as loosely constructed as his, but with tools barely adequate for the task of earning a respectable living, he was ready to explore the further horizon and leave Spain, which, in those days, was still wrapped in an introspective pall not unlike his own.

As he took the white road to Algeciras and saw the beautiful but poor countryside, with its medieval castles perched on rocky outcrops and mules, even at that late date, threshing and ploughing in the fields, he wondered what future awaited his parents' beloved and incomparable land, from which today, in a supreme effort and in recognition of their future's brevity, they had torn themselves to see the place where he had acquired an accidental permanence.

Soon after their arrival they became both pleased and saddened. Pleased that their son might one day return to his own country, because, as he reminded them, Hong Kong was not a place where strangers 'put down roots', but saddened that the contentment deserved by all children had passed him by.

'Tell me,' Feliciano had said, while pulling at his son's shirt in exactly the same way Eric had done with Vernon's, 'what keeps you een this place? Do you like eet here? From my short experience I can't but feel eet ees – how shall I say without seeming ungenerous? ... maybe ... inhospitable ees too harsh a word ... but for sure not so warm.'

'It's not a bad town to earn your keep and it's safe; I'm not sure you can say that much about most places these days, including Madrid; advantages probably outweigh disadvantages,' Eric had replied.

'*Si*, I can see the practicalities, but what about your happiness? Where are your friends, your neighbours? Everyone is busy; rushing one way and another. There's no time to think. Een buses people sleep or play electronic games; do they have nothing to say? Where do they meet, share friendships, exchange views, humm?'

'I'd have had a harder time making ends meet elsewhere.'

'The Good Book has something to say about having too much money.'

'I don't have too much; I get by, that's all. Can't ignore economics altogether, or I'll starve.'

'True, true, but tell me seriously; are you pleased with what you have?'

'I'm not so sure anyone can say that, but I have Vernon and,' he added as if in afterthought, '... and Sigrid.'

'Are you playing games with me? We used to understand each other once.' Feliciano affected offence.

'And still do, but remember how you were with your father? You couldn't leave him with your burden; we have to shoulder our own. If I learned anything from you, it was how to stand alone.'

'Not quite alone, I hope; I am always here. And your mother, well, she ees what a mother should be and wants to believe een you.'

On the arm he was reluctant to let go, Feliciano's old hand shook. He wanted to throw his arm over his son's neck and pull him close, the way he used to do before the boy left on his odyssey, but in these tension-laden surroundings, where everyone seemed to be on a cliff's edge or ready to cut others down, he was not sure whether it was the right or even a good thing to do.

Feliciano could see Eric had added further complication to his undirected life by marrying a person in a place neither called home, where, in the absence of any real roots, all that could be expected for either was the beggarly comfort of sleep at day's end and painkilling inertia. Now, with so much time gone and with so many trees already swept past the express train's window, his journey was approaching the buffers. The listless stare in Eric's eyes seemed to scream out for courage to walk away, but with life's baggage weighing so heavily on his back the alternatives were few and far between.

And what could be said of the others in this incoherent gathering? Were any of them, other than the apparently radiant Jintana, remotely content with what their lives had brought?

What of his daughter-in-law's strange parents? They were so inflamed with unreasonableness he couldn't believe they really enjoyed anything. Outsiders walking onto the roof would be hard pressed to make any link between the woman scowling into the night air and the man aggressively wiping his soup plate with a bread roll's broken end. Just one similarity, a sour and angry disposition, joined them like two aging pugilists exchanging blows for the tenth time. Did some form of bonding lie in the familiarity of daily hooks and jabs? And what of Sigrid or Vernon? Hands were reaching out everywhere, but none were being grasped.

Despite the night's sultry warmth, the old man shuddered.

Having cleaned away the last traces of pumpkin and parsley, Jakob writhed about in his complaining plastic chair and, with nothing else to do until the next course emerged from the stairwell, turned his attention to Jintana.

'What do you do with yourself?' he asked.

'Me? Oh, I'm a student; one-year exchange from National University of Thailand.'

'Uh-uh; what's your subject?'

Jakob Odergaard could not have cared less what course Jintana was taking, but he did like the way she looked directly at him and how her very full lips moved when she spoke. He had always found women in this part of the world appealing; their colouring, build and how they all managed to look no more than twenty years old. But this one really was no more than twenty. Dark skin may not have been a virtue among the people of South East Asia, but to Jakob it was irresistible.

'English literature; Mr Manley stood in during one of my electives. That's how I came to meet Vernon.'

'Vern –?'

At the far end of the table Vernon was watching carefully. His youthful sensitivity was outraged that a girl, his girl, was being sniffed over by a man not only old enough to be her grandfather, but, in this unconventional family, bearing almost exactly that relationship to his daughter's husband's son.

'Me, I'm Vernon,' he called over the dishes and assorted cutlery.

'Yeah, I know,' Jakob answered as if the interruption had not made the slightest register in his train of thought. 'So how do you plan making a living out of that?' he continued, watching Jintana's perfectly shaped mouth deliciously enunciate its syllables.

'She'll teach; same as your son-in-law. How else do you think?' Dagmar, having lost interest in the black stirrings of foliage on the hillside and the hissing and crackling of flying insects in the overhead ultraviolet lamp, offered an un-nuanced perspective.

Ignoring her even more emphatically than Vernon, Jakob pondered on the beautiful teeth possessed by many Thai women. They were larger and whiter than Europeans' and constantly showed in good-natured and unabashed smiles. With a slight narrowing of his eyes he could see, not just the glistening enamel, but the moist pink interior in which it was set. Surely this was a ship waiting to be boarded?

'You'll get a squint if you're not careful,' Dagmar cautioned maliciously.

'Damn you, Dag, do you have to show your claws all the time.'

'An old dog who's forgotten how to scratch must surely need the reminder,' she shot back with unconcealed venom.

'And being married to a dog qualifies you as what?'

The dinner party was lurching dangerously out of control.

'Mother, we agreed ...' appealed Sigrid from the middle of the table.

'Why don't we move to the main course; duck or fish I'm told.' Eric began throwing life belts to floundering mariners, before calling hopefully over his shoulder: 'We're ready when you are, Lig.'

A bewildered silence hung over the table. Feliciano raised an eyebrow at Yessenia; Vernon bit his lower lip and Sigrid squeezed the paper napkin in her wet palm until it fell into her lap in flakes. Above his head Eric probed the abandoned heavens for signs of cosmic order.

'Look,' he called out hopefully, 'isn't that Jupiter over there, rising above the trees?'

'For God's sake!' Dagmar stood up, jarring the contents of glasses and bottles into agitated ripples.

Her shaking fingers wrestled open the clutch bag and tumbled its contents onto the multi-coloured tablecloth. From the heaped collection she picked out a packet of cigarettes and lighter and strode away to the rooftop's edge.

Nonplussed faces around the dinner table watched and wondered what had caused this bitter outburst.

But Jakob, accustomed to his wife's tumultuous rages, drew energy and strength from the angry barbs.

Yessenia twisted the tablecloth's corner into a knot and looked at her husband as if expecting him to remedy the disturbance.

'Should someone go to her?' she asked her son.

'Hmm?' he responded, as if the orbiting stars, in their cold predictability, were a far safer topic of conversation than the high-octane outbursts of an incendiary mother-in-law. 'I think … um … perhaps not; Sigrid, your opinion?'

'It'll burn out, just leave her. We are, after all, eight, not one.'

Shipwreck was temporarily averted by the bulking and severely out-of-breath Ligaya riding into sight at the top of the stair flight with the serving contraption in her wake. She paused, either in expectation of approval, or to satisfy herself nothing had been left behind, and, having set down four large dishes, containing sliced duck, an open-mouthed fish with needle-sharp spines and an assortment of vegetables and fluffy rice in the table's many open spaces, flipped a wet strand of hair towards the back of her head.

The faltering conversation died again, as if a pink-faced infant had been strangled in its cot, and Eric, devoid of social poise, wished he had a special place reserved in the twinkling harmony of the planets overhead. On his right the newly engrossed Jakob effectively built a fence round himself and Jintana, while, against the hillside, Dagmar retreated into a transcendental trance. Casting about ineffectively, he called down the table to his mother.

'Erm ... ah ... and so, Mama, what have been your impressions of Hong Kong since arriving?'

Startled by the sudden attention and turning heads, Yessenia Mantageras dropped her fork.

The loud rattle drew Feliciano from careful inspection of bones protruding from a sliver of fish and he enquired attentively: 'My dear?'

'Oh! I haven't thought about it really. But it's busy, very busy indeed and people stand so close. Why, only yesterday, while we were buying souvenirs, a gentleman trod on my heel and I lost a shoe. When I turned he didn't say sorry or anything else I could recognise; just looked straight through me as if I wasn't there. You could tell how close he was because I gathered he'd eaten a lot of garlic. Hong Kong is so full of people; do you think it is for the best?'

The question was typical of his mother's conversation, as if to express anything, even the most excruciating platitude, was somehow better than saying nothing. Was she just being polite, or was her mental capacity really capable of nothing better?

'Do I think ...? Well, er ... best for whom? Other than visitors like yourself, people seem to get along all right. Everyone is used to it being this way.'

Yessenia smiled benevolently as if her son's statement revealed the ages' wisdom. There had never been a time when she was not impressed by him, although she wished some things, such as the abandonment of his Christian name, had been discussed beforehand. But, while these few lapses were beyond her ability to prevent from the distance of Madrid, she still felt obliged to let him know, at the right time that was, of her objection.

'I'm sure you're right, but in Spain we don't like to be so ... cramped.'

'Sigrid,' Eric said, 'can you can bring Dagmar back to the table; she's smoked several already; perhaps we can have another go?'

By the time Mrs Odergaard resumed her interrupted meal only two thin slices of duck, the widely separated head and tail of the fish, and a few cooling vegetables remained. She spooned a broccoli floret and some snow peas onto her plate and began tearing them asunder with the side of a fork.

An unidentifiable insect, charred beyond recognition, circled in a fizz after encountering the electric fly-catcher and fell in a twitch among the bread basket's scattered crumbs. No one appeared to notice. At one end of the table a conversation of sorts staggered into half-life between the Mantageras and their daughter-in-law. At the other, Jintana laughed frequently, but whether from natural exuberance or nervousness at being hunted by her boyfriend's grandfather-in-law, was impossible to say. Jakob watched her with the unblinking inexorability of a riverside anaconda. The dinner party, at last, settled at a level, which, if not tranquil, had moved on from outright belligerence.

The labouring Ligaya returned with a bowl of fruit and a dome-shaped pudding smelling faintly of almond essence and hot butter. On a second journey she held in her tight grip two bottles and a clutch of tinkling glasses.

'Ah,' said Eric with the relief of a long-distance runner sighting the finishing line, 'we are coming to the end of a great meal!' He looked at the domestic help before adding, 'Super job, Lig, but how about some of that strong coffee from your neck of the woods?'

Ligaya grasped her floating apron and returned the artificially enthusiastic gaze as if to say that dinner on the ground floor, notwithstanding the semi-permanent smell of incense pervading the airless interior, would, in her opinion, have been a much better choice.

Like rock fragments under a collapsed cliff the guests lay where gravity and the evening's circumstances had thrown them. Until, out of nowhere in particular, Vernon called across to his grandparent-by-marriage:

'Any advice for someone just starting out on how to become successful? Some of us would like to hear how it's done.'

Fearing a return to the earlier unruly exchanges, Feliciano attempted a diversion: 'Why don't you tell us about your plans after university?'

Eric grabbed at the interruption and, without realising how nearly he was copying his mother's unconscious prattle, set about burying the closing hour of a desperately awful evening with incongruous verbiage.

'If you ask me, the suggestion that a young man should have a plan must be an oxymoron.'

'Oxy-what?' remarked an astonished Yessenia.

'Jesus, just listen to him,' Jakob added unhelpfully.

The dinner party had resumed its downward spiral, as though the personality mix inescapably created a brew so toxic that conflagration was inevitable and the earlier lull no more than calm before the gale's loudest blast.

'Youth,' Eric continued, determined to make the most of his opening, whether anyone other than his mother wanted to hear or not, 'is all about exploration, and immature minds – sorry, son – don't develop completely if the chance is missed. Take mine as an example, which you could say I've seen up close over a very long time.'

'And are you saying someone, anyone should take you as a role model? In a pretty empty-headed evening that's just about the most stupid comment we're likely to hear,' Jakob remarked.

While doggedly clinging to his theme, Eric, to his surprise and annoyance, found himself unwittingly agreeing with Jakob's censure. 'I never had a serious thought about what to do until the age of thirty-two and some would say even that was too early, although' – he gave a nod towards his father-in-law – 'I suppose you could say I took an unreasonable length of time.'

Jakob, although neither philosophical nor spiritual, assumed everyone saw 'success' in the same naked terms as he. If the way to the ultimate goal was made possible by determination and consistency, what was holding others back if not ineptitude and laziness? He was not inclined to think this restricted definition had the least deficiency.

The discussion's turn, however, seemed to demand an explanation beyond a few off-the-cuff sneers, so, without taking his eyes off Jintana, he called back: 'Screw poncing about and go for what you decide is important. Nothing else is material; don't let anyone or anything get in the way. Life's what you make it.'

'Do you treat women the same way?' Vernon asked, hoping the reply would bring Jintana to her senses.

'Sure, why not? Never lost one I didn't want.'

'Oh! But that is too ... uncompromising,' protested Feliciano, unable to pretend courteousness any longer.

'More like depraved, if you ask me.' The mixture of South African wine and his vanished mother's feisty disposition carried Vernon past the point of return.

Jakob stood up.

'I don't know what it is with you people. Let me tell you something: you hide behind your silly beliefs and daft dogmas as if any of them mattered. There is no book, or church, or cult that will save you from your inadequacy. You make a virtue out of poverty and obscurity and have the gall to criticise me – me! – a self-made man who could buy and sell you a score of times while you were still working out what the hell was going on. Why am I spending my time with you? Huh? Why? I've got better things to do.'

With his back to the table he took two short steps towards the spiral staircase. At the head of the well a thought struck him and he retraced his path to lean low over the astounded Jintana and with one hand uplifting her well-shaped chin gave her a slow, open-mouthed kiss.

'You dirty old man!' yelled Vernon. 'I'm gonna ...'

'Just try, you pathetic little pip.'

Except for Sigrid and her stepson the guests had no idea how to respond to a situation so outrageous that the usual apparatus of human intercourse was rendered totally useless. At the heart of the paralysed assembly the hostess pressed the tips of her long pale fingers against her hairline in a last-ditch attempt to steady her reeling sanity.

But Vernon, being suddenly more amenable to the sort of remedy favoured by angry young men, cast about with wild eyes for something, anything, that would assuage the overpowering fury unleashed by his grandfather-in-law's affront. What should he do? Follow the older man into the street and heap abuse on his arrogant head; knock him into the broken poinsettia pots stacked around the yard, or ...?

Caught between indecision and boiling point and with the triumphant figure rapidly receding from sight, Vernon snatched up Ligaya's sponge pudding and ran to the stairs.

'No, not that,' cried his father.

But incensed beyond reason and oblivious to restraint, Vernon hoisted the dripping dessert over his thin shoulders and hurled it into the gaping hole at his feet.

Full satisfaction would have required the crash of Jakob knocked from the stairs, or at least a howl of pain, but the only sounds sidling onto the roof were a mixture of puffs, gasps and bumps, as if several elderly ladies dressed in fluffy slippers and smocks were engaged in a pillow fight.

With the dessert's departure, dinner guests, excepting the

detached Dagmar and dazed Sigrid, gathered supportively around Vernon and peered with him into the open well.

Spiralled stairs blocked a complete view, but on the floor of the living room several limbs could be discerned in a dusting of caster sugar.

'I have seen men killed for less,' said Feliciano, who, more than most, was prepared to excuse a crime of passion, although whether he was referring to Jakob's contempt or the pudding's dispatch was not immediately clear.

None of the outstretched limbs below moved.

'Is he conscious?'

'Bloody hell, I hope so.' Vernon's anger evaporated in the guilty thought that he had gone too far.

'Guess we should see?' suggested Eric.

Under the sticky disorder Ligaya lay spread-eagled on her back with Jakob Odergaard's head between her knees. As the concerned diners drew closer, Ligaya's popping eyes signalled her distress.

'Am I all right, Sir?' she asked plaintively.

'You sound OK; let's take a look,' encouraged Eric.

'Of course you are. Just winded that's all,' Jintana added with reassuring kindness.

'Winded? What's that?'

'I mean your breath has been knocked out of your lungs. You'll be fine in a moment.'

'Jakob doesn't look so great. He's not moving.' Eric, who would never have made a schoolmaster, was beginning to hope someone else would take control of the situation.

'Oh, I don't know. On top and head down there; should be just what he likes.'

'Vernon, that is not helpful,' his father admonished. 'We need something constructive here.'

'Heh, heh!' Feliciano was more relaxed than his son and was starting to enjoy the situation.

The inert body was turned and manhandled onto a settee

smelling of cats and cauliflower. Jakob sank into the cushions and his trailing arms were lifted alongside by a disconcerted Ligaya. The comatose form woke up and let out an unexpected shriek that rang in the heads of those closest to him.

'Aaargh!'

'I suppose that means he's not dead.'

'You're sounding a shade disappointed.'

Eric turned from his son to the gummy figure on the couch.

'What's hurting?'

'Fuck you, fuck your stairs, fuck your son, fuck all of you,' Jakob protested with even more than his usual feeling.

'That's not going to help focus our search. Look, why don't we begin by removing the dessert from your hair and work down from there?'

'Don't touch me, you clown, you moron! I don't need any help from … aaargh!' Jakob let out a second scream, which brought a casually interested Dagmar to the overhead opening.

'I'm ready to go,' she called. 'What's your plan?'

'Probably we need more time,' Eric said as he methodically squeezed the protesting Jakob's parts until arriving at the middle finger of his right hand. Holding his discovery by its adjacent wrist, he offered it up for general inspection, as though sharing the sight of a pottery fragment from an archaeological dig. 'Here you go; this is what we are looking for.'

The rigid extension's blue-black contrasted sharply with other unblemished, almost white, fingers.

'How come we didn't see that straight away,' continued Eric, as if the body stretched along the settee had been a sentence with a missing verb.

'Because he was lying on it?' hazarded Feliciano.

'Lying badly seems to be a habit,' Vernon concluded resentfully, forgetting that his grandfather-in-law's astounding bluntness was anything but lying.

No event has a single beginning; that sort of solution was too clean, too neat. An airplane never fell out of the sky simply because it was struck by lightning; there was always something earlier that led it to a particular place at a particular time. Maybe a passenger hadn't shown up and delays had occurred while baggage was unloaded, or perhaps the pilot diverted because there was bad weather along the route. Sigrid's ill-fated party had not broken down because Jakob flirted, or because Dagmar wanted to be somewhere else. Right from the dinner's moment of conception its ending was fixed in warped and inescapable logic. If Sigrid had thought to make the connection, small though it was, she would have seen her father's broken finger and her mother's indifference in the hurricanes of childhood, and perhaps, if Jakob or Dagmar had reflected, they would have found the outcome stuck, like a bone fragment between teeth, in the circumstances of their own parents' lives.

Only Eric, Feliciano and Vernon escorted the Odergaards towards their waiting car. A suggestion that they all go as far as the hospital was roundly rejected. But, in spite of being sorely tempted to be completely ungracious, Eric wrapped a makeshift sling around Jakob's stiff and uncooperative neck.

Vernon pulled open a rear door on the Odergaard limousine and a faintly fishy smell, from a piece of sea bass spirited to the waiting driver by a considerate Ligaya, curled into the damp, night air.

'Uff!' remarked the affronted Dagmar. 'Open the windows or we'll smell like the evening market.'

'You should really let us drive you home,' coaxed Eric in a final effort of goodwill.

'Not the slightest point,' Dagmar retorted.

'Well, if you insist, but I still think we ...'

'Matilda,' snapped Jakob at the uncomprehending head behind the driving wheel.

'I'm not sure I get ...' Anil hated abbreviated instructions implying he knew a lot more than was often the case.

'I said Matilda Hospital, you jackass; now step on it.'

6

The Sunday walk from Wai Pang's Yau Ma Tei violin lesson to the Kowloon waterfront was a muggy slog and, before he'd gone a hundred metres, dark patches of sweat showed in the folds of his school flannels and shirt. Uniform, even today, was inescapable, because, his mother insisted, no other attire was proper for a student receiving tuition. Discomfort, however, evaporated in the joys of liberty found between the end of class and a solitary lunch left for him by the obliging Budiwati, before she, too, escaped on her short Sunday outing.

Budiwati was good like that and always made sure he had everything her position was able to provide.

On his earlier visits to the waterfront Wai Pang had thought about staying longer, to buy a slice of pizza perhaps, at one of the takeaways dotting the tourist-frequented streets. Luna New Year cash given by Grandma Tung and held for safety in his mother's musty dressing table would have paid for the treat. But taking money without permission, even when it was more or less his already and disposing of Budiwati's lunch in the rubbish chute, were bridges his courage had so far failed to cross.

Other than these few clandestine outings and some equally furtive diversions to an arcade, every breathing minute of his day and night, from getting up at first light to late arithmetic and character writing drills, was regulated to the point of exhaustion by his parent's unyielding belief that unfilled hours led inexorably to misbehaviour and society's ultimate collapse.

How the undetected intervals had crept into his schedule was difficult to explain, although Wai Pang guessed it lay in his mother's assumption that a school as reputable as the Panda Establishment for Musicality must surely require practice after class. Whatever her reasoning, the mistake had become so fixed in her mind that she gave herself leave to explore North Kowloon's marts during identical hours in search of products capable of enhancing her disadvantaged body and wardrobe.

Not wishing to curtail his parent's sad pleasures, Wai Pang decided honest disclosure of the Panda Establishment's precise timetable was not in anyone's best interest.

At the end of his damp trudge down Nathan Road he took the pedestrian tunnel leading to Victoria Harbour's northern promenade, from where he could view a littering of lighters, ferries and, occasionally, a single high-standing cruise ship on the choppy, grey-green waters. Today, as on most visits, he could see on the other side of the busy sea lanes and through the light-obscuring heat, expensive hillside homes struggling for visibility behind the walls of Hong Kong Island's throbbing financial and commercial hub.

Indolent crowds meandered round the esplanade and Wai Pang steered to a point hard against the harbour rail. From here he turned to watch the city's varied communities flow on their separate but complementary journeys.

Runners for low-cost tailors concealed in the warren of shops near by handed out flyers advertising rapidly assembled bespoke suits; migrant domestic helpers, lucky enough to have a whole day to themselves, ate and laughed raucously and parents of a sort he recognised fussed and dabbed at the perspiration on coddled children's shining faces. Tourists from a cruise ship pointed, talked louder than was necessary, and photographed everything from the old Star Ferry clock tower to the Falun Gong adherents meditating on the pavement.

Wai Pang came to see and think, and now the waterfront had become his favourite place to look for answers to questions never raised in the tiny Shatin apartment. The realisation that he was sixteen and far from an obdurate mother touched him with a kind of magic and he drank back the sights and sounds as a shipwrecked mariner would fresh water.

Many of those ambling up and down, or in some cases just lolling about, were quite foreign and could have flown in from the outer reaches of space for all Wai Pang knew. How, he wondered, could you explain the differences and the odd stickiness that made these groups hang together like ducks and geese around the ponds in his grandparents' Hunan village?

No one seemed to mind or want anything different, and he knew, if he had been in need of help, that he would have instinctively sought the type of face that was familiar and not one of those mysterious tailors or tourists or even an imported domestic helper, even though his daily life depended on exactly such an individual. But why? Surely other lives were as real with stories as compelling?

With the exception of these few truancies his thoughts and actions were not as much his own as he wished. A small, confined space seemed to contain him, which, whatever its origins, held him separate from many other passers-by. He was not just thinking of obvious things like language, although that, too, played a part, but more especially of what people thought of as OK, or not OK. How many times had he heard the phrase 'That's not the correct way' used as a sharp stick to make him conform, or drive him into his bedroom, or across the arm of his mother's sofa, or any other place desired by those who said they knew best?

What, he asked, was the point of the violin lessons? His mother wouldn't understand how he detested them or that he hadn't an ear for music. To her, skill followed hard work and had nothing to do with liking or disliking, and so he was obliged to persevere and spend endless hours achieving nothing he valued. The whole charade was just too depressing.

Who and what exactly, he wondered, was Wai Pang and why was his lot so limited?

A few feet from where he stood a young couple lounged over

the harbour rail. They looked like visitors. Further off a boy of about five or six, with no immediately discernible connection to the pair, ran about until, on an impulse, he climbed with his shoes on into a water fountain and waded to the opposite side. Wai Pang looked at the couple, as there were no obvious alternative parents near by, and then back to the child, who had started tugging at something he'd found at the bottom of the pool.

The father half-turned and without raising his elbows called half-heartedly across to the boy.

'Hey! Matt, come out of there.'

The mother was even less fascinated by her son's antics and pointed excitedly at an ocean liner swinging away from its moorings.

'What about some ice cream?' the father asked.

Fingers grown green and slippery from submerged exploration were wiped over an already grubby T-shirt.

'OK,' the child said slowly, as if not quite convinced the offer held as much attraction as the one about to be forsaken.

Wai Pang couldn't remember the time, even as a small child, when he had been allowed to behave with such indiscipline, or, more strangely, ever wanting to. There seemed to be a boundary, then, not only on what his world permitted, but also on what he felt he should desire, and to some extent the two had, until recently, been in harmony.

The worst of his youthful 'wildness', other than these secret outings was surfing on the Internet and watching television when he was supposed to be doing homework. But what could be truly offensive in those minor transgressions, when all he sought was the chance to see and compare and find some brief relief from monotony? Would the ungoverned child in the pool be able to say as much, or as little, when he reached Wai Pang's age, or would he be heaping grief on tolerant parents in a way their lassitude seemed to invite?

Between a finger and thumb he took a pinch of his forearm

and wondered whether he existed as a separate human being, or whether he was just an extension of his mother, her family, or maybe something even bigger, like Chineseness, or the rocks and soil on which he had been born?

Was there a choice? If there was, he would have preferred the shared discovery to belong with his father, who had gone away and never come back, and not with those others whom he scarcely knew or liked and who were just parts of the wheel that held him fast on impersonal, iron-clad spokes.

When he was really young and Man Kit still spent every weekend at home they read stories and devised small rituals together that only they understood. Other events in the household had their routine, but none like the one bitter-sweet tradition, which owed nothing to order or discipline, developing, as it did, a secret bond between them.

On those Sunday afternoons, when Man Kit waited for the lift that took him down to the street and to another week in the far-off China factory, a fumbled search took him through first one pocket and then another for something that somehow always managed to get misplaced. But Wai Pang knew no departure was complete until a much tarnished ring dotted with blue-and-red inlay had been located and placed in the boy's expectant hand.

'This ring,' his father would say, 'is enchanted and while it's held by the man of the house the home is safe. When I am gone everything is in your charge. You are to take care of it and your mama and make sure no harm comes to either. Do you understand?'

The wonder-struck child never spoke while the pretended burden moved to his tiny shoulders, even as his impatient mother watched the make-believe and breathed noisily in the background. After the lift door closed and his father departed to the mystery of 'work' in a faraway place, Wai Pang took the ring and hid it in a cup on a shelf high above his bed until, on the following Friday, he'd return it to his proud and loving father.

That was all a long time ago and at some indefinable point Man Kit had stopped coming home quite so often and the ritual had died. Now Wai Pang had forgotten what had become of the blue-and-red ring and to his father's wish for Mama's care.

The place on the harbour rail, previously occupied by the couple with the scruffy child, was now filled by a man in a dirty baseball cap. In complexion, he looked like the tailors' runners, but, rather than carrying leaflets, or watching the crowds intently, he lounged by the barrier and stretched his limbs more than the time of day seemed to demand.

''Oo are you staring at then, eh?'

Wai Pang was startled. He couldn't remember being in a conversation with an unknown foreigner before, or having a question thrown at him quite so brusquely. He goggled at the tall and slightly sinister figure with its muscular arms bulging from an uncomfortably tight shirt.

'Wassa matter? You deaf or sunnink?' the bulking Anil Patel enquired.

'Oh!'

'All right, calm down. Just wonderin' what you're lookin' at.'

'Oh! Sorry, sorry. I ... er ...' Wai Pang stuttered as if his tongue had lost contact with his thoughts.

Casual teasing with a complete stranger was an unknown experience and quite different to the solemn exchanges constituting conversation in the Shatin apartment. He struggled for a way of describing the verbal communications he was used to, until coming to the conclusion that they travelled vertically and not from side to side as this one seemed to be doing. Yes, that was it; schoolteachers, the violin instructor, his mother and relatives, they all spoke as if they were standing on chairs. Perhaps that was because they were adults and were expected to give directives. But this careless person was something entirely new and not at all the mythical caricature he had been led to expect.

'It'll come back, buddy; don't worry. What a great day; just what's needed to get my afternoon in shape.'

'What do you do ... on a Sunday afternoon ... that is?' Suddenly curious, Wai Pang wanted to know how far removed another young person's behaviour, especially an alien's, was to the normality explicit in his mother's reminders.

'That's a long ways from "Oh", an' what makes you think I'd want to discuss?'

'Do you play the violin?'

'Are you takin' the piss?'

A surprising surge of interest ran through Wai Pang's veins as if spring water had burst from thawing ice and rushed downhill to find a river. There was a complete absence of consequence and he suddenly felt able to say and do anything he liked. He was pulling faces and nobody was complaining or saying how silly he looked.

'Sorry, pardon. It's just that I've never spoken to ... to ... an Indian before.'

''Oo said I was a Hindian?'

Who indeed? On the waterfront in daylight people looking like this man sold tailoring services and after dark along the full stretch of Nathan Road hawked counterfeit watches, or, when a sudden shower drenched the street, cheap, collapsible umbrellas. Wai Pang's understanding would not stretch past what he had been told by his mother and seen during half a dozen walks from Yau Ma Tei.

'Aren't you?'

'No ... well, yes ... sort of, although my sis might have a different view.'

'You don't seem very sure.'

'It's a lot more complicated than how a fella looks.'

'What are you doing here?'

'You've got an awful lot of questions for a lad who couldn't say boo a while ago. But, if you must know, I'm waiting for a mate.'

'Is he ... like you; an Indian, I mean?'

'Him? No he ain't, an', as he's that bloke coming over, you

can check him out yourself. I keep tellin' him he should get a bit more colour in those cheeks of his.'

'Am I late?' Isidor Nash asked.

'Late for what?'

'Dunno; don't we have a plan?'

'Maybe, but a plan ain't an event, an' without an event there's nothing to be late for.'

To Wai Pang the conversation lacked purpose. Words seemed to fly back and forth to fill space and not to carry information. Most of the adults he knew spoke to give instruction or demand answers, although Budiwati was different. But as she wasn't a grown-up in quite the same way as his relatives and school-teachers she couldn't really be counted. Her long stories of the villages and rice fields in Sumatra went on for ever, unless someone turned them off like a tap. His mother was good at that.

But with these two, this Indian and his friend, the urge to laugh at something or someone, even if it was themselves, seemed more important than having anything sensible to say.

'Why are you rude to each other?'

Realising he and Anil were not alone, Isidor asked, ''Oo's 'e then?'

'Search me, just some nosey kid, or ... now, how about this? ... p'raps he's a police spy checkin' on the unreliable foreigners hangin' around the pier?'

'But he's too young to work for the pol –'

'Shut up, dickhead.'

The Star Ferry tower clock struck eleven thirty and to confirm what he had heard Wai Pang looked at the watch on his wrist.

'I must go,' he said, knowing lunch had to be eaten and cleared from the table before his mother came back from her foraging expedition.

'OK ... wouldn't want your ma to think we kept you.'

'But you don't know my ...'

'No, course I don't,' Anil replied soothingly. 'It's just a manner of speaking; see what I mean?'

'I ... see,' said Wai Pang without being sure he understood. 'Where are you going from here?'

'Stone me; don't you ever shut your bleedin' row? If you must know, I'm gonna test a theory an', as it only just came into my 'ed, there're still some details I gotta think about.'

'But I thought we had a deal?' protested Isidor.

'Now don't you start? Look, make yourself scarce, kid; I've got stuff to organise.'

The promenading crowds were denser than an hour ago and Wai Pang dodged and bumped in zigzags towards the nearby terminal and a double-decker bus preparing to leave for remote Shatin.

'Queer lad,' said Isidor Nash.

'He's awright; just a bit lost if you ask me. Probably needs a firm 'and on his shoulder.'

'So, what's the form then, eh? I've put on a silk shirt special like.'

'Well, you don't need finery to pull in the chicks. You must have learned that by now?'

'What are you sayin'?'

'In a nutshell, my dear Watson, some are born winners and others are not, and it takes more than a shirt and smellin' good. You gotta bait the 'ook. Doesn't the record speak for itself?'

'Absolutely! So where does that leave the afternoon, then?'

'I've been thinking; if you were to put a cool 'undred on the table, I'm prepared to bet I can lay the most unlikely bird.'

''Oo's that, then? The vicar's daughter?'

'Nah! Nothin' like that; I'm talkin' big league and movin' upmarket to give the shop girls a rest. How about Odergaard's fancy woman for a real long-odds game of skittles? I've decided anything is possible.'

'And how do you intend doin' that when 'e's splashing money and eau d'Cologne all over 'er lily-white bod?'

'Today, that's just what 'e aint. Last night I had the pleasure of takin' 'im to the 'ostpital wiv a bust finger and now 'e's at home feelin' all poorly and not able to do 'is push-ups, while his bird, 'oo I've seen, is waiting lonely and unserviced.'

'What makes you think she'd fancy you? What 'ave you got to offer?'

'You should know that by now. I've got a way wiv wimen, that's what, which, at the right time, is all a bloke needs.'

''Ow am I goin' to know if you score? You could just spin me a yarn?'

'Don't know yet, but if you're on, bar that, I've got some work to do. Probably got no more than three days and then 'e'll be sniffing around agin. It's not as if 'e's broken his neck, which would have given me several days longer.'

The abandoned Isidor watched Anil retrace his steps to the Star Ferry and board a vessel for Hong Kong Island. Stripped of ideas to fill the coming afternoon, he sat at the end of a concrete bench next to a cluster of chirruping domestic helpers.

'Like it here in Hong Kong, do you?' he enquired with some awkwardness.

For reasons he was not able to comprehend, the women shrilled with laughter and, in a body, turned to stare at him as if he had just swum the harbour fully clothed and climbed unannounced onto the promenade deck. One of the women said something in a language he couldn't recognise and turned down the corners of her mouth. The wild laughter, of a sort he'd never heard before, again convulsed the group.

How, he wondered, did his friend make the pursuit of the most unlikely girls so effortless?

Part of the reason was that Anil never lost more than a few minutes worrying about what he was doing or how he looked; by nature he was not a planner or worrier. Isidor, on the other hand, spent hours agonising over tiny details before failing to implement a fraction of what he had carefully rehearsed.

On the short ferry ride back to Central District, Anil decided to walk the half-mile to the Harbour Hotel and from there allow his wits and spontaneity to take charge. More than that would have clouded his brain and got in the way of an adventure's full appreciation.

Only as he parted the glass doors and stepped into a gust of air-conditioning did the next step begin to form in his mind. He'd have to find out if she was in and then pay her a visit. Once he got to the room a story could easily be concocted of why he was knocking uninvited on her door. Plumbers, electricians and dozens of other plausible callers roamed hotel corridors at will and in his jeans and stained T-shirt he could pass for any nameless artisan.

The Harbour Hotel was built at a time when only the width of a street separated its imposing façade from Victoria Harbour. At the moment of construction significance still hung on the name, but, like much else in Hong Kong's febrile development, a good concept soon disappeared under swathes of reclaimed land and behind ranks of intervening buildings.

Anil was at ease in the warm concrete canyons but still felt relieved to shake his clinging shirt loose in eddies of carefully controlled air. Behind the concierge's desk the eyes of a middle-aged employee narrowed in recognition.

With just an inconveniently absent name and a forgotten room number obstructing progress, Anil accosted the suspicious functionary.

'Messenger for ... ah ... guest of Mr Jakob Odergaard. OK to go up to ... er, which room would it be?' Mixing confident explanation with enquiry was, he felt, the best way to yield results.

Without bothering to look at the visitor, or implying willingness to help, the attendant consulted a desk computer in the same unbending manner of several nights before.

'What name give?'

'Er ... Mr Anil Patel.'

'... No one of that name in register.'

'Course not!' Anil said, suppressing a desire to kick the man. 'That's me.'

'I see, then how wish Harbour Hotel to be of service?'

'I'm delivering a message ... to a visitor booked in by Odergaard's – you know, Odergaard Holdings? We do the crappy furniture you see everywhere ... yes? She's stayin' at the top of the building here; only I 'appen to have forgotten 'er room number an' just need your 'elp finding it ... and whether the lady's in or not ... that's all.'

'Hummm. No name, no room number. Lady, you say?'

Demonstrating professional proficiency to locate a missing person for the wonder of an audience, any audience, even one as inconsequential as Anil Patel, was a momentarily more satisfying activity than blatant obstructionism and the concierge returned to his computer screen and keyboard, with sudden if temporary purpose.

'Would that be ...' the reply came at last after much clacking of keys, 'a ... ah, Ms Mandy Plumpkin ... room 2018?'

'Yeah, yeah ... got it! Well done, mate. You're an ace.'

The official straightened his back and, with the job done, reverted to his former self.

'Will check if expecting you.'

'I'm a bloody messenger with a message, so 'ow d'you think she's gonna know I'm comin'?'

Anil was hushed into silence by the palm of an authoritative hand.

After no more than two rings the desk telephone was hung up.

'Out,' the concierge snapped with satisfaction.

'Shit!'

'What?'

'I said I'll wait.'

'Loitering not encouraged.'

Four or five possible expletives sprang to Anil's mind, but, rather than diverting energy into verbal expression, he nodded and backed out of audible range to wait and watch for the tasty Ms Plumpkin's return.

'Now where'm I gonna sit while she's frolickin' in a hot tub, or doin' whatever gels do in a place this fake?'

A lounge at the far end of the lobby, enclosed by low partitioning and lines of palms in brass tubs, murmured busily under the guiding hands of half a dozen waitresses in abbreviated forms of Victorian servants' costumes.

'In there might work.'

Over fronds yellowing in unnaturally cool air he counted the glossy heads of customers enjoying sumptuous late-morning refreshment.

'Nah! Maybe not. Them fluffy ladies'll be askin' me to buy sunnink I can't afford.'

Anil cast around for an alternative and decided on an unattended bench marooned between condensation-spotted windows and the unhealthy palms. With his back to incoming daylight and an unrestricted view across the lobby and reception desks, he took up a strategic but uncomfortable position.

''Spose this'll have to do then ... thhhs ... so 'ere's where we are ...'

Caught in a vacuum between preparation and action, like an infantryman waiting for orders to advance from a waterlogged trench, he put a foot up on the bench and then put it down again. How much time, he wondered, would have to pass before Mandy Plumpkin reappeared? He was not a reader; in fact, he had never once read a book from beginning to end, not even during his perfunctory schooling. Hard pressed for an agreeable distraction he pulled a *Stiff* centrefold from a hip pocket and spread it across his knees.

The air-brushed smooth figure looked back at him as she had done on a score of previous occasions, but today her winsome smile and eye-poppingly large breasts failed to strike the usual beguiling notes, and his mind drifted to the edge of sleep, where reflection of a sort that rarely troubled his mind, bubbled ponderously to the surface.

For no reason, other than the recent wager, Isidor's wan and irresolute countenance swam into view, like that of a drowned man floating up from the bottom of a stream. By any definition his friend was a hopeless case, depending for fun more on the enterprise of others than on any personal resolve. There probably hadn't been one occasion when, left to his own invention, he'd had a really good time.

'What,' Anil wondered, 'might 'e be up now since being stood up on the waterfront? Attempting to waylay a desperate woman most likely and, in the process, managin' to look like a total creep.'

Like the droplets forming and running on the window pane behind him, Anil's deliberations continued their wandering journey from his friend to the odd encounter with the inquisitive boy.

In his adolescence Anil had benefited from a relaxed and undemanding father. This lad seemed to have no one to trust or share his passage over the tumultuous threshold of adulthood, a fact underlined by the guilty scamper to the bus depot.

What the young lad needed was another version of old Hari Patel, who, while producing an imperfect son, had made possible the chance to grow without restraint. Upbringing, Anil decided, was not just a matter of lecturing, but of knowing when to lay off. The process might be haphazard, a bit like laying out articles on a bazaar carpet for customers to think about, but at least it offered choices of what to take up and what to leave behind.

With the benefit of time and distance Anil had no reasons to regret absorbing his father's detachment in the same way that yawning sucked in air.

He couldn't find the right words to describe what he'd learned – he hadn't had that sort of education – but he could see there was more than met the eye in the notion that most matters were what you made them and that there was nothing to hold you back, unless you got imprisoned in a cage of your own creation.

'Bet JBO doesn't let himself get boxed in either and that's

what made 'im a star, an' why I'm gonna be right up there wiv 'im. Maybe not by havin' 'is cash an' all, but sure as hell gettin' as much out of recreation as he does.'

The closed lids on Anil's eyes fluttered to a standstill. Too much thinking was spoiling his afternoon.

From out of the dreamy void a voice coaxed in just the same way as his father's once had.

'We are not dealing over here with an insuperable problem; the right approach, if carefully managed, can arrange anything, absolutely anything.'

Was the old man nudging the owner of a pair of soft, suede shoes round to understanding there were better ways to handle an oversized carton than shoving it through a sub-post office's window grill? Even a dozy bulldog, the distant tones seemed to imply, could see the folly of that assertion.

Instead of the surly reply of ages ago an arch, female trill identical to the one he'd heard pulsating on the twentieth floor club-level air brought Anil's slumbering wits back to wide-awake consciousness.

'I'd be most interested to hear what you have in mind.'

The first voice, no longer speaking in a common-sense monotone, turned into the wheedling caginess of a man with an agenda.

'We will come to that, yes, we will come to that, but I'm sure a lady of your commendable ... attributes will not be found wanting when the moment arrives.'

Above the partition a crooked index finger rose to summon service. Whether physically afflicted, or temperamentally disinclined to be straight, was impossible to tell, but the extended hand described a semicircle of imprecision before retreating tortoise-like into the pink cuff of a sleeve bearing the monogram 'CCH'.

The elaborate initials, Anil realised in a shock of recognition, belonged to Claude Cordell Halt, the Odergaard Holdings Chief Financial Officer.

Anil lived for the hours he spent chaotically juggling his countless female attachments and nights on the town. But an enterprise this large required a certain amount of underpinning. Work and everything associated with it were unavoidable necessities, but they were brushed to one side and away from the things mattering most. Division of the good and necessary was the closest thing to structure in an otherwise messy existence. The parts, so long separated, were, however, beginning to converge.

'Didn't expect to be up against pansy-boy Claude as well as the guvner, so am I gonna keep soldiering on wiv this, or go back to lyin' low? Big question for the day, my son.'

In the huge sprawl of London, Anil had taken pleasure in the city's anonymity. Up until today Odergaard's had been no different and because no one knew him, other than the girls and fellow messengers in dispatch and a few compulsory contacts like Carol Tung and Johnny Lau, he was free to go anywhere, like a fly bouncing on and off the walls. As long as he delivered the post and completed his errands, no one was wiser for his passing. Anil knew them all, from the cleaners in the basement to the Chief Executive in his eagle's nest, and none lowered their voices, or changed topics, when he was present, because he was only a messenger and not expected to have ears.

Right at this moment he could have put his head over the rattling palm stalks and said, ''Ello, Claude old lad; I see you're up to no good agin', eh?' and, while the CFO would have flinched and wondered who this vagrant was, the errand boy could have fallen back under his cloak of obscurity and enjoyed the jest. But for how much longer could this continue when the two ends of his existence were about to be so inextricably intertwined?

With one side of his face in and the other out of hiding, Anil knelt on the bench and watched a waitress's hat turn and hop away. Behind, on the far side of the lobby, the concierge fell into earnest conversation with the green-coated doorman. Stooped heads and snatched looks told the messenger that he had become the subject of a hastily convened conference.

'Something needs to 'appen soon or I'll be getting the 'eave-'o, but in for a penny, in for a pound.'

Without warning, Claude Halt and the companion, with whom he had been sharing the late-morning break, emerged from the secluded lounge almost within touching distance of Anil's newly enlivened form.

'Then I will meet you here at ten thirty tomorrow?' the CFO confided.

'Wait for me inside, just where we were now. That way there will be no need to search for you,' the woman replied.

Long fingers extending in the direction of Mr Halt's chin were taken by their polished tips. After a moment's consideration of the correct protocol for attempted seduction of his employer's paramour, the CFO took the offered hand and held it tightly, as though it was an unexpected gift a breathless child had no intention of sharing.

In a single easy movement, the woman beamed in a manner implying the conferring of special favours and lowered her face and eyelashes. Basking in the promise's warmth, Claude Halt's heart collapsed in dust.

'Of all the bloody ... toerags!' Anil stumbled over restricted vocabulary and impassioned feelings.

By itself, the spectacle was ludicrous, but, because it involved the occupant of room 2018, whom he'd set out to ensnare with nothing in his arsenal except a sense of pure devilment, it was contemptible competition.

'Surely any bird,' he thought, 'especially one 'oo knows the tricks of the trade can tell what's goin' on? But ... hang on half a mo ... P'raps that's the point ... p'raps she does know and, wiv a bit more cunnin' than old 'Alt's got goin' for 'im, is gonna make him pay through the nose?'

To be in her position, Ms Mandy Plumpkin would not only have had to understand what she was, but also where she wanted to go. And, in truth, she did and had done ever since setting out on her bumpy road to stardom, and in spite of several annoying missteps along the way.

With dreams at once so lofty and so unimaginably prosaic she had faced the reality of toiling up the professional ladder, or employing her many assets in a less strenuous assault on a much sought-after celebrity. A girl with massive aspiration and severe financial constraint had a longer way to go than most and while many of the avenues open to her were insufferably laborious there was one with tree-lined paths and distant prospects that seemed set to carry her to Shangri-La.

She had met Jakob Odergaard a short while ago after arriving at a minor Scandinavian film festival in the company of an avant-garde and entirely unsuccessful director who viewed art as more important than an ability to fill theatre seats with ticket-purchasing audiences. When the relationship with the director failed to provide the desired 'kick-start' to her unlaunched career, her attention rapidly turned to figures of greater promise.

On the festival's fringe, where she and other hopeful starlets added glamour, but not much artistic commentary to the many conversations, Ms Plumpkin marked out the wealthy Odergaard entrepreneur as a person capable of supporting her interests.

'I hear you are a very influential man in Asia,' she had said.

'And where did you learn that?' he replied.

'Festivals are full of talk. You'd be amazed what can be picked up.'

She stretched out to place an empty glass on a passing waiter's receding tray and, as she twisted away, her strapless evening gown exposed naked shoulders and the full length of an unblemished back. Jakob's cold blue eyes explored each powdered hill and valley along her spine before coming to rest, like two exploratory fingertips, on the spot where a red satin bow sat loosely between very full hips.

From across the crowd the director, who liked to wear a beret and sunglasses even on the darkest night, returned Mandy's leisured wave.

When she turned, Jakob's lower lip, which he had momentarily sucked in between his teeth, protruded abruptly in a moist, shiny line. During months in the vicinity of a film set the only lesson she had taken to heart was that a good pose could be milked for more than just its initial effect.

'Have you visited Asia?' he asked.

'I don't wander away to remote parts of the world without invitation. And, besides, I have my work here to think of and couldn't be gone long.'

'Oh, I'd make a few weeks very worthwhile. Some introductions might be just what you're looking for.'

In the subsequent visit to Hong Kong, she met a number of local film-makers. One, who seemed particularly well acquainted with the Odergaard Chairman, promised her exposure in a Cantonese production requiring a white moll to speak a dozen lines during an on-screen performance of roughly twenty minutes. Not, she concluded, a role to define a star's reputation, but just enough to add some desperately needed padding to an admittedly slight record.

Jakob would, of course, have to be looked after, but fulfilling that part of the bargain required more effort from her patron than she contributed to the proceedings. 'Alas,' she thought with an inward theatrical sigh, 'this most recent attachment is not proving any more agreeable than the recently discarded director whose cinematic and romantic predilections were best left to collectors of minority tastes.'

A second trip, although undertaken for the specific purpose of filming the Cantonese part, was even more dissatisfying. Admittedly, a once anaemic bank account showed signs of weak recovery, but in most other aspects the tide was running out and at a comparatively mature age of not quite thirty the fantasy-laden barque carrying Oscars and truly masculine relationships was in danger of being stuck at the jetty.

Her feelings thus jaded, she had minimal expectations of the introduction to Claude Halt in spite of the assurance that he boasted connections to the art world of an even greater stature than Lam Qi Fat, the Cantonese film-maker, over at Starburst Pictures. Although sceptical she listened with staged enthusiasm and resolved to make the most of an unconvincing situation.

'It's like this,' Jakob explained, as he looked at his grey face in the bathroom mirror, 'Halt has been out here an age and knows people I don't bother with.'

In the reflection he could see a bed and two naked legs casually bent at the knees. Twenty years ago the sight would have consumed him with fire, but this morning, after a demanding and strangely unfulfilling night, he could only stare with an unaccustomed feeling of deep pessimism. A splash of aftershave lotion trickled from the creased chin to a spot on his left shoulder where it stung horribly.

'Jesus Christ!' he hissed through inhaled breath.

Bending sideways he found an inflamed patch glaring back at him.

'What the fuck's that! Hey! Come and tell me what this is.'

The legs straightened, but remained on the bed.

'Something up?' her lazy voice called back.

'Do you think I'm shouting blue murder for the fun of it? Come here!'

'What's the problem, my dear Jakob?' Mandy asked, entering the bathroom.

'Look at this, will you? What is it?'

'Hm! I'd say it was a two-inch scratch, put there by the fingernails of a woman craving excitement.'

'I don't remember.'

'Perhaps that's because you were half asleep and had made an early exit from what under most circumstances is considered a joint activity.'

The perfect truth of the mockery was maddening. In a reflex

action most men would have regarded as shameful Jakob raised his hand.

'Really?' she said. 'Has it come to that? I'm not your wife, you know.'

He was not used to being cowed by someone who should have been content with the crumbs tossed in her direction. People's sensibilities were there for him to bulldoze, not for them to manipulate in a way that made him feel both a cad and, because he'd held back and missed the pleasure of a resounding slap, a confirmed impotent.

Mandy Plumpkin had suddenly become more trouble than she was worth and handing her off to a credulous CFO was an opportune relief.

No one, it had to be said, was more adept than Jakob Odergaard at spotting other people's hidden weaknesses and he'd seen quite a few in his business associate of thirty years.

Insight, outside his small sphere of expertise, was not Claude Halt's forte, but, if he had stretched his imagination beyond the combined effects of debit and credit, he would have recognised corporate advantage rested foursquare on the CEO's astute and very individual assessment of public and private foibles that had little to do with the prevailing market and business circumstances.

'Then ten thirty it is. I shall wait for you in the vicinity of our table,' Claude said ingratiatingly.

Mandy Plumpkin gently withdrew her hand from the manic grip and lifted her smile from his glowing, schoolboy stupor, before retreating coolly across the hotel lobby. Behind her, in a haze of happiness and hope, she left a new and devoted admirer rooted to the marble flagging and wishing tomorrow had already dawned.

The transfixed figure breathed as if his lungs would never fill. Metres away the messenger snorted in derision.

'What a bleedin' pantomime!'

A member of the hotel's floor staff, clad in blue jacket and yellow-frogged chest suitable for the torso of a Hungarian hussar, circled the ménage. Above his head he carried a message board supported on a short pole and periodically rang a small bell.

'Telephone for Mr McAlister; a call for Mr Alistair McAlister,' he announced as if the initial absence of a given name was significantly remedied by its later inclusion. Casting around eyes that struggled to appear engaged, he alighted on the visage of Anil Patel, but realising the improbability of the connection turned instead to the static figure on the marbled floor.

'Would it be Mr McAl–?'

Claude Halt's thousand-metre stare swept over the hussar as if he had been invited to confession after a night of paralysing debauchery.'

'What?' he asked with bewilderment.

'Mr Alistair McAlister ... Sir, please?'

'Ah! Unfortunately, no I'm not. But, if I may ask, what would your name be?

'Pardon? Oh, here ... on name tag ... Wong. Are you complaining? Hope nothing wrong?'

'Well, ah ... so Wong; in a town of six million where five point nine have the same label, that won't tie anything down a great deal. Look, Wong, may I call you Joe just to help me out here? I need some assistance. If you are open to a small incentive, say ah ... one hundred, no, fifty dollars ... I'd like you to keep a watch out for ...'

What Joe Wong was being asked to observe was lost in hushed confidence.

Although Anil couldn't exactly say why, a window seemed to be closing and three days shrinking into a matter of hours. What he needed was a bit of that fast thinking that normally came so easily.

With censorious stares from the concierge and green-hatted doorman, who thought they had seen it all, he walked across the lobby and into an open lift. Behind him, and across the polished and spacious distance, Claude Halt withdrew from sight with an arm thrown casually over the pliable bellboy's shoulders.

Anil stabbed briskly at the illuminated lift display and was whisked in hermetically sealed comfort to the twentieth floor, club level. Room 2018 was twenty-seven paces away; why on earth had that fact been there to recall when previously he hadn't remembered the room's number?

Facing the wooden door he took a deep breath and tapped.

'Yes, who is it?' a faint female voice called.

'Floor service for Ms Plumpkin, M'am,' Anil replied as steadily as he could. 'I've come to check your lights.'

7

The Shatin flat was still in early-morning darkness when Budiwati finished polishing and neatly laying out shoes for the family's approaching day. School regulations chose the boy's unvarying black, but, as whim and choler dictated Mrs Tung's choice, hers was never final until her moment of departure. To cover more than one possibility, Budiwati put out a tan pair, with dainty leather bows on each instep and, next to them and after some careful thought, the much favoured open-toed, green ones that were badly scuffed around the heels by petulant walks across Odergaard's steel warehouse floor grills searching for Johnny Lau, who never seemed to be around when he was wanted.

Without envy, but with a great deal of curiosity, Budiwati placed a flat, farmhouse foot on top of one of the green shoes and wondered whether balancing on four-inch heels was as much fun as magazine and shopping-mall advertising implied. At first only four stubby toes found their way into the soft leather interior; the fifth hung loose over a protesting rim. Standing on her full weight she studied her well-muscled calf to see how a leg's line should blend into the straightness of a highly fashioned heel. Not quite satisfied with what she saw she wriggled and pushed until her smallest toe, which suffered chronically knotted joints, unexpectedly found room alongside its so far estranged companions.

The shoe emitted a faint groan and, from a previously impeccable seam, released a black cobbler's thread, which curled spontaneously round the, until then, unhoused toe's horn-hard nail.

'Uh? ... Oh, dear!'

Taking curved scissors from a pocket under her apron Budiwati trimmed away the strand and wiped over the abused leather with a puffy sleeve, as other daily chores waited for her attention.

Last night's drained dishes still stood by the sink and the newly dented wok rested empty on the tiny kitchen's one cold gas ring.

After last night's commotion and missed dinners stomachs would need filling. Budiwati looked through the window at the black morning and wondered who in her Sumatran village family would be up first. When she was at home it had always been Grandfather, whose bucolic habits were so engrained he could not have slept one minute longer even had he wanted.

She turned back to the wok and after a sad sigh splashed in some corn oil, some noodles, a sprinkling of chilli, and some chopped vegetables and soon had a rich, sudsy smell rising to her nostrils that recalled the huge breakfasts her brothers ate before leaving for work in the rice fields.

On the wall above her head a cheerless clock looked down in utter irrelevance. To Budiwati the day, and indeed her entire life, was moved by compulsions quite separate to the order and timetable of her employer. Not that she was a slacker, far from it; tasks that crowded in were tackled ruggedly one by onerous one, but they were performed at a pace and rhythm within and around her and not on the false demands of fingers on a dial.

When daylight outside the flat was of a certain intensity and colour Budiwati knew instinctively what she should be doing. The clunking sound of the lift rising in its hollow concrete column told her a security guard was making his first round and by this time Wai Pang's clothes should be pressed and hung. At the moment the bathroom door bumped into muffled place her mistress's first jasmine tea of the day should be standing cooling near the bedside and, in the neighbouring room, Wai Pang's leaden shoulders must be shaken. The banged doors and shouts from across the landing not only confirmed the neighbouring Mr Chan's departure for his computer repair shop in the New Territories and his angry preparation for managing undocumented labourers, but also that Wai Pang should be finishing his breakfast or about to break the golden rule of being first to leave.

If that breach occurred, there was no knowing exactly how Mrs Tung would react. She might just sulk, or more probably throw a violent fit, but whatever happened the aftermath hung in a pall over the house for days or sometimes weeks on end until everyone felt so disconsolate they'd do almost anything to dispel the toxic cloud.

In the short space of time between getting up, which Budiwati did at the same minute every morning without any form of mechanical assistance, and polishing shoes, she usually took the pet schnauzer for its early toilet outing. Scrapes on the ceiling overhead indicated another home helper was also preparing for the ritual of gathering, like Budiwati, with others of their profession in separate national groups, to talk and discuss employers and their most recent days off and, almost incidentally, to purge household pets.

In the street and on the ends of slack leads, dogs of various breeds and sizes, scratched, sat down, yapped, occasionally fought and intermittently relieved themselves. None, however, walked anywhere, until, at a time determined by a sudden lack of cohesion in the group and an imperceptible shifting away of handlers, the charges were dragged reluctantly back to their pokey apartments high in the hot, dirty sky, where they would remain until joining an identical gathering at noon and again at day's end.

But this morning, search as she may, Budiwati could not find the schnauzer anywhere. Noticing her employer's locked door she suspected the creature had sought refuge inside and must be left unevacuated until its mistress was ready to stir.

When left alone Budiwati was expected to make decisions

coinciding with Mrs Tung's unambiguous likes and dislikes and unpredictable temperament; a tricky proposition at the best of times. Independent thought and, more importantly, independent action on any subject under the sun were strictly forbidden, and entering the confines of her mistress's bedroom while it contained the mistress's person was a decision no employee with any sense, let alone the long-suffering Budiwati, would wisely contemplate. The disagreeable schnauzer's toilet outing was therefore, inevitably, but somewhat unadvisedly, shunted to one side until, at a later time, the animal's pestering would bring it back into the helper's mind.

A bump and drone from the lift reverberated through the flat's cramped rooms and Budiwati hung Wai Pang's uniform on a rail above his bed before giving the boy a brisk shake.

'Yaawh ... euh ... What time ... is it?'

'You should be washing and getting ready for school. Look,' she said, pulling back threadbare curtains that shed a fine dust film onto the window sill, 'children are already out and waiting for the buses.'

'They're going to Hong Kong Island and have to leave early.'

When she looked back Wai Pang's head was under his pillow.

'Your mother will want the bathroom, so better move quickly now.'

Of all the imaginable horrors capable of wrecking a teenager's day, maternal ire before his trousers were on was the worst.

'Have you made her tea?' he asked through the bedclothes.

'Yes, but I'm still waiting to give it to her, so get a move on or you'll be in all sorts of trouble.' Half-truths were usually sufficient to pry apart his sticky eyes.

Raised voices on the landing and a door slam, dulled by travel through several wood-and-cement obstructions, echoed in Wai Pang's bedroom.

'Who's ...?'

'Mr Chan.'

He scrambled free and rushed away to return seconds later with water on his chin and dry night-time secretions still clinging undisturbed to his long eyelashes.

'Where's my shirt?'

'On the bed.'

'Is she up yet?'

'Her door's closed.'

'What's for breakfast?'

'Noodles; I've put some on the table.'

'I'm going to be late.'

'Yes.'

Dragging a satchel into the living room, Wai Pang stood in front of the table and chopsticked several coils of fried vegetables and noodles into his mouth.

'Um, good.'

She glanced at the growing light on the other side of grime-smeared windows.

'You should sit down'.

'Can't.'

'Why?'

'Bum hurts.'

'Oh.'

'Gotta go.'

He closed the apartment door with a soft tick and, in the subsequent whirr and bump of the lift, fled towards school. From the tiny kitchen's window Budiwati watched Wai Pang run across the street and in between double-decker buses until he disappeared among the bustle of food hawkers setting out their early-morning trade.

A shadow from a tower crane's jib caught in the last blaze of night-time flood lighting swung over the road below and glided up the side of a neighbouring block of flats. In his windblown turret the driver juggled with an array of levers and several brown objects pierced by a barbeque stick. 'Fish balls,' Budiwati surmised. The operator grimaced over something not suiting his taste and spat a long stream of stained juice through a ventilation opening at his elbow. Momentarily held together by internal tension, the spittle arced away until gravity broke it to a million invisible droplets that drizzled dew-like onto the bent necks of the growing throng below.

The sky was almost light now, but no sun shone through the industrial fug blown down from China. In the near and further distance, uniform and sentinel high-rise apartments, as grim as tombstones, glowered on the new day.

Rapid frothing on the stove behind her pulled Budiwati away from the window to lower still further the blue gas flame under the damaged wok. She was not yet ready to set about the rest of her mounting chores, but, to prepare her mind, walked from one cramped room to the next. Work was a fact and an inescapable condition, but in her native village, which seemed years and lives away and not just a few hundred air-miles, it was undertaken without the soul-crushing melancholy found in Hong Kong. Reluctantly, she stooped to pick up Wai Pang's more than usually soiled underwear and yesterday's discarded flannels that were still sticky from spilt soda. Several times she thought she heard a movement in Mrs Tung's room, and the muscles in her shoulders contracted. But, although no one emerged, she still let fall a gentle breath that, despite its lightness, was full of the weight of pointlessness.

The crowds in the street outside began dispersing to offices and factories and, at the construction site opposite, a line of ready-mix cement lorries ground to a stop beneath the tower crane's turning boom.

As she deliberated over whether to postpone vacuum-cleaning until later in the day or risk Mrs Tung's displeasure for being noisily woken from sleep, the bedroom door lurched open and the pet schnauzer bounded forward in a state of great agitation.

'What's going on?' boomed the flat's mistress.

Was the question asked in anticipation of an answer, or was it framed so widely that it would deliberately prevent any acceptable form of response? Previously, Budiwati's employer's dissatisfaction had not required real or even manufactured causes, because just being felt was more than enough to bring thunderbolts down on the heads of all the Shatin flat's occupants regardless of guilt or innocence.

While pondering on the possibility of a repetition of last night's pitiless outbreak Budiwati tilted her head to one side and studied her employer. The long sleep had not been entirely beneficial. Puffy eye-shadows marred the usually tight skin, and the normally well-groomed hair, on which a modest fortune had been spent, stood out in strands as if the body beneath had undergone nocturnal electrotherapy. 'That's what comes,' the domestic helper decided, 'of going straight from bath to bed without using a dryer.'

'Shall I repeat?'

In Budiwati's estimation, duplication was most unlikely to shed light on anything and, after noticing the pet schnauzer's agitated circling of the living-room rug and ominous stiffening, she sought refuge in the uncontentious.

'Your tea's ready; in fact been ready a long while. I'll put it by your bed and take the dog down.'

'Do you realise the time?' Mrs Tung's voice was quivering with feeling.

'I … er … I know his walk's past due and he should go now or …'

To emphasise just how far advanced day had become, the schnauzer squatted down with forelegs tucked tidily between its rear paws and, with painfully expressive eyebrows conveying both relief and remorse, flooded the rug's central lotus blossom motif with more bright yellow liquid than the tiny proportions of its body seemed capable of containing.

Mrs Tung placed both fists on her narrow hips as if to say, 'And on top of everything else you allow this to happen!' and, with a hitch of the perished elastic in her nightwear undergarment, she returned to the stewed and unventilated privacy of her bedroom.

Before the domestic helper had time to sink to her knees and roll up the fouled rug, her mistress returned to the living room.

'And! ... I will be leaving late this morning.'

What had led to this unusual pronouncement was not of the slightest interest to Budiwati. But that her morning was becoming progressively more complicated filled her with nervousness. The hair in front of her that once spoke of no more than a restless night now suggested a fragile state of mind with unpredictable consequences.

'In that case, what do you want me to prepare? Would it be fine if–'

'Stop! ... Not finished yet. Iron tan skirt and white blouse, the one with frilled cuffs and front and put out green shoes.'

'But what about ...?'

The late hour had forced Mrs Tung into making an odd decision. In all her years with Odergaard Holdings she had never once been unpunctual, not even when the cross-harbour tunnel had been blocked by a punctured poultry transporter and commuters were escorted on foot for the last half-mile, and had certainly never contrived a day off when there was nothing wrong with her. Arriving late after oversleeping was so pathetically commonplace she could not bring herself to say that was what had happened. She had become a victim of her own savage standards, where anything less than perfection would cast her as a figure of fun. So, instead of committing the small and everyday sin of oversight, she opted for the greater and more reprehensible one of deception.

'As soon as you've done ... down ... there ... give me breakfast. Presume something is ready?' And then adding as an afterthought: 'What did Wai Pang eat?'

'Noodles, but there's plenty left. I knew you'd be hungry too, so ...'

Since her early twenties Carol Tung's disposition never flirted with exuberance. The nearest she had ever come to that exalted state had been in the moment Jakob Odergaard waved and smiled at her from the junk and in the few days immediately after when a glow of a kind she had not previously experienced gave her existence unusually vivid meaning and purpose. Since then she had descended by degrees into a state of permanent peevishness. No respite was offered to her family, her colleagues or herself, and her crankiness varied only in its severity.

After rising and realising how late she was her mood was as low as could be. The sudden wild idea of an illicit day chasing unspecified pleasures, however, gave her spirits an unaccustomed fillip. But, in her bathroom and after throwing her nightclothes to one side and recalling the previous evening's morbid soak, her thoughts once again began to spiral downhill. She pressed her sagging stomach with both hands and stood a little more erectly to tighten its loose folds. At the sink she washed her hands thoroughly and then, dissatisfied with the result, washed them a second time before getting into a blisteringly hot shower.

'Is this what Wai Pang ate?' she asked later.

'Yes, M'am.'

'Wonder he wasn't sick.'

'Said he enjoyed it he did, M'am, but didn't have time to eat a lot.'

'Don't believe you. He doesn't like chilli and always gets up when told. Uhh! Too hot; can't you cook without killing food with spice?' She pushed away the almost untouched plate of noodles. Servants were no better than children and firmness was the only way to keep them under any sort of control.

'Can I get something else?'

'Leaving now; where are my shoes?

'By the door. The tan ones would look best with that skirt.'

The best response to effrontery, Mrs Tung decided, was to ignore it altogether, cut it stone dead, as if it had been penury pleading for alms on the pavement.

'Yes, yes, of course,' she said to herself. 'Exactly as expected; green contrasts beautifully, and brings a splash of colour to a moderately stylish outfit. If only the heels weren't so badly marked ... ah, well.'

For the sake of her looks Mrs Tung was prepared to suffer and couldn't understand why only one shoe pinched. The last time she had worn this pair both had given her considerable discomfort. 'Do feet lose weight?' she wondered, 'And if they did, shouldn't they do it together?'

As she studied the single lacquered toe on her right foot it was joined in the open vent by a second, third, fourth and then fifth extremity until her entire foot slid though the broken seam onto the flat's cold floor tiles.

'Oh!'

'Then I suppose ... you'll want the tan ones, M'am?'

Escape into truancy was presenting a great many more obstacles than traditional departures from the flat, but having set her mind on a course Carol Tung would not be thwarted and vigorously snatched at the recommended tan choice before flouncing away to the landing and her abruptly devised mission.

Originality and spontaneity were not traits typically associated with a dogmatic mind. But heavy sleep and lifeless bedroom air had somehow combined to spawn dank toadstool imaginings she could scarce believe to be her own. Some irresistible force, like a man's hand on her naked breast, had taken control. She wanted to turn and flee shrieking to the security of her fusty room, but, in spite of almost crippling misgivings, her outstretched tan shoe stepped over the lift's sill and touched the threshold of a guilty journey that made her flesh tingle with secret, wicked thrills.

From the street she looked up at the elevated flat's tiny windows and, for a moment, thought she saw a face staring back at her. Instead of waiting at the bus stop, where she could still be seen, she turned right and walked until the apartment block disappeared from view and boarding the number 343 double-decker, which would take her through the cross-harbour tunnel to Hong Kong Island and Central District.

For no other reason than the name's familiarity, she decided to take tea at the Harbour Hotel. Never having been picked up by a man before she was not at all sure how she should advertise her availability. Hanging out in places ostensibly more respectable than establishments along the Wanchai Do, which catered for clients with unreconstructed morals, struck her as a novice's best way to begin.

The hotel's secluded lounge at the lobby's farthest end was more crowded than she expected and, although not a disappointment in itself, the heavy preponderance of women was a let-down.

Several pairs of tai tais, dressed in the sort of designer clothes never found in upper Kowloon's discount stores, were gossiping over teacups, before setting out on another round of therapeutic purchase and a group of foreign tourists waited noisily for an open-topped vehicle to carry them round the city. Without exception the holidaying men were fatter and heartier than she liked and their women were all under-dressed, with ugly lines of white flesh showing where thin shoulder straps had kept out yesterday's ultraviolet rays.

'A table for one or are you meeting ...?' asked a tactful waitress in a lace cap and short black skirt.

'Oh! Ah ... for one if ...'

'This way, please.' Number Twenty-seven server, who for public purposes lacked a human identity, circled away towards the clouded windows.

'No, not over there; this instead?' Mrs Tung pointed to an alcove fringed by thirsty palms on the edge of neglectful death.

Success in this abnormal excursion demanded visibility, but exposure to open gaze was more horrifying than exhilarating. 'Perhaps seclusion and reticence,' she thought tremulously, 'would add to my appeal?'

'I'll come back for your order after you have had time to consider,' Number Twenty-seven confided.

'I'll have tea.'

The request was greeted by an indulgent smile.

'Yes, Madam. We have Chinese and English. If it's Chinese, we have Oolong, green, chrysanthemum, Pu'er, jas –'

'Jasmine,' Mrs Tung interrupted before the tide of choice drowned her ability to listen.

Among the tourist and all-female groups a solitary male leant over a laptop computer. His shirt sleeves were unevenly rolled to the approximate middle of thickly haired forearms. A tie, which may have started the day under his chin, hung loosely to one side. Over the back of a neighbouring chair a creased linen jacket had, by its appearance, been thrown there carelessly. He didn't have the look of a businessman, Mrs Tung considered, but with foreigners, who were so negligent of how they appeared, one could never tell for sure.

If Mrs Tung was to guess, he was somewhere in his late fifties. But she could be ten, fifteen or more years wide of the mark, because, as everyone knew, heavy people, unlike those of a slighter build, had a way of aging rapidly. 'Not surprising considering the food their bodies are expected to digest.' Apart from a few comparisons at Odergaard's she had no means of verifying whether this often repeated line was true or not. But what if it was? Mrs Tung had not embarked on today's outing in search of weight or age compatibility. Put simply, although the thoughts clanged like cymbals in her head, she'd come 'to find a man'. The admission, even at the core of her repressed emotions, was so appalling, so sinful, she pretended the temporary nature of the hoped-for encounter would somehow diminish its iniquity. 'Not long-term thing,' she kept telling herself. 'Just once and then go home to wash and sleep.'

'Jasmine tea, Madam,' the waitress announced majestically before putting down a cup and pouring into it steaming yellow-green liquid. 'Will there be anything else?'

'Yes ... er ... is ... ,' Mrs Tung screwed up every last grain of courage and almost choked on the words, '... is ... er ... that gentleman over there resident at the Harbour Hotel?'

The head under its frilly lace hat lifted a fraction before turning along the line indicated.

'You mean Mr Keso; Mr Geoffrey Keso? Yes, he is staying here. Are you meeting him?'

For indeterminate reasons the courtesy of 'Madam' had disappeared.

'Yes, maybe ... but not now ...'

Having made up her mind exactly which game this casual visitor was playing, Number Twenty-seven server looked down with all the disapproval four feet ten inches could bestow before turning away to assist customers possessing worthier motives.

From the obscurity of her corner and while observing her declared, but oblivious, target, Mrs Tung was unsure what to do next; perhaps catching Mr Keso's eyes in cold cod-fish stares and coat-button smiles across the intervening rows of furniture would be a start? However, the lifelong degradation of her emotions and the chaos of the surviving rubble left her, at the age of not yet forty, totally unequipped to entice. She was like the hulk of an abandoned foundry built in pristine parkland during the 'Great Leap Forward' that had been left to rot and leach poison into the surrounding soil and air.

Shifting her chair to one side she opened up a direct and unobstructed view to Mr Keso and, while fixing him with lustreless leers, pulled her skirt hem to the top of her knees.

Without at first being aware of the intense interest near by he leant back to retrieve a pen from his discarded jacket and met Mrs Tung's almost unhinged gawp.

Thinking that, by negligence or oversight, he had somehow unwittingly offended a person sitting close by, he smiled back hoping his courteous action would moderate any unintended fault. The coat-button distorted sideways and up and down, without being in sufficient control to fully reciprocate his gesture. Trying to diffuse what was becoming an embarrassing situation, Mr Keso pointed to his chest as if to ask, 'Me?', and by implication offer over the yards an apology.

In reply, Mrs Tung slowly raised one leg over the other permitting Mr Keso a leisured view of her thin, silk-stockinged thighs and a suggestion of whatever else may lie deeper in the gross and inhospitable shadow of her tan skirt.

'Mah good Lord!' Mr Keso gulped, for he was a God-fearing man, dedicated to his wife and five blue-eyed children in rural Utah, and, while not beyond the capacity to recognise beauty, or to enjoy female company, he was most unlikely to join, without the least introduction, a casual lady in an unpremeditated escapade.

But, he conceded, graceful legs, even without the benefit of elegant clothes, could have a certain – he searched for a satisfactory word – charm that should not be altogether ignored and on this trip he had seen many from behind the dark glasses he habitually wore to protect his sensitive eyes. But, alas, this female opposite, who seemed bent on something quite ugly, was neither good to look at, nor improved by her selection of bargain apparel.

'Ah! Geoffrey how good to see you back with us again. How are you; how are you?'

The thighs slapped shut and, as Mrs Tung spun round to face the parched palms, Claude C. Halt, the Odergaard Holdings Chief Financial Officer, strode forward to effusively greet Mr Geoffrey Keso.

'Ah'm well, well ... or at least Ah was up until a few minutes ago. Ah don't visit the East as often as maybe Ahd like, but Ah have heard tales and seen sights that are downright unexpected and would make Mrs Keso's dear hair stand on end, and Ah believe you may just have saved me from a very unusual, can Ah say quite unsettling, incident.'

He looked back at the neighbouring alcove, where only an

untasted and still steaming cup of jasmine tea suggested the table had recently been occupied.

'I'm sure we can help you with anything you care to name, in the same manner as you will help us. Now, I have someone I want you to meet. She'll be here very soon; splendid lady, simply splendid, but totally unfamiliar with Asia. In fact, so much so that I'll be taking her off in a few minutes to see the sights. But meeting her, before we set out, or I hear your proposal, is I suggest an early priority.'

'Ah have to tell you there are limits to how far we can go.'

Although Geoffrey Keso was glad of Claude Halt's financial support and this afternoon's timely appearance, which had saved him from the discomfiture of who knew what, he was not pleased to be confronted by the – as yet undefined – price for sponsorship of the Provo Repertory Theater Company's return to Hong Kong. He felt like a dim-witted goat which, having once escaped death with only a few scratches, had walked into a tiger's ambush that had been signposted several miles back.

The previous visit had been clouded by Odergaard Holding's insistence that the semi-professional group would perform *Peer Gynt* in its entirety. The choice was communicated very early during eighteen months of negotiation and, although protestations were fulsome, Jakob was adamant and unprepared to change his mind.

'They say it's an impossible play, goes on for hours and needs an orchestra,' Claude Halt had cautiously advised.

'I don't care if they have to play Norwegian bagpipes, if that's what Dagmar wants and I'm paying for it then that's what they provide.'

The decision was communicated to the Provo Rep, which, in view of its ambition to 'go international', succumbed with grumbles to the blatant arm-twisting. Financial backers, they kept repeating, had no right to interfere with artistic choice.

'And I say artists can go and fuck themselves' had been JBO's disobliging reply.

'Yes, to be sure, but let us try and steer the conversation towards expressions of cooperation. Sounds so much better, wouldn't you agree?' Claude had suggested.

'My word is "fuck"; you use whatever you like.'

The intervening year and a half and frequent contacts with the troupe's sponsor should have made Geoffrey Keso a little more worldly wise and a lot more sceptical about Odergaard's corporate integrity, especially when at the end his backer and spouse omitted to attend the opening night and all subsequent performances of the famously difficult play. But Geoffrey was a trusting soul who assumed people were essentially good by nature, even while being sometimes perhaps a shade misguided in their actions.

In the confusion of Mrs Tung's precipitate departure she came close to colliding with a blonde woman gliding immaculately across the lobby as if on ice skates. Scarcely noticing the beatific smile that fell on her and the patronising nods to left and right, the flustered office administrator hurried to the door and the squalid safety of Wanchai's streets.

Behind the troubled exit and before Mandy Plumpkin had spotted Claude Halt, he was out of his seat and rushing towards her.

'Ah! You are looking positively wonderful today; an alpine breeze wafting though our sweltering city. How are you? How are you? Come, we are lucky to have with us our friend Mr Keso who is visiting from overseas to discuss our support for next year's programming. What a stroke of good fortune to have you both here at the same time!'

Not knowing quite what the day held in store, Ms Plumpkin had dressed for effect rather than comfort, or, for that matter, in expectation of a guided excursion to local tourist spots. A tight skirt and flowered blouse, matched in subdued blue shades, accentuated her fledgling starlet's already exceptional figure and provoked sniffs of disapproval and jealousy from the less well-blessed tai tais.

'Pleased to meet you, Mam,' Geoffrey Keso said, rising unsteadily from his seat and extending a fat, dimpled hand embellished by a college graduation ring as big and brown as a walnut.

'Geoffrey is the programme director for the Provo International Theater Company, my dear,' Claude explained, with a sly, sideways look to judge how the suggestion of intimacy had been received, little realising the world of performing arts was awash with meaningless expressions of deep affection, which, in other walks of life, caused stomachs to heave. But, being green and obstinate in his objective, he let the endearment dangle before lamely adding as if to disguise his intentions, 'Provo is in America, Utah; not far from Wyoming ... umm ...I believe.'

Although not a question, Mr Keso felt obliged to proudly confirm the veracity of the comment: 'Yas, Sir, and close to that great metropolis of Salt Lake City, of which Ah'm sure ya'll have heard.'

Ms Plumpkin may not have been one of the movers and shakers of stage and screen, but she had, in a manner of speaking, touched the hands of many who were and this provincial impresario appeared cast for work of a different, even lesser, stamp. While clearly not of the same gangster mould as Lam Qi Fat, his eventual worth might not be much greater.

'Hello,' she said.

A shade crestfallen at the lack of instant rapport Claude sought to invigorate the conversation.

'We were just about to hear from Geoffrey what he will bring to next spring's Arts Festival,' he said, before adding threateningly, 'once we have settled sponsorship terms.'

'If we are lucky enough to return, we'd want to do something less complicated than last time out.'

'They brought *Peer Gynt*; it was a tremendous success. Geoffrey is just too modest. That's a play you should try; with hair the colour of yours you'd make a delightful ... er ... who's the heroine?'

'Solveig,' returned Mr Keso, as if the name had been etched into his memory with a hammer and chisel and adding, in view of where the conversation appeared to be heading, 'Might you be an actress bah any chance?'

'Indeed she is and fresh from a filming assignment in Hong Kong before returning to Europe. How really fortunate your visits coincided.'

The right presentation, spin if you will, was necessary in dealings between these artsy, fartsy folk, or they were likely to get themselves into trouble. Unmanaged aspirants were clearly not the best people to answer for themselves and allowing too much opportunity to speak was fraught with risk.

'Yes, Ah'm sure you're right,' replied Provo's theatrical agent, without the least evidence of conviction.

'Now tell us what delights you will be bringing to the next Arts Festival?'

'Oh! Ah don't know yet, Ah'm sure, but maybe something from Stateside.'

'Wouldn't that be too – how shall I say? – regional, for broad-based taste?'

Mr Keso found the off-the-cuff remark a shade condescending, but having decided he needed the Odergaard CFO he held his tongue.

'Nothing final yet, but it'll be twentieth or maybe twenty-first century.'

'Good, good. Well … I'm glad you had the opportunity to meet Mandy here.' Claude turned to Ms Plumpkin. 'So shall we "do" the town now if the heat permits?'

Having not been directly spoken to since the very beginning of the conversation, she had contributed nothing apart from topical matter, but as the spotlight swivelled back in her direction she instinctively sat up with a backward curve of her spine. The movement thrust her chest forward and provoked an involuntary twitch under Claude Halt's left eye.

'Perhaps,' he suggested, 'a change into something less

warming ... would make you more at ease ... hum ... in the sun that is; what do you say?'

'I'm sure you are right. Then if you'll excuse me ...?'

Why men were captivated by a beautiful woman's breathless but slightly vacuous statements was beyond comprehension, but they were, and that was enough for Ms Plumpkin. She nodded at Geoffrey Keso.

'Is it possible we will meet again soon?' she asked.

'Nothing, nothing at all would surprise me,' he found himself saying, as if the matter was somehow inescapable.

'Claude, I will be back shortly.'

Although both men were past the time of youthful gallantry, they spontaneously rose from their chairs, a gesture hardly ever made to female friends or relatives, as if in the circumstances of this young lady's departure no other behaviour was possible. They watched the rounded hips recede from view and she, knowing where their eyes rested, rotated her tight blue skirt in slow, artful motion.

'That's quite a woman,' Mr Keso observed before adding, with the recollection of an earlier brush with feminine wiles fresh in his mind, 'One thing for sure Hong Kong ain't Provo.'

'I knew you'd like her instantly.'

'Ah did not exactly say that, but Ah can see she has merits. However, setting that to one side Ah prefer to talk about sponsorship.'

'And so do I, so do I. But to be quite plain there is the matter of what we'd call "linkage".'

'Ah see,' said Geoffrey carefully, as he started to realise what demands were being made of the Provo Repertory Theater Company. 'But we do have our regular players.'

'But all theatre companies, especially those stepping up from a local to an international level, have guest appearances, to give them – shall we say? – cachet. There must be hundreds of amateur wannabes out there and only a few break free from the herd. This could seal your place among a minority.'

'Ah see what you are getting at, but that would be a decision made bah the committee at home in Provo.'

'Of course, but a committee you advise and which can't but move without your guidance?'

'Then Ah'll have to get back to ya'll.'

'There now, isn't that all I've been asking?'

Pleased with his performance, Claude Halt settled back into his easy chair and pursed his lips smugly as if he had just found an irregularity in the canteen's petty cash float. 'Well,' he thought, 'old JBO might fancy himself as a master negotiator, but when push comes to shove the Odergaard CFO isn't so far behind.'

With business effectively concluded and with nothing left in common, after the encounter at the crossroads of Hong Kong's and Provo's theatrical ambitions, conversation dried up. If thrust upon each other at a cocktail party, they would have briefly exchanged the smallest of small talk before discovering the pressing need to circulate. Round contentment, faith and family, the chance to do good work and serve his god and church were almost all Geoffrey Keso asked, but Claude Halt had been schooled in a more sophisticated world and under wings he envied and sought to subvert. For years he had served in the shadows, 'But,' he reflected, 'even this self-effacing, number-crunching, backroom boy would have his day.'

'So, that's about it for now?' said Mr Keso, peering intently at his computer as if in search of a phrase requiring a pair of commas.

'I guess it is. When are you heading back to Utah?'

'Monday. Ah'm just about wrapped up here.'

'Good, then that's all right.'

'Yas, you could say so.'

'OK, well ...'

Claude, impatient for Ms Plumpkin's return, tapped the arm of his chair and Geoffrey went back to staring into the lid of his computer. They exchanged a glance as both waited for the other to leave.

'Got to send some emails, so Ah'll be on my way.'

'Right you are. Then we can expect to hear from you?'

'Yas, sure, but just give me some time.'

The hotel lounge was filling with late-morning traffic and Mr Keso's departing plod left Claude Halt in sole possession of a table and five chairs. The diminutive waitress in the frilled cap bounced into sight again followed by an elderly woman helped along by a brightly dressed girl of about twenty and a short stooping man with lengthy hair hanging along the fringes of a wide bald patch.

'I think this table has space, if you don't mind?' the waitress said, addressing first the new arrivals and then the already seated CFO.

'I'm expecting someone,' Claude snapped.

'Oh, but do you require all the seats?'

'Don't disturb the gentleman, Enrico. We can find another place,' implored the older woman, who was not inclined to make a fuss.

'There's nowhere else. Please help the lady; she is a visitor,' coaxed the girl.

Repetition was not going to make his statement any clearer, or change no into something softer, so Claude just turned away to consider matters far more important than minor conflicts with deaf tourists.

'Just sit down, Mama; he's hardly likely to throw you out,' Eric said firmly.

'Now look here!' protested Claude.

'No, you look. What's the matter with you? Can't you help an old woman?'

'Please, please ... this is not how ...' Eric's mother was becoming agitated.

'If I may suggest, I believe the lady across there is waving to you.'

Timely intervention from the laced waitress indicated Mandy Plumpkin approaching from the far side of the lobby flourishing above her blonde head a yellow-tinted sun visor.

Competition for the table and surrounding chairs ended as abruptly as it had begun. Having no need to retain possession, Claude, without apology or hesitation, sped purposefully away with a spirit made light by the oncoming countenance.

'What a bloody jerk!' Eric said.

'Oh dear, oh dear ... I'm just not used to argument, Jintana. In Madrid people are not like this.'

'And nor are they here, except for a few difficult people. Sit down and tell me what you'd like.'

In the few minutes of her absence Ms Plumpkin had dressed in yellow cotton hipsters, the visor had been chosen as a matching accessory, and a white tank top that showed her breasts at their sculptured best. Her navel had a silver stud, which from a distance and under the right light sparkled like a diamond.

Claude Halt was speechless with joy.

'Ah! ah!' was about the only comment he could muster, as if he were a recently caught carp panting away his last moments on a riverbank, under a blazing and indiscriminate sun.

While he made ineffective efforts to articulate she smiled and gave him time to fully appreciate the spectacle. With undisguised camp she turned a little to her left and then to her right, put a knuckle on her hip and tilted her nose and Claude Halt absorbed every last movement as if no one had ever before been teased.

From the inside of the lounge, the concierge's desk and the glass entrance door, a very small waitress, a brittle caretaker and a top-hatted doorman observed the public entertainment and said nothing.

'Taxi, taxi!' Claude cried out.

As he and the delectable Ms Plumpkin swept away from the forecourt and through the hotel gardens towards the byways of Wanchai and beyond, they passed a row of summer-bleached stone benches and a seated figure in a white blouse and tan shoes. Under enveloping thorny arches of scentless bougainvillea Mrs Tung had not yet decided whether her quest for male company was still within the capacity of her battered self-esteem or should she call it a day and return frustrated to the confines of the Shatin flat and the unavoidable wretchedness of life with Wai Pang and Budiwati?

8

Through the trudge of years since leaving Spain Eric had seen his mother rarely. Infrequent contact should have made the prelude to their meeting bright with anticipation. Why, then, was his heart so heavy from before the moment of her arrival and why were his filial greetings more compulsory than affectionate?

He acknowledged she had once given him life and kept him warm and dry, but that was a long time ago and now just the sound of her voice started sensations in his extremities that drew closer and closer to his chest until he could barely breathe. What a difference to the surge of warmth prompted by his father's genial face, which in childhood had not often been present.

While Papa had been away his mother provided every source of comfort, until the moment he had been sent – yes, that was the inescapable word – *sent* away into the company of teachers with vocational instincts as finely tuned as those belonging to roof builders driving nails into beams of wood.

Much, much later and long after leaving home, the unsettling idea occurred to him that in the remote days of his childhood he, rather than his father, had been the chief focus of her suffocating love. When the thought first occurred to him he hadn't been at all sure whether this was a normal maternal behaviour or just an idiosyncrasy peculiar to Yessenia Mantageras. But, as later experience expanded to two mothers, his own and his son's, he recognised a common loss of interest in the means by which their children had been acquired.

Was that why, with his many obvious imperfections and in spite of all the chidings waiting on the tip of her tongue as if he had never quite grown up, she still managed to talk about him to others as if he was a man they should admire? Perhaps she saw him as her legacy to an enthralled world, who, with a little bit more prodding and doing as she asked, would one day become a surgeon or a famous lawyer?

But, instead, the reality was he had become a small-time purveyor of something passing for education and an itinerant, with one slight volume of unreadable, self-published verse to his credit, and this plainly was not enough. He was incapable of scaling her visionary heights, although, once in a while and in moments of self-deception, he persuaded himself that the book's trifling achievement was a lot more than it seemed.

No son – or poem, for that matter – was free of the deliverer's expectation. Was there a possibility she had never read the book, or perhaps, if she had, found it incomprehensible, or, less pessimistically, had seen enough to positively loath every last syllable. She really couldn't have it both ways: either he was a credit to her, or he was a waster. Together the two were an illogical absurdity.

Her contradictory ability to build him up and simultaneously put him down left him irresolute and quite accepting of the fact that he had never measured up, and now that she was here the feelings had intensified until they were just too much to stomach. Her reproachful face brought back tenfold the ultimate futility of that youthful decision to flee to the other side of the planet to exorcise his insufficiency, or at least push it so far down in his consciousness that it became indistinguishable from dozens of more humdrum neuroses gnawing at his ragged self-belief. Since she had arrived the remnants of his confidence flaked away to leave only tiny pinpricks of light blinking in his mind like glow-worms speckling a cavern's vaulted gloom.

His time for 'making it' to a level she would accept had slipped inexorably by, and now, in her presence, he felt in the dock for failing to be as she wanted and for having been raised so high and achieving so little. Freedom to be inadequate, he decided, was allowed only to those orphaned at birth and happily denied the tyranny of a mother.

The sense that she deserved better or at least merited an explanation was just too exhausting to contemplate. Why on earth couldn't she have been as oblivious of him as she had been of his father? Looking back, that first step on the white ribbon of road to Algeciras was not a studied decision, but just an emotional rebellion against distorted maternal affection, which starved as much as nourished and prevented him from being only what he was able to achieve.

Although Papa Feliciano had not been about the house to anything like the same extent as Enrico's mother, his easy, untroubled way made no demands and took the boy for what he was – the son of an averagely middle-class and moderately intelligent couple experiencing hard times and lost romantic love. There was no hounding, just gentle, if old-fashioned, encouragement and humour, a bit of a yearning for more certain times and a private and careful conservatism never pushed on others.

When Enrico became a teenager he had begun to ask questions about his father's absences and the vague replies led him to conclude they had something to do with the work gripping so many friends of his parents' early days. Why the subject was not openly discussed he never quite understood, but, because Mama liked to be free of contention, politics was beyond debate and, like religion, in an inflexible state which everyone was assumed to accept. The stars, in her view, were fixed and so, too, should be the ways of society. Deviation was an anomaly right-minded people strove to repair; that it could usher in change for the better was beyond her range of possibility. She was, he decided, an infant's mother; nothing more and nothing less. Friendship with her own growing children, who might have sought reasoned answers, was not a faculty she possessed.

Enrico's unobtrusive father never had the same difficulty and evolved in step with the boy, until neither felt indebted to the other, nor unable to meet as adults just for the sake of tapas and a glass of wine. Continuity and fondness without any form of obligation kept their relationship in a kind of symmetry.

Not that their views had been identical, far from it: while one had been intensely, although silently, political, the other had not bothered to cast a vote for any party throughout an apathetic life.

Maybe men were only in true harmony with their own and needed no more than rough honesty to make an understanding whole. Could that explain the comfort induced in him by the old man's image, when visions of his mother flapped untidily in his head like wet laundry chilling in the wintery gusts blowing all the way from the Guadarrama?

From a hodgepodge of reminiscences he conjured up long-dormant pictures of a summer vacation to Andalucía and Alamar Mares, a many-times-removed farming relative. In retrospect, the visit had been as significant as those first steps on the southern road. Just he and his father had made the journey, while Mama with her habitual air of martyred necessity took care of the suburban home and protected the standards her class had once done with better means.

Instead of the thousands of open-range acres familiar only to the very old, young Enrico's far-removed cousin cultivated and defended on horseback a sunset domain of less than one hundred, which, against the odds, still produced small quantities of dark Oloroso wine.

The skill to ride, once a rural second nature, had all but died out among a newer, urbanised generation. But his father, having never lost the art, took the young boy by the waist and hoisted him astride a white-fetlocked bay stallion and into a deep, creaking saddle. On the great, proud back, father and son rode together as one.

Enrico's childish spirit leapt from the rough and tumble of blighted city wastelands into a storied canter through wooded valleys and up sun-speckled slopes covered in fruit-laden vines, to the summit of a tiny ash-brown hill. In the afternoon distance the far, grey ocean was still and winking with golden Atlantic lights. Through veils of imagination the world's other side beckoned excitedly.

The eastern enigma which eventually claimed Eric had, alas, neither magic nor mystery. Toil at the rainbow's end, he concluded, was still toil. But, if there was one saving feature in an otherwise shattered vision, it had to be Vernon whose bright lantern lit the way for a very tired and footsore traveller.

A doorman in a green overcoat and preposterous top hat swung on the glass door's huge yellow handles with his full, perfunctory weight. There was no joy in the tedious gesture's one thousandth repetition and perhaps never had been even in the first. To a grown adult, more or less capable of managing his own exits, the bored offering was worse than no service at all and Eric dispensed with even a rudimentary nod of thanks.

For a few hours he was on his own and out of reach of his mother's bizarre alchemy of emasculation and maternal pride that withered his soul. He must remember to tell Vernon how much he appreciated Jintana's offer to take the old lady to morning tea, while he fabricated preparation for yet another day of ad hoc freelance lecturing.

Teaching was not a profession he had deliberately pursued; it had crept up on him while his mind was elsewhere and being thus waylaid by the lures of minor responsibility and very long holidays that exactly matched his pace, he tumbled in without a backward glance. Thank God, he thought, for that hard-won university degree, which had drained him of every urge for graft and which, since its acquisition, had been all that stood between him and empty dishes on a bare kitchen table.

Without that basic level of competence, who knows what might have happened after the de rigueur sixties bus trip around Morocco with companions fuddled by pot and poetry read to the open Sahara sky? From that seminal foray into carelessness, the 'East' and what it seemed to be was the next best place to pedal a slim portfolio of unremarkable wares. English literature, a few electives in social anthropology and sports coaching, he discovered, with gratified surprise, were an attractive mix to the hard-pressed private school establishment.

On the coming late afternoon the Tai Po Chinese English School had him listed for a grammar tutorial after their regular lessons and, because the parents of his pupils sought any means to cram the heads of obedient offspring, he was ready to oblige. If the choice had been his, he would have preferred a lecture or, better still, a debate on the merits of twentieth-century playwrights, but lessons in Hong Kong had to be ultimately bankable and streams of consciousness were patently not of that category.

His hopes for the continued flow of occasional employment at this institution would, however, have been greater if Dr So, the school principal, had liked him better and the buzz of parental discontent about unproductive hours had not been so loud. Not that he had received anything like a direct complaint – his paymasters were not that sort of people – but there had been inescapable whiffs of uncertainty floating, like forest murmurs, in the passageways and galleries of this centre of academic ambition.

But no one could argue with the visible progress made in last year's Fung Kei Soya Sauce inter-schools football Challenge Cup, when Tai Po's improvement carried them for the first time as far as the knockout stage – before elimination, in a seven–nil thrashing, at the hands of a gang of border-line hooligans from one of the international academies – or with the hardly wavering term-end Eng. Lit. results to which he believed he had made a measurable contribution.

And if there was no outright failure to speak of, nor open parental rebellion to record, what was to stop him from making the most of this empty morning and early afternoon, before he slid surreptitiously into whatever awaited at Tai Po. Doing absolutely nothing for six hours, now that he had handed off his watchful mother to a very considerate and engaging young woman, was Eric's idea of a nearly perfect day.

On the other side of the hotel's purpose-built driveway a collection of unruly bougainvillea shrubs clustered in manicured clumps to half-conceal the views of nearby Wanchai. This, he decided, would be a good spot to eat his breakfast granola and let his thoughts run over subjects unconnected to the enormity of filial deficiency.

Chaotic foliage, held in check by vigorous pruning, festooned a plethora of notices put up to remind visitors of correct behaviour in public facilities. A nap under the *Morning Post* at this warm time of day would have been a good idea, but sleeping in municipal areas, the red-crossed circles warned, was a punishable act likely to bring down on the head of any miscreant expensive retribution.

Behind trellis-work and multi-coloured blossoms Eric glimpsed a head of tousled dark hair and heard something rasping on the granite pathways. A gardener, he speculated, getting to grips with the necessity of controlling rude nature in its many uncooperative forms.

Under the systematically tended arbours, unsteady shadow and sunlight fell in patches that filtered out the morning's harshest glare. This quiet corner of an unabashedly hustling town seemed to fall between a variety of purposes. Too much was disallowed for carefree recreation and too little offered to make a worthwhile visit any more than transitory.

Eric sat down on the first in a line of hot stone seats. Stored sunlight radiated vertically through his unseasonably thick slacks and into his lower back.

'Thhppt!' he gasped, shuffling painfully from one buttock to the other until, unable to escape the discomfort, he slid to the ground and leaned against the bench's mock-Grecian legs.

The first bite of the granola bar, picked up hurriedly while herding his mother and Jintana into the lane in Sai Kung, confirmed he had made a mistake by leaving behind the soft oaty kind he preferred and bringing along one built to splinter into a dozen gritty pieces that became embedded in his cheeks and palette the moment it was bitten. Tilting to one side, he spat away the offending debris and returned the unchewed remains to his trouser pocket.

From the angle his inclining body had assumed, he could see beneath contorted bougainvillea stems to the approximate spot from where he imagined the sounds he'd first heard on entering the garden had emanated. There they were again – tap, scratch, tap, tap, draaag, scratch. Because he had nothing better to do, he lay flat on his ear, looking for the weeding hoe and pair of gardening boots he expected.

His eyebrows lifted.

A small bundle of off-white material, looking like a blouse or something similar, lay at the centre of what could have been a one-person dance, or at least a series of deliberate steps made by a pair of sinewy calves and bruised green shoes. A voice from somewhere higher up, out of Eric's sight, hummed discordantly.

'Lah, dah, hum, ha.'

With curiosity overcoming his reluctance to be involved in anything out of the ordinary, he edged forward on elbows and knees and began wondering if he had discovered a throwback to the times when some of his contemporaries sought life's meaning in the woods of California and gatherings on Salisbury Plain.

'Is that a half-clothed woman?' he wondered somewhat breathlessly. 'Experiencing the same fantasies in the heart of metropolitan Wanchai as those one-time flower people?'

The weariness of an old dog whose sight had faded from many years' incarceration behind concrete barricades fell away and he scented open country and the lure of a fox's trail, until, in the tangle of overhanging bougainvillea, a thorn caught his scalp and drew a smothered expletive.

'Ferkin' hell!'

Carol Tung's prancing and partially clad form froze.

'Would you believe it; I … I think I've cut my head,' Eric offered, hoping a status report would substitute for an explanation of what he was doing under the hedge.

'Eureech!' she wailed and sank to her haunches in a howl of humiliation and anger that reverberated from the Harbour Hotel's steel and glass walls across the street, until, suddenly released from her coil on the hot paving stones, she sprang upright with a high-heeled shoe in her grasp and her chest and black-bushed armpits exposed to the humid air.

Realising an attack was imminent, Eric attempted tactical withdrawal.

'Don't do that now; I'm going. Look, see – I'm out of here.'

Unpacified, Mrs Tung flung her shoe with as much vitriol as her indignation and naked shame could generate. Incapable of stopping the incoming missile, Eric ducked into the ground, but took the blow's full force on his balding and already scratched pate.

'Ah, ow! Oh, my Christ.'

Snatching up her discoloured blouse and clasping it to her shrunken chest, Carol Tung fled towards the sound of traffic growling in the adjacent driveway.

Eric's escape, however, was frustrated by determined bougainvillea clinging to his shirt and corduroys as if collectively marshalled to punish civic trespass. After seconds of fruitless writhing about, he decided, instead of backing out, to drag forward onto the very spot where Mrs Tung had performed her strange Druid jig and, with his already weak stamina ebbing away, he stretched full length on the hard granite floor and fell asleep.

How much time passed he didn't know, but, however long, it was brought to an abrupt end by a resounding kick on the rope soles of his feet.

'No allow,' a quavering voice said severely.

Eric was stiff all over and one side of his face stung from the effects of vegetation, insects or too much sunlight – he wasn't sure which. To alleviate his many discomforts he rolled onto his back and saw the upside-down face of a very old and sunburned man peering at him from under a large straw hat.

'Sleep in bed, not park.'

'Give over, will you? I'm in no condition to be knocked about.'

Eric sat up, pressed his tender cheek carefully and folded one of his abused feet into his lap.

'Uh! Can you believe this place seems to breed objectionable characters? Should we put up a sign saying "bad attitudes welcome"?'

'What say?'

'Oh, nothing, nothing.'

Satisfied with the rebuke he had delivered, and entirely unperturbed by contrary points of view, the old man hawked noisily and, while still keeping his yellowing eyes on Eric, gobbed emphatically into the neighbouring fauna in almost the exact place where Eric had deposited the pieces of his granola bar.

Government employees at any level, even a humble gardener, expect to hold sway, and whether a situation applied to unruly plants or inconsiderate visitors made not the least jot of difference.

Although still several hours from his scheduled lesson at the Tai Po Chinese English School, Eric was persuaded he had outlived his welcome and should move on. Against his inclination he got to his knees and flapped at the prickles and leaf mould dotting his clothes. Without thinking he fingered the top of his head and winced at its tenderness. The green shoe responsible for most of the damage had ricocheted from his crown into the tangles of spindly bougainvillea hanging disconsolately an arm's length away.

'You should pick that up and seek out the owner after midnight; she'll be just your type.'

Having the last word made him feel better, even though it fell on deaf and uncomprehending, ears.

Since stepping hopefully from the Harbour Hotel, events had not lived up to the early promise inseparable from jettisoning an inconvenient mother. But, Eric speculated wistfully, a slow ride across the harbour and Kowloon Peninsula to Tai Po and a plate of wet noodles in a hole-in-the-wall eatery might just elevate his mood a fraction, although the way things were going it wasn't worth an even-money bet. And what if his guess was accurate, would anyone, other than himself, care the least little bit?

Unlike the first leg of his journey the last was completed at break-neck speed aboard one of the Territories' life-threatening minibuses. Reckless stopping and starting and jostling of other vehicles contesting passage ended at Tai Po a good thirty minutes earlier than intended.

Bringing the heedlessly propelled minibus, which collected and deposited passengers on request rather than at predetermined places, to a halt at exactly the right spot required fine judgement and more subtlety than the few words of Cantonese Eric possessed.

Street lampposts and overhanging signs hurtled by until he thought he recognised a cooked meat shop on an approaching corner. Steamed chickens and smaller birds looking suspiciously like sparrows on window hooks flashed alongside and with only two linguistic options at his disposal he called out.

'*Yau lok ngoy*; stop, stop here, please!'

In a pressure cooker of uncompromising capitalism, entrepreneurial speed of delivery trumped customer comfort every time and, instead of experiencing a gentle glide into kerbside safety, po-faced travellers, conditioned from birth to swallow anger, were thrown forward in the din of squealing brakes and smell of smoking tyres. Where seat backs were absent, hands clawed frantically at the unhelpful air. But no one scowled or complained, because that was not the way things were done.

Endeavouring to achieve a safe exit, before the bus took off again, Eric disentangled his bony limbs from under and beside the tiny rear seat and, while the vehicle was still in mid-slide, tottered along the central aisle towards clam-shut folding doors. In the commotion he knocked askew a woman's wide-brimmed hat.

'Oops, really sorry; goddamnit, man!'

Neither his smiled apology nor furious glare received the slightest acknowledgement. The inconvenienced woman tilted back her head and continued her scarcely interrupted mobile telephone conversation and the driver impatiently revved his already overheated and groaning engine. Before the soles of his feet struck the pavement the folding doors smacked shut and the minibus hurtled away pursued, not by Beelzebub and his hordes from hell, but by the prospect of the far worse damnation of losing fares to a faster rival.

Further along the street a few students, with no formal afternoon activities, trickled out of the Tai Po Chinese English School building. All the others would remain for at least another three hours, before they too went home to a quick meal and a long night's homework.

Family control, Eric reflected grimly, had some compensation. He'd never seen any of the adolescents from this, or any other local school, dressed scruffily, on the streets, or in anything like an unruly state. None of them ever seemed to step out of line. Perhaps an iron hand really was a better way than independence, with its attendant risks of shameful behaviour.

When he saw the scrubbed and studious faces attending his tutorials he wondered whether Vernon, too, would have benefited from a father's firmer direction. But then, was the permanent separation of a teenager's shirt-tail and trousers of any real importance, or was the view that a missing belt soon dragged the whole family into disrepute more realistic?

In these schools, the youth who had problems with authority was, as far as he knew, non-existent and even the few that turned to crime were probably just as much at ease in the Triads where iron-fisted clout was only an exaggerated form of that meted out by unwavering parents.

Outside the gates several luxury cars driven by hired help waited for the sons and daughters of owners too busy making a killing to trouble with the minor chore of shepherding children back to the family home, and, just inside, a knot of shrill mothers conversed in the falsettos of classic opera. Some of the women he recognised from last year's parent–teacher meetings and they knew him, but none turned or offered a greeting. His cords and ponytail, he suspected, could have been the reason for and the content of their solemn exchanges.

'Probably planning a bit of pedagogicide,' he speculated and walked straight on, past the staff common room and up three flights of stairs to class 303.

In his pupils' minds there was no distinction between the appearance and substance of teaching, so he took his expected place at the head of the room and scanned the twenty or so inexpressive faces. What a depressingly top-down process this was; not one where exploration threw open doors to understanding. He was expected to be infallible, the font of all wisdom, a sage who would lay before them a basket brimming with the 'right' way, which these sponges would absorb and on later periodic regurgitation use to make money.

With nothing prepared he turned to the blackboard and wrote: 'Bird, flock, sheep, bacteria, stadium, fruit.'

'Right,' he said, wiping chalk from his hand on to the backside of his humus- and Campari-stained trousers. 'This is a list of nouns; who can tell me which is singular and which plural?'

Not a hand rose. He looked round the class and waited.

'OK, I'll make it easier; which are plurals?'

Children in Hong Kong didn't learn this way. They wanted to be told and to make the knowledge of the teacher their own. Encouraging any youth to have an opinion, to stand out from his peers, was just inviting disharmony with consequences lingering long after lessons were done. Relationships made in the classroom, he should understand, while not equal to those of extended family, would continue into adult life and provide part of the network essential to future success. Because no one was prepared to imperil that balance every single face stared down at the unmarked desk-tops.

'What about you, Lam?'

Singling out one person in this way was too direct and several feet shuffled in coded reminder.

From the third row, the first two being empty, Patrick Lam raised his head slightly and looked toward the front of the room. He was not attempting eye contact – that would have been too disrespectful – but he was signalling involvement.

'Perhaps, if you wrote it down, Sir, we'd understand.'

'Oh, come on, this isn't something new. Doesn't anyone have any idea?'

The twenty faces stared down as if all eternity would pass before a disruptive personal point of view was released into the proceedings.

'Let's go round the room. As you can at least speak, Lam, we'll start with you. *Bird* ... what is it?'

The boy waited until Eric's impatience escalated into irritated snorting.

'... Singular, Sir.'

'Thank you, yes. Next: Leung ... flock?'

'Singular also, Mr Manley, Sir.'

'Excellent, excellent; now doesn't that feel better?'

None of the pupils had the least idea why they should feel anything but a lot worse than at the start of the lesson.

'But tell me why a word that describes a lot of things isn't a plural?' Eric continued.

Again, no one responded.

'Yes, you, Leung; you can't give up on a theme you've helped initiate.'

The boy wondered what crime he had committed that forced him into this intolerable breach of etiquette and moved his gaze from the floor between Eric's rope sandals to the ceiling above his head.

'Because the word describes the many things as a singular group and is called a collective noun, Sir.'

'Good; very, very good. Cheung, tell us about sheep.'

Of all the boys in the late-day grammar class at Tai Po Chinese English School only Cheung Wai Pang stirred any positive feelings in Eric. He was one boy who could be said to have a personality; all the others were a composite of some remote concept outside Eric's comprehension and without any individual identification.

Unusually, the boy was not a particularly good student, his homework was often late and his attendance unreliable, but behind the shortcomings and while others went about their studies mechanically, he demonstrated human frailty and, when not wrapped up in his own thoughts, an engaging spark of curiosity.

'Sorry, what did you say?'

'I asked,' Eric said, struggling with a smile, 'whether the word "sheep" is singular or plural.'

Before being pulled into participation Wai Pang had been drawing on a sheet of paper. At the sound of his name he slid a page under his homework folder and looked up to meet Eric's amused face.

'Err … don't plurals have "esses" or something at the end?'

'That's possible, so are you suggesting singular and "sheeps" for the plural?'

'Yes, I … think so.'

'In that case would our next example, bacteria, have a plural and become "bacterias"?'

The only hint that the boy was experiencing any emotion was the tiniest, between-the-eyebrows shadow in an otherwise steady expression. If this, thought Eric, had been a lesson among a rag-tag group of youths found at some other school assignments on his circuit, or in the places of learning he'd attended as a child, a publicly floundering student would have prompted sniggers, or, in the worst cases, gales of laughter from the rowdier elements of the class. But here, in this setting, there was not a flicker of anything, least of all entertainment. Students, with the possible exception of Cheung Wai Pang, were in the class to learn and acquire the means to ascend a ladder, not to mock or challenge the pillars of social order.

'I ... suppose ... so ... I don't know.'

'What about the others – stadium and fruit?'

'Umm ...'

'Let's try this. Sorry, I realise it's not your preference,' he said to the whole class, 'but discomfort is often said to be the condition in which people actually learn things. Write an essay ...'

There were no audible groans or exchanged glances, but, before continuing, Eric detected a shifting of bottoms on chairs.

'... with the title "Forces that make language change" and specifically include the words "stadium", "stadiums" and "stadia". We've got about an hour and a half left, so three hundred words should do it. Drop your papers on my desk as you go out.'

Although none of the students openly grumbled, there were ways disapproval could be communicated and, after all the boys except Cheung Wai Pang had completed their written work and left, a note was delivered to the classroom asking Mr Manley to stop at the Principal's office on his way out.

'What's the hold-up?' Eric called across to Wai Pang.

'Almost finished ...'

Another fifteen minutes passed and still the boy scribbled.

'Look, Dr So is calling for me and as he has a thing about being kept waiting I need to go. Give me what you have.'

The off-hand, almost comic reference to the headmaster puzzled Wai Pang. Superiors – and surely Dr So was one – were privileged and deserved the respect inseparable from their positions.

Scooping up his folder and untidy papers he walked hesitatingly forward with the whole mess pressed against his body.

'OK, hand it over.'

'Pardon?' replied the boy as if he were startled by the request.

'Your work, you ninny; the stuff you've just written.'

'Oh.'

One hand fumbled to find the right paper and place it on the teacher's desk and the other struggled unsuccessfully to prevent the rest of the bundle slithering into a heap on the floor. The sketch Wai Pang had been busy with in the early part of the lesson came to rest on top of the chaotic pile.

'What's this?' his tutor enquired of the essay assignment.

'Nothing,' replied Wai Pang from his knees on the floor.

'It's as good as nothing. There're only about twenty-five words here, if that. You're going to get me into a whole lot of trouble producing stuff like this.'

'Couldn't think of anything to write.'

'And what's that you've got there; anything that needs my attention?'

'No, no; not really.'

Eric decided to simplify matters and leant down from his table to pick up the paper Wai Pang was returning to his folder. He carefully studied the sketch of a naked woman.

'I didn't know you had an artistic bent; this is very good.'

'You won't tell Dr So or my mother, will you?'

'Your mother? Wouldn't she be pleased to know you have a talent?'

'She'll think it's obscene.'

'If your intention was to be obscene, then, yes, she may have a point. Was it?'

'No, well, not exactly, but it felt good while I was drawing; you know, a sort of tingling.'

'I do. So we could say motives are mixed? Does your father talk to you about girls?'

'He's not home much and anyway he wouldn't want to discuss such things. Families like mine don't talk about, you know ... sex.'

Wai Pang's eyes widened at his daring use of a forbidden word.

'In that case you wouldn't like to hear about what happened to me today.'

'Have you ever seen a woman without any clothes, Mr Manley?'

For a second Eric thought his wry smirk may have given away something of this morning's monstrous incident in the garden outside the Harbour Hotel. But what he knew about the nature of this environment was that most people didn't expect or want to read the minds of others any more than they were prepared to disclose anything of their own interior debate to near strangers. Was that why Wai Pang, with his startlingly innocent questions and approaching manhood, was so different and easy to like?

'At my age if you haven't had the pleasure something is seriously missing.'

'When was the first time?'

'Well, you're a nosey one, but if you want to know the first real occasion was when I was a bit older than you, maybe seventeen or so.'

'And since then?'

'Whoa, wait a minute; not sure I should give you unrestricted access to my sinful past.'

'What about a naked man?'

'Eh? I'm not sure where this is going, but that's an altogether different proposition. Are you sure you want to ask? But if it's any help, being on a football team introduces you to a lot of new experiences.'

'Funny how you people talk. A man I met on Saturday was

just the same. Sometimes I wish we were like that, not so, so …' Wai Pang couldn't find the right word.

'Bottled up?'

The slight figure of Dr So's personal assistant appeared in the doorway. She said nothing, but waited to be noticed.

'We want everything to be in the correct way; it isn't the same for you.'

'It is for some of our mothers believe me, but mostly we like to be self-reliant, although that gets you into a deal of trouble, because you don't know beforehand if a thing is any good until you try it; like booze or girls.'

A scuttle of tiny footsteps hurried away along the corridor, as if a rodent, detecting the approach of a terrier, had fled to safety.

'Seems to me,' continued Eric, 'you have a lot to say, but as El Comandante wants a word in my ear 'ole it'll have to wait. Do you want to get into the Tuesday soccer practice? We could catch up after.'

'Sport's a waste of time; won't earn a living Mama says.'

'How many millions does she make, I wonder. Look, enough chat, or I'll have to explain my misdeeds to the governor. See you next week?'

The Principal's office was on the fourth floor and to get there visitors to the school had to climb open concrete stairs from a car park and through the intervening levels where classrooms were situated and subjected to the heavy aromas rising from an adjacent meat and poultry market. Dr So's choice of location for his headquarters had been inspired by his wife, who, being both a spouse and an inveterate control freak, reasoned that parental grievances would lose focus during a strenuous and poisonous ascent to an altitude where, at last, the air became just about breathable and where they could not but feel thankful for a safe arrival.

As a eunuch might defend the peace of an imperial master, so the Principal's proscriptive assistant obstructed audience to all but the most suitable, irrespective of whether a prior appointment had been arranged or not. Her task was to inhibit, or to confer arbitrary favour on those she instinctively felt upheld the indisputable way. She knew better than anyone that, while modernity had merit, the Tai Po Chinese English School's older mechanisms, which had functioned adequately since long before open-door policies became fashionable, were as much as anyone should required.

'I'm wanted,' Eric announced without elaboration.

Disturbed from an absorbing project requiring the application of correction fluid to a stiff document with serrated edges and a red seal, the personal aide sat up sharply and, for unknown reasons, fixed her narrow stare on the upper centre of her visitor's abdomen.

Whether his shirt was unbuttoned or egg-stained was not a subject to exercise Eric's mind, but he did object at having to crouch to engage the assistant in direct conversation.

'Have you got a problem with me?' he asked over bent knees.

Higher authority permeated the room and insinuated its way from behind the assistant through hairline cracks in the doors and walls. Secure in her reflected power she expected and demanded the same respect that fell on the master she served. Some arrogant people, who could not see beyond themselves, had, in her opinion, much to learn. Why were they so overbearing? Had they no sense of the natural order of things, or how to blend into a community until there was no such thing as individuality left? And then there was the right procedure for every situation which they just couldn't grasp ... tch!

'Please to sit down.'

'I haven't come to sit.'

'Dr So will let me know when he is ready.'

'Look here, young lady; he called me, therefore ... I assume he's ready. Get it?'

As Eric stood back and the middle of his torso again claimed the aide's pinched look, a telephone rang. She turned to answer the interruption and listened attentively without giving her name or office.

'Yes, she said at last and took up from her desk a polystyrene food box and a plastic folder containing several sheaves of paper. A strained voice answered her timid tap and she disappeared into the inner office at her rear.

An odour combining recent furniture polish and ancient household dust reached Eric's unusually flared nostrils. He couldn't tell whether they wafted in from the Principal's room, or had been stirred into the air by the assistant's sudden movement in the disorder of her workstation.

Except in the stairwell, the Tai Po Chinese English School's hermetic sealing and outrageously cold air-conditioning kept inmates a million miles from the rest of the world.

On the other side of filth-encrusted windows and under smudgy factory haze, Eric could see burnt hills tumbling down to Tolo Harbour and the flat oily waters of Plover's Cove. He remembered seeing similar, but cleaner, stretches of country from the safety of his father's lap and the back of a massive bay stallion stirring and pacing under his boy's thighs with the strength and potency of a bull. On that unforgettable occasion, the western sun had sunk in wine-coloured shades through copper-coloured beech trees, but today it frowned between ranks of grey, untenanted buildings in an angry white ball.

What, he wondered, had brought him to this? Not a carefully thought-out plan, that was for sure. Since the first sign on the Algeciras road the mileposts of teaching, that other woman, Vernon, Sai Kung and Sigrid had followed as inevitably as what had gone before. Every lurch into this soulless corner of the globe and the perpetual sloth that followed had been predictable. Even in her dotting ambivalence Señora Mantageras would never quite realise how decidedly she had placed the pins in her unremarkable son's road map.

Perhaps he should have set out to shock her by taking work as a dock labourer on the Mediterranean coast, or by sailing with one of the tramp steamers to South America? 'But, if he had, would Enrico Mantageras have been a noticeably different or more contented person than Eric Manley had turned out to be?'

The personal assistant's smells and rectitude snaked back into the room.

'Come through to Dr So.'

She stirred some papers on her desk while waiting for Eric's compliance. The disturbed air irritated his breathing and he pressed a nicotine-coloured finger to the underside of his nose. Anticipating the worst, she turned to a metal cabinet and took down a cardboard box.

'What's this?' he demanded as she thrust a surgical mask towards his face.

'Stops germs spreading.'

'If I'd got a cold, lady, I wouldn't want to shut it in. Even the sort of air you have in here would do it some good.'

The aide stared. These people were incorrigible. They refused to do as they were asked and never began to understand behaviour that best suited the community.

Eric shoved the outstretched arm aside and walked into the Principal's office.

Dr So was a small, almost elfin man, whose feet struggled to touch the floor when he was seated on the summit of a cushion-packed chair behind his desk. If students or parents had seen more than the proffered head and shoulders, they would have realised he was not the forbidding administrator his position implied. But assailed by symbols of status, the posed photographs with established government and education figures, a doctorial certificate and a board listing all fourteen past and present principals including the waistcoated founder of 1923, visitors were deterred from expecting an equal exchange of views.

But, thought Eric, remove the most egregious examples of authority and what remained? A threadbare little man, with a miserable job, who carried about a plastic umbrella as if it was a monarch's sceptre.

'Sit down, Mr Manley, please.'

A second churlish refusal would do nothing to extricate a part-time tutor from the slough in which he'd struggled all day and perhaps all his life.

'What is it?'

'How long is it you have been in Hong Kong, Mr Manley?'

So it was going to be one of those strangely circuitous conversations. 'I don't bother to keep count, but long enough.'

'Mmm, yes, and having many assignments like Tai Po Chinese English School?'

'Some.'

'I see.'

The interview seemed to lose momentum while Dr So pondered on issues known only to himself, before continuing,

'This school, you understand, is a private establishment, not funded by government?'

'I hadn't the remotest idea, but what if it is?' Eric didn't have any other matters to attend to, but his private time was valued more than anything else and today he preferred conclusion to wandering dialogue.

'Time,' said Dr So, as if hoping to read the other's thoughts, 'is infinite …'

'Funny, I've always found it in rather short supply; especially to do the things I want.'

'… But money is not.'

'Can we get to the point?' Eric was thinking by now he could have been on the roof back in Sai Kung with a cigarette and an early frosty in his hands.

'The Steering Committee has been forced to decide …'

'Who?'

'… for business reasons you understand.'

'Oh! I get it, you're firing me. Is that what all this is about?' Eric stood up abruptly.

Half expecting a beating, the startled Principal pushed vigorously back from the huge desk and completed his statement from the protection provided by the rear wall and an adjacent hatstand.

'A necessary financial step; not connected with performance; your bank account will be credited after security clearance with … .ah … with …'

Now the painful message had been delivered, Dr So was in a hurry to get through the closing formalities, but having become separated from the apparatus of his position, he was having trouble reading the notes on his desk.

'… Ah … your final settlement … of … hmm …'

Man, what a tosser!

On his way through the outer office he sniffed at the air, which had now acquired the additional odour of roast pork, from the empty polystyrene lunch box, to its already mixed themes. The personal assistant had completed her task with the correction fluid and, with head down and thoughts concentrated, she was engaged in replacement of the stiff document's offending script with her preferred wording. Deep inside Eric's nasal cavity the earlier itch moistened into a trickle and he let forth a showery sneeze that shook the room and released upper-level particles, normally beyond the cleaner's token attention, onto surrounding papers and furniture.

'Ah-ahhchwoohah!'

The engrossed assistant flinched and her nib end, which had been employed in studied creativity, shot in a crescent line across the serrated certificate.

'Oh, 'scuse me,' Eric said, dragging an entire forearm across his wet upper lip and turning to the concrete steps and the afternoon's weakening sunlight. 'I guess I better be off.'

9

After sunset Mong Kok's seething activity hardly dipped below the uproar of mid-afternoon. While there were services to be sold and money to be made, work continued through every hour of the twenty-four. No one sought work–life balance, because work was life and the question of balance never entered anyone's head.

Delivery vans discharged cargo into backstreets no less congested than six hours earlier and hand-held trolleys, like so many mechanised scavengers carrying morsels of rotten fruit towards underground nests, trundled in and out of the many alleys and unlit doorways. Bare-chested shopfitters, paid by the project, not the hour, cut wood, marked glass and twisted metal at kerbside fabrication benches and let fall odds and ends for municipal sweepers to gather into the bulging black refuse bags infesting every untidy corner.

For meagre rewards, men and women too old for traditional employment, threaded through the chaos dragging heaps of collapsed cardboard cartons and recyclable drink containers towards distant collection points.

Late-night labour in Hong Kong moved with a pace and din of its own. Boards were hammered, trolley wheels creaked, shouts conveyed instructions and demands when whispers would have sufficed, electric drills whined, doors banged, engines started, and, to the rhythmical clack, clack of something beaten on their metallic sides, lorries reversed into the tiniest of spaces.

An elderly sheet-metal worker with a half-smoked cigarette

behind his ear and a pencil stub between his teeth sat back from a panel he'd been beating and wiped his face. In the deafening clatter he detected a pounding he couldn't quite identify; it was not loud like the other noises and seemed out of place in the surrounding bustle. He listened; there it was again ... pat, pat, pat, pat ... At first he thought rain was starting to fall and began gathering his scattered tools. But the noise was too regular, too insistent, to be an approaching shower.

Realisation that the sound belonged to running feet came at precisely the moment a young man, with scared eyes and a bright gash on his left cheek, sped from a narrow opening on the far side of the street to vault over garbage bags and shopfitting apparatus before disappearing into the dark space between two neighbouring buildings with the same pat, pat, pat fading fast behind him.

The metalworker and a youth, standing on top of a container lorry's hydraulic tailgate, looked at each other. The cigarette and the pencil stub switched places and their owner patted his pockets in search of a lighter.

Through the smoky exhalation two more runners erupted from the passageway opposite. Both were in nearly uniform black, from the bristling manes of their hair to lizard-skin shoes. Such relief as there was came in ginger highlights on top of one head and a silver tie, held by a very thin knot, beneath the chin of the other.

'Where go?' demanded the highlights owner.

The youth on the elevated lorry platform ducked from sight into the container's interior.

'You, where go?'

A finger shook threateningly at the metalworker's face to emphasise the peril attendant on incorrect or incomplete answers.

After another deep pull on his cigarette, which circulated comfortingly around his lungs, the shopfitter flicked the hissing butt into a roadside drain's open grill and without commitment said, 'What say?'

Setting aside social nicety, the figure under the streaked thatch stepped forward and cuffed both cloth ears.

'One more time,' he shrieked. 'Where went?'

The old man, whose head rang like a fishwives' debate over this morning's grouper pricing, hesitatingly pursed his lips at a ninety-degree angle to the one taken by the fleeing man, but said nothing. Unaccountably, he seemed to be the only person left in the previously crowded lane.

Before resuming his chase the ruffians' spokesman gave a final warning.

'Know you and know where work,' he yelled before pursuing his partner as quickly as elegant footwear permitted.

Some way behind him and at the end of another unlit alleyway dripping with water and echoing with intermittent splashes, Vernon scuttled into the sodium glow of streets surrounding Prince Edward and descended the tiled steps of an underground train station three at a time. On the eastbound platform he walked as far from the entrance as he could and hid behind a pillar.

His heart stopped beating with any regularity and escalated into a flutter. Reels of nausea overcame him and he vomited onto the track. Further along the platform two women turned their backs and moved away.

Later, when he disembarked at Diamond Hill, a clock overlooking the concourse showed the time was five past two. Buses for remote Sai Kung had finished long ago.

'Damn, that means a taxi.'

He searched his pockets and painfully counted just fifteen dollars and twenty cents; not even enough to cover the flag-down fare.

'Suppose I'll have to wake Lig when I get home.'

When the green-and-white vehicle rattled to a halt beside the wilting poinsettias and flaking paint of the family home he called over the front seat to the driver,

'Wait a bit; I'll be right back.'

'Where money?' the driver asked, sensing Vernon was not as well equipped as customers ought to be.

Vernon rubbed a thumb and index finger together and pointed at the house.

'In there ... there; won't be a sec.'

The lock rasped unhelpfully and he pushed the door back just far enough to allow access for his shoulders. In the confined space a smell of curried vegetables, sucked from fusty wall hangings and curtains, collected in a pungent yellow-green halo over his head.

Two lights shone at opposite ends of the house; one above the spiral staircase leading to the rooftop garden and another in Ligaya's room next to the kitchen. Not that the lower one meant the home help was still awake. Her rest was taken when it was needed, not when the hour said it was due, and whether the light was on or off was neither here nor there.

Vernon knew Ligaya's daytime things had a way of happening at night and vice versa and that she could quite happily fall asleep at ten in the morning and walk about the house when everyone else was deep in habitual slumber.

'Lig!' he called softly towards her bedroom and then more urgently: 'Lig! Lig!'

A head appeared in front of the light.

'What? What are you doing and ... uhh! ... what's that ugly thing on your face?'

'Tell you later. Look I need sixty dollars ... for a taxi ... it's waiting outside.'

To reinforce his request, a horn blast fractured the droning, insect-filled night.

'Geez! Listen to that; hurry, hurry!'

Vernon snatched at the three notes Ligaya pulled from her bag.

'It's all I've got.'

'I'll pay you back, honest.'

'What's going on down there?' a voice called from above.

'Nothing, Dad, it's OK. Be up in a minute.'

The taxi disappeared in a spray of gravel and Vernon clicked the front door back into place.

'Who's that?' Sigrid called from somewhere in the darkness.

'Only me, Vernon; go back to bed.'

'Oh.'

One part of the house returned to sleep and Ligaya, in the room beside the kitchen, put away whatever had occupied her, her bible or a letter home and lay down fully clothed.

Vernon put a foot on the staircase's first rung and it moaned unmercifully. He half-expected his stepmother to start from her bed a second time. Every joint and hinge in the old building had seen better days and the whole pile deserved demolition.

On the rooftop and slumped over the outer parapet, Eric gazed out to sea.

'You OK?' Vernon asked.

'Had better days, but, yeah, I'll survive. How about you? Kinda late to be on the streets, ain't it?'

'Yup, ran into a spot of trouble. Might have to discuss it when you've got time.'

Revolving thoughts internally and at each other's elbow was their first step to sharing difficulties.

'Sure, plenty of time to spare, especially over the next few days.'

Eric was never fully occupied, but he wasn't often caught making it quite so obvious.

'Something happen?'

'Well, yeah, now you ask … it did.'

'Uh-huh … ?' Vernon waited.

'Couple of things. Ran across a real weird woman in Wanchai, dancing about with hardly a stitch on.'

'That doesn't sound so bad. Was she a looker?'

'No, terrible, and she gave me this.' He lowered his head towards Vernon. 'Bloody hurts like hell.'

Vernon suppressed a snort of laughter. 'Could have been

worse if she had a boyfriend with her or the police thought you were up to something.'

'No joke.'

At three in the morning Sai Kung's distance from the rest of Hong Kong's frenetic, round-the-clock grind was more marked than ever. Apart from gentle, breeze-borne heaving in the woodland behind and bobbing lights on the marine inlet in front, nothing else moved. The single road below, which led in one direction to the dead end of High Island Reservoir and in the other to some forms of employment, was deserted. Not one vehicle had passed through the entire short length of Sai Kung's main street in the last three hours.

'Quiet, en it?'

'That's what Sigrid and I were looking for when we came up here. But, sad to say, you can't keep the world at bay all the time.'

'Ain't that the truth.'

A sudden stronger gust blew in off the sea and trees on the black hillside nodded furiously.

'Rain coming?'

'Yeah.'

Behind, in the thick forest, a sudden crack followed by a rushing sound, as if one of the walls of an ancient culvert had broken, rattled windows at the back of the Manley residence.

'What's that?'

'Tree gone down, I 'spect.'

'Could be.'

'Look, Dad, I need to talk about something.'

'Yeah? What?'

'It's about Jintana ...'

'Nice girl that; got me out of a hole this morning taking your grandma to tea, while I did my thing.'

'Yeah, she's great, but ...'

Eric lifted himself from the wall and looked into his son's face.

'You haven't got her ... I mean, she's not ... is she ...? Heh! What the hell's that ... on your cheek?'

'Oh, nothing much ...'

'Nothing much! It sure as damnit is!'

This was not the way Vernon intended the conversation to develop, or how he wanted to reveal his financial overreach or the tale of what, but for an exceptional turn of speed, would have been a severe drubbing at the fists and feet of uncompromising gangsters. He knew his father would have to know, and have to know soon, because there was no one else who would want to get him out of a very big mess.

'Well, see, it's like this ...,' he began cautiously and by a roundabout route.

One of Eric's routine openings, he reminded his father, which was as hackneyed as it was convenient, began with a request for students in a new class to introduce themselves by relating some aspect of their background that no one in the room knew. What was revealed usually produced light-hearted exchanges, maybe some laughter, and succeeded in breaking the tension of the first few hours with a tutor they had not met before.

Jintana had startled the group into 'ohs and ahs' by saying she'd been in jail for six months following student riots in Bangkok. When Vernon heard her story of dangerous idealism he was swept off his feet. But so were others and, being as immoderate as the mother he'd hardly known and the grandparents to whom he had no blood tie, he went about repelling the competition and landed in several bruising scrapes along the way. And having come so far and having fought to win her, the excitement of possession inexplicably transformed into something closely resembling responsibility.

Going back further still he'd heard Eric remark, in a late-night session where confidences came easily, that involvement with a woman meant accepting all the baggage she had picked up along her way. The older they were the greater the trouble they brought with them. But whether they were forty or twenty years old, they all had a history that weighed like millstones as well as parents and siblings and cousins and aunts, who had situations to deal with or something to ask, or to say, which was often worse and unlikely to be their business.

'There is no woman I've come across in all my years who travels light.'

While Jintana might have been a stunner with a head on her, those virtues, in Vernon's assessment, were at risk of being outweighed by an extended family that seemed to go on and on for ever and connect to every resident in the small town she called home.

'You know, Dad, she's got half a dozen brothers and sisters and God knows how many cousins and nephews and nieces and everyone is crying out for help, and because she's out of the country they think she's going to make it all right for them, even though she's still studying and making only a few dollars doing waitressing and that sort of stuff.'

'And how does any of that put a four-inch gash on your face?'

Vernon took a long time to reply while he drew in the warm air that had aromas of decaying leaves and beach shingle on its breath.

'... I borrowed money for her, so she could get them started with a good plot of land by the river to grow their own rice and farm chickens or something.'

'Uh ... I see and ... where did the money come from?

'Some guy in Mong Kok ... a classmate put me in touch with him.'

'And how much may I ask?'

'Fifty thousand dollars.'

'Hong Kong?

'No, US.'

'No shit! Sounds bad; someone connected to the Triads, you reckon?'

'Who knows!'

'And the cheek?

'Went to his office tonight; he runs other businesses; money lending is just one of many lines he's into. Told him I needed more time to start repaying. He took me to a back room to meet what he called "repayment advisors". One swung a knife at me. I bolted and lost them in the backstreets.'

'Christ, doesn't sound good.'

'No.'

A waxing moon rose over the hills on the harbour's far side and its silvery glint speckled the ruffled waters unevenly. Eric and Vernon watched the waves twinkle like diamonds shaken in a bottle and wondered what the next day would bring.

'Forgot to tell you; I got fired from Tai Po Chinese English School.'

'Oh … big problem?'

'Not really; there's others like it, but in the short term it doesn't help much.'

'No, s'pose not and … I borrowed sixty dollars from Ligaya … for a cab.'

'Tell her to take it from the house float.'

'OK, but marketing money and her own are all the same and it's gone. Her purse is empty; I saw it.'

'Uh.'

'A bit of sleep might make things look better. Shall we crash?'

'Sure; don't have any ideas right now. Let's think about it tomorrow.'

Wind picked up in what remained of the night and by the time morning arrived a steady drizzle was falling from the outer fringes of a cyclone crossing the China coast near Hainan.

When Eric got up around eleven o'clock the house was empty. Sigrid had taken Feliciano and Yessenia to buy gifts for friends in Madrid, Ligaya had gone to the shops in search of fish and vegetables for the evening meal, and Vernon was walking on the hills hoping to stumble across a solution to his problem.

'Been thinking,' he announced as Vernon came in, kicking off a pair of mud-splattered walking shoes and pulling a soaked T-shirt over his head.

'About last night?'

'Yeah, perhaps old Jakob could be part of the mix. In fact, he'll have to be, because no one I know of has that sort of money to spare except him. What do you think?'

'Can't see him lending a hand … especially after the pudding and his bust finger.'

'Yeah … see what you mean, but let me talk to Sigrid; she's probably got some angles I haven't thought about.'

Sigrid had no real affection for Vernon; he belonged to a period of Eric's life she preferred not to recognise or discuss. But for good or ill Eric was the partner she had taken and after he brought the matter up she felt obliged to show interest to avoid appearing the iceberg of his imagination.

'Hong Kong may look like a city, but it's a village really,' she said. 'And Jakob knows people who pull strings, or people who know people who can do as much. Instead of asking for money, which he'll never give to anyone let alone you, you have to find out what could be in it for him. Get him interested in a deal of some sort where payments are made and you'll be halfway there.'

The conversation left Eric feeling stupid. This wasn't the first time he resented her condescension.

'Blast it, why did she always manage to treat him like a nitwit?'

Even in the middle of a crisis Vernon was so much more agreeable than any of the others, except Papa Feliciano, who, after one more week, alas, would be in the air and heading back to Madrid.

The address Vernon gave was at the top of a flight of stairs in Stanton Street. The entrance, sandwiched between a shop selling every conceivable brand of running shoe and another crowding the narrow walkway with racks of so-called 'export-quality' childrenswear, gave access to a passage that had recently benefited from an application of a pale-green wash repaint covering everything. Walls, skirting, electrical wiring, a noticeboard lacking notices and the parts of the floor close to the walls; all had been liberally slapped with the same utilitarian hue.

Eric wasn't at all sure he wanted to go further, but, after elaborate equivocation, he stepped across the threshold and under a low-watt bulb hanging at the end of a spiralling green wire.

At the end of the hallway a flight of stairs ran up to a first floor and a door made of clear plastic sheeting, bearing the names in red-and-gold lettering of several commercial enterprises – Lam Qi Fat Financing, Universal Sea Food Wholesalers, Starburst Pictures and, mysteriously, High Returns Beauty Products. Through the plastic Eric could see two women working at desks and one man walking about with a mobile phone to his ear. There seemed to be a lot more furniture than the size of office or the number of people warranted. Some, straddling little paper cups holding blue pellets of rat poison, were stacked against the walls, while others on the left side of the entrance propped up a display of coloured marketing photographs of a factory's premises.

Through the plastic screen's distortions the man with the mobile noticed Eric's wavering figure and thrust his highlighted head on to the landing.

'What want?' he snapped.

'I ... er ... wondered ... if ...,' Eric trailed off. He was not at all sure what he wondered or wanted.

The man's mistrustful eyes narrowed.

'Borrow money?' he enquired.

'Er ... no ... definitely no ... but ... urm.'

'What then?' the eyes widened fractionally. 'Shark's fin?'

'No, no, now see here ...'

Whether his nerves were equal to the occasion or not, Eric decided an unambiguous response was the only way of making progress. 'I want to talk to Lam Qi Fat.'

'Mr Lam know you?'

The representative was not convinced.

'We have mutual interests. Let's leave it at that, shall we?'

'Not in.'

The news came almost as a relief, because an immediate conversation with Lam Qi Fat, or anyone who could call off the Triad dogs was a discussion Eric had, as yet, no idea how to handle.

'Ah! I see ... then you have a phone number or a business card, maybe?'

A call to the rear brought one of the women forward with a small piece of folded card, which she offered to her colleague holding up the plastic screen.

'Him,' he said without removing his stare from the caller.

Eric took the card and, as good manners dictated, studied it carefully, in spite of its Chinese script and the urge to turn and run as fast as his poor physical condition allowed.

'Thank you ... er, Miss, thank you.'

His smile was intended to be warm and disarming, but, in this unusual situation, it had quite possibly come across as an anxious and unsteady grimace.

'What name give?'

'... Huh?'

Unpleasant interviews had become daily events, which, some of the time, could be closed with a snappy one-liner. Disengagement from this one, however, seemed to require a level of finesse capable of steering this ginger-streaked lout's mistrustful extrapolations into something advantageous.

Without thinking, Eric responded with the first thought that came into his head.

'Say ... say I'm from ... Odergaard's ... Odergaard Holdings, that is, and have business of a very attractive nature to discuss.'

The convenient lie produced a slow nod of recognition and was the cover for a more or less graceful exit into the havoc of Stanton Street.

'Who will ...?' the highlighted head asked.

From the foot of the stair flight Eric called back, 'Tell Mr Lam we ... yes, we, will be in touch imminently.'

The minibus journey back to Sai Kung was not an ideal place to weigh the very little information he'd gleaned or consider what to do with the name Lam Qi Fat, so Eric got off early and walked the last three miles deep in worried thought.

Making an irresistible business connection between JBO and a Triad money lender was beyond his modest creativity. He loved the invention of others, but had, alas, no personal gift of originality; even his poems, in Sigrid's view, owed more to T.S. Eliot than to a fresh mind.

Of the many obstructions to progress, involvement with a crook was not going to be Jakob's objection, because as long as people gave him what he wanted he never wasted time worrying about whether the source was virtuous. If he had any morals at all, other than those of his own making, they were determined by the value a particular connection offered. Jakob's relationships, except for the weird one with Dagmar, were conducted as transactions in which everyone was considered to be either a merchant or a consumer: 'I'll give you three dollars for that screwdriver. Are we agreed? Yes, OK, here's your money, or no, then I'll go somewhere else.' End of story.

The dealings he had with women, again with the exception of Dagmar, were just the same and that's why they were so simple. There was no way of guessing what he would have done had he a son for whom he held deep affection, of the kind Eric felt for Vernon. Who knows, he might have turned out to be a better and more public-spirited man with a life others would be sorry to see ended, instead of the present unloved degenerate whose departure would attract little sympathy?

Three miles was a long way and Eric wasn't used to exercise. Under the end of his ponytail tiny dribbles of sweat pricked and ran into his shirt. Struggle as he might he could think of nothing that would fascinate Jakob sufficiently to raise money and pay off a loan shark about to reel in his pound of tuna.

What could finance racketeering, seafood, beauty products or film production offer an already ostentatiously rich man, who could afford to eat any endangered species, soak his women in ass's milk and sponsor art, and ignore the results of his investment? None seemed anywhere near Jakob's narrow range of interests and, reluctantly, Eric put the question to Sigrid.

'You look as though you've been swimming,' she said as he puffed out of the spiral staircase's opening on the roof at Sai Kung.

The descending sun cast shadows through stacks of plastic chairs, flower pots vacated by dead plants, bamboo canes and bicycle parts. In the centre of the dappled chaos Sigrid lay on a lounger and pushed a pair of sunglasses into her tousled hair.

'Walked a bit of the way back,' he explained.

'What on earth for? Summer's not the time for athletics.'

'Look, help me with this. I've been checking out the moneylender that's after Vernon.'

Sigrid lowered her sunglasses back on to her nose and pressed flat the open place in the book she had been reading. An iced drink that had kept her company dribbled beaded spots over the cracked cement beside her.

'And what have you discovered in the mazes of Mong Kok?'

'Not a lot, except some guy called Lam Qi Fat runs four businesses that he's willing to advertise: moneylending, wholesale fish distribution, film production and cosmetics manufacturing. But there I'm stuck. How do I get your old man interested in any of that and ready to fork out a tidy sum of money to get Vernon off the hook?'

The steady gaze over a faint smile had the effect of making Eric feel more than usually inept.

The book Sigrid had been holding was turned over and placed face down on her lap and she leant over to pick up her drink.

'You know, in my estimation, but this is only my point of view …'

'Yes, that's what I need,' Eric said eagerly. He always knew she had a fertile brain; wasn't that one of the things that had attracted him ten years ago, when that other dull woman was driving him to despair with her inability to talk to him constructively about a football club's chances of promotion, or the quality of a rhyming couplet and for insisting marriage was something to be stuck on the side of a person's life, like yoga or pottery lessons.

'… I think you should leave young Vernon to sort out his own mistakes.'

'Oh!'

'He's an adult by most definitions; he can vote, join the army, be sent to jail, make a girl pregnant …'

'What? Has he? I was going to ask him about that last …'

'I'm talking figuratively, Eric. Please don't go flying off at a tangent. And, besides, is your son likely to open his heart to me when he has you around him all the time?'

'He's family and therefore I'll be helping,' he replied sulkily, as if he was a pupil struggling to make a valid point to an overbearing schoolteacher.

'I see, well, if you insist, think about this as an illustration of what could be done. Jakob despises many things, but he likes the glamour that attaches itself to what he'd see as ridiculous activities like the performing arts. You remember how he was with the programme he sponsored last year; went to the cocktail parties, but not the show. I've never heard of him watching a film for amusement, but he is ready to bed the sort of women who hangs around a production set. If I were you, I'd ask him if he wants to finance something this Lam Fat, or whatever his name was, has on the go. Once you have them together, it will be a simple thing to persuade Lam to accept part of the financing as payment for your son's debt, or maybe just write it off because of the connection, while Jakob runs amok among the girls in the make-up room.'

That was what he liked about her. She wasn't exactly smart, but she could contrive convoluted solutions to almost any problem no matter how complex, as if she had never lived anywhere other than Asia; it must have been a faculty acquired from her father. Too bad she hadn't got his urge to make ludicrous amounts of money and maintain a semi-idle spouse as well.

Tomorrow, Eric decided, he'd call Jakob.

10

'So pleased to see you, Mrs Odergaard. What can we help? Autumn collection displaying all this month, down in upper basement. Orange and mauve are season colours. This way, will you?'

The store manager's thin frame shivered with excitement at Dagmar's unannounced appearance in the boutique. No upmarket retailer was more aware of her visitor's spending power or more knowledgeable of the fashions most likely to appeal to this notoriously picky client. If only fickle attention could be held for an hour, she thought, it could translate into a sale covering this and maybe next month's exorbitant Central district rent well before their distressingly early due dates. In shameless anticipation of getting a head start selling next season's wear long before summer peaked, her abnormally long tongue reached out and licked the end of a very cold nose.

In the same way as devotees of other lifestyles sought status in computer and motor-car technology, Dagmar demanded possession of the season's most recent designs, and this, almost as much as her quarrelsome nature, was what defined her.

But nothing held her interest for long and, except for a few handbags and pairs of shoes and half a dozen garments of classic cut, nothing remained in her wardrobe from one year to the next, nor adorned her pampered body for more than one glittering outing. Articles that bored her stiff were cast aside to be fought over by poorly paid members of her female staff, who, being less exalted, happily incurred laundry and dry-cleaning charges in exchange for a dash of reflected glamour. Those enjoying figures approximating to their employer's tall, slender form became, as a result, the best-dressed envy of the City's domestic helper community. Only the cook, who relished the fruits of her profession too much for her own good, was left to patch and recycle apparel purchased years ago to accommodate a once-younger girth.

Distaining the noises of obsequious encouragement, Dagmar, with a turn of her heel here and a tested fabric there, circled racks and mannequins with waxing and waning attention.

'Nothing entices,' she murmured before halting close to the glass entrance.

Fearful of losing her best opportunity for months to make a real killing, the unctuous supervisor protested, 'But Madam has missed downstairs. Come this way, come please,' before breathing an aside to a lethargic junior, 'Tea, fetch tea immediately!'

With her gaze floating over the heads of boutique staff and repeated diversions along the way, to fluff at and then pass over skirts and scarves and any other momentarily eye-catching object, she dispelled any notion of being under control, but nevertheless allowed herself to be drawn inch by vacillating inch down a flight of stairs into a beige crypt hung about with the clothes and colours of European autumns.

'Show me,' she demanded abruptly and sat down on a chaise longue of a sort that could once have borne the negligible weight of half a dozen nineteenth-century gadflies.

A dainty burgundy handbag, matching the shoes on her feet and belt at her waist, was put to one side and her beautiful legs were crossed with the precision of steel scissors.

'Well, I'm here. Come, excite me.'

The presence of a famously free-spending customer should have given the floor manager's spirits a lift proportionate to the size of her anticipated sale, especially as, in the accepted wisdom of retailing classes taken at the vocational trades polytechnic, decisions to buy were taken at the moment a prospect sat down, not at the moment a cheque was signed. But, if that was true, why were the penetrating stares and chilling smiles so daunting?

'I ...'

'Yeassss?' Dagmar drawled, before placing an elbow lightly on her uppermost knee.

The jumpy junior attendant, who shared her boss's anxiety, but not her experience, hurried forward with a tray of pale Chinese tea, which she placed at the very end of the chaise and no nearer to the customer than she was prepared to advance.

'Pleased to take tea?' she whispered before backing away into obscurity.

The assistant's suggestion passed unheeded and, with the emotion of a crocodile counting wildebeest at a watering hole, Dagmar moved her elbow to an open hand and an index finger to her lower lip.

'Do you have something to show, or am I in the wrong place?'

'Yes, yes; the latest ... hmm ... yes ...' Recovering traces of composure, the manager took several long strides to no real purpose and, returning, clapped her hands.

Two helpers hurried forward carrying selected costumes.

'And from Milan we have jackets and coats in shades of autumn; there are oranges and browns and a charming mix of all the colours seen on Tuscany's hillside slopes during October.'

The manager's limping English had transformed in an instant to something memorised from a promotional card.

Several more customers entered the boutique; some strolled around the carefully constructed displays; one purchased a fashionable but impractical belt made with loose strands of knotted leather, which, in an emergency, could have doubled up as a cat-o'-nine-tails and another, after regarding the impromptu fashion show enviously, departed bemused into the sweltering hordes of Central. A blonde woman, with a body that turned a dozen heads in her short walk from a kerbside taxi to the glass entrance, swept into the basement with a sharp-visaged man hanging on her arm. But the cluster of activity surrounding Dagmar carried on as if none of these comings and goings was of the least consequence to an establishment depending for its life's blood on the contentment of many clients.

Intermittently, the premier patron flicked her wrist and directed another article to the growing pile she intended trying on.

From somewhere in the maze of racks and mannequins a ripple of female laughter rose and fell, like a wavelet slapping on the sands of a tropical bar. The blonde woman was enjoying her outing.

Never missing anything detrimental to the conclusion of a major deal, the floor manager observed the cloud passing over Mrs Odergaard's concentration.

'Apologies for annoyancing,' she said and dispatched one of her many assistants on an errand to quieten the disturbance trilling behind rails of weekend outfits.

Dagmar had visited this particular boutique perhaps six or more times during the last year, but today she refused to recognise any of the staff or details of the premises. A different admission would have denied her the power conferred by wealth, which fed on the rabblement's toadying as a blind mole grew fat on earthworms. In Mrs Odergaard's estimation, shop personnel served, but, like all commonplace things, had no right to be noticed.

'And the fitting room is ...?'

'Ah! Yes! Over here, behind Place der ... umm ... Boo-loin.'

Scenting the transaction's approaching consummation, the manager navigated around an elaborate mid-floor arrangement of dried leaves and branches mimicking an autumnal Parisian park, having at its centre a dressmaker's dummy decked in a yellow three-quarter-length coat. Rapid-fire commands sent underlings scurrying ahead to gather up and hide loose clothes hangers left over from previous fittings, boxes of stored garments and small stainless-steel canisters containing today's lunchtime soup that together risked troubling a thin-skinned, but irreplaceable, client.

The startling colour of the centre display caught Dagmar's eye and she stopped to examine the yellow coat's sweeping folds that fell like a rider's cloak from the mannequin's perfect shoulders.

Another distraction was not what the floor manager wanted and she scuttled back to refocus Dagmar's wavering attention.

'Not autumn,' she said emphatically. 'Special spring number; keeping theme of seasonal change; from one colour to next.'

'Really? In that case shouldn't ice blue follow the fall?'

When customers challenged promotional verities, a nod, smile and saying nothing were the best responses. The manager tried her best.

'Wouldn't you say?' continued Dagmar with a pause just long enough to discomfort her audience.

'Umm ... as Madam likes.'

'Whether I like it won't help too much. But ... never mind ...'

The unhurried eyes again fell on something of interest and Dagmar, veering away from the fitting rooms, strolled towards the back of the shop where the tinkling laughter had risen moments earlier.

Behind her a plaintive voice called out, 'Here, all clothes ready.'

A rail bearing no more than six costumes hung diagonally on the far side of the fake French park. The lowest item, a dress with vaguely square patterns of amber, mauve and white mixed with splashes of dull red, would be just the sort of luncheon outfit Dagmar's social circle would admire.

She extended a hand to lift the article from its perch only to see it rise in the grip of the boisterous blonde woman, whose joyful show of white teeth Dagmar suddenly found profoundly vulgar.

'Mine I think,' Dagmar said, snatching hold of the moving costume and calling across the floor, 'Add this to my fitting.'

'But I believe I had it first,' the woman replied without letting go.

'Slut!'

'... Ooff! ... Aren't you a tart one?'

Actresses, even aspiring ones, have more to their make-up than mere exhibitionism. Their metier was the cut and thrust of competition, seasoned, more often than not, by the disappointment of unfulfilled ambition. Mandy Plumpkin maintained her grip with determination.

Unseemly female commotion, however, would not facilitate closure of the year's most spectacular sale, so the floor manager, with thinly disguised partisanship, joined her special customer at the shaking clothes rack.

'What is problem? Can I help to you, Madam?'

'Have this put out for me to try,' Dagmar said with the finality of a space engineer counting down – two, one, zero – and blasting a satellite into an orbit from which the only return possible was as a fiery ball and particles shot over the length and breadth of the Pacific Ocean.

'I think you'll find ...,' Mandy began.

'Deal with it,' a fading but inflexible voice called back from the other side of the plastic-and-paper woodland and the mannequin in the yellow coat. 'And have someone walk around in that, will you? I want to see how it moves.'

'Agnes will help,' the manager called as control of the suddenly tumbling events cascaded over her unprepared head.

'Agnes? And what does she have to do with ...?'

A rattle of curtain rings and thump of a door at the far end of the basement guillotined the sentence's end.

'Now, heh, what about some of these to add a few splashes here and there?'

The gentleman who had accompanied Mandy Plumpkin into the boutique, but who had been elsewhere during the unedifying spat, approached with several costume jewellery necklaces trailing from his outstretched fingers.

'Just the stuff for a fun day; what do you say?' he blustered.

The ability to make a stand or inspire others to follow his lead was not a feature of Claude Halt's personality. He preferred to work in a back room and under cover of secrecy and larger personalities where he could bore and grind his way out of sight and, like a weevil in inky silence, contrive to send the sturdiest ship and all its company to the depths of a bottomless sea.

But he knew his weakness and compensated for its imbalance with a sort of flourish that surprised onlookers and gave them the momentary illusion that he was, after all, in some command.

Mandy's tight lips and evident huff was not the reaction he anticipated.

'Hello, hello? What's happening here?' he asked.

'That awful woman snatched away something I was about to try on.'

A dramatically thrust chin pointed accusingly.

'Well, then, we'll get it back for you. So ... what about it, then?' Claude said, delegating the problem to the attendant manager, who was beginning to wish a telephone call from head office or an arrival of new merchandise would unexpectedly call her away.

'Some time, please.'

'That's the ticket. We have to be fair now, don't we?'

'Hum ... yes. Must attend now to Madam Odergaard.'

The nervous muscle spasm under Claude Halt's left eye started up and Mandy's perfect mouth opened just as far as a theatrical gasp prescribed.

'Whoa! In that case, then, perhaps we should ... But you didn't say what you thought of these things.'

'Claude!' Mandy protested vehemently. 'You can't let me be treated like that, whoever she is. Do something!'

Confronting and ritually pummelling subordinates was well within the CFO's capacity, but tackling his employer's wife over a matter as minor as her rough handling of another shopper, especially when the wife was of Dagmar's disposition, was altogether beyond his ability to contemplate, still less initiate. The head that only ten minutes ago had been thrown back in the excitement of his escapade slumped forward despondently.

'Look,' he said, 'why don't we just wait this one out. She probably won't like it and, anyway, in a shop like this there must be dozens of other things you'd fancy. It is, after all, a boutique and anything you buy here can't help but be unique; isn't that the way it works?'

Other than the totally unexpected and scorching encounter with the dusky electrician at the Harbour Hotel, Mandy had not met one man on this Asian trip worthy of the name. But, while the handsome artisan may have stimulated her animal instincts, he was patently incapable of advancing her career.

That was the long and the short of it – men were such limited creatures; some good in bed, others influential, but almost never both at the same time.

'If that's the best you can do, I suppose I'll have to look around,' she said petulantly.

'There you are; that's a good girl! Now, what else can we find?'

How feeble, how depressing and how thoroughly predictable, thought Mandy.

'Will send help,' announced the manager happily, now that her listing ship had miraculously righted itself without her having to put one hand on the pump.

Released from the threatening situation, she sped away in the direction of the fitting rooms and her delayed, but still keenly awaited, retailing triumph.

Behind her, Mandy's gaiety, like lights dimming in a theatre's emptying auditorium, lost its sparkle, while Claude, knowing he should have done better, struggled to regain the ground lost in a moment of weak compromise.

'I say, what have we here? What about this then?' he called with unreal enthusiasm.

Dispatched as a painkiller from the other end of the shop, an assistant shambled forward to provide support. Like other staff, she wore a navy-blue uniform of jacket and skirt, which, in her case, had grown creased and stained with frequent wear, because the boutique's restrained generosity stretched no further than one free outfit for each member of staff. Her slack shoes, which were entirely her own, clacked noisily on the floor's high-gloss surface, and with no natural grace or manners in her she said nothing and picked at her fingernails.

'Oh! I don't know. There's nothing here. Let's try somewhere else.'

'But you are not looking,' Claude complained hopelessly. 'How about a dress, a coat? See ... this yellow one here, for example.'

'No, it's not right; no one would ever wear it in this weather; they'd cook.'

Put out, but not completely put down, Claude battled on.

'You could save it for winter. These things will always keep.'

'You haven't shopped with many women, have you? We don't buy things to store; we buy them to wear, now, not a second later.'

'I do understand really, really I do, but this is Hong Kong and the season's could change. You'd be surprised how quickly that happens. One day it's baking hot and then suddenly, bingo, winter's here and we're all freezing and putting on a thermal layer or two.'

Claude's insistence was becoming just too tiresome. Had he no idea it was a spring coat? How could he babble on about wearing it in the winter? Who, I ask you, ever wore buttercup yellow in the middle of anyone's winter? Wearying of the argument, Mandy gave up.

'OK, give it to me,' she said with a sigh of resignation.

'Only one,' the assistant said unhelpfully.

'Well, get it, get it. We're customers, you know; we need attention and don't have all day.'

Untroubled negotiation of the artificial Parisian woodscape

demanded greater dexterity than the loose-shoed shop assistant possessed. She wriggled between a couple of brown trees and over the plinth, which carried the full weight of the mannequin in her yellow coat. The untidy navy-blue shoes fell free and landed close to Claude. In the otherwise clinically cool showroom he detected a warm, faintly vinegary tang that was more than a scent; it left a bitter taste on the tip of his tongue as if he'd licked his fingers after handling small change from a wet market vendor.

'Errph! Let's wait over here, shall we?' he said, beckoning at Mandy to join him in the lee of a large hatstand and before they were pursued by the bare-footed assistant clutching the yellow coat.

'Can I suggest, my dear, you would be better able to assist with ... ah ... your shoes on ... humm? Prevent you from sliding about the floor, you know; highly polished and all that,' he urged, before changing his tone for the still unpacified Ms Plumpkin, 'Try it on, try it on. Ah, ravishing, absolutely ravishing! You are really, if I may say so, quite exquisite. A mirror, a mirror.'

An audience of one was all the young starlet required to perform and suddenly, setting aside her huge displeasure, which was as much theatre as what came after, she walked round the rustic centre display and tossed her hair about with a laugh, held the coat close then threw it open with abandon, arched her back, covered her face with a sleeve until only her eyes showed, pointed her toes and swayed her hips. First she was a model, then in quick succession a duchess, an Oscar recipient, a heroine, a goddess and a temptress. She was Ophelia, Isolde, Andromeda, Scheherazade, Elizabeth, tragedy, comedy, pastoral all rolled into one.

'Do you like me?'

The question was redundant; Claude loved her and would have carried her on his back to the outer rim of the universe; she just had to say the word. She was the most extraordinary creature, who seemingly could change her mood at will. Was that, after all, what being an actress meant?

'Yes, yes, magnificent. I adore you,' he cried.

The flummoxed assistant construed nothing of any sense out of these mysterious changes of mood – from what one minute earlier had been a serious rift into what now seemed inexplicably transformed into intoxicating foolishness.

'Card or cash?' she asked, assuming the visit to be at, or close to, conclusion.

'Yes, indeed!'

Exuberance had overtaken Claude's dour logic and he pulled a wallet from a rear pocket before waving it around his head in festive victory. One, two, three, four credit cards were extracted from normally impenetrable depths and thrown in quick succession onto the woodland platform, like playing cards in a poker game.

'One enough,' remarked the assistant, picking up one branded by a bank she recognised.

Claude signed the credit slip without reading its details and without realising he hadn't spent that much in one go since purchasing a second-hand, but still newish, German sports car three and a half years before. Expensive transactions usually received his strictest scrutiny and only today had he neglected the personal commitment to squeeze a merchant for every last drop of available discount.

'Pffpt' – the perfectly fitted boutique door gasped into place and, as the ecstatic pair of customers disappeared from view, the assistant explored an itch in her underwear with the ball-point pen Claude Halt had forgotten to take with him.

A clamour of voices punctuated occasionally by one shriller than the rest rose from the fitting rooms. The harsher tone suddenly escalated and was followed by what sounded like a slap. The floor manager with her face shaded to pink on one side hurried into view.

'Get Agnes into yellow coat, quick.'

Agnes, following hot on the heels of her superior, started to unbutton her jacket. A crash and bang reverberated from the fitting rooms as if the premier customer had been replaced by a spitting, kicking mule.

'Quick, quick quick.'

'Not possible.'

'No insolence; get immediately.'

'Can't; coat sold.'

Sale of the single most expensive garment in the shop would at any other time have been a cause for happiness, even celebration, but today the news hit the manager like a thump on the end of her blue nose. She reeled backwards under the blow's colossal impact.

'But wha … to … how … I …?'

The ball-point pen had not cured the shop assistant's discomfort and she exchanged it for the greater precision of a sharp, green fingernail. Subdued eyebrow movement suggested the spot had been correctly located.

'Stop doing that, will … The coat where gone?'

Where the garment had gone was of no possible importance. But that it had been spirited away from under the covetous eyes of one of the City's most demanding and liberal-spending shoppers was a matter of gravest concern.

The inquest's thread was terminated by a rasp of curtain runners pulled aside at unusually high speed and the stormy debouchment of Dagmar clothed in a wrongly sized dress of amber, mauve and white squares, which was evidently designed for a figure fuller than the one she was ever likely to possess.

'Get this ridiculous costume off me this instant. And where is the coat? I want it paraded,' she commanded before returning to the fitting room.

'Ahhrr!' wailed the manager.

'Look, credit card payment – forty thousand.'

'Stupid girl; away with paper.'

All of the boutique's staff, with the exception of the store manager and untidily shoed assistant, suddenly discovered the urgency of tasks other than attending to the one customer gracing the premises and began variously to pack shelves and check the till. Agnes fled to the ladies' room and locked herself in. With their soldiers mown down by hostile gunfire, the general and her aide-de-camp turned to face the barrage together.

'What do you mean, sold?' Dagmar shrilled, 'How can it be? It was there seconds ago – I saw it; I touched it. I believe, young lady, you are trying to make a fool of me. Be careful, or you will regret such impertinence.'

'No, no. Look outside; gone ... this is the one. Ask her.'

Now that most personnel had fled, the checked dress was left hanging from Dagmar's narrow shoulders as if she had been a clothes-horse.

'This is too much; I'll teach you,' she yelled, before catching the dress's hem and dragging it over her head.

Boutique clothing was not built to withstand demented rage and the stitches of the delicate garment began to whimper and ping like guitar strings plucked by an angry ape.

Tearing herself free, Dagmar screwed the outfit into a ball and hurled it in the face of the long-suffering junior store assistant. Not even exotically stippled bikini underwear and a fifty-year-old's enviable figure could render Dagmar attractive at the height of her wrath.

'Damn you, damn you ... where are ...?'

Being a salesperson the manager assumed that her enraged customer was enquiring after the recently selected purchases and with an upturned hand indicated a stack of cardboard boxes neatly secured with ribbons in branded carriers.

'You must be out of your tiny mind,' fulminated Dagmar and she took several enraged kicks at the diligently prepared pile.

Tissue paper, boxes, ribbons, costumes and carriers flew in all directions and the two remaining staff fled like geese before an approaching butcher's knife.

'Where are my clothes!?'

But there was no one to hear, still less help.

Faced with the choice of waiting for the shop staff to emerge from their hiding places or carrying out an independent search, the seething Dagmar stalked from cubicle to cubicle until she located her carefully hung clothes.

The tempest of Mrs Odergaard's passion was not just a sudden cloudburst that blew itself out and left the hills fresh and sparkling in its wake; it was a poison that dripped infection into her blood and stayed there for hours.

Anyone who crossed her path that afternoon was subjected to the worst of her madness. Taxi drivers, servants, her so-called friends, the relatives who had not deserted her, excepting one, even people on the street whose behaviour in some way displeased her were lashed with a razor-sharp tongue.

Once the rage had passed she never stopped to question her unspeakable behaviour, or wonder what people had thought of her at the time. If she gave her outbreaks any reflection at all, it was that the occasion had deserved her anger. The event was at fault, not her, and this reasoning distorted her reality into one only she recognised. She never doubted being true to herself, but things outside varied and oftentimes conspired against her.

From the boutique she took a taxi and railed at the driver for driving too fast and then for getting in the wrong lane, until, in the way of Hong Kong taxi drivers, he refused to go any further and received his fare in a hail of coins propelled from the rear seat.

When she got home later that night Dagmar had a meal sent to her room and, after abusing the cook for her cold food, went to bed with a large tot of Scotch whisky and a pile of fashion magazines.

11

A few miles north of Sai Kung and near the end of a dirt track leading down from High Island Reservoir's arching road, a dilapidated Victorian house, with roof tiles torn off by seasonal typhoons and windows shuttered against incursions by vagrant bats, mouldered away sedately, like a dowager at the end of her society career. Just as the ruin teetered on total collapse it was saved by the Friends of Pak Tam Au and converted into a refuge and counselling centre for the region's abused and homeless women.

The 'Friends' were volunteers from surrounding neighbourhoods and just what anyone would expect of the Sai Kung vicinity's residents. They were serious, well-meaning, more hardworking than practical, and full of compassion and blind faith; not the sort found in established religion, but one more in keeping with free-thought and travel along the sylvan routes by which neglectful humanity could, if it listened attentively, grope its way out of the mire and towards a better future.

These wide-eyed devotees sought utopia in organic food, green energy, Buddhism and abstract ideas of love. Family members, with their infinite capacity to exasperate, were not included in great but discriminating affection, because, not being anonymous casualties of life's vast battlefield, they failed to qualify for liberality and spontaneous kindness.

The 'Friends' and their like, however, were a tiny rivulet feeding an already minor tributary of an undeniably bounding flood. The mainstream community, where unrealistic folly had not yet become common practice, ignored such groups and went about its business as usual. Those born to three thousand years of instability knew more than anyone the importance of a full rice bowl and of keeping an unabashed foothold, devoid of fanciful ideologies, on capitalism's charging chariot.

And, besides, the charioteers might have said, shouldn't embarrassing deficiencies, deviations, handicaps, malfunctions and the inconsistencies no one wanted to acknowledge, be dealt with in their proper place, in the seclusion of a family circle where intervention by disassociated intermediaries was doubly unnecessary?

Sigrid Odergaard, who held many marginal and sometimes unreasonable views including an insistence on being right and dislike for the name Manley with its unintended chauvinism, was not one of the 'Friends' founders. She joined soon after arriving in Sai Kung, with Eric trailing along behind like a watery-eyed beagle in search of a home. Within days, minutes almost, of seeing the Victorian house and meeting its impassioned volunteers she became, like any new convert, more committed to their cause than any original member. In the long, sorrowful sessions that followed, she soaked up tales of women caught in bad relationships, where financial and emotional bonds so strangled self-expression that nothing but the tiniest whimpers of protest, escaped. To these wretched wives and girlfriends she gave the same stock advice – make a stand! Bullying men, she said, may have strength, but their brains were no better and they certainly had no rightful claim to the privileges they enjoyed in a lopsided world.

She would have liked to give more time to the refuge, but being involved in so many other activities – volunteering with a charity for mentally handicapped children and running a side-street, herbal medicine and Indian ornament shop with Ligaya – her concentration, while total at any exact moment, was never quite constant enough to gain her indispensability. In that way, as with a host of others, she was her father's opposite.

From its opening the shop had focused on nature cures and

only after a few disastrous months, when the harsher aspects of marketplace economics imposed its unrelenting logic on her cash flow and undeveloped philosophy, had she expanded into South Asian knick-knacks. Realisation that her freshman's project lacked novelty, in a city where alternative treatment was already an age-old tradition, came slowly. Only Vernon's timely but uncharacteristically shrewd suggestion had saved the fledgling business from crushing debt and an abbreviated lifespan. But, such was her contempt for her husband's son, she refused point-blank to admit he had been, in any way, the saviour of her incoherently undertaken adventure into commercialism.

If the truth was told, a good return, or just doing better than break even, was not a matter to spark her enthusiasm. Her purpose was to be immersed in something intriguing, and the East, with its innumerable mysteries, piqued her interest like nothing an upbringing in distant boarding and finishing schools regarded as normal, so she threw herself headlong into every engrossing discovery that passed her way, while her jaded husband juggled with poetry's troubling metres and forgot that he, too, had once been captivated by the same fairy story.

But, like most unsuccessful people and although brimming with ideas, her shortcomings were beyond her comprehension and getting to the very heart of the things she craved brought her up against the brick wall of her own limitation. She was bright in many ways and, as Eric knew, her mind had flexibility, which his hopelessly lacked. She could instinctively sense the many varied ways to a single destination, while he only visualised moving forward in the steady, unimaginative plod of putting one thick-soled boot in front of the other. Without her prodding, divergence from a straight line would never have occurred to him.

Not that Sigrid was exactly a dilettante, but she was apt to allow her focus to wander when confronted by unappealing work, and, like a bright child tiring of a sudden curiosity or unfamiliar food, she began looking elsewhere for her taste to be excited. She had tried to learn Mandarin and Hindi and, for a while, was captivated by both. But there were simply not enough hours in the day for either to be pursued with the industry they deserved and so, after a few lessons, she gave up in disgust and blamed her tutors for improperly conveying their messages. Similarly, the thrice-weekly dramas heard at the institutions she frequented held her serious engagement for as long as she was on the premises. Under the eaves of the old Victorian house the dreadful tales of privation and sadness became hers and every repeated blow and curse struck her until she wanted nothing more than to illuminate the path by which her charges would escape their oppression and resolve their hundred crowding dilemmas, until, that is, she returned to selling South Asian brassware.

'I'll be at the refuge,' she told Eric one morning. 'Ligaya will be at the shop. We'll be back in the evening; I don't know how late.'

'OK, but look, I'm contacting JBO this morning. Got any advice about how I talk to him?'

'I hope it'll be face to face and that you have found something irresistible, or we might next hear of you as something shovelled away from the bottom of his stairs.'

Sigrid sniggered at her own flippancy and Eric's discomfiture.

'Yeah; I'm sure you're right, so what do I do?'

'Of course I'm right. So, you should surprise him when he's feeling comfortable, over lunch, after an evening with a woman or something. I don't know; you think about it. But if someone like you called out of the blue asking for a loan, what would you say?'

'Hmm … see what you mean, but I've got to help the lad.'

Sigrid had never understood Eric's devotion to Vernon or the rush to bail him out of every crisis that he seemed to attract. Hadn't the time come, she wondered for the tenth time, for the boy to stand on his own feet? At the refuge she had seen the worst effects of cloying dependency and no one, absolutely no one, should live, still less choose to live, with the damage it inflicted.

There was no noticeable traffic north of Sai Kung and only hikers and farmers took the reservoir path past the junction where a rare minibus terminated. Further on still, the level way swept into empty parkland and the 'Friends' rock-strewn track broke down to the right. No one found their way here, other than the few wretched women in need of counsel and those with the urge to talk to them.

In the earliest morning, when the sun still slept and foliage was thick and inscrutable on the hillside, the walk soothed Sigrid's spirit. There weren't many places where she was at peace; her family, such as it was, gave her too much anguish. Jakob and Dagmar were so far beyond the pale with their irrational selfishness that she preferred not to be in any form of contact except in the direst extremity, and Eric and Vernon needed more propping up than was healthy. The virtuous family of her experience was an absolute fraud and any time she could get away from them and be about her own business was a blessing that never came often enough.

Sigrid would like to have said her volunteer work also left her untroubled, but that, too, would have been a lie. She was intermittently stimulated by it, admittedly, but that was a far cry from tranquillity. The plight of these women was too intense for comfort, and for a while at the end of each day she felt their suffering was hers. Their husbands' or fathers' absences, the rejected kindnesses, the betrayals they endured and yes, their chains and inability to break free, she recognised them all. Each blow and angry word hit her until she gasped. Sometimes, when she looked in her mirror before leaving for home, she was surprised and perhaps a little dismayed to find there was no torn hair, no split lip and no bruising. How could she feel the thing so utterly and, yet, not have it show? she wondered.

'Hello, Sigrid. Do you have anyone coming in? We've had

several calls already and one is being picked up and brought over. We are short-handed again and could do with your help receiving.'

The sun burst over a nearby hill and blazed into the room through an ancient lattice window. Black, hatched lines fell across the face of the young woman seated at a donated computer where she typed notes extracted from a cheap register bought at one of Sai Kung's supermarkets. Her hair was almost naturally red, but her features bore the evidence of mixed parentage.

Dawn birdsong and the momentary serenity of the gravel track evaporated as if they had been torched by the new day.

'I'm available for whatever turns up. Do we have a translator?'

'Great! Archie will be here in about an hour; had to take the van almost as far as Shatin. Don't know the story yet, but sounds like she's taken a beating and might have to be admitted. But you'll work out what needs to be done. And yes, there'll be a translator in around ten, but you may not need her.'

Archibald Chan and the two permanent nursing staff were the only paid employees at the refuge. He was no longer a young man and wasn't always prepared for the physical challenges of the job. But as a former office worker he spoke beautiful, if quaintly period, English that endeared him to the younger women giving their time to the refuge. The modest salary he received and a tiny pension from his last full-time employment just helped him get by and avoid being a serious burden to his willing but unusually impecunious son with whom he lived and who constantly urged him to stop work.

Archie's job was to drive the 'Friends' van, bringing in supplies and taking out laundry. When a traumatised caller needed help getting to Pak Tam Au he was dispatched. With his steady reliability, avuncular manner and gentle driving he was often considered the best introduction to a type of support traditional society found alien.

'Which room?'

'Take three. We'll have the medic assess her when Archie gets here and then take it from there.'

Although Sigrid had taken two cups of strong coffee before setting out that morning, she poured another from a large percolator in the kitchen under the rambling mansion's winding staircase. Good coffee was not a luxury in this line of work; it was a necessity and kept her unblinkingly attentive during what was often a very long and emotionally exhausting day.

Before she had set down her cloth bag the telephone rang.

'Archie thinks he'll be here in thirty minutes. Do you want to stand by in the medical room after your coffee and take it from go?'

'OK.'

Sigrid blew into her hot mug and took several blistering sips. With a note-pad and pen in her hand she walked across to the nurse's station.

The white-uniformed and crop-haired attendant was laying out a stainless-steel dish with the tools of her trade, a syringe, a bottle of alcohol, tweezers, scissors, swabs and bandages. Sigrid nodded at her, but got no response.

'Know anything?'

The nurse's head moved imperceptibly in what was neither a nod nor a shake.

Sigrid stepped out of the door and called to the woman at the computer who was speaking on a telephone in Cantonese. She waited for the conversation to end and spoke again.

'Did this one call, or did we find her?'

'Called in; she's Chinese, but speaks pretty good English, Archie says, so you'll be OK.'

The nurse, having finished her preparation, looked at her watch and then out of the window.

A bell rang and above the medical room Sigrid heard the tread of feet. Residents were making their way back to the dormitory after a communal breakfast. Soon they'd be out on the rear veranda and in the vegetable garden where the stillness necessary for rebuilding lives shaken to the roots was readily found.

Through the window Sigrid could see the speck of a bird's wheeling silhouette high in the brilliant sky; it was not one of Hong Kong's ubiquitous fork-tailed kites, but another lofty and impartial observer of lost fortune, maybe a harrier or hawk.

Pebbles and rubber scrunched on the track leading down from the reservoir road. A vintage Japanese eight-seater, manufactured in a time long forgotten by Hong Kong's shoving classes, edged cautiously towards the refuge's front door. Archibald Chan was back from his errand across the New Territories and the edge of Shatin.

On the entrance's lower step the red-haired woman waited for the vehicle doors to open. Archie wound down his window and spoke to her.

'I think they need you,' Sigrid informed the nurse.

With support at each elbow, and Archie following quietly behind carrying a handbag that looked as if it had been dragged through filthy gutters, a bloodied woman limped into the medical room.

'Lie down,' the nurse ordered as softly as she knew how.

The woman curled agonisingly up to the bed in too much pain or embarrassment to make the movement in one clean turn.

'Come with me, Archie,' the red-haired woman said and turned to go.

'Is this a police case?' Sigrid asked. 'Looks like she's taken a real battering.'

'No, she doesn't want anyone to hear. Archie, now please!'

Sigrid turned to the spotlessly white couch and the prone figure.

'No need to say anything right now; we'll just clean you up a bit.'

Anyone who has been injured or beaten had licence to complain, but this person with her matted hair, contusions and streaks of blood apparently had neither the strength nor the inclination to protest. Sigrid watched from behind the nurse's assured moves. No woman deserved to be in this state, but wouldn't you expect her to be crying out at the pain and injustice inflicted upon her?

Without resistance from the passive figure the nurse cut away soiled clothes and threw them into a steel bin.

Who, Sigrid thought, would ever want to see them again or be reminded of what was happening when they got into that awful state.

Alcohol-soaked swabs, which usually make patients flinch, but left this one unmoved, wiped away the worst grime and blood from wounds on the woman's arms and face. She must have been defending herself, warding off an attack, to receive damage like that.

'No bones broken, just bruising, lacerations ... can see? Leave here, till bed's needed. Later take bath. Want me anymore?'

What the nurse lacked in bedside manner, she compensated for by efficiency.

'No, thank you. I'll wait with her.'

Sigrid looked at the tortured form, now lying naked under a freshly laundered sheet. You'd think she'd want to sleep, she thought. But the heavy breathing, if not her closed eyes, said that she was unlikely to do so for some time.

'Can I get you something; water perhaps?'

The woman on the bed said nothing, but rolled away and faced the wall.

'I'll just wait here; you let me know if you want anything.'

Two hours passed and the overhead footsteps returned. Residents were coming in from the garden and cleaning up before lunch. Smells of soup and fried vegetables intruded under the closed door. Sigrid stretched and stood up. Through the window she noticed the old Japanese van had gone. Archie was out on another errand.

'I can't, can't!' the suddenly roused patient screamed.

Sigrid sat down again and took hold of a hand that had fallen free of the covers.

'Tell me what you can't do?'

'Go home! How can I, like this?'

'Who needs you at home, your husband?'

'No, no, no; it's my son. He'll want me.'

'Your son? Is there no one to look after him?'

In her free hand Sigrid's pen hung over an empty page waiting for something, anything that would help this woman climb out of the abyss into which she had fallen.

'No, yes, not really.'

'I'm not sure I follow, but we can check if you like. How old is he?'

'Sixteen.'

'Sixteen? I see; then he'll be at school? Does he have a key, or is there someone in the house?'

'Yes, but I'm his mother.'

'Steady up now. Give me your address, a phone number and we can make sure your boy is taken care of. Then we can talk about you and getting you back to rights.'

Slowly, carefully, Sigrid drew the information she needed and took it to the red-haired administrator. The boy would be cared for – there was no question of that, especially as he lived with a domestic helper who, reading through the outpouring, sounded more than capable of managing his daily needs. He might be surprised, even curious, why his mother was not at home, but at sixteen and if Sigrid new anything about teenagers, gratitude and relief at the sudden absence of governance would be a more spontaneous reaction.

'We have everything under control,' Sigrid said. 'Your son will be looked after, but now we need to help you rebuild. Shall we talk about what happened and why you called the refuge?'

'Owwh!' the woman moaned and rocked backwards and forwards in time to the rhythmic wringing of her dry hands.

'Were you at home yesterday?'

'Aarrh!'

'Then these ...' – Sigrid pointed at the bruises disfiguring the face in front of her – 'happened at home?'

The patient sat up unexpectedly and the sliding sheet revealed a thin and shrunken body that should have been in better condition for a mother of just one son.

'No ... I ... no, I can't tell you.'

'Don't worry now. I'm here to help, not sit in judgement. What you've done or can't talk about is immaterial, but when you leave here I want it to be to a place where your problems are made easier. Do you understand?'

This was Sigrid in her element. Her own relationships could crash and burn, and had done so many times in the past, but with total strangers and, when not distracted, she could gather them up and carry them on a road to safety. Perhaps her skill came from the absolute shambles of personal history, but there was no denying she had nursed many hopeless cases back from the brink with surprising art.

The pitiful creature on the bed lifted the comforting hand to the pounding deep within her heaving chest. Slowly and fitfully, with many diversions and apologies, an unremarkable account unfolded of disillusionment, desperation and bad decision making.

Over her years at the refuge Sigrid had heard the tale a hundred times, of how women, either unwilling to lose what they had invested, or, having become trapped in an emotional prison, became doomed to repeat the same mistakes and, as often as not, bequeath identical misery to the next generation. There were variations, of course, but they all had the same roots. So-called love or biology wearing different guises lured women into relationships no one with a clear mind would contemplate, still less prolong and then, when their ship foundered and they had neither the courage nor society's approval to leap clear, went down with the stricken vessel, or simply fell overboard as it sailed from sight.

Few people in this woman's world ever frankly revealed their innermost thoughts to total strangers however impartial they seemed, and so the story Sigrid would later tell contained as much of her own biases and convictions as the woman's indirect revelations.

There was apparently a marriage, she surmised, although one hardly worth the name, from which intimacy had not simply faded; it had failed to exist since the conception of a son many years before. Even at the beginning romance had hardly been a factor and what was shared revolved around the practicalities of maintaining jobs and income, running a home with traditional observances, and, later on, ensuring the education of a single child.

While daily bills were paid, frustrations gathered like infections under an outwardly healthy skin. The husband had gone away to work in China, as many did and came home less and less frequently, while his wife managed the family household and, to her horror, discovered the ache and heat of sexual deprivation and longing. The longer she waited the more unbalanced and distorted the solution to her agony became. Only yesterday she had lowered her guard sufficiently to test the means by which her hankering could be satisfied.

But judicious management of urges she found almost repellent had proved more difficult and humiliating in this highly connected town than she imagined possible. Instead of seeking quick and easy gratification near by, which, although accessible, was too close to people who knew her, she deliberately looked for a remoter association, preferably one unlikely to stay long or think of an extended dalliance.

Only on the third encounter, the first two having left her feeling soiled and more than a little deranged, had she progressed as far as a conversation. The chance meeting had taken place on the Kowloon waterfront, where backpackers and Tsim Sha Tsui louts came looking for easy and inconsequential scores.

An unattached woman in such a setting, other than lonely domestic helpers on a day off, was unusual, and few would suspect her of harbouring the preposterous motives that were quite unconnected to taking the sea air. She walked up and down the waterfront for some time and watched other women sitting singly or in groups under the vigilant eyes of prowling males waiting to pounce.

Observing the patterns of an ancient ritual to which she had never openly subscribed, she decided her availability was undermined by constant nervous movement around the promenade deck. Stationary targets enabled the hunters to sort through choices and make their moves. A gazelle that stayed still browsing was, as far as she could determine, the one that got eaten first and she was just about in a mood to be devoured as one luscious mouthful.

A seat chosen on the corner of a low concrete wall separated her from knots of chatting women and conveniently thrust her into the path of milling walkers. Although this South Kowloon tourist spot was not a place she, nor many others of her kind, much admired, today, for no more reason than her necessity to quench the fires of frustrated lust, she was prepared to suffer its disreputability.

The afternoon ticked steadily on until the clock overlooking Star Ferry chimed three thirty. Only four hours left to the time she was normally expected home from the full day's work everyone, except Budiwati, expected her to have completed at Odergaard's and still there was a forty-five-minute journey separating her from Shatin! Was there no way she could strike up a passing friendship or was the whole idea just too sordid and foolish?

Doubt and a numbing sense of stupidity flooded her mind. She could feel the strain dragging at her cheeks and eyes. A small make-up compact taken from her handbag was not at all reassuring. Wasn't she looking older than yesterday evening when her face had shone in the bathroom mirror and, oh, my, were those leaf particles still hanging in her tangled hair?

While she concentrated on flicking away the offending debris a cloud of liberally applied male fragrance swept over her and made her nose curl. Ugh! How can some men wear such stuff; it makes them stink. Even the parlour where she took her beloved pet schnauzer smelled better.

The compact snapped shut and she stood up. This entire adventure had descended into absurdity and she was ready to go home.

A second deluge of male fragrance made her cough and she put a hand to her mouth.

The odour had come from a thin man, shaped like an archer's bow with both ends apparently drawn towards each other at the nose and toe by an invisible cord and wearing hideously violet trousers and a frilled white shirt. What a ridiculous spectacle. No self-respecting person she knew would be caught dead in such apparel.

But her brisk verdict, which at any other time would have been unarguable, was, today, not quite so clear cut. In fact, such was the opposing pull of her emotions, she could not but notice that from the rear the elaborately dressed figure looked young, at least younger than she was, and possessed remarkably narrow hips and, given his repeated and solitary passage, probably on the lookout for companionship.

The presumption of his intentions coupled with a vision of firm buttocks under the garish costume brought a rush of blood to her face and she sat back on the concrete bench with the same peremptory suddenness with which she had left it only seconds earlier. To calm her confusion, she agitatedly set about smoothing her unruly hair.

The man, sensing his showy parade had made an impression, stopped, turned and retraced his steps to within a few feet of the concrete wall and its edgy occupant. He lent forward and leered in a grotesquely toothy way. Quivers of trepidation shook her stiffening body and she stared back in dull but hopeful astonishment.

''Ello, darlin'. Mind if I sit down 'ere?' he enquired from the centre of his musky cloud.

Carol Tung was speechless with fright and joy and edged a few centimetres away.

'Well,' he said, 'that's right hospitable of you; don't mind if I do.'

Like an inexperienced angler fearing the loss of a promising catch, or a man who had repeated a 'come on' a thousand times without much success, he yanked at his line and began roughly hauling on it. A steady patter, he decided, was the best way to occupy his audience's attention while he spread a net under her awkward flapping.

'Stuff bleedin' Anil Patel; I'll show him he ain't the only bloke who could land a herring and turn it into a kipper with a pat of butter on top.'

Incapable of almost any utterance or recognition of what she was doing or hearing, Mrs Tung writhed about uncomfortably and, to minimise her spectator's perceptions that she had the personality of a plank of wood, gave him an occasional nod.

'Fancy summat to eat, then?' he asked, believing the route to a screw, even one as ugly as this, required some formalities of behaviour.

The American fast-food joint to which he steered her was quite without appeal, but her inability to eat had nothing to do with the cuisine or the ambiance and everything with her jangled nerves. A cup of jasmine tea, which remained untouched throughout the meal, was the extent of her expressed appetite, while he, preparing for a trek up mountain slopes in cold weather, devoured a heaped plate of spaghetti and minced beef awash with tomato sauce.

A fulsome belch returned traces of paste to his lower lip and Mrs Tung watched in fascination as a line of tiny dots swayed to the irregular tempo of mastication and tireless monologue. If this had been her son, a reproachful word and forceful wipe would have removed the bobbing specks. But an inexplicable yearning to lean forward and lick away the scarlet fragments from the moist mouth made her veins throb like pipes bursting with steam from a groaning furnace.

'Not bad,' he said patting his belly with both hands. 'For fuck's sake, I'll have to let my belt out after that lot. Sure you're OK with just a cuppa then, eh?'

After the meal they walked twice round the municipal park behind Nathan Road mosque. Near the end of a second circuit he moved round to her left side and took hold of the hand not desperately gripping her handbag.

Neither responding nor withdrawing, Mrs Tung let her companion determine whether his advance was making progress or not.

'Let's sit over here for a bit,' he said, pulling her towards a garden seat dotted by the secretions of a banyan tree's hanging roots.

'Sheesh! Gonna fuck up my pants that is ... Don't suppose you'd have anything we could put ...? No, that'd be askin' too much.'

Without letting go of the rigid hand he sat down and dragged Mrs Tung into place by his side. She could make this easier, he thought, but at least she hain't bleedin' bolted. Just needs to be reassured that I ain't a pig, that's all.

He reached out an arm to put round her shoulders, but stopped in mid-passage as he felt the awkwardness of a right-handed man embracing a woman sitting on his left.

''Scuse me,' he said and clambered over her knees.

The warmth and closeness of his breath, mixed with smells of meat and light ale, which at any other time would have appalled her, had the effect of electricity on a cadaver. Her legs twitched and she squeezed his hand as if wanting to crush its bones to splinters.

'Oww ... oowah! What yer doin'? You gonna bust something if you ain't careful darlin'.'

A youth and someone who could have been his grandfather passed by on their way to the mosque. They were dressed in the loose cotton suits and round beaded caps of the Punjab and moved at the old man's faltering speed. He was staring fixedly ahead, either because his eyes had dimmed with age, or because he wanted to avoid the city's rambunctious distractions. The youngster observed the spectacle of a man in violet trousers straddling a seated woman's strangely contorting knees and wondered if this was an education he should ignore.

'Look, it's like this ... I ain't got much of a place, you know; it's what you'd call like ... shared accommodation, so how about we go back to yours and really get to know each other, eh? What do you say?'

His pungent aromas beat down on her forehead and eyelids in short warm bursts. The suggestion was not altogether ludicrous. She could phone ahead, yes, that was it and make sure Budiwati and Wai Pang were in their rooms and tomorrow morning, when the girl was out walking the dog and her son had left for school, the man could slip away into the morning crowds and need never be seen or heard of again. If only she had known an affair was not so simple and that, once in, it would hold her in its teeth as fast as in a famished hyena's.

'I ... let me ... make a call,' she stuttered.

On the bus ride under the harbour and all the way back to Shatin she held the man's hand and dragged at it intermittently as if afraid he might change his mind and get out at one of the many intervening stops. Sitting at the back of the bus, where she could be as far from other passengers as possible, had been her idea. If she recognised anyone along the way, she'd just have to let go and then no one would be the least bit wiser or suspect she was riding a roller-coaster that left her clutching at the walls of her stomach.

Over the last few miles the shops became more familiar. She

hadn't realised before that within a three-mile radius she could recite from memory the name and business of every small shop, especially in the market's cluster of stalls, where each proprietor was known to her. There was Chan Leung the vegetable dealer, Wing Fau Lai and his 'Golden Returns' pawn shop and Mr and Mrs Foo at the California Laundry, and then the larger shops, with branches in other parts of Hong Kong, which closed at the same time every night and left the small family traders to keep going until no customers were left on the streets and no takings left to ring into a till.

The double-decker turned over a canal bridge and into the Shatin terminal. A loud gasp of airbrakes, a final lurch into an open bay and the journey was done.

'Me first, you follow,' Carol Tung said as she disentangled her fingers from her escort.

'Uh? Wassa matta then?'

Without bothering to explain, she hurried away.

On the bus station's apron a wizened couple who looked as if they had been left out in the sun and rain for weeks on end sold sweet potatoes and chestnuts cooked over a still-red charcoal brazier.

'Cor! Fancy some of them?' the man in violet trousers called towards Carol Tung's disappearing back.

She slowed for a second but then inexplicably moved into a higher gear and crossed the road in front of a construction site before turning into a darkened gap between two buildings.

'Hey! Where are you off to then?'

A short sprint to catch up made him breathe rapidly.

'Please stay behind. Mustn't look like we are together.'

'Why? Who gives a shit?'

'That couple; I see them every day.'

'So? What's the big deal?'

'No one must know.'

Back there in Kowloon she had almost bitten him, so strongly had she wanted to taste the flavour of his body. But here, in her own neighbourhood, she was not willing to be seen, still less recognised in his company. If she were to open herself to him, it had to be on her terms and in the utmost secrecy.

He, however, was puzzled. She had accepted, albeit stiffly, the pass he had made at her and was now getting weird and playing hard to get. Well, bugger that for a game of skittles. No bird was going to lead him on, get him all fired up and then back off at the last minute. No sir, if she ain't going to give it, I'll just have to take what's due and what was as good as promised a couple of hours ago.

There were no lights in the alley, except a few broken fragments from apartments high overhead, which fell in a patchwork through tangles of metal fire escapes and retractable laundry lines.

She wanted to stay far enough ahead, so that no one could possibly believe they were connected. Rasping pants fell on her neck and she speeded up again, hoping the presence of other people in the blur of the distant street would force his better behaviour.

But he was too inflamed, too excited to be put off now and he caught at the back of her ballooning blouse as she hurried away. With the exhilaration and recklessness of a schoolboy enjoying a playground scuffle with the class dish he hauled her back to where he could grip her with both hands and control her suddenly wild swipes with all his animal strength. Under his greater weight he wrestled her to the wet pavement, rolled her face down and placed a knee in the small of her back.

But restraint failed to prevent her furiously wielded high-heeled shoes from landing painful blows on his chest and arms.

'Bleedin' cat,' he yelled and knocked the weapons away from her writhing legs. 'There, that'll do ya.'

Rather than calming the man's instincts, the bruising tussle raised his mood to fever pitch and he dragged Mrs Tung's arms behind her shoulders and held them together at the wrists. With a free hand he took a handful of hair and pulled her, still face down, wheezing like a bellows and flailing like a windmill, towards a stack of cardboard cartons piled up behind a skip overflowing with several days' fruit and cooked-food stand debris.

'Bit smelly, aih? But we'll be nice and cosy in here, darlin', trust me.'

The man had never been a successful womaniser, much less a rapist, except in swirls of fantasy where every imaginable perversion had been explored, but, having come this far and with his blood boiling, he could not draw back, even though the next part of the manoeuvre required a degree of deftness his curved frame found demanding.

Still holding her firmly, he took up a better position astride her lower limbs, where she could no longer move so freely.

'Well, here goes,' he muttered and let go of the black hair to unbuckle his belt and wriggle the outrageously coloured trousers below his buttocks.

The bony knee that suddenly forced its way between her thighs stung Mrs Tung into a paroxysm of demented twisting and heaving that would have done credit to a rodeo mustang precariously ridden by an inexperienced ranch hand.

Succumbing to the violent convulsion under him, the man flew upward and forward in a tangle of his own clothing and into abrupt facial contact with the skip.

'Yow! Fuckin' Geez almighty. You stupid cow!'

Enraged and shamed beyond words, Mrs Tung sprang forward and sank her extended fingernails into his pitted cheeks and, to the accompaniment of maddened shrieks, hauled them down to the end of an agonised and twitching chin.

'Owwahh! Bitch! ... Bitch! Just you bleedin' ...!'

Without being able to see or take clear aim his fists flew about, colliding first with the heaps of cardboard boxes and then something soft and knobbly, which he hoped was the woman's head, although he wasn't sure.

Neither the man nor woman were in a condition to run, but,

while he fell back into the trash tumbling across the alleyway and clutched at his bloodied cheek, she limped away down the dirty lane towards far-off lights.

As occasional traffic and even less frequent pedestrians drew closer her steps slowed until at the very end she discovered an entrance to a basement stockroom enclosing a few square metres of grubby space and, at the rear side, a pair of windowless steel doors. She pulled herself inside and curled up in the farthest, darkest corner. 'Rest, rest' was what she needed, where no one could see her and where she could gather her desperately racing mind.

Hours later an almost imperceptible greying in the severity of the night woke her. She had no idea of the time and, as the full horror of the Kowloon encounter and its aftermath rushed back into her mind, she was overtaken by panic that constricted her chest and neck until she retched over the windblown litter at her feet.

Day and renewed street clamour crept slowly into the soiled recess. Light touched her cramped toes and rose deliberately over her huddled legs as far as the sore hips that had been so summarily wrenched apart by the thrust of last night's uncouth knee.

'What will I do? Where can I go?' she wailed.

A bang and clatter at the far end of the alley way bounced along the high, unwelcoming walls. Refuse was being collected and she could no longer postpone a decision. Without looking towards the approaching noise she stepped out of her night-time shelter and turned into the main street and away from her apartment.

She walked and walked without the least idea of where her steps were leading, until stalls and buildings lost their familiarity and instead of the grim towers huddled over a maze of tiny shops in the centre of Shatin, she found herself among low-rise shanties festooned in criss-crossing power cables.

The electrical threads were held aloft by steel-and-wooden

poles plastered with layers of advertising for every known freelance service – plumbing, painting, waterproofing, air-conditioning, automotive repairs, travel, tutorials for adults wanting to get ahead and children not already leading the pack, pet grooming, freight forwarding, picture-framing, 'magic hand' massage, herbalism, yoga, acupuncture, hairdressing and satellite dish installation.

Stuck in the wind-battered and rain-stained notices was one for the 'Pak Tam Women's Refuge' counselling service. At her wit's end Mrs Tung peeled away a phone number and, from an adjacent mini-mart, made an anguished call.

12

'This is the first time in more seasons than I can remember when performers have been called to return for a second straight year, which only goes to show how esteemed the Provo Repertory Theater Company has become and how well targeted and prescient our sponsorship has been. It is an accolade for them and a public-relations accomplishment for us.'

No one could say Claude Halt was a truly persuasive man; he lacked the necessary sincerity, but, once into his stride, there was no doubting the persistence he brought to any task, especially ones of serious personal interest. He was like water seeping through a rocky crevice; unnoticed for the most part, until, in the fullness of time, capable of cutting a mountain in half and changing the entire landscape.

Huh! JBO thought. Half Claude's trouble was he's been in Asia too long and has started to acquire local characteristics. Next thing I'll know he'll be recommending a medicinal poultice for a broken finger.

'Who gives a shit?' he said out loud. 'Do you remember any of last year's sponsors? I'm sure I don't.'

'Oh, but surely you must; look at the impressive line-up in last year's programme, which I just happen to have here about me … somewhere and … Ah! Here we …'

'When I say I don't, I mean "give a shit", not "remember the sponsors", although, seeing you've raised the topic, it does apply to both.'

'Oh, I see … then …'

Seeing his second shot fall short of its intended target, the

CFO sighted another shaft. He rarely entered a debate with a single arrow for his bow; he came with a whole quiverful.

'... In that case, let us explore another avenue. Hong Kong is a small place where reputations are of inestimable value.'

'That's your opinion; mine is they don't matter a toss, unless you're talking about what our customers think of a delivery. I ask you, how's footing the bill for this bunch of hay seeds on a good time going to make the quarter's bottom line, or my life any better?'

'At the corporate level, yes, yes, you may well be right and, as we have seen, successful sponsorships do require protracted periods of time to fully realise the returns investment in them warrants, but, on a personal level, they can, in the right circumstances, be assured of a quick and beneficial outcome.'

The penchant for elliptical communication left JBO unimpressed.

'What the fuck does that mean?'

'Well, it seems to me, but only as an observer of what may well be construed as a potentially annoying situation, we could take this opportunity to open a door and give a gentle push, shall we say, to allow a difficult party to move on in a preferred direction.'

'For Chrissake, Halt, what are you blathering about?' JBO was getting impatient.

'Let me be clearer ...

'I doubt you know how.'

Claude's lips parted painstakingly, as if he was posing for a studio portrait he intended attaching to his mother's Christmas greeting card, and he drew a slow breath through his teeth. The preamble to an admittedly sensitive subject had been, he felt, a necessary precursor to playing the highest card in his hand.

'Hssss ... for many months Geoffrey Keso, the director, you recall, of Provo Repertory Theater Company, has experienced a dilemma.'

'Uh-huh, so?

'And I have been happy to put forward a solution, which I believe will resolve his quandary and coincidentally – correct me if I'm wrong – tidy up an inconvenience which has consumed your valuable time.'

'Oh yeah? And seeing you know so much, what's bothering me?'

'I speak,' and here the CFO paused and puffed out his cheeks as though preparing to eat a super-heated baked potato, 'of the resolution of a certain lady's ... ah ... status.'

At this advanced stage of JBO's relationship with the actress, her mention should have left him unmoved, but to have it enigmatically tossed into the conversation by this necessary nuisance in a voice that for inexplicable reasons had fallen a full octave hinted at issues the Chairman should better comprehend.

'You mean Plumpkin? What's she got to do with any of this?'

There was a distinct edginess to JBO's tone that may have come from an alpha male's atavistic posturing or, alternatively, total weariness of an adventure run to the end of its natural course. But without insight into his superior's waning powers Claude looked no further than the virile defence of property rights, before continuing cautiously.

'Would I be correct in suggesting that while you have deep affection for the lady her theatrical ambition has strained your ... er ... eagerness to guide ... umm ... her career and thus become, shall I say, too ... time consuming? If my impression is indeed accurate, my duty to you, as a loyal and trusted advisor of many years' standing, is to facilitate freeing you from this not inconsequential burden ... is it not?'

'What on earth are you talking about?'

'Succinctly put, if Odergaard Holdings sponsor the Provo Theater's Festival entry, I can obtain their agreement to engage a star of international repute, I mean of course the talented Ms Plumpkin, in a role which will establish her position where she will no longer require your extended patience and kindness and thus leave your relationship to rest on its ... hmm ... merits and

… without the complications of what you may be pushed to provide. Her career, in other words, will be under way and your attachment to her may continue unfettered by side issues, or not, as indeed the case may be …'

'And what's in it for you, or is that a silly question?'

'How long have we known each other, Jakob old man?' the CFO simpered.

'That's exactly what was going through my mind,' replied JBO, who recognised thirty years' service in the highest reaches of his company had not satisfied this subordinate's high-stepping ambition or made him any more trustworthy.

Rough manhandling of Claude's interesting idea was, from the Chairman's perspective, a good tactical move; it disguised where he stood and left this craven and obstinate contender no certainty of how battlefield formations could be deployed.

There was, however, no denying that the Plumpkin woman had become an irritant. At the beginning and before developing doubts about his ability to carry off a fiery affair, she had seemed exactly the type of recreation he relished. But since then, and in parallel with his decline, she had become too stridently demanding and too aggressive in the promotion of her professional aspirations and, it need hardly be said, too difficult to shake off. If ever there was a mercenary woman, she must surely be it.

JBO's views of women had never been clouded by sentimentality, but the recent impairment of a once-consuming instinct revealed the pathetically amateur actress in a newer, starker light. How could he tolerate a situation where she provided nothing of the slightest value and strove to milk him at every verse end? Should he have just stopped paying the hotel bills and answering her calls? That would have sent her packing.

Summarily terminating an affair was not beyond him and countless discarded women littered his impersonal social and business circuit, like leaves fallen at the rugged roots of the biggest beech tree in the wood. But the sadistic pleasure of seeing his CFO, whose romantic experiences stretched no further than gawping at Wanchai whores from the safety of a passing taxi, taken for a ride by a scheming tart more than offset the powerful urge to toss her on one side.

'So, let me see if I've got this right; you and this ... this Geoffrey Keso are ready to come riding over the hill and roll out Mandy Plumpkin's red carpet to stardom and leave me to call on her if I feel in the mood for a matinee – is that it?'

The image of JBO and Mandy locked in yet another amorous embrace pained Claude Halt more than he cared to admit and he squirmed unhappily under his employer's piercing stare.

'Yes ... er ... pretty much.'

'Well, is it or isn't it?'

The same intake of breath that first accompanied the subject's delicate introduction sucked in again between and under Claude's clenched incisors.

'Thsss ... yeahs ... you are indeed correct.'

'OK, so what's Keso got in mind? Needs something with a small cast, or we'll be covering holidays for every alfalfa farmer's wife in Utah.'

'Something American he said.'

Claude took his arms from the edge of the Chairman's desk and a misted patch from the warmth of his skin evaporated under chill air-conditioning.

'Didn't know there were any American playwrights. But tell him to nail something down for me to look at.'

The twisted smile conferred on Mrs Chou as the CFO slithered through her outer office was so hard to interpret that she glanced behind her through the separating window to reassure herself the Chairman was still at his desk and untroubled by his blackened finger.

In his own room and behind the security of a closed door Claude Halt put in a call to Geoffrey Keso.

'Yah, who is..?'

'Hello, old man; wanted to bring you news as soon as our decision was made.'

'Uh! You are?'

'Halt, Claude Halt at Odergaard's. You were expecting to hear from me, no?'

'Give me some space here, Ma; you're leaning on me.' Geoffrey's voice was barely audible.

'I couldn't quite catch ...'

'Sorry, kinda late. Just let me sit up and find a pen.'

The muted grunts and rustles of a heavy man heaving upright from the embrace of too many mattresses and pillows, followed by a rattle of disturbed coathangers, drifted down the line from Provo.

The favourable report, which had required no little outlay in time and effort, dangled cooling in the trans-Pacific void, while Geoffrey Keso, wrapping himself in the folds of a copious bathrobe, rumbled to attention.

'Yah, right; what've ya'll got.'

'If you're not ready, I can come back later.'

Glad tidings should be greeted with enthusiasm, Claude felt, whatever the time of day or night.

'Uhh? Whatever ... let's have it.'

Like a woman, who's first wedding anniversary has been forgotten by an inconsiderate husband, the sponsor's spokesman would not let his pique drop.

'After taking pains to inform you immediately, I hoped you would be as excited to learn of our deliberations as I have been to press your cause.'

'Sure, just need to get oriented here and ...'

Realising the relationship required some stroking, Geoffrey continued deliberately: 'The whole association and their families have had lives on hold waiting for this one, to be sure.'

'In that case ... tch ... I can tell you a board meeting has been concluded this very hour in which our support for the Hong Kong Arts Festival was discussed in great detail.'

'Uh-huh and ...?'

'As profit, and therefore control of costs, is part of my official brief, a key part I should add, sponsorship stands or falls by my ability to link expenditure to corporate objectives.'

'Ah see …'

Whether the explanation of a CFO's role facilitated a better understanding of the destiny of Provo's amateur theatrical aspirations was unclear, but having had his habitual nine hours of sleep next to the mother of his five children shattered, Geoffrey Keso listened as well as any man could at three o'clock in the morning.

'We are a frugal organisation and watch cash-flow with extreme care. Irregular or substantial expenses have to be fully vetted. You appreciate our difficulties?'

'Yeah, so … the answer's "no"?'

'What? Good lord! Haven't you heard a thing I've been saying? The root and the essence of my message is that, mindful of my recommendation, Odergaard Holdings has agreed to underwrite your proposed participation in the forthcoming Arts Festival in Hong Kong.'

'Yer? … Man, that's great! Really great. So we can go ahead and put together a plan for the Organising Committee? No remaining issues?'

'No, none whatever, other than … that is … those touched on during your last visit to our glorious city.'

'Ah! yes, Ah remember that conversation, Ah do indeed. Remind me again of what ya'll were asking.'

'Some very minor matters that'll take almost no time to approve; just the question of clearing your programme choice through Odergaard's before we sign off and your agreement to our nominee playing the lead female role.'

'From where Ah sit those could be a couple of mighty big obstructions.'

'Come, Geoffrey, we are both men of the world. You know what you want as much as we do and that means providing leadership to those around us so they can make proper decisions. At this end the ground work is complete and now, for the project's happy launch, we require you to do your bit.'

Chill desert air lapped round Geoffrey Keso's unclothed ankles and insinuated its way into the gaping legs of his pyjamas. He wanted to lift his feet into the bedside chair and under the warmth of his vast weight, but middle-aged bulk was not at its most supple in the depths of a sleep-deprived night.

'Urtt ... pffth!'

'Shall I take that as confirmation? Subject, as always, to a formal exchange of letters.'

'Look, give me a week to get a wrap on this, OK? And then if we're ready here Ah'll draft something for the Festival Committee.'

'Excellent, excellent! But to save you the aggravation of dealing with too many parties you can confide your entire proposal to me ... in my capacity of financial advisor to the Festival, you understand?'

The Pacific Ocean and Utah's wilderness yawned expectantly.

'It's a voluntary position,' Claude Halt continued, 'with a great deal of onerous work, but, I have to say, prestigious appointments even while unpaid do have the capacity to influence decision-making.'

'Ah see; wha'll you're quite a guy; gotta hand it to you, Claude. So if we come up with decisions you like we can say we're in. Is that how it goes?'

'Well, I don't like to overstate my contribution, but, yes, I believe that would be a fair assessment of our process.'

Without removing his bathrobe Provo's theatre director rolled back into the warmth of his king-sized bed and voluminous wife and plotted a route for Hong Kong through the maze of overhead ceiling patterns and the intricacies of thespian group politics, while, across the sea, Odergaard's CFO sought out Mandy Plumpkin.

Company performance standards insisted incoming calls should not be allowed to ring more than three times. Offenders against this strict practice were quickly invited to pursue their futures at less exacting establishments.

After allowing eight rings to the telephone in room 2018 at the Harbour Hotel, Claude took a pencil from the tray in front of him and began revolving it round his thumb.

Where could she be? he wondered. Under a masseur's oiled hands perhaps, or stretching that blissfully leotarded body in the gymnasium?

The images were just too inflammatory.

'Aarrhh … hrh,' he sighed.

On the twelfth ring he leant forward to disconsolately return the receiver to its rest, but, just as he was about to let go, a soft 'hello' fluttered at the end of his outstretched arm, as if a threatened maiden had called from a crag in the storm-blown waves.

'Yes, yes,' he said with the telephone back to his ear. 'Is that you?'

'Hello? Yes … Mandy here, is that Claude? Oh, hi, I wasn't expecting you. I was … I was taking a nap.'

'What? At this time of day?' He looked at his watch before remarking incredulously, 'It's almost five thirty!'

'Claude, darling, I'd lost track, but you know how Hong Kong is, so sultry and soothing. An afternoon swim and the soft air just make me want to … to … lie down.'

The thought of Ms Plumpkin's mouth-watering limbs lying stretched and naked on white sheets was almost too much for the CFO's composure. The turning pencil inexplicably snapped and fell in a shower of splinters over his open computer.

'Damnation … fuff … fuff …' He blew at the wooden particles lodged among the keys.

'What is it, Claude dear? Are you unwell?'

'Huh? No, I'm fine. Just need to make sure the file I was working on wasn't corrupted; that's all.'

'Sounds awfully boring; not something I could take care of for you, is it?'

'No, yes, well depends ... fuff ... got it. Look, forget that; I've got some news.'

'Wonderful, I like surprises, especially from nice men.'

If she had said 'from a nice man', Claude would have been better pleased, but he knew beggars and those standing in a queue could not always be choosers and accepted the qualified compliment with the best grace at his disposal.

'Then that's good to hear. So this is the state of affairs, I've been able to guarantee you a ...'

'Hold on ... hold on a second ...'

There was nothing Claude Halt loathed more than being told to wait when he was about to reveal breath-taking news, or in this case a *coup de théâtre*. In that, if not in much else, he shared the performer's art; timing was all and he knew a punchline's separation from its supporting story was the kiss of death on any delivery.

Unidentifiable noises, not unlike the fussings that had welled up out of Provo's small hours minutes before, fell on Claude's distressed ear.

'Yes ... OK ... I'm ... uh ... ready now; what is it, my dearest?'

'What's going on? Sounded ... like ... you know ... sort of strange.'

'Oh, nothing to bother about, an electrician was here ... wanted to look at the fuse box or something. I had to shoo him away until later. Now, what is it, what do you want to tell me? I'm all ears.'

There was no mistaking the pushy, and so far unsuccessful, actress for an innocent; no one understood that reality better than Claude Halt, who had waited patiently for her previous entanglement to dissolve, while at the same time expediently conniving in its continuation by writing off countless private expenses to the company account. But the thought of her conversing with an artisan, however briefly, in sleeping attire, or, hideous thought, with a towel or something equally bewitching around her slender waist, filled him with raging jealousy.

'Were you … did you … ?' he blurted incomprehensibly.

'Pardon? Was I … did I … what? … Dear boy, don't say you are asking how I sleep?' she teased. 'That's an awfully direct question between people who only began spending time together a week ago.'

'Ten days actually, although we had spoken several times before. It was Thursday the seventeenth … that was when we first met at the Harbour … I remember it quite distinctly because that was when I introduced you to Keso.'

'Who?'

'Sorry, I mean … you know … the director … Geoffrey Keso.'

'Well, never mind the date, or who was around,' Mandy Plumpkin purred. 'Let's just agree on one thing and that is, if you want to make the same sort of enquiry again, you should do it while looking straight into my eyes and then we will understand each other fully. Can I be any clearer?'

If the CFO had been as discerning as he was scheming, he would have immediately recognised the actress's lavish mockery. But, while believing he was about to storm a citadel, rather than fall into a trap capable of engulfing an entire cavalry regiment, he merrily accepted the invitation at face value.

'Yes, yes, of course, and, with Geoffrey Keso finding his way into our conversation, can we start over dinner and a bottle of Château de Ferrand, say, tonight to celebrate the double pleasures of sharing, yes, sharing intimacies and …' he paused for effect '… your selection from a very competitive field for the lead in a coming Hong Kong Arts Festival … dare I say it? … premier theatrical production? Now … what do you say to that?'

The artless blending of hyperbole and downright lies should have elicited raptures of appreciation from the underachieving Ms Plumpkin, but she was perceptive enough to know men promised the earth and more frequently delivered an arid plot.

'Let me check.'

The telephone bumped down on a hard Harbour Hotel table top.

'What? What is there to check?' he screamed at the rustle of flicked pages and distant murmurings.

'Tonight's no good; do you want to do tomorrow. I'll be free from about eight and we can make it a long evening if you wish and you can tell me all the details.'

'Details, ah, yes. What exactly will you require?'

'Oh, you know, basic information; name of production, role, script if it's something new, dates of performance and anything you have on terms being offered. Nothing more complicated at this stage. Then I can give this Mr Keso my reaction; is that who I'll be dealing with?'

An inordinate sense of anti-climax assailed Claude Halt when, a few minutes later, he heard the telephone's terminating click. He slumped despondently against the rigid form of his patented backache-proof office chair and let the telephone handset slip from his grasp to spin at the end of its greasy, coiled cord.

What was it with these people? First there was the bloody-minded Geoffrey Keso, who should count himself lucky that he and his troupe of country yokels had secured corporate sponsorship for the Festival, following their horrendous struggle last visit to get to grips with a play that must have been staged a million times by ten thousand companies and when, this time, no one had so much as a clue what they wanted to perform. And, if he wasn't enough, Mandy had also taken it into her pretty little head to start acting up!

The CFO was not at all sure what he should think. Was she playing hard to get? Neither the news of her role nor the suggestion of a dinner celebration appeared to bowl her over. But how could any of that be true, when her invitation to look deep into her eyes during the hush of a long evening and to understand her couldn't have been more explicit?

On the launch pad of fine food, wine and improbable hope he could still convince himself that the threshold of an imminent journey through the firmament's sparkling stars was but a step away.

The recurring vision of Mandy Plumpkin's cascading blonde curls on soft bedroom pillows and the sight of her perfect body as he drew away a clinging silk sheet sent waves of excitement shuddering through every particle of Claude's anatomy and he licked his dry lips one after the other as if they had been coated in sugar.

But the afternoon had been a lot more trying than his dedicated effort deserved, and every muscle and limb ached in exactly the way they would after a driving session at the Society of Financial Executives' indoor golf range. The thrills and disappointments of these past few hours combined to rob him of his customary sense of control and good order and, if that damnable spasm in his left cheek was not bad enough, another had begun buzzing on his upper thigh.

'Blast ...' he said, slapping distractedly at the tremor until realising the source was not another overtaxed muscle but an incoming text message on an under-utilised mobile telephone kept inside his trouser pocket.

From in between a neatly folded handkerchief and business-card holder he extracted the pulsing instrument won in an interdepartmental raffle three years ago and read on its flashing face: '7 visits room 2018 – Wong J.'

13

An inexpertly but enthusiastically kicked football sliced across the outer field and, after several squelchy hops, slid to a stop at Wai Pang's feet.

Before Eric Manley's dismissal became public knowledge, the unremarkable pupil from the late-afternoon English grammar tutorial had accepted advice and added his name to the Tuesday and Thursday evening football roster displayed outside the Principal's fourth-floor office.

Aware parental opinion condemned sport to a place beyond the farthest periphery, Wai Pang's planned explanation for his delayed homecoming, should his mother ask when she reappeared, was the necessary consequence of weak performance in mathematics and science and the inevitability of yet more remedial sessions, which, coincidentally, were scheduled on training days and at the very moment players assembled for departure to Hong Kong University's borrowed pitch.

With the school getting by without its usual, although, as far as Dr So was concerned, patently inadequate coach, the Principal, on top of his already gruelling burden of academic and administrative responsibility, took into his charge the football team's supervision. For a man with sporting views closer to Carol Tung's than Eric Manley's, this self-imposed addition was seen by many as unnecessarily perverse and by a few as completely self-defeating.

In reality, however, and, although superficially out of character, the new task simply furthered the pedantic pedagogue's uncompromising precept that scholastic endeavour must count above all things. Selection for representative matches would henceforth, he decided without any form of discussion, go to those achieving impressive classroom and homework marks. The neat trick of turning vice into virtue suited the diminutive Principal's sense of morality and, while his manner gave away nothing of his satisfaction, somewhere deep inside he managed a wintry chuckle of righteousness.

Wai Pang's poor educational record initially disqualified him from even the halfway house of participation in practice sessions, until his fluency with computerised Excel spreadsheets came to the ambitious Principal's attention and opened a path, first to a supporting role as the team's statistician and then, on the occasion of the first knockout game in the prestigious Fung Kei Soya Sauce inter-schools football Challenge Cup, as unplanned replacement for the centre forward and top-ranking physics student whose twisted ankle forced a potentially calamitous retirement ten minutes from full time.

With the game's one–nil score tilting inexorably towards the East Island International Academy and Tai Po Chinese English School's survival hanging by a frail thread, the statistician was belatedly thrust onto the field to plug the unscripted vacancy in a pair of boots hastily borrowed from an absentee's changing-room locker.

After the new coach's first two preparatory games in charge, which had been lost by near-record margins, he had plenty to contemplate, not least in the disappointment that few others shared his long-term vision of building a squad based on scholastic merit. One particularly scornful parent, who failed to understand what was required to get on, had the insensitivity to refer to the second trouncing as a rout, as if pig-tailed militia-men carrying opium pipes and umbrellas had been chased into the South China Sea by invading barbarians. How could anyone be so myopic to have missed the team's one-hundred-per-cent composition, until today that is, of Tai Po's top-performing pupils?

'If today's game has not shown marked progress,' Dr So remarked to his statistician, 'I don't know what will. And I'm sure your continuing analysis will support my assertion.'

But the yawning gulf between swots, who were good at algebra, but not at breaking out of their own half, and roughnecks concentrating on goal-saving tackles that hadn't a hint of beauty or structure about them, was lost in the later study of unsecured possession, incomplete passes, lost tackles, missed shots and metres retreated.

Tai Po's scrambling defence, urged to unwilling gestures of engagement by a sparse crowd of unconvinced parents and disbelieving junior boys, sloshed and slid into place behind Wai Pang's back. Knowing the expanse of territory to be defended and looking in turn at the heavy ball and the mud-and-sweat-spattered player galloping mercilessly towards an untried reserve in freshly laundered strip, the team collectively gulped.

'Wassa matta? You just goin' to stand there like some kind of wuss, or summat?' the overweight East Island wing bellowed as he bore down on the new arrival in a shower of coarse language and turf particles.

Toeing the ball forward, Wai Pang realised that most of the opposing team's players were also clustered in Tai Po's half of the pitch waiting for the easy glory of thrashing a dispirited opposition and that nothing, apart from the charging loud-mouth, stood between him and the distant goalkeeper. He avoided the incoming express train in a gently described arc and jogged forward into the vast acres of empty space.

'After the game arsehole, you watch out,' a threatening voice called out from somewhere behind him.

The East Island goalkeeper, who had been untroubled throughout the afternoon, looked around for help. But, as none was within supportive reach, he withdrew apprehensively to a trampled white line where he had paced for the best part of eighty minutes and where decisive action against this first serious incursion from Tai Po's end of the field could no longer be delayed. The keeper's fearful backtracking and waved extremities opened up even more ground to the spotlessly dressed and suddenly quite upright Wai Pang than had already been evident and the deft shot between his two widely separated legs carried unmolested into the net. To ward off later accusations of stupidity or funk the beaten defender hurled vigorously into the rain-churned sod in a late and largely symbolic act of heroism.

The first goal of Tai Po Chinese English School's Cup challenge caught Dr So and his team so much off their guard that within seconds of the restart they were incapable of preventing justice being executed by the stout East Island wing who hustled over several prostrate figures before banging in his second and, this time, winning goal. With arms outstretched he planed in a weaving run back towards a mobbed and mud-caked celebration. Fists punched the air and cries of joy whooped around the hero and Wai Pang hoped someone would remember to tick the 'tackles lost' box three times.

What sort of new openings had Mr Manley been thinking about when he suggested participation in football? Surely he hadn't just been talking about scoring goals, although stabbing in that one had felt better than almost any previous school experience, even if the team's first knockout match had ended only minutes later in peremptory elimination from the calendar's most important competition. There must be more to it than that! What he needed was an experience to shake off the unrewarding predictability of each day, in which he could gasp with exhilaration and fly like a seabird caught on the winds of a gale.

'What does your data examination reveal, Cheung?' Dr So enquired.

'Too early to say, Sir, but two statistics we should add are fitness and weight. The East Island boys train daily and they are all at least twenty pounds heavier and ...'

'Nonsense, boy; sixteen-year-olds don't need exercise, when

sitting still is already completely beyond them. We are not developing professional athletes here; we are rewarding academic application. You'll be telling me soon we should monitor diet. Ha ... ridiculous thought. My job is to achieve good grades and get students ready for the best universities. Whatever serves that aim is worth while and your task in this endeavour is to give me the numbers to support my objective. Do you understand?'

'Yes, Sir, but losing every game doesn't build confidence.'

Dr So bit his lip. The trouble with Cheung was he lacked obedience and thought in an unregulated fashion when he was supposed to be doing as he was told. He'd never make a responsible member of society that way. Dr So wondered why his mother hadn't got to grips with such obstinacy long ago.

'Advancement is plain for all who wish to see it; there is a world of difference between losing two–one and being thrashed seven–nil.' The Principal winced at his own unfortunate choice of expression.

'Yes, of course, Sir. Shall I send the information as an email attachment?'

'Hmm ... what? No, don't do that. Print, boy, print the spreadsheet! Never lose sight of the value of the printed page. Even in these indiscriminating times.'

At the end of most matches Tai Po boys usually wrapped their boots in plastic bags and slid quietly towards buses and underground trains, while still reeking of the game's rigours and humiliations until bathing in the quiet of their family homes. Only the rowdy extroverts from visiting international schools showered in full view and took pleasure from exhibitionist masculine flaunting.

Without stopping to think why, or having an obviously good reason, as he hadn't played long enough to feel more than warm, or get mud-flecked by the game's hurly-burly, Wai Pang took off his clothes. Not just his unmarked upper shirt, but everything and dropped it piecemeal in a casual circle of abandonment, right down to the last ugly green sock that rounded off the school's pseudo-Premiership League strip.

At first he expected to feel shy and ready to take a rushed shower, but he was astonished to feel instead an immense wave of liberation carrying him to where time and possibility were endless.

Other members of Tai Po's squad were too busy concentrating on their personal rituals and a speedy return to inflexible and syrup-sweet homes to notice the replacement centre-forward's changed mood; drying, fumbling in bags for bus passes, carefully lacing school shoes, or informing Dr So of their departure with respectfully averted eyes, they shut out not just the East Island boys at the opposite end of the changing room, where soap, towels and bags flew about in a havoc of catcalls and laughter, but also the players on their own team.

Alone among the twenty-odd teenagers Wai Pang had not become irreversibly conditioned to either studied correctitude or compulsive riot. For perhaps the first time he had a dawning awareness of who he could be and was starting to understand its dissimilarity with any of the labels he had been told to expect. He raised his chin and stood up to his full five feet four inches, just as he had done when he flicked the football between the goalkeeper's legs, and, without modesty or show, walked the length of the dressing room to the open showers and soaped his entire body and short, stiff hair.

The leisurely strokes over his firm shoulders, chest and thighs and the warm water splashing over his upturned face gave him a sensation of uniqueness – he was no longer part of a community, but travelling alone on a road waiting to be defined. Streams ran between the folds of his skin and touched the gateways to his inner being as if fingers searched for a sensation no parent or schoolteacher could explain.

Eventually and more than a little reluctantly he turned the taps off and stood for a while to drip and allow the steam to twist and coil around him, like mist circling from the floor of a primeval, rainforest.

Most of the players had left by the time he stepped back into the changing area. All the Tai Po boys had gone quickly and just a few East Islanders, under the rough supervision of an assistant coach, remained picking up possessions scattered by end-of-match jousting.

During the game trainers, supporters, the few Tai Po parents and many more from East Island had drawn up on opposite sides of the pitch. From where he sat recording data for Dr So and before replacing the distressed physics scholar, Wai Pang had not recognised any in the sparse crowd, except for several vaguely familiar junior boys and mothers, who at lessons' end habitually waited by the gates for their sons. But, now that the game had ended and because the two teams were gathered into the same room, if not in one group, he realised he was familiar with the East Island assistant coach's exaggerated stoop and bad complexion. Since their meeting on Kowloon's waterfront, the coach's hollow cheeks had become hideously marked by welts, so regular in pattern they could have been placed there by primitive rites of initiation.

'Git yur rear end into gear an' go 'ome, will you? I've 'ad just about enough of you lot today,' the assistant barked.

'Aw, come on, coach, we're celebrating a famous victory here. Where's your appreciation?' retorted the team's heavy, free-scoring wing.

''Ow is it you can move after a ball, but when you're in 'ere you turn into bleedin' snails, eh?'

'We're going, we're going. Hey! Look at him; how come a five-second substitute needs a shower? Must've got hot counting all those goals I kept whacking in; ahaa … ha!'

The attempt at ridicule had not the least affect on Wai Pang's changed frame of mind and he looked straight back at the querulous group with hands on his naked hips as if he had descended from the clouds to puzzle over lower life forms.

Isidor Nash squinted towards the new distraction and, while letting a ponderous memory chug towards its destination, ran an appreciative eye up and down the entire length of Wai Pang's unclothed body.

'Go on; git out,' he growled from the side of his mouth at the slothful remnants of East Island's football team.

Rancid strip was scooped up and shovelled into gaping sports bags and the last players clattered towards waiting rides.

'See ya,' a voice called back.

'Yeah, right, Thursday; an' don't forget,' Isidor replied.

But, with none save Cheung Wai Pang left to hear, attendance at the next scheduled practice went unconfirmed.

The headlights of a car snaking round the far side of the pitch flashed through the open doorway and puddles dotting the changing room's length cast up temporary golden flashes. For a few seconds Wai Pang's damp torso and youthful limbs were lit by reflected beams before returning to the hues of a darkening dressing room and incoming breaths of early evening.

This was the moment when day tipped into night, when the still woodland on the hill slopes above stopped drawing in birdsong and the sun's warmth and began exhaling the odours of fungus and decay; when creatures of the light fluttered to safety in upper branches and night-borne things stirred among tree roots and subterranean burrows.

'Well, and where might you be heading on an evening as fine as this one, young man?'

'Hm? Oh, home, I suppose,' answered Wai Pang, holding a cotton shirt by its neck as though unsure whether to put it on or not.

'Uh-huh. Round here then, is it?'

'Home? No, no; I live over by Shatin.'

'Oh, Shatin? That's an interesting place ... Know a girl from around there I do ... Spunky sort of bird she was and no mistake,' he added, touching at his disfigured cheeks.

'Can I ask something?'

Isidor leaned forward and the scarred tram lines on his white face flushed darkly.

'Me? Oh, yeah … anything you like … go ahead … I'm open to anything.'

'Can I draw you?'

'Uh? … Can you what? Are you … I mean, weren't you askin' some weird questions before, when I was out with that there Patel … you know … over in Kowloon?'

'Yes, yes I was … I remember. But you have a really interesting face, especially now that it's … it's … and I like to draw, so … would you mind?'

'You're an odd bloke to be sure. So … er … OK, where do you want to go an' do it … I mean … your drawing?'

'Where? No need to go anywhere … I can do it right here. Look, I've got pencils.'

Wai Pang dipped both hands into his school case. He had not been given one of the new sports bags, provided at no cost to the Tai Po Chinese English School by a local athletics equipment manufacturer, whose name and logo, 'High Jump Apparel' and 'Leap Higher Together', proudly adorned both sides of what became another of Dr So's incentives for impressive classroom scores and starting team selection. Statisticians and reserves, the Principal's unsympathetic decree ran, would by definition fall outside carefully modulated munificence.

'Uh! … I see. Well, in that case … have you got a preferred position?'

'No, just stay where you are … you have to look as if you were caught unaware; seen as you are …'

'Uhuh, gottcha.'

The cotton shirt was thrown carelessly across the assistant coach's end of the bench and Wai Pang spread his feet wide to support a sketch pad lying in the crook of his left arm. In total absorption and driven by instincts beyond his power to explain, he lavished bold strokes across the virginally white paper.

'Fancy a burger … after, I mean … if, that is, you've got nothing else to do?'

'Mmm …' Wai Pang was too immersed to hear or respond.

'I said … never mind … later'll do.'

Only the top of the young artist's head and his trim below-the-waist body was visible from the seated coach's position, and what had previously received a cursory but approving glance was studied in prolonged and fascinated detail – the firm calves, thighs and abdomen that flexed involuntarily while Wai Pang swayed in concentration and the pleasure of drawing, and the glossy, brown skin, as smooth and shiny as honey, except for traces of hair marking ankles and in the dark bush beneath his glistening belly.

Youthful good health and innocence so close they could be touched prompted Isidor to fidget in his habitually cramped coil.

'Don't move … I'm nearly done.'

'Er? Oh, don't mind me. Just easin' about on my particulars here.'

'There … there … I think I've got it.'

'No rush now. I don't mind you takin' as long as you like, while I just … ah … do a bit of thinkin' an 'at.'

'Here … want to see?'

The minimalist sketch was offered for inspection and, although Isidor recognised at once the straight nose and fierce scars, there was something unexpectedly disturbing in the creased eyes and thin lips. Although fully clothed he felt exposed and, in a shocking way, more naked than the engrossed schoolboy in front of him.

'Yeah … yeah … you've got a bit of a touch there, sonny, if you don't mind me sayin' so … but … come on … let's get a better look.'

'It's only rough and more time would help … but … maybe … I don't know … if someone could tell me …'

'Tell you, tell you what? If it's any good? I'm a teacher, en' I? I should be in a position to know about this sort of stuff. Now come and sit over ’ere next to me, so I can point out a few things.’

The sporting tangle of bandages, plasters and surgical tape on the bench next to the assistant coach was pushed onto the floor with a sweep of a forearm.

‘Hold it up a bit … yeah, impressive … really quite fair …’

As they examined the drawing together their legs touched; at first with the merest brush, but then quite firmly until Isidor believed he could feel the boy’s warmth through his tracksuit. Counterfeiting serious contemplation, he put his free hand down on the knee beside him and waited. Getting no reaction he stroked along the smooth, brown surface; once, twice, three times, with each pass climbing a little higher until stopping at a bend just below the boy’s flat, guileless belly.

Was this going to be a hit? Isidor wondered, or just another of those frustrating experiences like the one in Shatin and so many others besides, where gratification was centimetres from his grasp and dashed at the very last moment when his rising pulse and hot breath could no longer hold back?

Every sinew in Isidor’s crooked length tightened as he prepared for what seemed the inevitability of a shocked rebuff. But no rejection came and, while his gaze held the boy’s sketch, unexpected fingers closed over his protruding knuckles and squeezed them kindly.

‘Like I was sayin’,’ he continued hoarsely, ‘do ya fancy that hamburger? We could do takeaway, if you like, an’ go back to my place. No one at ’ome this time of day; my mate’s on ’is part-time after abart six. Then, when we’re done with eatin’ an’ all, I can run you over to Shatin on my motorbike. If you don’t mind holdin’ on round my waist … that is?’

14

The restaurants frequented by Eric Manley served food incidentally and without compromising their primary purpose of delivering large quantities of alcohol to boisterous gangs of young men and their irregular female attachments. Fare found at venues such as The Sporting Bear, comprising flaccid chicken wings, fat, brown chips, suet puddings and the like, which were forked up by disposable plastic utensils, was known to subdue even the heartiest appetites.

Le Foie du Canard, with its futuristic steel and glass decor and recently enfranchised clientele, for whom staggering cost and discerning taste were indistinguishably merged, offered another class of meal altogether and only his son's present predicament was capable of forcing Eric to consume what was on offer.

A chance meeting in the Shau Kei Wan fish market during Mrs Chou's rushed lunch break provided the tip-off, just as Eric was circling the Odergaard warehouse for the third time in search of an improbable fifty thousand United States dollars.

'Well, hello,' he said, 'haven't I seen you before? Your Jakob's assistant, right?'

The nature of Mrs Chou's job allowed her to know Eric a lot better than he knew her.

'Yes, yes,' she said, happy for her backroom status to be recognised by a member of Mr Odergaard's immediate family. 'And you're Mr Eric, aren't you?'

'Yeah, correct and on my way to see your boss if he's in.'

'Oh! I don't think you will find him there today. His diary is very full and he's been engaged in meetings since this morning.

But I can make an appointment, or let him know we met if you wish?'

'No ... thth ... don't worry, it's only a small family matter and can wait,' Eric lied.

Facilitating personal arrangements was, however, what people like Mrs Chou did.

'Allow me to pass him a message. I'm sure he'll ...'

Eric was suddenly alarmed.

'No, no, don't do that either. Tell you what, though,' he continued, 'if you know where he would be over the next few evenings I can catch up with him when he's not quite so busy.'

'I'll check Mr Odergaard's schedule when I get back and give you a call if there is anything helpful.'

True to Mrs Chou's word and with a thoroughness she was proud to demonstrate, even while rattling her nearly sacred and preeminent duty of confidentiality, a call came later to say the Chairman would be dining alone that night at Le Foie du Canard.

'And that,' Eric thought, 'is exactly the sort of location Sigrid recommended for an encounter and the first bit of luck I've had in this whole sorry caper.'

Needless to say, what lay behind Le Foie's bronze doors, where the companionable delights of shepherd's pie and tomato ketchup were unknown, was as forbidding as the waters beyond Cape Horn to early sea-farers.

But, fortified by several glasses of flat bitter beer, he felt the test of his father-in-law's interest in financing a Lam Qi Fat film could be put off no longer.

His instinct, and, it had to be said, uncertain nerves, still leant towards a less 'in-your-face' phone call from the safe distance of rural Sai Kung, but, in the wake of Sigrid's emphatic reasoning, he conceded that purse strings protecting the old man's small change might be most effectively loosened in the unsuspecting ease of a CEO's after-hours.

And, because Sigrid had a way of sounding infallible, he

agreed, while knowing in his heart JBO had been disagreeable from birth and that to convince a man who castigated all humanity but one was a feat of salesmanship outside his usual compass.

But, to be charitable, there was an argument to be made for blaming his father-in-law's abominable attitude on the corrupting influences of wealth and power, although, in Eric's opinion, the causes went further back still to the formation of defective genes in a perturbed mother's acid womb and in the nurturing they received at her poisoned breast.

'Glad I never came into contact with Mrs Odergaard Senior.'

Diners entering Le Foie were dressed expensively and in costumes obtained from either a continental European catwalk or a science museum's boot sale. Eric, who was nobody's authority, could not decide which, but certainly lads at the pub would fall about holding their sides if one of these couples dropped in unexpectedly to watch a late-night football game.

'So what's going to be the reaction when I amble into this poseurs' den with my home-trimmed locks and Sai Kung cords?' he speculated.

'Do you have a reservation, Sir?' the lady in full-length evening attire asked from behind a wooden structure that looked startlingly like a church pulpit.

'Er ... yes, actually ... I do.'

'And the name would be?'

'I'm meeting someone who's already here, so ... no need to announce me I'll just wander in and find him, if that's fine with you ...?'

Eric craned his neck over the attendant's padded shoulders towards a cavernous and glitzy interior.

'Then his name ...?' she enquired without moving a millimetre.

'Er ... Odergaard ... that is Jakob B. Odergaard, to be exact.'

'Mr Odergaard, oh, I see and may I say who will be joining him?'

'His son.'

'Mr Odergaard has a son?' the astonished lady asked.

'Well, son-in-law actually, but in this part of the world it's more or less the same thing. We share a lot ... if you know what I mean?'

The begowned guest receiver had absolutely no idea what was meant, but, with forced meekness and disbelief held in check, she gathered up a menu and wine list and prepared to show the way.

'In that case, Sir ... please follow me.'

'Look, I know you have procedures and all, but this is a special occasion, yeah, and I've come to surprise the old bugger ... so just give me that.'

He removed the heavy cards from her startled grasp.

'If you don't mind, I'll find him.'

Unconvinced of any connection, let alone family bond, between the Chairman of a public company and this untidy ruffian, she allowed the discretion of an imperial palace servant to overcome natural inclinations to play detective and, with an expression giving away nothing of her opinion, stepped to one side. Later, she decided, would be time enough to reflect on the conflicting responsibilities of upholding proper practice and providing satisfaction to an elite clientele.

'As you wish,' she said, gesturing towards the spacious but thinly populated dining hall.

In the short while since opening Le Foie du Canard had been adopted by patrons prizing exclusivity and a fashionable reputation. This was indeed today's place to be seen. Glass table tops and shimmering arrays of cutlery and glassware under glaring white lights appealed to people not really there to eat, but comfortable with the dainty morsels of an Asian version of nouveau cuisine and an odd menu best legitimised by exorbitant pricing.

For Jakob Odergaard the restaurant was one of half a dozen places where hardly anyone of his acquaintance came to eat and where he was able to think and scheme in solitude about the business, the women in his life and how to get the most pleasure out of the vast quantities of money he had accumulated during his years in Hong Kong.

Tonight, while he poked at a sorbet with a long silver spoon, he thought of Dagmar and of how he and she had argued and yelled and come to blows and how years ago that rage had turned into the most tempestuous lovemaking he had ever encountered. The 'highs' reached were shots of cocaine that became an addiction and took him off in search of other women with whom he wanted to repeat the experience on an even grander and more promiscuous scale. But, though he had hunted everywhere, he had never discovered anyone with whom to share the tumultuous thunder created with Dagmar, or the explosive days and nights when he wrestled her to the ground and she tore and spat and he dragged her cursing from one room to another, until, at the end, they laid together, exhausted, entangled and bloodied.

There had, of course, been more women than he could remember, but loyalty to Dagmar as his ultimate goddess remained absolute. Only a relationship of such devoted singularity could forgive his rampant licence.

'Hello, Jakob old chap. What a coincidence finding you here.'

'Huh? Manley? Bloody hell!'

'You know I was just about to eat on my own when I saw you over here and thought well now there's a surprise, so why don't I join you and find out if you've recovered from that awful accident at our place? I can't tell you how sorry I was that we couldn't get you to the hospital. No one wants to end a party quite so badly.'

The restaurant staff, knowing Jakob's habit of dining alone, had prepared only one place. But the intrusive son-in-law, not wishing to be put off by minor organisational inconveniences, dragged over an unoccupied chair from a nearby table and sat down.

'I prefer to choose my own company. Wasn't that plain enough last time?'

'Heh! Come on, we don't hang out much; let's forget what happened.'

'You probably got in here by mistake; this place is a sort of club, where members come to avoid hanging out with the beer and baked beans crowd.'

'My, you're sounding in bad form; your finger must still hurt like hell. Look, I apologise for Vernon, he was completely out of order. We had a serious talk afterwards and he knows he was being an ass and wants the incident put behind him.'

'He might not want to think about it, but you can tell him I don't forget so easily.'

For an instant and considering the purpose of the call, Eric wondered whether he should just get up and write off the plan as daft and impractical daydreaming.

'Yeah, well, so I guess we'll just have to begin again and, in the meantime, why don't I get something to eat? See, I anticipated being self-managed and brought along the right kit.'

Eric ran an eye down the main courses; something to satisfy an ordinary man's appetite seemed to be out of realistic reach.

'They don't do scampi and mushy peas.'

'I thought you would have said paella was closer to my taste.'

'Oh, yeah, the former Spaniard; I forgot.'

'How can they justify charging fifteen hundred dollars for a piece of chicken?' Eric asked in amazement.

'I guess you'd rate that as quite a lot if it's from a kebab skewer takeaway.'

Nursing the conversation round from such a thorny start to where it would lead seamlessly and unnoticed into Odergaard's support for a local film venture was so improbable as to be hilarious and, despite Eric's sober intent, he could not restrain a chortle.

'So what's funny?' Jakob demanded.

'You'd think a place as expensive and affected as this could afford to have its menu copyedited by a professional.'

'Meaning?'

'What is anyone supposed to make of a dish called "black pepper cowboy loin"? Doesn't bear thinking about, does it?'

With the one exception of his angry and violent wife Jakob Odergaard shared no pleasurable feelings with any member of the human race, least of all humour.

He glowered stonily, while his son-in-law shook noiselessly and, in a show of cheerfulness, flapped the menu onto the table with a bump. If the broken finger had rested anywhere else, Eric's careless gesture would have passed harmlessly, but lying on the hard glass surface, with the stiff necessity of a butter knife, it took the bill of fare's full weight.

'Thssss!' JBO exploded. 'What the fuck! Are you trying to finish off what your idiot son started? I've a good mind to ...'

'Oh Christ! Sorry. ... Let me get you some ice or something.'

Aware, even before a hand was raised, of the unregulated exchange passing between his esteemed customer and this newcomer, the head waiter had been compelled to hurry forward.

'Something not satisfactory,' he said, addressing Jakob Odergaard with a trained memory poised to record any imperfections in Le Foie's extravagant service.

'Ask him – he's the lunatic crashing about and having trouble with what he wants to eat.'

The waiter lowered his hands to a less obsequious level.

'Sir is ... ready to order?'

'No, look, not yet; we need some ice and ...'

'Don't even try to help, just get on with it before you're asked to leave,' Jakob snarled.

Again, the waiter turned to Eric.

'Are you sure you are going to be ...? Yeah, well, don't want to miss out on all this unusual chop. What's good, anything you'd recommend?'

The mask of oriental inscrutability wavered.

'All good ... but depends on individual preference. Would Sir like appetizer? House speciality is foie ...'

'No, no, skip all that malarkey; let's go straight to the mains. Got a decent steak?'

'A dec –?'

In this establishment such questions were not asked. With a slight lift of his shoulders, which offered a thousand interpretations, the attentive maître d' lent forward and returned his diner to a previous menu page before continuing.

'We have sirloin; we have filet mignon, an unusual cut in Hong Kong; we have the black pepper cow ...'

'The cowboy's loin? Oh, so that's what it is.'

'It's the finest; prepared in our unique style. You like? Would Sir prefer well done, medium or undone?'

'Look, I'll read between the lines here a little and go for the undone and a lager.'

Thankful to have brought the order to a satisfactory conclusion the waiter sped away to consult his chef, who hailed from the remotest interior of Saône-et-Loire and to search for the requested drink, which he was sure would be available somewhere, although he could not remember having served one since Le Foie du Canard's opening several months ago.

While Eric wondered how to get to the fraught subject which brought him on this 'surprise' meeting, his cantankerous father-in-law unexpectedly provided an opening.

'If you're going to sit there in front of me upsetting my digestion, at least have the manners to say something of interest.'

'Oh, right. Yeah, well, er ... how's the Arts Festival going? Sigrid tells me you guys are sponsoring something again.'

'Don't ask me; that's Claude Halt's business. I don't get involved.'

'Halt? Who's he?

'My accountant, but he likes mixing with artistes, as he calls them and their hangers-on, although I don't suppose he knows a thing they're talking about half the time. You ought to meet him and give him the benefit of your education. You could start by explaining what the fuck the play is about that I'm paying for, because I doubt if he has any idea.'

'Oh, aih, and what's that?'

'Something so memorable it went straight out of my head the second he told me. Here, hold on, it's ...'

Jakob dug in his jacket and took out a mobile device. After a few aggressive prods, which were quite out of character with the finely manicured thumbnail making them, if not the owner of the thumb, he read out:

'*Moon for the Misbegotten*; for crying out loud. Mean anything to you?'

'Er ... yeah, yeah ... it's an O'Neill, I think.'

'Who? A bloody Irishman?'

'Irish descent, I suppose, but an American. All about alcoholism and fist-fights if I remember right.'

'That's what I mean by Irish. Who in Hong Kong will turn out to watch a thing like that? Only OK'ed it because it's a small cast and Halt's been yapping round me like a Pekinese for months.'

'You really like sponsoring art?'

'You are of course joking. It's done for bigger benefits. The first was for Dagmar. This time ... we'll have to see. But don't expect it to happen again.'

'How about turning your attention to something local? That'll raise your profile with the people who buy your furniture.'

'Since when did you know anything about my business?'

Eric decided that, if he was ever to make the suggestion that brought him to Le Foie this was the moment.

'I may be just a part-time teacher, but I ain't stupid,' he said carefully. 'But look, I er ... know some people in the local film industry who'd be interested in a big commercial name cooperating with their production house.'

'Cooperating, cooperating? Are you another one speaking idiotic local jargon?

'Oh ... I mean ... financing.'

Fearing the word was too stark and likely to scare Jakob, Eric searched in his head for the outlines of a plan to soften the blow and fell instead on the sword of his father-in-law's scathing interjection.

'And who in the local film industry do you have these friendly ties with?'

'I ... er ... well ... there's this guy ... Lam Qi Fat, who is a bit of a specialist in ...'

'How do you know Qi Fat? He doesn't move in your expaty, beach party circles over in Sai Kung.'

'No, true ... but that's not germane...'

'Germane? You're full of fancy words tonight. Look, I can tell you I wouldn't get into bed with Qi Fat at any price. Scratching his back occasionally after he's scratched mine is about as far as I'd want to go.'

'You know him? Oh, geez!'

'Look, stop fucking me about with dumb ideas. If you want to get on the right side of me – and I guess that's why you just happened to come in here looking for a meal you can't afford – then do this; I want someone to keep an eye on this entry of Halt's at the Arts Festival; and, seeing we are related in some sort of way, make sure I'm not getting short-changed and in particular ... that he's taking care of the leading lady in a way that will keep her off my hands.'

Jakob stood up to go just as the smallest steak ever to come under the hungry gaze of a man used to old-style cuisine arrived on the centre of a plate capable of accommodating twenty similar meals without a hint of overcrowding.

'Won't you wait while I finish this? It's hardly likely to take long.'

'Nothing to keep me here; I've got things on my mind.'

The waiter flustered forward at the sound of Jakob's metal chair scuffing over ceramic flooring.

'Leaving us so soon, Mr Odergaard? Will you not stay for coffee?'

'No.'

'In that case shall I put the charge to your account?'

'My son-in-law here,' he said, nodding at Eric, 'will pick up the bill; he owes me one.'

15

'Wa'll that Asia sure takes some beating,' Geoffrey Keso roundly informed his family when he sat down to breakfast the morning after Claude Halt's late-night phone call. 'But, setting aside local peculiarities, which'll always be beyond me, we seem to have the makings of a deal to take our players back to Hong Kong, China again in the spring; yes we do indeed.'

'Why, that's just wonderful, honey,' Mrs Keso called from the kitchen where she and her eldest daughter were preparing a stack of pancakes and bacon, which, by some assessments, could have filled the stomachs of every early riser in the next three counties.

'Just some minor details to iron out with your marm and the committee and then we'll be heading down the pike.'

'Do you mean we'll be on our own for a month again, just like last time?' asked Jake, the Keso's prematurely portly boy, who in frame, if not mellow contentment, was a carbon copy of his father.

So accepting were his parents of values instilled by the Church and its brother and sisterhoods that they mistook the fifteen-year-old's animated enquiry as apprehension and not eagerness for the time to elaborate on his overtures to the winsome Naomi Smith, who he had coaxed into conversation at the last Provo Repertory's support group event.

'Not quite alone, son; ya'll remember your Aunt Rachel stopped by twice a day, and what with your school and community work you'll be surrounded by safe and willing hands.'

Was that the sound of adolescent plotting escaping Jake's lips, or had he just enthusiastically greeted the pile of butter-and-syrup-soaked pancakes set down in the table's centre? Teenage communications were not the easiest to decipher, even by doting parents who claimed to know their offspring better than anyone.

Mrs Keso and Jake's twin sister hung their aprons on a rack beside a refrigerator the size of a Hong Kong family apartment and settled into the two vacant places at the table.

'May the Good Shepherd, who has returned me safely to mah family's bosom, bless our house and this table and accept His servants' humble thanks for such a truly bounteous feast ...'

Assuming grace was at an end, Jake took up his fork. But his father still had thoughts he needed to share.

'... and as we repledge our service to His great enterprise and while Satan in all his manifestations, for he is a very clever devil, strives to corrupt our minds and deeds and the minds and deeds of our children, we pray that He will light our way and keep us free from temptation and sin, yea, all sin; ahmen.'

Unburdened, Geoffrey sat back in his chair to let his thoughts return to Hong Kong, the people he had met, the incidents occurring in the course of his visit and the arrangement struck with Claude Halt to return the Provo Rep to Asia.

In the Keso household his many duties included handing out first helpings at mealtimes, but today he was inattentive and breathed more deeply than his morning activities of shaving and showering warranted.

His clan watched and waited for their plates to be loaded and permission granted to begin. Why, they wondered, was there this unusual break in family custom?

'Is anything the matter, Geoffrey?' Mrs Keso enquired over the cooling pancakes and bacon and through the steaming threads dissipating in the warm air.

'Hum? No, why, no. Begin, begin ... the Good Lord's food awaits you,' he said and waved a chubby hand over the lingering breakfast, before downing a large orange juice in one draft as if the flames of hell lapped around his vast belly.

'And will you ...?' the patient wife and mother enquired.

'Why, I do forget myself ... just too many things to digest right now. Here ...,' he said, and began doling out thick, puddingy slabs of pancake and slithers of crisp streaky bacon onto every waiting plate.

The five Keso children re-established routine at their sides of the table by chattering noisily through very full mouths. After a second and a third helping they stood up, cleaned their dishes at the sink and returned them to an overhead cupboard. With each child taking responsibility for the next youngest in line they filed in order of age through the bungalow's rear door and yard towards a promptly arriving yellow school bus.

Now that they were alone, Geoffrey decided to seek Mrs Keso's view of Odergaard's sponsorship offer before she submerged herself in the thousand and one household chores necessary for the maintenance of an already immaculate home.

Geoffrey's wife was a simple but mostly sensible woman, charged with the production and nurturing of children and in supporting her husband in the ways he required. She had little understanding of the world beyond Provo and next to none of what it was outside Utah. Her husband's ventures to Asia seeking to 'internationalise' the local theatrical association filled her with dread, and only after he had explained the spread of values as an evangelical duty, akin to preaching God's Word, had she come to terms with what looked like excessive and unnecessary risk. When he had reminded her that Mormon settlers came to the wilderness to build a city in praise of the Lord she had been appeased, because, she understood that he, like them, carried truth and beauty to those who knew none.

Along the way and as can happen in any marriage, there had been brief moments of doubt, especially a year ago when she had joined him at rehearsals for *Peer Gynt*.

'I don't see why you have chosen this play,' she piped. 'Some of the music is very pretty, I'll grant you that, but what have all those witches in caves got to do in the Almighty's parish?'

'Wa'll, it's a bit complicated,' Geoffrey had said, 'but it's what's known as allegorical, ya'll will understand. The hero's on a journey of ... ah ... self-discovery, yah, self-discovery after being a total loser. Not a guy expected to hit a homer, if you know what I mean? How's he gonna know how to change and where to begin without knowing what a two-timer he's been? Ya have to see yourself in the mirror before you start.'

'But it looks to me like he went to the hereafter unrepentant,' Mrs Keso quibbled.

'Thch,' he scolded mildly, 'there's hidden meaning there; you hafta see what the writer intends.'

'I'm sure you know best, Geoffrey,' she had said at last, as his explanation lost momentum.

He hadn't the courage to say the choice of programme had been thrust upon him by a sponsor whose wife was a lot less likely to be bought off with platitudes than his.

'But this time,' Geoffrey continued, 'I don't have to leave the matter to others in quite the same way and have a much bigger voice in deciding what we take out east.'

To Mrs Keso 'out east' was the east coast, New York and Baltimore, where towers of Babel swayed in the din of licence and havoc and from where her great-grandparents had fled in search of the new Holy Land.

'Isn't China in the west?' she asked in genuine confusion.

'Yah, sure; why?

'But I thought you said ...'

'This is not about geography, Marm; it's about carrying the Word. And as Ah say, on that Ah have total, Ah mean total control. Something 'erican Ah have been thinking; you know, Marm, like Tennessee Williams, or one of those other good old boys.'

'Was he God-fearing, too, Geoffrey?'

'Huh? Well, you have to look carefully at his message. But hold on, here's a thing Ah want to get your read on.'

He paused and studied his hands, first the backs with their flat, round nails and huge ring bestowed by Brigham Young University on his graduation, then the palms with their strange vertical creasing.

'We'll have to take a leading lady from outside,' he said as though wanting to get the subject out of the way as quickly as possible. 'Some of our women are not gonna like such an idea. But you have to take the rough with the smooth if you want to get on in this game, at least that's how Ah happen to see it.'

'Is she one of us, I mean does she belong to our Church?'

'What? I never thought to ask. But ... if you saw her you'd think so ... as blonde and blue-eyed as anyone ya'll will meet round here,' he giggled stupidly.

'What's her name?'

'Name? Well, it's ... er ... Plumpkin, Mandy Plumpkin, a stage name maybe; Ah didn't rightly hear.'

'Sounds more fashion model than Christian to me, Geoffrey. But if she will help spread the Word you should embrace her and take her into our company.'

'Don't know if that would be my approach exactly. But ... yeah, Ah see your angle. Great ... yeah ... great idea, Marm.'

Despite a largely provincial history, stretching back no less than eight years, the Provo Repertory Theater Company had, in recent seasons, become markedly outward-looking and to satisfy its ambitions the rising generation had sent Geoffrey off a year and a half ago in search of audiences beyond the fields of their pastoral home, where, as good fortune would have it, his dormant yen for travel found a looser rein.

When he first returned with an opportunity to produce *Peer Gynt* it had seemed a stunning triumph and only when the unwieldiness and complexity of the play fully dawned on the company had its members felt hopelessly out of their league. But, while the adequate if uninspiring performance, cobbled together with frequent heartfelt prayers and the incidental withdrawal of several key players along the painful route, was accepted as the worst experience the group could endure, Geoffrey Keso's second coming was anticipated to provide a comparative cakewalk.

If *Peer Gynt* had held any benefits at the time of the troupe's great trial, other than frightening lessons in experimentation with internationalism, it had been the large cast of small parts, which enabled just about everyone with theatrical aspiration in Provo who had stayed the course to get on board for the overseas trip.

But this time the emotional slide around the committee table began as soon as Geoffrey Keso revealed the terms of his agreement. From euphoria that he had come back with a deal, they subsided quickly into disappointment, when they understood only five or six players and a limited programme would make the journey, until finally slithering to a full stop at the revelation that a nominated player from outside their closely knit society would take the production's plummiest part.

'So no real new experience for anyone outside a handful, is that it?' opined the bespectacled Treasurer, who last year, at the apogee of his theatrical career and under heavy disguise, had played a troll delivering many unauthorised grunts and whoops.

'Wa'll,' said Geoffrey, sucking at the clinging flavours of maple syrup and bacon lodged between his teeth, 'it's like this ... mmm ... see, companies like ours have to be open to guest performers. That's what makes them international ... not just being seen in another country ... Am Ah making myself clear?'

'Who is this "lead"? Will she rehearse here? How do we know she'll meld?' the Treasurer complained, sensing the diminishing probability of a second visit to the fabled Orient.

'We're going to have to work around her some ... she's a film star ... got a full calendar ... and used to being taken care of. But that's the price we have to pay for doing more foreign tours.'

'You saying we don't meet her till we get out there?' another grouchy voice asked.

Doug Plat had been the hero, some would say saviour, of last year's production, with a performance of Peer that achieved mentions in state-wide press reports and his point of view deserved respect.

'Ah won't say that exactly, but she's a busy woman and may want to read the part and get ready to fit in when we git out there to Hong Kong.'

Hope drained out of the glum faces.

When selfishness crowds out good thoughts it's time to appeal to dooty, Geoffrey decided.

'Now, tell me, what are we doing here, huh? We ain't just pleasing ourselves, are we? This outfit wasn't slapped together just so yous and Ah could have fun; it's here for a grander purpose, why, so it is. Anyone going to tell me what it is, or do you want the Almighty to help you out?'

'You mean why we do theatre work?' Doug Plat asked uncertainly.

'Yeah, right and why we send all those young guys on mission work to carry the Word to the poor benighted heathen who don't know better and why we build churches all round the globe? What's it all about, eh?'

'OK, OK, no need to harp on, we get the message; we're carryin' a God-fearing and civilised society to where it educates and brings light.'

'Right on. So, here we are, another chance to do good work, but ya'll are going on and asking what's in it for you when our little provincial, yes, provincial company gets an opportoonity to take a programme we can choose out there and show people what it is to come from this great country and city of ours. Yeah, Ah agree, not many will go, but it's what we give that counts, not what we take away. At this level we are dealing with linkage.'

'Linkage?' the shocked Treasurer remarked. 'That doesn't sound altogether as upright as we should like.'

'Huh? Oh, don't worry over that; it's just an expression Ah

picked up while travelling. We must not forget we are dealing with foreigners here. So we've got a week and by then we have to make some decisions, before Ah go back to those good people who'll be vetting our final proposal, with sumthin' that's gotta include the name of the piece and the part we're offering our guest female lead.' He paused to let his message sink in. 'Other than that I guess we're just about done here.'

The room emptied and Geoffrey Keso was left to ponder on the meeting's progress. 'Yes,' he thought, 'Mrs Keso would be proud of me and so, too, might Claude Halt; I'll let them both know when the time is right.'

Sixteen years of marriage and the production of five children should have given Mr Keso a better understanding of how his wife's mind worked, but proximity had obscured more than illuminated. If they had seen each other less often, maybe their meetings, across the table and in the open spaces of a ludicrously oversized bed, would have contained intimacy, instead of an efficacy like that of a kitchen utensil.

After their first year, when the dulling really set in, breakfast and dinner times became way stations on the road from, or into, sleep. The hurried lunches, snatched while he built his legal practice, where he specialised in family, personal injury and real estate law, were originally conceived as 'together-time' but had evolved into midday refuelling containing hardly a scrap of conversation. But, for all that, he loved his family as well as a good Christian should and, while its members may have lacked poetry's white-hot passion, they brought instead the trust felt in an old jacket's worn elbows and greasy collar and they served his purpose and sense of what a man's life should be about. His thrills, such as could be contained in a wholesome and blameless life, were found in God's work and temperate support of the Provo Repertory Theater Company's contribution to the community.

Being moderate in his own sentiments he took for granted Mrs Keso was no different and that she would loyally traipse through the years at his side and tend to his flock's needs. But, while he was correct that she would never think of going anywhere else, she was propelled, not by his sense of responsibility, but by a different sort of fatalism which saw no alternative. Her part of the marriage bargain was delivered as if pleasure and choice were not, and could never be, part of the process and as if 'buckling down' to whatever had to be got on with was an irreversible fact no proper wife would contest.

Her only experience of romance had occurred in the first few months before children started coming and was to her a young girl's guilty secret shared with no one, not even her god. Now, when that single human weakness had withered and died like an untended house plant, her vestigial pleasures rested on a certain smugness that knew unquestioningly the Good Lord, for reasons known only to him, had condemned vast swathes of humanity to perpetual darkness, and that it was among these poor people her husband and his like had a duty to sow a little relief.

When Mr Keso told her his recommendation to the Organising Committee had been accepted he expected her to smile and say 'Well done, Geoffrey' as if his grade-school exercise book had received a stick-on star and happy-face from a teacher paid to read the standard manuals on child psychology.

Her economical 'There, and just as it should be' fell a long way short of the sort of praise he savoured.

If Mrs Keso failed to water her husband's thirsty ego, Claude Halt's reaction to the chosen play doused it in a cold deluge.

'I don't know why I've spent so much time getting sponsorship for such a rag-tag outfit.' Hard work, whether cloaked in altruism, or left naked in bleak self-interest, was, in his estimation, still hard work. Couldn't these country amateurs appreciate how lucky they were?

'Say, that's kinda harsh. Mah view, although Ah recognise some bias here, is we've a track record speaking for itself. Sure *Gynt* was a stretch, but your critics gave us marks for effort.'

'Huh! As if they had a clue what you were performing. So I suppose another work unknown to Asia will save you a panning? Is that how you see it?'

'Well, heh, hang on a minute; you've corralled us into a tough position. Small cast, strong female lead, something not done before; what are we left with? '

'But, I ask you, *The Moon and Ninepence*? Will anyone, other than one of your compatriots ...?'

'*Misbegotten*, you should say.'

'What?

'The title; it's not "Ninepence", it's "Misbegotten"; *A Moon for the Misbegotten*."

'Is that supposed to make me feel better? OK, OK, give me something to get hold of here; Ms Plumpkin's part ... what is it? She's an actress of substance, you realise, and'll be looking for something meaty.'

'Yeah, sure, Ah can tell yous this is a role for a pro not a vehicle for a bimbo, forgive mah expression, wanting to show off her looks. If what you tell me about Mandy Plumpkin is right, she'll lap this one up.'

'U-huh, u-huh, so ... details, man ... not publicity material.'

As chief representative and spokesperson for the Provo players, Geoffrey had first met the Odergaard CFO a year and a half ago. Then, dealings with Claude Halt had been bearable, even if serious decisions were clearly taken over his head and he was no more than a go-between. But this time, the agent had become the principal, the banker, chief handler and gatekeeper and the Good Lord knew what else and had more questions and opinions than were healthy.

'Wha'll ... the play is set in Connecticut and ...'

'Skip all that ... Tell me about Ms Plumpkin's part.'

'She'll play a sharp-tongued Irishwoman who's been around the block more than once and ...'

'I doubt if a lady of Ms Plumpkin's breeding will want to play a harlot.'

'Why not? She's an actress, ain't she? Look, anyone can do a heroine, but only a true actress can pull off a serious role and, believe me, this one is as serious as they get.'

'But I want this production to enhance her ... her ... stature, yes, that's it ... She's got to come out of this on a new plane ... Brand recognition is what we want to establish.'

'Uh? Well, Ah don't know how much of that we can give her when some people think folks from Utah ain't so sophisticated.'

If Geoffrey Keso hoped sarcasm would help his cause, he was to be disappointed. After a moment's reflection Claude remarked.

'OK, here's the deal. As I represent Ms Plumpkin's interests along with the Festival's and Odergaard's I'll pitch this ... this part to her and see if she is prepared to go along with it.'

'Yeah, I see, but how about teleconferencing me in as Ah have a better understanding of the play and playwright's reputation and am better ...'

'No, that would not be a good idea; you just leave Ms Plumpkin and her career choices in my hands.'

16

Seven visits! How can that be? Hadn't she effectively put JBO behind her as soon as she turned to me for counsel and support and we became seriously acquainted?

Claude Halt was distraught. Since his very first meeting with Mandy Plumpkin and the beginning of his foolish schoolboy fantasy, every waking minute had rested on the falsehood of her unfortunate captivation by a wily old fox that had lain waiting in the dust at the hen-house gate. Belief in this warped vision allowed him to submerge the truth of her seedy shenanigans, witnessed weekly in the passage of hotel bills across his desk, and cling to the hope that he had become the sole focus of her affections.

Yes, she had been taken advantage of, he told himself – almost as if repetition of the lie would turn it into fact – by a lascivious cad, who caught her in a moment of desperation and vulnerability and when at her wit's end she grappled with trying to make a living on her own in a notoriously competitive and fickle profession. Yes, that was it. At heart she was a good and decent woman who hadn't realised hungry predators had their way of getting into the farmyard.

If Claude had been aware of the film director, with his underground tastes and the numerous temporary facilitators of Ms Plumpkin's thespian voyage, his ability to find convincing explanations for her widely dispensed favours would have been severely strained. But, being more easily influenced by affairs of the heart than many would have expected for a man used to the cold, hard realities of income and expense, he continued to relieve his doubts with tidy and insupportable reasoning.

Conviction in daylight hours, however, was not the same as certainty at midnight, when he had put away his briefcase and switched off the bedside lamp and let insidious suspicions flutter around his unsteady mind, like insects over a garden picnic, which, if not swotted away before the sun rose, would buzz, gorged and incorrigible, to sting and plague his waking hours.

'But seven visits was a distressingly large number,' he grumbled to himself as he pulled a purple-flowered duvet close to his unshaven chin, 'when I, with my special and growing relationship, have yet to accomplish one.'

He paused, fending off sleep and the uncertainties of his ambiguous status in the lady's life, until he hatched a contradictory solution.

'Stop! Why, I forget myself; does she not reside at the Harbour Hotel, an institution famous for the finicky way it looks after guests? The entire place must crawl with cleaners, maids and handymen, who make countless room-calls each day to make beds and replenish minibars. I wonder how I could have been so slow, so unthinking, when the number ought to be much higher and when I should be asking why service was apparently not all it's cracked up to be. I'll call the manager directly and, if he can't tell me light bulbs and shampoo bottles are inspected daily, he better have a good reason, why, so he must.'

'Get me the head person at the Harbour Hotel … instantly,' Claude snapped at the timid assistant as soon as he arrived in his office the following morning. Unsure to whom precisely her supervisor wished to speak, the assistant, who kept office affairs in the best order her modest skills permitted, opened her mouth preparatory to forming a question.

'And before you ask, no, I don't know his name; why do you expect me to keep trivia in my head when there are people here paid to do it for me?'

'Not good mood,' the assistant confided to the woman

vacuuming carpets along the executive suite's corridor, who, minutes later, conveyed the same news to Mrs Chou; just to be sure those who should know were properly informed.

After delivering a forceful reminder of who paid the guest's bills for room 2018 and a suggestion that the Harbour Hotel's manager shape up, Odergaard's CFO felt more relaxed than at any time since receiving Joe Wong's plainly inaccurate message.

'He's just getting carried away, that's all. Perhaps some other person would look after my interests more reliably? I wonder if…'

A vibration on his left thigh, to which Claude was becoming accustomed, interrupted a comforting train of thought.

'Not that damned bellboy again, is it?'

Another text from Joe Wong, revealing visits to room 2018 had now risen to eight, was initially dismissed as further evidence that the mole's condition remained unduly excitable and still dependent on defective powers of observation. Or had he, perhaps, seen evidence of the beneficial effects of the admonition recently heaped on the Harbour Hotel's under-performing customer welfare manager? As mythology in this part of the world regarded eight as an augury of luck and prosperity, Claude was inclined to believe the latter, so he held the lighted mobile at arm's length and smiled a satisfied smile.

'I'll tell Wong he's off the payroll from tonight. Misleading information and mindless panic were so unconstructive and certainly not the services I'm paying heavily for.'

But, long after the mobile light blinked out, its capitalised image hung at the back of Claude's thoughts like an exclamation mark.

'Well, why don't I call him now and hear the complete story?'

At the Harbour Hotel Joe Wong snatched up his phone from the concierge's desk before it had completed two rings.

'Wei, wei? Mr Halt sir? You pay today, yes?'

'What? You've got some nerve … pay a dunce for rubbish? Pshaw! Whatever next?'

'Huh? Job finish. I no like more. So seven day times fifty; owe me three hundred fifty.'

'Look, young man, what I said was fifty each time you have something critical to relate, not as a daily rate. You have sent me two texts of dubious value, so at the wildest overestimate you are due one hundred. Your engagement was not a request to convey details of how many times a waiter delivered a croissant. Do I make myself clear? Hum? Answer me.'

'Oh, this not waiter thing; this real visit. You know jig jig? Eight times, lucky man. She very beautiful lady; him very happy, yes?'

Claude Halt's blood froze. Nothing could hurt like this. He'd set his heart on winning Mandy Plumpkin and had done whatever he could to encourage reciprocation. Hadn't he been a constant and considerate escort; spent lavishly on her and, above all, fixed – that was the only word to describe what he had done – yes, fixed a leading part at the Hong Kong Spring Arts Festival in a production by a company of the brightest international stars visiting the city, only to be rewarded with this ... this betrayal? And what was worse, yes, far worse was the discovery of her infidelity from the mouth of a common bellhop with neither the charm nor manners to soften his appalling revelation.

'Uhh! Uhh!'

'So you pay now and we quits?'

'Uhh! Yes ... no ... not yet.' Claude clung desperately to the wreckage of his fragmenting dream. 'Specifics, boy, give me specifics to ... understand fully and ... better assess the quality of your numbers ... No one ... no one ... thsss ... is struck down until proven guilty.'

'Oh oh! She guilty, all right. Right up to neck.'

'Will you stop that, damn you! You sound as if this was a joke.'

'OK, OK ... see here ... Man not Chinese, not white. Look like he work on Nathan Road. Black, yes, very black. And I know his name and ...'

'Aah! Give it me, blast and damn you, give it me!'

'... No, no, not yet.'

'What! You can't leave it there? I'm paying for this, this ... this sordid story.'

'You pay three hundred fifty dollars for what Joe gave and five hundred more for man's name, yes?

'That's outrageous ... I'll have you fired if you don't ...'

'No can. Joe done nothing wrong. And you pay ... in cash,' the bellhop said in a voice that indicated negotiations had reached an end.

Whether an Albert Rawlings, Jose Aguirre or Ho Jiang had come between the struggling actress and her thwarted suitor was of course totally immaterial. But, with hopes atomised, Claude Halt needed a name, or better still a form into which he could stick the needles of his disappointment.

'OK, OK ... I'll pay. Now ... who is it ... the name ... the name at once, do you hear?'

'Money first ... then name.'

'Why, you ... blackguard! You're going to regret this to the end of your days, my boy; see if you don't...'

Unmoved by the threat Joe Wong conceded nothing.

'In cash ... no cheque ... leave at concierge. Call you back after receive.'

Several banknotes, taken from the CFO's float for handling miscellaneous discretionary expenses, were folded into a sheet of copying paper and shoved into an envelope. The fearful assistant was called to arrange dispatch and sent on her way with a no-nonsense 'And do it this second!'

'Yes, yes, Sir, yes,' she responded from a crack in the doorway as she closed it hurriedly behind her and fled from sight.

The vacuuming lady, who had her own thoughts about the CFO, was entrusted with the document's safe delivery to 'Administration' three floors below. In the stairwell's seclusion she sniffed the envelope's edges and held it up to an electric light.

'Money,' she announced authoritatively to Carol Tung as she

handed over the envelope. 'From Mr Halt to Joe Wong, low-level employee at Harbour Hotel. He waiting.'

'Who?'

'Mr Halt,' and after a pause, '... and Wong Joe.'

Messages conveyed by cleaners that sounded like directives had to be put in their proper place and this one was tossed, face down, into a tray marked 'For Collection'.

'Oh that not good ... must deliver now,' the vacuuming lady insisted.

'Will be dealt with.' The frigid glare was unequivocal. 'May go.'

As soon as the messenger was out of sight Ms Tung picked up the envelope and ran her fingers over its exterior, testing the folds and edges of the contents. The cleaner was almost certainly right; money was passing hands, but news to the office administrator was not for passing on in titillating gossip, but kept for safekeeping, so she, better than anyone, would know the business of her superiors.

There was a score of urgent office matters waiting that afternoon for Claude Halt's attention, but in the interval between Joe Wong's call and waving away the envelope, he was incapable of any semblance of intelligent deliberation, other than of the pictured horror of Mandy's repeated ravishment – if the bellhop was to be believed – by the most envied man in all the ugly world.

Shortly after two o'clock the telephone on his desk rang. Quite forgetting his informer had only a mobile contact, Claude grabbed at it with the eagerness of a man hoping for a lottery win.

'Joe?'

'Hello,' whispered the timid assistant from the shelter of her workstation's partitioning, 'should I order lunch, as you have ...?'

'No, no,' he bellowed, 'I'm busy; stop intruding on my thoughts, will you?'

The solicitous secretary reeled under the verbal barrage and replaced the receiver, as gently as a gecko removing moccasins, and dabbed away several salt tears from the fluttering ends of her eyelashes.

Unable to sit still, Claude Halt got up and paced backwards and forwards across his office. He still wanted to believe there had been some kind of mistake; that the bellboy had got the room number wrong, or hadn't actually seen anyone visit at all and was just guessing to claim the money and end his assignment. Maybe he had asked others to keep a lookout and, without checking, treated their observations as his own and took the easy path to squeeze his reluctant paymaster. 'Yes, that was it; he's a crook. I'll get on to the Harbour's manager in a day or so and have him sacked. They always listen to their customers, especially ones providing repeated business.'

When the expected call eventually came through Claude was weak from speculation and tense with anxiety.

'Joe here,' the voice said. 'Got money; now give name.'

'Yes, OK ... who ...?'

'Got pencil?'

'Stop sidetracking and just give it to me! I haven't got all day here.'

'Oh! It's ... ah ... Anil Patel.'

'Who?'

'Say again; Anil Patel.'

'Ani ... never heard of him. Who the hell is that?'

'You not know? Heh, heh, heh! Should do; works at Odergaard.'

'How can he when I sign the payroll and don't know him from Adam?'

'Drives Odergaard van; comes here in afternoon, sometimes evening ... and stays all night.'

'That's just about the most ridiculous thing I've ever heard. Are you saying a woman of Ms Plumpkin's professional celebrity, who is about to appear at the Hong Kong Arts

Festival's premier production, is having a liaison with a common artisan, a lorry driver. How absurd! You're fabricating a yarn here to get me to pay up. When I'm done with you you'll be carrying your sorry tail down the road and that's as certain as you can get.'

'What mean?

'I mean, goddamnit, you are going to get your arse kicked into next week, so you better get ready for the ride. Do I make myself clear?'

'Suit self. Name given; job done.'

A rattle in Claude's ear ended the conversation. A tiny wave of exhilaration, like the tingle from a first sip of champagne, rose inside him. The tale was so preposterous it was beyond the invention of anyone in his right mind. Only a devious street boy trying to make a fast buck would have dreamed up such nonsense. He'd like to have told Mandy the story, for surely she would see its funny side. But, unfortunately, given the delicate nature of his enquiries, he'd have to forgo the pleasure of seeing her laugh and having Joe Wong ridiculed.

Claude suddenly felt a surge of hunger and sent his assistant for an omelette sandwich.

'And sprinkle some chilli over the egg; I like some spice,' he said to the retreating head.

When lunch arrived it came wrapped in thin tissue paper, over which cooking oil spread in dark patches, and was accompanied by a glass of aerated water rapidly losing its sparkle. Notwithstanding the meal's plainness the CFO devoured it with gusto under the nervous eye of his desolate assistant.

Preoccupied with his thoughts and intent on scraping a few remaining chilli fragments together with the ends of his fingers, he ceased to be aware of his assistant's continuing presence, until she managed a mostly tactful attempt to clear her sinuses.

'Arrum … huk.'

'Well, what is it; what are you waiting for; this? Here take it,' he said, shoving the plate at her.

'Mmm ... yes and ...'

Her contorted face looked towards a heaped in-tray at the end of Claude's mahogany desk, on top of which rested a crowded folder marked 'Immediate Return' in unapologetic red letters.

'You want my signature ... on these? Is that what you are after? Speak up, woman, or no one will ever know what you are after.'

Claude removed his glasses, polished them with the end of a silk tie purchased cheaply at a tourist souvenir shop in Stanley market, and dragged over the paper mountain.

'Pen.'

He held out a hand and waited for the black one he used for signing important documents to be placed there, before flipping back the cover of the dense folder of payment instructions.

His customary practice was to examine every numerical detail. In the past, such careful attention had yielded many arithmetical errors a more attentive accounting staff would have detected without his intervention. He loved the figures' form and shape, their smooth curves and emphatic lines and the mechanics of their additions, subtractions and percentages, so much that sometimes he lost sight of what service the payment covered, or whether it had even been requested. But not one calculation, he firmly believed, escaped his thorough review, or left his office inaccurately totalled. But today, while other obsessions claimed his attention, he was just not up to his usual level of diligence.

'Want tea?'

'Uh?'

'Tea, clear head if not feeling good.'

The audacious advice just slipped out as if the frightened assistant had been addressing a sibling many years her junior, or an infirm elder relative. But she need not have worried, for Claude's mind had not fully returned to the arena of his expertise or employment.

'No ... no ... but I may leave early tonight.'

The first voucher in the pile sanctioned payment to Wah Lin Garages, where Odergaard's sent its fleet of aging delivery vans and where, with a nod and wink and a five-per-cent surcharge, they avoided the risk of failing government inspection tests. Numerous fuel and spare parts dockets and a covering note, signed by five members of the Accounts department in descending order of authority, were gripped in the black jaws of a spring clip to support details of Wah Lin's monthly invoice.

'Fffff.'

Claude scribbled on one of the dockets to make sure the ink in his pen was flowing satisfactorily and signed the payment instruction in the space marked 'Approved – Chief Financial Officer'. The size of the bundle was just too daunting for today's mood and he sped on through the folder's contents, just stopping to notice the name of each payee – Shoestring Air Freight, Thomas Ting China Appointed Attesting, Faithful Traders, Glorious Jobs Employment Agency and so on – until, at the very bottom of the pile, he reached one for the Harbour Hotel.

Here, in the mass of recorded events and calculations, were papers from kitchens and bars that she had touched and where she had written her name. If he bent closely perhaps, he could pick up a whiff of her scent or detect the impression of her fingertips where she had signed her initials.

'Wait a minute, look at this ... Can it be ... a blonde hair!' There was no mistaking which golden head that had fallen from!

With his pen stuck in the bundle to mark his place, Claude extracted the brilliant strand and straightened it out along the edge of his desk.

'Could anyone believe such a find?'

'Come back later?' the assistant whispered, as if anything louder than her stifled mouse's enquiry would rend the welkin.

Too engrossed to notice her interruption, he delved into his desk in search of an envelope in which to delicately place the prized thread. Instinctively, he carefully folded the paper and began sliding it into his suit, until concluding its rightful home was in his shirt's breast pocket, right over his beating heart. In his pulsating imagination an exhilarating wave bore two bronzed and laughing figures on its frothy summit towards a tropic sand spit. He settled comfortably back and closed his eyes and across his inner retina he and the luscious Mandy Plumpkin were cast by booming rollers onto a white beach awash with rays of summer suns.

A rabbit's sniff broke into the corner of his dream. He opened one eye and looked out.

'Mmm ... must collect ... payment file ... urgent ...'

Her voice rose higher and higher until either it disappeared in an inaudible register, or ended in an absence of constructive things to say.

'Here, take all this away.'

Claude put his hand into the wad of Harbour Hotel memoranda to retrieve his pen and stopped with a voyeur's curiosity at the theatrical sweeps of an elegant signature. He felt as if he had caught her raising a smooth leg before she stepped naked into her bath.

'Let's see what the lady likes to eat for breakfast. Hmm ... cereal, eggs, bacon, sausage, pancakes, coffee and tea? My word, she rises hungry. But, of course, she does sleep late and an army's appetite is forgivable.'

The sea billows sustaining Claude Halt's fantasy crashed over rocky headlands and ebbed in a churn of tumultuous green-and-blue water.

'But ... served at midday for two ...!?'

He flipped back to the preceding night's dinner chit and found room service orders for Duck *à l'orange* and Lobster Thermidor. Madly dashing through the Harbour Hotel pile he discovered seven occasions in the preceding month when dinner and the following breakfast had been served for two.

'Arrhh! God damn all women!' he roared and, gathering the twenty or so payment instructions and their supporting documents into the red-lettered file, he hurled them in a cloud over his assistant's bowed head.

'Gone mad!' she said as she passed the vacuum lady humming through her afternoon ritual in the executive suite's corridor.

'Ah! Chilli,' the cleaner replied. 'Give body too much heat.'

17

Straddled across its mistress's sleeping body the pet schnauzer cocked a fretful ear. Early-morning petting was how the day began and inattention was perplexing. When whines failed to rouse Mrs Tung's prostrate form, the highly strung creature explored other tactics and snorted crudely into the one visible ear. The, so far, inert figure smiled gently, but remained in a state of semi-conscious collapse. Becoming more frantic with each passing minute, the animal pranced and licked at the coating of surgical spirit on the face below until an unnatural drizzle of saliva splashed over its battered cheeks and mouth.

'Mmm ... again,' she drawled and rolled on to her back.

The schnauzer sat on its haunches, threw his head back and yapped, not once, but over and over until Carol Tung sat up fuddled with sleep and Budiwati hurried in from the kitchen twisting a towel round her wet hands.

'Uhh! What are you doing?'

'Doing? Why cleaning, M'am, and laundry. I have the washer on daily as I like to have everything back in the drawers by ...'

'No, no ... meaning here in my room ... when I woke.'

'Oh, I see, but that's not your bed, M'am,' the domestic helper tittered. 'Look, it's the sofa. When you were dropped off late yesterday by that old gentleman, Archibald he said his name was, such a nice man too, you just fell down there and slept the clock round, eight to eight. Didn't want to disturb you and Wai Pang just slipped in and out and went to school and ...' She paused. 'But your face, whatever happened to it?'

Without thinking Carol Tung's fingertips explored her abrasions.

'Oh ... it ... was an accident; yes ... a man ... on a bicycle ... that's all ... nothing worrying.'

'We did worry to begin with and before you came home as well, but after the lady rang, she was very nice as well, to say you were staying with her we felt better. But three days is a long time to be gone, M'am, and Pak Tam Au such a long way away.'

Budiwati knew people outside the family, even ones of many years' service, had no right to information, but hoped an explanation or at least a hint would reassure her that all was as well as this abnormal household permitted. But Carol Tung's missing days and nights were a closely protected secret, so awful in detail, it could not be admitted to anyone, much less an unrelated employee, even one sleeping under the same roof and eating food served in the same dishes.

'My son ... has been on time ... for school and doing homework while ... while I've been away?'

'I can't say anything about his studies, except he's been working long on them extra classes of his. Got home really late on Tuesday, though, and funny thing, next day he says he wants to learn to wash his own clothes. Not happy letting me do them anymore. Independent young man that one, to be sure. And then last night, Thursday that is, a teacher called to say they had a science camp and several boys would be staying over if parents gave permission. As you weren't here and the teacher was so insistent, I said you probably wouldn't mind, it being serious schoolwork and such.'

If the same account of her son's comings and goings had been made a week ago, Carol Tung would have pored over its implications like a forensic scientist sifting grains of sand in a trouser turn-up for evidence of damnation. But, drugged with sleep and drowned by anguished reflections on the last few, torrid days, Budiwati's astounding revelation fell into the refuse heap where all her mindless platitudes and empty air ultimately came to rest.

The domestic helper's presence suddenly became intolerable.

'Return to work; will call if needed.'

'Then I'll just be over there in kitchen doing the ironing and when I'm done …'

'I don't care what will be doing, now, or after ironing; just go and do and leave me alone, understand?'

'Of course I do. You want to think in private after a bad experience; that's what anyone would want, although sometimes a bit of company and someone to talk to helps … Did I tell you about my cousin when she came back to the village after working in …'

Was there no way to silence this garrulous woman, who never knew when or how to stop?

'Take dog out, now, this instant.'

'… But he's been out already! I took him down at …'

Swollen with rising blood, Mrs Tung's stiff wounds were ready to burst. The ominous signs were beyond mistaking, even to Budiwati's slower than usual appreciation, so a fat finger was hooked under the unwilling animal's collar and pulled towards the outer door. Not used to unscheduled exercise, or having less than his own way, the creature thrust out four unbending legs and, like a windsurfer propelled by sea gusts, sailed across the lounge floor aboard the stained central rug.

As lift sounds receded, Carol Tung fell back into the sofa's comfortable embrace and ran both hands through her knotted hair. What a turbulent few days these had been. Her feelings were unlike anything she had ever experienced, except, perhaps, that time during the still vividly remembered junk trip, when Jakob Odergaard had unwittingly set her heart alight with flames that still sparked intermittently two decades later. Nothing, until today, least of all in the wearisome marriage to Cheung Man Kit and its dutiful production of a son from furtive fumblings under shrouded sheets, had scorched her with such white heat.

The first feel of a man's hot breath on her neck and his grip on her frightened limbs had shocked her to the core. But she would be lying to herself if she said the tussle in the black alleyway, among the refuse bags and abandoned cartons, had been only awful. Her feelings were a lot more complicated. In the desperate flailing, clawing and scratching there was a kind of deliverance and tearing at the hair and clothes of the man by whom she wanted to be violated was somehow an inseparable part. Debasement and intercourse were a pair unlike humiliation and love. Dare she admit that in the heart of her terror she had found the road to unspeakable pleasure and discovered the object of her search?

There was no question, of course, that probity had its place. How else would families hold together, bring up children correctly, perform filial duty, work and prosper? But what if she had allowed the hideous episode to continue to its final barbaric conclusion? Who, in other parts of her life, would have heard, or been affected? Face down on the sofa, with arms behind her back she imagined the thrusting knee separating her thighs and groaned aloud to the silent furniture and the tiny flat's four mute walls.

The only answer was to find him again and let raw nature take its course. She stood up, straightened her twisted clothes and, smoothing away creases in the skirt she had slept in for over twelve hours, went to her bedroom to paint her lips scarlet and powder over the bruises on her discoloured face.

If she hurried, she could be out of the apartment block and well on her way before Budiwati returned with the dog and launch into another stream of endless yattering. But where should she begin, when even his name was a mystery? Finding one ready man among the city's millions had already been a difficult task, but locating this one, unless he was in the habit of returning to the haunt where she had first found him, would be impossible. But that was surely the answer; yes, she'd go back to the Kowloon Waterfront and, if he wasn't there, she'd come again the next day and the next until he reappeared. In time she would find him.

By the bus station, the man and woman who had occupied the same patch of pavement three days ago, turned maize cobs, instead of sweet potatoes, over their charcoal fire. The woman raised her eyes from the stinging smoke and gave a minimal nod of recognition. Across several parking lanes buses, with closed doors, were drawn up and lines of would-be passengers waited on the warming concrete in drifts of cooking smoke.

The roar of an approaching motorbike engine somewhere beyond the stationary double-deckers added foreign and self-promoting notes to Shatin's daily clamour.

Mrs Tung walked to the end of a long-suffering line snaking back from the Kowloon express bus stop. A shadow from an overhead tower crane swept over the press, which, intent on keeping hard-won places, let it pass unheeded.

On the terminal's perimeter, the motorcycle rider, in a fluttering white shirt and violet trousers, pulled over and let his engine idle into subdued phut-phuts. Wai Pang alighted from the pillion and unlaced his hard hat. His tousled hair fell over a face lit by adventure.

Maize from the corner brazier sold briskly; the busy owners were having one of their better mornings. Stirred charcoal embers were revived into glowing life and the sun-dried man pulled his last remaining cobs from a sack at his feet. He had planned to share the best tonight at dinner with his hard-working wife, but, anticipating one more sale, he decided, for today at least, vicarious pleasure would take second place to additional profit.

Close to the back of a meandering queue and impatient with her wait for the Kowloon express, Carol Tung could not remember the last time solid food had passed her lips. There had been some thin and well-intentioned soup at the Pak Tam Au refuge, but that had been an age ago. Recollection of that evening's course of events should have submerged a normal person's hunger under an avalanche of shame. But, today, Carol Tung was not a woman of ordinary sentiments reflecting on abhorrent mental images. The unlit alleyway's hot pursuit and its violent tumbling aftermath quickened her desire to eat and coloured her face with such alarming shades that those closest to her in the waiting crush backed away in alarm.

More knobs of fuel were thrown into the glowing stand and more maize was stripped of its stiff green coating to reveal hard shiny centres ripe for consumption. The very last one, once destined for pride of place at a private meal, was turned, examined in detail and cast along with all the rest across a blackened grill plate.

With hunger getting the better of her and, to the relief of those in her immediate vicinity, Carol Tung broke from the line and made for the cooked food stall.

The motorcycle, having let its pillion passenger dismount and slip from sight into the swarming multitudes, resumed a full-throated roar and weaved in revving snarls across the bus terminal tarmac.

Although the rider's head was encased in a helmet, his familiar hollow chest, covering the vehicle's petrol tank as if it had been shaped for the purpose, and his flamboyantly coloured slacks squeezed Mrs Tung's heart to suffocation as soon as she saw them. Tottering back from his oncoming rush she let out a yelp of shock and gratitude.

While her thoughts for three days and nights had been seared with his image, his had moved with the ebb and flow of fortune to an alternative, but still gratifying, experience. She had been so far from his mind as he rounded the corner into the bus depot that her sudden ghastly appearance beside his growling machine blinded him to obstruction and he struck the pavement in front of the glowing brazier in a burst of invective and rubber.

Without the benefit of slow-motion replay, the anonymous crowd heard only a screech and a bump and saw nothing of the open mouth, goggling eyes, inverted flight over suddenly stationary handlebars and subsequent crashing descent. Only the strewn hot coals of the street vendor's smoking stand and litter of motorcycle and rider explained the commotion.

'Aah! *Fai te ah* ... what you do!?' yelled the hawker as his livelihood and best ears of corn disintegrated and rolled under the wheels of the oncoming Kowloon bus.

Muffled howls seeped from inside Isidor's damaged helmet, and his bony fists thumped at the smouldering patches on his much prized violet slacks and baggy shirt that were singed and so far twisted round his body and protruding ribs that he had the appearance of a broken lampshade abandoned on the municipal landfill.

'Mmpff, mmpff; holy, f-fucking Christ!'

'You pay; you pay,' shrieked the hawker's wife, while passers-by and the bus queues watched from intrigued, but uninvolved, distance.

Whether providence played a part in humanity's journey to the grave was not a question to resonate in Mrs Tung's circumscribed intellect. Until now, her world-view extended no further than being correct, working invisibly under JBO's imperious direction and pressing her feelings into dark recesses where none, other than herself, would expect their melancholy existence, but as she witnessed Isidor's unimpeded trajectory across the terminal concourse she could not but help think there was a great deal more in his arrival than mere chance.

Their first meeting on Kowloon's waterfront could have been dismissed as pure coincidence, but today's, embellished by exploding colour and smoke, proclaimed a fateful entanglement only the foolish would attempt to deny. Higher authority, mindful of the right way, could not have indicated the course with greater precision, and if destiny governed the orbiting planets' melodies why should it not influence her lowly existence? Remaining shreds of her usually iron-clad restraint fell away and she sank to her knees at the feet of a wildly gesticulating Isidor.

'Will someone get me outa this bleedin' thing,' the trapped voice protested indistinctly.

'Let me help,' Carol Tung purred.

'No pay; call police!' railed the hawker couple.

'Don't do that; I pay; live over there. You've seen me and can trust.'

In addition to rendering Isidor's speech barely audible, the broken helmet also affected his hearing.

'What's goin' on? Is someone gonna do somethin'!'

'Yes, yes. Help here, please?' the uncharacteristically gentle Mrs Tung asked the still-bubbling, but partially pacified, roadside cook.

'Uhhff?'

Together they twisted and prised at the helmet until it and Isidor parted with a pop.

'Fuckin' hell! Think my bloody head just come orf and look at my clothes, will yer? I'm in a right bleedin' mess.'

And so he was. Almost every hair on his head had been dragged into a waxy crest, as if he'd spent the last hour in a wind tunnel, and his red and swollen ears resembled cauliflower florets dipped in cochineal. The distinctive outfit, once the high-water mark of a limited leisure collection, had been sliced into ragged strips by the barbecue's sharp edges and left on the verge of ruin.

Automated doors on the express bus to Kowloon wheezed apart and impatient travellers, keen to get about their delayed business, shuffled up two steps into rows of empty seats. Interest in the street-side incident evaporated in the concerns of daily necessity.

'Look, live near here. Come and patch up.'

'Aih? You serious, or what?'

'Need some help and it's close.'

'You don't say so? If I remember right, you weren't so keen on hangin' 'round a few nights ago, or particularly worried if I got some cuts.'

'That different; had time to think.'

'Cor, will you listen to her! Too right some things have changed. And what might you have been thinkin'?'

'That ... you distressed me and ... I shouldn't be ... so alarmed.'

Realisation that he was back to where he started with this strange creature spread over Isidor's bruised and shaken countenance with a smirk of disfigured blue lips.

'Well, you're nuffink if not surprisin', my girl. So where is it then ... this ... place of yours? I don't want to be pushin' this bleedin' bike too far, you know, cause it ain't goin' nowhere under its own steam.'

Because it distracted from the main problem, this sudden outbreak of friendliness bothered the cook and his partner. Full and rightful compensation was toting up to quite a large sum if replacement costs for the appliance and maize and lost earnings were included. To add emphasis to arithmetic, the brazier's charred wok received a sharp kick that sent it clattering across the depot.

'There,' Carol Tung said, while keeping her eyes fixed on Isidor, 'see the building ... it's on thirty-fifth floor. Let me take care of ...'

From a green leather wallet in her handbag she took out a five hundred dollar note and handed it to the hawker. His pupils dilated, but not one muscle on his face moved.

'Not enough,' he said categorically.

'Not enough! What mean? Just a box on wheels and ...'

'Can't work for a week, while repair. Him,' he pointed accusingly at Isidor, 'must pay more.'

'Don't look at me, old son; I ain't got a ha'penny to my name and now I gotta fork out from next month's pay for the bleedin' bike.'

'Call police!' shrilled the wife.

'No, no need, here's five hundred more,' conceded the more flexible Mrs Tung, who was anxious to close a conversation inhibiting her beached ship's relaunch on the crest of a romantic spring tide.

Without a flicker of appreciation or thanks the old man passed the money to his mate and set about recovering what he could from the broken remains of his enterprise. Ears of corn, whether edible or not, were dusted free of litter and dropped into a wide apron. One, partially crushed by the incoming Kowloon express, before it loaded up with passengers, was sniffed hopefully and eaten. The broken struts, spokes and stays of the charcoal burner were sorted into separate piles on the pavement for later, careful reconstruction.

Isidor heaved his damaged motor bicycle upright and, with Carol Tung's considerate hand in the fold of his wet armpit, limped in the direction of the tower block to which, only minutes earlier, Wai Pang had walked.

The damaged bike was propped against a basement car-park wall and, with Isidor's willing arm, feigning more than his condition deserved, transferred to her shoulders, he allowed himself to be escorted towards the entrance of a lift.

'You know, it's nice being alone an' leanin' on you like this?'

'Not yet! Wait till upstairs.'

'Not sure what you've got in mind here, but 'spect you'll make allowances for a guy who's had a couple, yeah a couple, of pretty demandin' days, eh?'

'Can wash if want.'

'You don't say so? Now if you could manage a shower an' somthin' to eat that'll get me right back to my fightin' best.'

The fitfully maintained elevator rattled open, groaned, closed and chugged upwards. Mrs Tung cringed at the noises that must have been heard up and down the entire building.

'Fuckin' hell, what a din.'

On the thirty-fifth floor one rumpus was replaced no less noisily by scuffling and bumping from the interior of Mrs Tung's flat.

'Shss ... someone in,' she said.

'Who's that, then, aih?'

Before Mrs Tung's key made contact with the lock the apartment's door flew open and an ugly schnauzer, gurgling deep in its throat, squeezed between Budiwati's plump legs and began snapping dementedly around its owner's ankles.

'Just gone out again … science camp experiment finished,' the home help announced quickly to pre-empt any investigation into Wai Pang's night out. 'Wanted a shower before going to school he said. Not like him to be late. No time to eat … I wasn't going to force him, although I knew you'd be angry and so … oh! You've brought company with you?'

'Not company … traffic accident downstairs. Need first aid and …'

Carol Tung was surprised by the ease with which she began steering her story.

'Another one? Every one getting run over these days. Cuts and bruises, is it, or anything worse? … Did you know my mistress was hit by a bicycle only three days ago?' Budiwati informed the visitor. 'Got lots of cuts, too … You can see on her face, look … Shall I get some hot water, or …'

The non-stop prattle and the yelping dog were not making Carol Tung's path to abject surrender easy.

'Geez, what a zoo!'

'Get lead and take him out,' Mrs Tung commanded, indicating the family pet.

Budiwati's eyes opened wide.

'Again? … But that'll be three times this morning and it's still only …'

'I don't care. Just do what told. Go to market and buy some … some …'

For the life of her Mrs Tung could not think of anything that the house urgently needed.

'Oh … anything you find,' she added in desperation.

'But there's no balance in the petty cash … and nothing that …'

'Then go out and … take phone … I'll call when time to come back.'

'I see … yes … OK.'

From under her thick black brows the domestic looked up slyly.

'You don't see anything,' Mrs Tung snapped sharply.

For the first time the schnauzer's pitiful whimpers left its owner unmoved and, as its snorts and yelps faded, Carol Tung leant against the apartment door with her hands behind her and sighed with the relief and anticipation of a convict breathing open air on the opposite side of prison gates.

18

Summer and most of winter passed and Mandy Plumpkin had not seen fit to travel to Utah. Instead and although not a skier, she spent her time around the slopes of the Tyrolean Alps in the company of a middle-aged gentleman from Innsbruck, with whom she had shared the Harbour Hotel's breakfast buffet and discovered interests in common.

Her companion owned a niche business making advertising videos for manufacturers of China-made fashion goods. While he edited videos in what was once his darkroom, she read her part and rehearsed moves for *Moon for the Misbegotten*.

In the spring that followed her long vacation, and as a result of her work in the Tyrol, her hands and feet acquired prominence in several ladies' glove and shoe commercials and later became items of discussion in the broader topic of her expanding professional portfolio.

Being a realist as well as an aspirant, Mandy recognised the Festival role as heaven-sent and for reasons of insurance and good management exchanged essential correspondence throughout her travels with Geoffrey Keso, to work herself into her first 'starring' role, and with a surprisingly petulant Claude Halt.

Her first call to the disgruntled CFO, designed to test whether the safety net under her theatrical take-off was ready to catch her, should her flight be aborted, was not as she expected. He was unaccommodating, almost rude, as if his advances had been rejected by a woman of whom he had the greatest expectations. But, after several more solicitous calls and words enough to sooth a grizzly bear's interrupted hibernation, he grumbled to heel and redirected his ill-will at other less mesmerising targets.

'"A return built on last season's popular and critical acclaim", my foot!' he remonstrated, tearing the offending article from his Sunday newspaper and hurling it in a ball over the boiled egg and hot toast carried to his bedside by an uncomplaining housekeeper.

If inclination to overstate the newly rechristened Provo International Theater Company's credentials was to be found anywhere, other than in the troupe's country opinions of itself, it was surely in the copious column inches of the Festival's 'official' newspaper.

'So much for objective reporting,' he thought.

Others may know pieces of the story, but only he knew how completely the rustics of Provo owed their selection to his artful manipulation.

'Insightful critics and quality performance? My Aunt Fanny! Only the strings I've pulled have brought this motley band of wannabees to within a million miles of Hong Kong.'

But, while Provo Theater's winning inclusion in the Festival and the fillip to Mandy Plumpkin's career had indeed been brought about by Claude Halt's devious contriving, he could not eradicate the nagging feeling that everyone, including that unrepentant bounder Jakob Odergaard, was benefiting from the arrangement while he languished in mud at the starting gate. Unfairness of this magnitude brought tears to his eyes and chagrin to his soul and made his nose wet with powerless frustration. In mute protest he slapped butter on his bread under the pained watch of his puzzled chatelaine.

Only weeks ago a seemingly perfect plan had given him endless satisfaction together with sporadic fantastical dreams of the most heavenly creature stepping into his arms from a sumptuous palanquin. Today, however, the litter-bearers had so much grit in their sandals their early arrival had fallen into serious doubt.

With nothing and no one on his side he had moved mountains. Sponsorship like blood had been squeezed from a stone; superannuated members of the Arts Festival Committee had been bullied into accepting a production none of them liked or considered suited to local taste; Provo's journeymen had been coerced into giving their lead role to an unknown starlet; Mandy Plumpkin had been jostled into taking the role, after a show of indecision, when all along she wanted to grasp the gift with both outstretched arms, and he had assiduously courted her at some little cost to his peace of mind and credit-card balance. Hadn't this unswerving dedication, this dogged pursuit, which should have benefited everyone, deserved a better outcome for its chief architect and pilot?

Ah! If only that wretched Joe Wong had not muddied the water with contemptible insinuations and outrageous behaviour! Without him, Claude would still have raised her up with an untroubled mind from the feathered cushions of her cavalcade and to the fanfare of trumpets and booms of canon, instead of suspecting he was beginning to look like the fairy tale's chump.

So smitten had the Odergaard CFO been and continued to be that, even at this advanced hour, he could still not quite believe in Mandy's flagrant disloyalty, which, to other people, was as plain as if she had dispensed tickets and front-row views of her gross infidelity. His blind refusal to accept the obvious even while approving payment for her shared bedroom suppers and breakfasts led him, not just to deceive others, but to perpetrate the greatest deception of all upon himself.

The palanquin might sway in sandy gusts but, by an effort of will, it could still be held upright. When the dust settled the angelic woman who so rattled his fragile reason would be there, glimpsed behind her silken curtains, beckoning to him.

Subordinates, who knew the CFO's steady resourcefulness and dreary communiqués, were amazed at the sudden polar extremes of his moods. One minute he teased playfully and with humour foreign to everyone's memory. In the next, when he was sapped by thoughts that maybe Joe Wong and the Harbour Hotel's room service vouchers told the real story, he barked at even the most inoffensive employee, who might well have concluded that Mr Halt's life's savings had disappeared in ill-considered, cross-border speculation.

Before the advent of Mandy Plumpkin, Claude Halt's mental well-being had been grounded in order and method and in knowing things had their place and assets a book value. Nothing, least of all the alluring and vexatious Ms Plumpkin, should appreciate or depreciate just by thinking about it. If his investment return – and yes, he was not afraid to describe his efforts as exactly that – was in any way calculable, her stock should be steadily climbing, not fluctuating through dizzying highs and lows reminiscent of a balance sheet riddled by bad debt.

But now she was back and preparing for the Arts Festival's opening and he was overwhelmed by a desire to see her immediately and set the matter straight once and for all. The congealing egg and cold toast were pushed away and he resolved to make his way to the hall lent for rehearsals to the Provo International Theater Company free of charge by the local chapter of the Church of Jesus Christ of Latter Day Saints.

Instead of pulling up at the hall's side entrance, as he had instructed, the unwilling taxi driver insisted on dropping him on the opposite side of Gloucester Road, which obliged him to take a walkway running over the bustling thoroughfare.

'No, no, I didn't say stop here,' Claude protested. 'It's too damned inconvenient to climb across the bridge.'

'Traffic too much; you *yau lok* here.'

'But can't you keep going with the goddamned meter on? I don't see the problem.'

'No problem, if get out now.'

The threat reminded Claude that, in Hong Kong, passengers had no rights in spite of by-laws legislating differently and that expostulation from the back of a hired taxi-cab cut no ice whatever.

'What's the matter with you people?' he fumed as he stepped out. 'No wonder you can't get a real job. Why, in my company ...'

Unconcerned by what took place at Odergaard Holdings the taxi driver jerked the rear door to with a thud and, in a stench of diesel smoke, sped back to the noisy flow of vehicles passing beneath the concrete-and-steel overpass.

By the time he descended on the street's far side, Claude felt numbed by the cool winds swirling round Gloucester Road's bleak government towers. His wispy hair blew about in untidy threads and he hurried to be out of the weather. But, because air-conditioning was rarely turned off in this city, the second he tugged open the church hall's side entrance he was assailed by an even colder blast from the bowls of holy sanctimony.

'Shheewutz!' he gasped as the freezing draught raced through his lungs and over his face, prompting the wet trickles of breakfast time to reassemble and run along the entire length of his nose.

'Why do they insist on such idiocy?' he complained.

As he strove to regain composure, indistinct voices reminded him of the purpose of his visit and drew him towards a vast auditorium, where, at other times, faithful crowds of believers gathered to celebrate. At the front and surrounded by ranks of sloping seats and hot arc lighting, Geoffrey Keso, dressed in shirt sleeves and travel-stained slacks and with spectacles resting in his tangled eyebrows, was speaking to an undistinguished but slightly arty middle-aged man.

Claude knew the type; they were always to be found hanging around the fringes of festivals and rarely contributing anything worth while. The specious pleasure of being with stage folk and treading the same boards was as much as they asked and more than they deserved.

'Where's Mandy?' he called from far beyond conversational distance.

Geoffrey's large head turned lugubriously.

'Huh? Oh, that's you up there, is it, Claude? Hi, Ah guess we weren't 'specting you at rehearsal.'

'Is Mandy about? I want to talk to her?'

'Mandy? Yah, she surely is; can't rehearse without the leading lady. Mah expectation, however, was you'd meet up with the crew on sponsors' night? Am Ah correct?'

Undeterred by the rebuff, Claude was not in a mood to give up.

'Well? Where is she?'

'We're on a schedule here and Ah'm going to have to ask for some space.'

'This is important.'

'An' so bah golly is our preparation. Lookee here, Claude, you can stay an' watch if you like, but Ah don't want you getting in the way of mah actors.'

'She is an actress,' Claude, ever the stickler for form, corrected, 'and one of the highest order.'

'U-huh, whatever, but you see mah point? So Ah'll get young Mr Manley here, who you may not know, to sit and answer any points you have, but Ah can't have you ruffling performers' feathers during rehearsal. You can speak to her afterwards.'

'Hello; I don't think we've met, or ... have we? You seem a bit familiar. Do we ... were you ...?'

'No.' The reply was unambiguous.

But Eric remained unconvinced and thought for a moment. Hong Kong was a small place and social circles even smaller. A meeting in a pub or at a football match was quite possible, or was it?

'Do you watch foot–?'

'I'm an accountant,' Claude said with feeling, as if the condition excluded all forms of pleasure.

'I see. Anyway, I'm Eric Manley, sent here as a sort of local liaison chappy for the Provo people who don't know their way around town ... and to look after a few bits and pieces. Jakob sent me over; I'm his son-in-law. Want to sit at the back, to give Geoffrey and his team room to stretch?'

A dainty handkerchief was taken from Claude's trouser pocket and flapped energetically to loosen its compressed folds. He sensed conspiracy in the air and blew hard to clear his nose and suddenly wary thoughts.

'Who? … then … I … should … aarrffoo! … Do you know someone called Anil by any chance?'

'Anil? Anil? Can't say I do. Has he got anything to do with the Festival?'

'Not as far as I'm aware, but never mind, just a thought.'

From half-light at the auditorium's rear the sunken rehearsal platform appeared as the centre of a bright bowl through which Geoffrey Keso swam distractedly. With his spectacles now pulled down from the overhang of his brows he looked like an anxious guppy plotting a course through inhospitable waters.

From out of the shadows a man and a woman moved to centre-stage holding hands and waited for Geoffrey to stop reading from a sheaf of notes.

Claude jumped out of his seat.

'What's she doing with him?'

'Shush … sit down. He's one of the main male parts … bloke called Platt, Doug Platt I believe … Supposed to be very dependable … They're creating atmosphere,' Eric advised.

'But they are not acting yet … Nothing's happened.'

'Not so loud … Emotion takes time to build. Just watch … It'll take shape as they start reading.'

'Where does her part begin? She'll bring glamour to anything.'

Eric looked at the agitated face and the crowning top of thin hair, which, in the coldness of the hall and in the space of a few minutes, had fallen into all sorts of ungainly and irregular angles.

'Possibly, but there's not much need for it in this play.'

On the stage Mandy kicked off her shoes and wrapped a blue, cotton shawl round her throat. Doug Platt exchanged places with another young man who moved alongside the actress.

'OK, from the top, go,' Geoffrey Keso growled.

Mandy, shaking her hair free of the shawl and in heavily accented tones that travelled through the frigid hall like ice cracking on a high snow field, called, 'Ah, thank God.'

'That's good. "Ah thank God"– that was well said,' Claude observed and leant forward into the back of the seat in front of him.

He was suddenly absorbed, as if her lightest word was spoken to him alone and that he was bound to listen. Eric observed the concentration and wondered if this was something he should note, although if JBO was worried about his CFO's commitment to the programme's success there was no obvious reason for him to lose sleep.

'You don't have to sit through the whole rehearsal. Repetition gets pretty tedious and could spoil opening night for you.'

'Umm? Oh, don't bother about me. I have a very particular interest in this production and its cast.'

'Yes, so I understand, but ...'

Mandy's voice carried over rows of seating to the back of the hall with the clarity of a bell.

'I know what a trial I've been to you, Mike, having a sister who's the scandal of the neighbourhood.'

'How could such a lovely creature be the scandal of anything? The audiences will guffaw in their sleeves at such a suggestion,' Claude protested.

Not wanting to stare, but fascinated by the strange fervour consuming this unprepossessing visitor, Eric shot repeated glances at the figure next to him.

'God forgive you. You've never cared for your virtue, or what man you went out with. You've always been as brazen as brass and proud of your disgrace.'

'That's too strong. Who is that blackguard?' Claude yelled.

'Quieten down; you'll disturb the reading. Do you mean the actor, or the part he's playing?' enquired Eric.

'Huh? Why him … that man!'

'Ur … well in the play he's Mandy Plumpkin's brother, but apart from that I don't yet know as I've only met up with the group today. I've been too busy reading the script. But I can find out later … if it's important?'

'No matter, look, he's leaving … and good riddance to a bad lot.'

Another man stood up and ran across the stage, with power and strength in every stride.

'Haven't you a tongue in your head, you great slut you?'

'Ahh!' Claude whimpered and fell back with his fingers pressed to his lips as if wanting to prevent whatever was inside from escaping.

'Are you ill?' Do you want some water?' Eric asked considerately.

'Mmm!'

'You look as though you are going to throw up or something. What about getting out in the open air?

'No, no; too windy and, besides, I must talk to Ms Plumpkin in the interval.'

'Oh, I don't think there will be an interval. This first reading is scheduled to go through to four o'clock, just to make sure everyone has a shared feel for the play. Then they'll break up to work on their lines independently. There'll just be five-minute breaks here and there to take care of biology and parched larynx.'

'But Mandy and I have something we need to settle, something most desperately urgent.'

'You'll be running into trouble with Geoffrey if you're not careful. Is there anything I can do? I am here to iron out difficulties, after all.'

The beleaguered CFO turned to Eric and then to the radiant but distant Mandy who was obviously having the best time of her career. The blue shawl was thrown back over her shoulders and her yellow hair tossed in make-believe sunlight and the parched winds blowing off the endless prairie's rattling cornfields.

'... that I'm the scandal of the countryside, carrying on with men without a marriage licence,' her voice rang defiantly.

'Hell roast his soul for saying it. But it's true enough,' the second man said scornfully.

Claude clapped both hands to his ears and raised his knees, as if there was simply just too much pain in the words for mortal man to endure. In spite of the excruciatingly cold auditorium, sweat had broken out on his bloodless forehead.

'I'll have to make a decision here, if you don't mind. There are rooms upstairs where you can rest and where someone can take a look at you. We don't want our sponsor's representative having a heart attack in the theatre's best seats, now do we?'

The hand Eric took hold of was so firmly clenched to the side of Claude's face that several pulls were needed to prise it free. His next move was even trickier as the hand and arm to which it was attached sprang back whenever Eric's grip relaxed. But after some heaving and puffing and with his head inserted into the stricken CFO's armpit the recently appointed liaison officer struggled upright and dragged his load to the exit.

From deep in the auditorium pit Mandy's crystal tones overtook them.

'That's because I soon get tired of any man and give him his walking papers.'

The speechless body in Eric's arms twitched as if a dagger blow had struck an already wounded heart.

'Just up to the top of the stairs and to the left, then there's a lift and ...'

'So the only hope, he thought, was for me to catch some indecent man, who'd have money coming to him I could steal.'

The unrelenting voice rode in a triumphant finale until cut short by the emphatic 'fftph' of closing acoustic doors.

Beaten into insensibility and incapable of any response Claude hung on the semi-obliging neck.

'Here you go ... up to the next floor. There's plenty of space there where we can take a breather.'

They emerged into a deserted area of low tables and easy chairs lit by a wide expanse of window overlooking the busy traffic convergence below, where grinding processions descended into the cross-harbour tunnel. The Church of Latter Day Saints understood better than most how to insulate their brethren from the turmoil of Hong Kong's frantic journey.

At the first chair Eric dropped the numb body and hauled its two feet across a neighbouring armrest. This was not the sort of task he enjoyed. Responsibility for his own problems was usually put off for as long as possible and until action of some sort became inescapable. Other people's crises were intrusive and he hated having to be involved. But Vernon's financial difficulties and the circuitous course by which he hoped to overcome them had conspired to trap him in a Mormon tabernacle with his father-in-law's near-comatose accountant – he wanted nothing more than to run down to the ground floor and hurry away.

Only his son could have compelled him to such uncharacteristic action and so, calling him for advice, rather than the unsympathetic Sigrid, seemed not only the best way out of a jam, but a just solution.

'Got a bit of a situation here that needs your careful thinking.'

'Huh! Oh, hello, Dad, what's happening?'

Without getting into every detail of why he was caught up with a visiting theatre company or what he hoped to gain from it, Eric moved quickly to the part-time coordinating work for JBO and the present predicament of an unconscious CFO.

'So there you are, I could call an ambulance, or old Odergaard ... The first is way over the top when all that happened was the bastard more than likely fainted, although why I can't work out, as this building's as cold as an ice-box and

... I don't want to drag JBO into anything more or he'll feel its confirmation that I'm an idiot who can't get anything organised.'

'No problem, I was coming into town anyway with Jintana; we were going to buy some cheapies for her to send home. We can stop off at the warehouse and bring someone to pick him up and take him home. What was his name again ...'

'Halt, Claude Halt – one of Odergaard's big wheels, I guess – but doesn't look too impressive with his mouth open and tongue lolling out.'

'... Right, Halt. We're as good as on our way.'

In the hour that passed between the telephone call and Vernon and Jintana's arrival with a company car and driver, Claude Halt had woken twice from his perturbed slumber to stare and cry out: 'No, no, it's just that she'd soften any man's heart' and 'Who would not love her?'

Apparently dazed by the implication of his own words, he pulled fitfully at the buttons on his shirt and sank back into another round of disturbed sleep.

'Just looks like he's had a rough night and is sleeping it off, if you ask me,' Vernon said as he and Jintana observed the suffering figure.

'Sober as a magistrate when he arrived this morning. Got a bit sweaty and yappy, but the rehearsal really seemed to bother him.'

'Been watching Mandy Plumpkin, has he? That's not good. P'raps I should get 'im 'ome to his 'ousekeeper; she'll know what to do for 'im.'

Three pairs of eyes turned to the burly driver, on to whom the problem was now swiftly unloaded.

'Yeah, right, good man,' Eric agreed thankfully. 'Where are you parked?'

'Right at the side entrance here. Up on the kerb, so we shouldn't 'ang about, if you know what I mean.

'Yes, yes, of course. Let's move him then, shall we? Can you take the heavy end? You look better equipped than the rest of us. Vernon, get hold of his feet, and Jintana, the lift, please.'

Now that Anil Patel's finely developed upper body provided the physical means to conclude an arduous episode, Eric's energy recovered.

'Probably best if you back in, Vernon, and you ... er ...'

'Anil.'

'OK, Anil ... Anil? ... Well, that's a coincidence.'

'Why?'

'Well, just before he got bent out of shape Claude Halt here asked if I knew anyone called Anil. Perhaps he was expecting you to pick him up, seeing as you both work at the same place?'

'Really!? I 'ope 'e wasn't and anyway I'm too 'umble. Guys in his position ask for drivers, nothing else ... and staying out of the spotlight suits me fine. Look, let's get 'im in the car and 'ome before he wakes up, shall we?'

'Right, yeah, follow Vernon into the lift holding your end ... be easier to extract our man when we get to the ground floor.'

Back on the street with one arm round the incapacitated CFO the driver leant against the silver limousine and pulled a set of keys from his hip pocket for Jintana to take.

'Open both the back doors; we'll just slide 'im across. I'll drive nice and slow, so 'e won't roll off and wonder what's goin' on.'

Luxury automobiles have many beneficial features, but even the best accommodate prone forms with difficulty.

'You'll have to bend his knees, or he won't fit in,' Vernon suggested.

'Yeah, just squeeze him round here a bit an' tuck his arms in like so an' we'll be ready to roll.'

The CFO was coaxed and chivvied into position.

'Well,' Eric said, 'they'll be waiting for me inside. Don't want to neglect them any longer, so ...'

'I thought you said these were your duties, at least, as far as this job goes?' Vernon asked unhelpfully.

'I'll be OK from here. Is there anything you want me to say back at the office?' queried Anil.

'I'm more or less on the Odergaard payroll as well, so you can leave that with me,' Eric replied.

As befits a man whose livelihood derived from the judicious management of money, Claude Halt resided in an area known as Mid-Levels, which, as the name implied, was not at the top or bottom of anything and offered a comfortable haven to middle-class professionals enjoying middle-class tastes and middle-class incomes, which they spent while living in middle-sized flats, usually with middle-sized families.

In this, as in many other things, Claude was an exception. By virtue of his long and prosperous years with Odergaard Holdings he had amassed a small fortune and, because he had invested it inventively, while having none of the personal responsibilities of most men his age, he could with justification have chosen to live in the greater spaciousness of South Bay, or on the Peak, which rose above the cramped concrete homes of Mid-Levels where every spent penny was counted carefully.

The drive from the Mormon tabernacle on Gloucester Road would take no more than twenty minutes, and before long Anil expected to have returned his unsuspecting rival to the safe custody of a housekeeper on whom the few demands made by an unexciting bachelor imposed negligible inconvenience.

But, on the steep road just below Mid-Levels, the clouds of distress lifted from Claude's brow and shredded wits and he sat up with a start.

'Urh ... what ... and who the devil ... Oh, my suffering head ... Where am ...?'

Anil looked up into his rear-view mirror and the bleary eyes of his passenger.

'You're OK, Sir. I've just picked you up and we are headin' to your 'ome. You've 'ad a bit of a turn and need rest. I called ahead to your 'ousekeeper an' she's waitin' for you with somethin' to settle your stomach. We'll be there soon, so don't worry now.'

'But I was ...?'

'Yeah, you were watchin' some actors rehearsin' for ...'

'Oh God, yes! Mandy ... saying some of the most terrible things no one would believe. I am aghast.'

'Well, no need to worry about that now. Let's just get you 'ome and then ...'

Their eyes met again in the mirror, Anil's half-covered by lazy lids and Claude's racked with pain.

'You ... you work for Odergaard's?'

'Yeah, been there since ...?

'Do you make deliveries to the Harbour Hotel? Answer me! Answer me now!'

'Go wherever I'm told, Sir.'

'And your name, goddamnit, man, give me your name.'

'OK, OK, take it easy now. It's ... er ... Anil ... Anil Patel. But ...'

'Ahhhh!'

Oblivious to the rush of traffic sweeping down the hill, Claude threw open the passenger door and fell into the street. Although the Odergaard driver had been driving carefully, his speed threw the CFO into a roll. A minibus swerved round the fallen man, who, staggering upright, ran across two lanes of vehicles, vaulted a fence into Saint Joseph's Catholic Church and disappeared.

19

The grinding pre-war trams snaking their way between Kennedy Town and Shaukeiwan were, as rickshaws had been in the age of horseless carriages, anachronistic blemishes on the face of a city determined to be one step ahead. In the rattles and bangs rebounding from city skyscrapers stale custom and leapfrogging progress coexisted incongruously. Businessmen and their families travelled in the padded style of private automobiles, while tens of thousands of domestic helpers, the modestly resourced majority and tourist hordes craving novelty were conveyed in varying shades of bone-jarring local colour.

Out of struggling congestion that was midway between a queue and a brawl, Budiwati's wide frame cleared its own path through a turnstile and the jam-packed press of the rear platform, in the way a visiting battle-cruiser jostled a course between Victoria Harbour's sampans and tugs.

By the standards of her home country Budiwati was a tall woman, who, in crowded places, rested her ample chest and arms on the heads of shorter bystanders and avoided air-polluting lower levels with their flavours of manual labour, garlic and unwashed teeth.

The district surrounding Kennedy Town was a long way from the Shatin markets where Budiwati usually shopped. But today's errand was not a typical outing to buy household necessities, which, after so many repetitions, she could have done with her eyes closed. This morning she had been dispatched immediately after the schnauzer's first walk by a strained Mrs Tung, to a place where hardware and plumbing merchants were known to huddle to search for a replacement pilot light for the bathroom gas heater, which, although old twenty years ago, had survived against the odds until last night's inconvenient explosion rendered it inoperable.

'A handyman's the best person to mend it,' Budiwati had advised her employer, while peering into the appliance's soot-stained interior and twisted tangle that once had been an adequately functioning appliance.

Carol Tung, however, was not prepared to allow a stranger's greasy hands unrestricted access to her bathroom, nor was she ready to hear comments, which she knew were inevitable, on why the heater had caught fire in the first place.

'It's overuse I'd say,' the home help ventured.

'Rubbish,' Mrs Tung had countered. 'Who ever heard of heating equipment wanting days off.'

Since her momentous meeting with Isidor Nash at the bus depot, their clandestine retreat to her apartment high above Shatin and subsequent twice-weekly meetings that continued uninterrupted through the late summer and winter, she had alternated between heights of indescribable ecstasy and depths of blackest despair. Racked by the fullest range of emotions she lost all sense of principle and proportion and was condemned to two opposing lives travelling at speeds and trajectories where neither touched. In one and while at his side, she was Isidor's rapturous devotee, singing mental hymns of exultation through every blissful hour that called for repeated shots of poppy juice to stop the spell from breaking.

Down in the other, especially when alone with her thoughts, she staggered and fell into a snake-infested pit of shame and self-loathing and heard above her head hell's gate crash and steel keys grind in locks.

And from somewhere outside this nightmare her maid was making the indecent suggestion another man should be invited into her private rooms to touch her taps and bath and look upon the towel she used to wipe the most secret parts of her person.

'No, no, no,' she had nearly shrieked, 'You will have to go and find a new part and repair it yourself.'

'But, M'am, I don't know nothing about heaters, or how to patch them up!' Budiwati wailed vainly, while inwardly complaining how some folks brought plumbing disasters down on their own necks by letting their minds wander and going to bed before turning off the hot water. Maids, she confided to herself, were not the people to put those mistakes right.

Although her mistress's behaviour had always been odd and often downright lunatic, Budiwati had learned to recognise most changes in the approaching weather, which, like squalls clouding the Java Sea, could be avoided if timely precaution was taken. Urgent visits to the market to remedy sudden shortages of salt or washing powder, or an outing, at precisely the moment thunder was about to break, to collect suddenly remembered dry-cleaning was an often used expedient.

But, while infinitely subtle in her own country way, the one thing she could not do was hold her tongue, and when Mrs Tung's daily ablutions first turned from one to countless scalding showers through the day and night she could not but question the necessity.

'I was wondering about the gas bill, M'am; it must be going through the roof these last months since … since … and I wouldn't want you to be thinking I wasn't looking after the house properly, if you know what I mean. And then there is the effect it might have on you. Too many baths, my grandfather used to say, takes all the oils out of your skin and lets in river fever, especially during rains when mosquitoes are as fat as sparrows round a rice mill and …'

This advice was given a half-day before the bathroom heater incident and just as Carol Tung prepared to leave for a rendezvous with Isidor. She was riding high on excitement and had absolutely no time for the sort of blather always on Budiwati's lips. Her thoughts were on her destination, the hotel off the Chatham Road, where rooms could be rented by the hour, or even less for busy executives juggling crowded calendars.

'Uhh! I don't understand a word you say. If something I must hear, tell later, when I come home.'

'And then there is this.'

The servant waved JBO's severely crumpled photograph over her head. But if she expected thanks for rescuing this once-prized memento from its latest repository in a waste bin under the bathroom sink she was about to be corrected.

'What doing with that?'

'Found it mixed up with tissues and cotton wool and other bathroom rubbish, but I know how important it's been ... seeing that it has been kept under your undies in the top drawer for as long as I can recall, and before I came to the house, too, more than likely, and I don't want you losing it by mistake ... so I tried to straighten it out by running a warm iron over the back and, although it's not as good as new ...'

'Give me!' Mrs Tung seethed.

'Don't worry I can put it back snug and safe and all, if you'll just ...'

The photograph was snatched from Budiwati's well-meaning grip and torn to as many pieces as trembling fingers and fulsome outrage could manage and, to ensure finality to the action, it was flung in the face of the bemused helper.

Mrs Tung turned to go, but, believing her message had not been driven home as vigorously as she required, spun round again and gave the ingenuous helper a slap that resounded round the apartment's walls.

'Will discuss gas consumption later.'

But when Mrs Tung returned from her assignation and had taken yet another scalding shower she was in no sort of mood to discuss household utilities, or anything else that the domestic helper might have wished. In fact, the cycle of the mistress's mood had carried her so far from the dizzying summit of earlier in the day that she had become almost unrecognisable as the same person.

With the fluttering of a cockroach threatened by a rolled newspaper, she slipped out of the bathroom towards her bedroom and past a startled Wai Pang, who was busy at the round dining table with subjects not in the school curriculum.

'Hello,' he called cheerfully. 'Do you want to hear what happened to me today?'

Mrs Tung flinched and looked back at him as if she had been caught shoplifting by a policeman carrying handcuffs.

'Wha –?' she moaned in a voice scarcely her own.

The conversation, however threadbare, brought Budiwati from her kitchen with a smudge of flour on her face.

'Do you want to talk about it now, before I go back to my dumplings?' she asked.

Baying hounds were closing around Mrs Tung and her wobbling cheeks were criss-crossed by lines of tears. Without dropping her distressed gaze she tore herself free and backed into her airless bedroom. The pet schnauzer, which, until its mistress's emergence, had fussed at the steam coming under the bathroom door, dashed determinedly towards its owner and the familiar luxury of a place on her bed, but a foot under its belly and a hoist into the air sent the suffering animal skidding and yelping towards her baffled son and domestic helper.

And that night, after another purgative shower taken when most occupants in the apartment were fast asleep, hot water was left to run and the overheated appliance to burst.

The boom rattled up and down the tower block's metal piping and shook Budiwati from her drowsy thoughts of driving her father's ducks to the paddy field where they fed on frogs spawning in pestilential thousands under Indonesia's seasonal rain.

Strangely, the billowing smoke and abnormal noise disturbed no one in the flat, except the housekeeper. On the far side, in the apartment's un-insulated walls, none was willing to be disturbed, and, inside, the hormone-drenched Wai Pang slept on through the earthquake epicentred metres from his pillow as if it had occurred in another country altogether.

Budiwati shuffled off her mattress below the kitchen sink, expecting her touchy madam to charge angrily from her room in a blur of indignation and scorching blame. But no one rose from their rest and no one knocked at the outside door.

Next morning, before anyone was up, Budiwati walked the pet schnauzer to the corner of the estate and joined other chattering domestic helpers. They shared the usual stories of economic hardship that brought each of them into reluctant servitude; of being parcelled out to employer's relatives in other parts of town and compelled to work illegally in shops and factories; of food and sleep deprivation; of beatings, sometimes by children, and of fines for coming home late. All the tales were of lost dignity and often, when not the speaker's own, almost comic in their exaggerated tragedy.

Her anecdote, of the nocturnal detonation and deafening silence that followed, was a new one that kept the group guessing as to what might happen once the madam rose.

'Won't notice,' said one.

'Make you pay for it,' said a second.

'We're above and heard it,' added a third. 'And everyone was talking when they got up and said whoever was responsible should be fired.'

'She'll bath in cold water and wash away her sins,' suggested the last, and everyone in the group trilled with the sort of laughter only the hopeless can appreciate when confronted by others' repulsive truths.

Retribution Budiwati took for granted, so she had thrown every window wide before returning to bed the previous night and had taken a bucket of soapy water and wire wool to the blackened heater to remove what visible damage could be changed. But, at the end of her labours, she realised a fragmented pilot light was beyond her capacity to amend and nor could she make cold water hot in the quantities required by Carol Tung.

When Mrs Tung did at last drag into sight the next day, she was in a similar condition to the broken heater. Her outward appearance may well have been improved during the night, but internally damage was beyond estimation. In the absence of any alternative remedy to purge her remorse she yearned for another badly needed wash.

'What mean; how can it be broken?' she demanded in rising panic.

Before answering, Budiwati looked at the tortured face; it belonged to a woman standing before the unflinching court of lost causes from where she would be hauled away and stoned in the marketplace for a betrayal of village morals. Was any reply possible, she wondered, that wouldn't get her into trouble?

'The gas, it ran all night long,' Budiwati began slowly, as if looking for barefoot passage over a wasteland littered with flint and thorns, until overtaken by her enthusiasm for monologue.

'Until the fitting got so hot it blew up and filled the house with clouds and clouds of smoke ... I'm surprised you weren't woken ... I'm sure the people upstairs heard it, because their maid told me this morning when I was out walking the dog and we, that is me and the other girls ...'

With both hands pressed against her temples Mrs Tung slumped into the settee, which, over recent months, had witnessed so much that had brought her to this present fevered pitch.

'I need to bathe, not later, now. Boil water, quickly, now, on gas ring in kitchen, as many pans as you can find and fill tub.'

'But can you wait while I find a handyman? He'll be the best person to mend the pilot,' Budiwati had urged.

'No, no, no' was the obdurate reply and so, after toiling to fill the bath and dismantle the old pilot light with tools borrowed from the upstairs domestic helper, she had set off on the mission to Kennedy Town in search of a replacement.

The hunt had taken an interminable time as she passed through a dozen different shops and broken conversations with unhelpful proprietors, until now, with a second-hand part taken from a scavenged unit in the straw bag on her hip, she stood wedged into crowds on a screeching tram threading through a maze of streets and under overhanging viaducts towards Star Ferry and the bus routes back to Shatin.

At each stop a wave of passengers, dressed in the uniforms of Hong Kong's multinational have-nots – soiled vests on elderly men; slippers and stiff collars for their wives; anything remotely fashionable, false designer labelling and garish colour coordinations included, for housemaids, or head-shawls and jeans for their Muslim cousins – disembarked in turn to be replaced as quickly by another identical surge. Bilingual signs pleading consideration for those wishing to get off were left ignored.

With each exchange of humanity, first boarders were pushed closer to the centre, until lucky ones found spaces on lines of hard wooden benches.

Keeping a tight grip on her basket and relieved that the hardest part of her journey was done, Budiwati found a seat and wriggled her full hips in between an immovable matron and an effusive tourist.

'Colourful place, Hong Kong, heh?' the vacationer observed.

To Budiwati the city was many things, frequently modern, more often than not primitive, bewildering, unfriendly, hot as a furnace in summer and unpleasantly cold in winter, oppressive, unforgiving, but 'colourful' was not a word she would have used. She smiled and nodded back.

The mass of standing passengers sandwiched between her and the bench opposite thinned out at the next stop. People on the far side were of the same cosmopolitan appearances found in any other tram. A young office worker of some sort, maybe a salesman, cradled a briefcase on his knees. His grease-marked collar and frayed shirt cuffs suggested difficulty in selling his product. Next to him, a very old man, with white, stubbly hair, held a plastic bag containing a papaya and a bunch of green-stalked onions between his calves. He was either on his way to sell what he had grown, or returning to enjoy a purchase to satisfy a very small appetite.

Further along and on the other side of the old man was a woman in her mid-thirties. At first glance she could have been from Budiwati's homeland; her features certainly had that mark, but the canvas bag with its optimistically brilliant sun motif suggested otherwise.

When she was alone and running errands Budiwati liked to play this guessing game with herself to see if she could decide what country people called home; whether they were single or married and whether those in an identical station in life to her were better off or treated more kindly.

The woman with the sun on her bag caught Budiwati's eye and made her own assessment.

'Indonesian,' Ligaya decided, at the same time as Budiwati determined 'Filipino'.

'Country girl,' thought Ligaya, with a little puff of pride at her small-town origins. 'Just look how short and far apart her toes are; must have grown up on a farm, or in a fishing village.'

'Huh! Filipino maids always dressed better than they can afford just to hide their poverty. Look at her; she's on the tram like the rest of us ... She'll sleep on a shelf over the toilet. At least I have my kitchen floor.'

'How black she is; never been taught to use an umbrella in the sun. Wonder why her hair's not covered like the others? Maybe she's Christian?'

'She'll be working for a foreigner or they wouldn't let her dress like that on a work day. Probably gets her food paid for as well.'

'She'll be working for a local family, who'll have her on minimum wage and make her shop in Kennedy Town to save a penny.'

Their eyes met again until, pretending disinterest, they turned to look at opposite sides of the street.

Rounding the corner at the end of Des Voeux Road the tram clanged through a set of traffic lights and drew to a halt on the edge of Chater Square. Ligaya was off first and in the crowd Budiwati followed some way behind. At the entrance to a tunnel leading under the road towards Star Ferry and the harbour, a man with a lank ponytail greeted Ligaya and took her bag.

'Hello, Lig,' he said. 'Let's get you back in time for dinner.'

Budiwati stood and watched them depart with a frown on her face.

'Perhaps she's living with a foreigner, not just working for one. That shows you just how some girls lose sight of what's right once they are away from their families.'

The woman and the man with the ponytail disappeared into the tunnel chatting amiably and Budiwati, tossing her head disapprovingly, followed on behind.

20

Close to the winter sea, where rocks and vegetation dripped sadly into briny puddles under a weeping heaven, there was no clear distinction between sky, sea and land. The elements had fused into uniform grey and the ocean, despairing of brighter days, heaved round granite boulders as if surface oil subdued its natural vitality.

Above tidal reach, the beach, such as it was, ended in a chaos of broken black rocks, algae-coated litter thrown up by the choking sea and tangles of low green undergrowth, which alone thrived under the great dome's wet shroud.

Nestling among the fragments, a temple's mossed walls and roof blended into the shoreline so completely, they could have been thrown up in the same convulsion that once delivered South China's coast from the abyss.

Scented smoke from a pot of smouldering joss sticks rose into the windless air and, at the entrance to a dank interior, two stone lions roared in mute ferocity. The cold, cloistered temple scowled unwelcomingly as if it was a place few should enter.

Although drenched to his skin and unlikely to get any wetter, Eric took shelter from the rain beneath incessantly dripping eaves. He should have worn more clothes, but hadn't expected the weather to stay inhospitable and, besides, sharp walks near the sea, where humidity hung so heavily, were sticky whatever the season or time of year.

With his back to an unyielding wall and knees drawn together as tightly as the few inches of dry space allowed, he watched disconsolate drops fall around his worn sandals and frighteningly pale feet, where, just above his heels, thin blue veins criss-crossed in the intricate patterns of middle age.

Away to his right and over the rubble-strewn beach and fringe of ragged greenery he could see the low-rising jumble of Sai Kung. Behind and further up the hill was his own house and in the middle of its potted shrubbery a figure dressed in white cheesecloth was bent almost in half. That, of course, would be Sigrid tending to her plants in a never-failing early-morning ritual. Would anyone, other than her, think of watering plants in the midst of a downpour?

The rose petals that once seemed to strew the meadows of their early romance were not as plentiful as they had been. Criticisms surfaced more frequently, and not just in private where the jarring sometimes felt like outright contempt.

What had happened to the time they used to hang on each other's words, when they thought their meetings were steered by gods? Shouldn't the move to the semi-rural world of Sai Kung, which so fitted their refusal to be wage-slaves, have capped a perfect union?

Instead, the adventure had lost its appeal. He had begun to bore her and she exhibited her mother's aloofness and ready tongue, although not, thank God, her evil temper; that would have been too much. As time passed, separate interests drew them apart even while they inhabited the same few square yards of a shabby house they referred to as home. Would another child on top of Vernon have made a difference? Eric doubted it, because by the time they met he was too tired and she too disillusioned by her one ghastly experience of motherhood.

On the beach nothing much stirred except for some wading birds probing the grey ooze for lugworms. But, in the rain-speckled distance, as workers slipped away on bicycles and buses to daytime jobs, a man stepped down from a barnacle-encrusted jetty.

The figure's hand rose to shield its eyes and locate landmarks, before moving slowly, with an umbrella held high, in the direction of the temple.

The upright posture and natural elegance, in spite of a trailing raincoat, were recognisable as belonging to Feliciano. He trod deliberately round shallow pools and over the various bits of muck and rubbish dotting the water's edge, until he came upon his son.

'I thought I'd find you somewhere here.'

'How would Sai Kung's backwaters occur to you; I've never brought you this way?'

'Ah, we fathers have a way of nosing places our sons might find attractive. Ees there room een there for an old man to shelter from this rain?'

A pair of abandoned earthenware pots lay near by and Eric rolled one into the narrow space where he had been sitting, turned it upside down and brushed the earthy underside with his sleeve.

'Try that. Not luxurious, but better than a wet step full of arthritis.'

'Thank you, thank you,' Feliciano said, undoing the one button of his raincoat and wiping at his forehead with a large bandanna. 'One does not search for comfort een such places.'

'Not a great morning to be out walking. What brings you down; don't you enjoy sleeping in anymore?'

'When you have seen as much as eighty years allows, you will realise every morning, whatever the weather, can be considered a blessing. I thank God for giving me time to appreciate so much and for being with my son.'

'You don't have to get wet to be with me, you know?'

'But your house, it ees ... how shall I say? ... too full of women. Your mother, your wife, that lady who does your cleaning and cooking; they all expect something from you and sometimes I wish not to share. You understand my meaning ...?'

'Yeah, yeah. That's why I left early to be out of their way.'

Feliciano folded his umbrella thoughtfully.

'… And I need some time, before we, your mother and I that ees, get ready for our return.'

'Do you have to? It's not as if you have a job or anything; can't retired people take endless holidays?'

'*Si*, my boy, they can, if they have the means, but … there are many reasons … You have your life – I can see that better now we have been here – and sometimes, especially for a mother, a reminder is necessary. You need to be with your wife. She should be the single most important person to you; the same as my wife was for me … Yes, as she *is* for me. And then there is Vernon and, if I do not misread his intentions, he, too, will soon be building something with a woman for whom he feels much devotion and you should enjoy him before eet ees too late.'

'I'll miss you when you go.'

'Yes, yes … eet will hurt too much and eet ees at times like this that I regret you leaving Spain. If you were een the next city, visits would be so easy, but out here, so far away, we have to make do with what we can, no?'

After a momentary lull, drizzle began again and Eric's elbow and shoulder, which hung out of the temple's shelter, now that his father had joined him in the narrow space, were quickly sodden again. The ocean swelled and subsided and waders scurried into muddy patches left by retreating waters.

'Have you not been made welcome?'

'With you I am always at peace. But we can't, nor should we attempt to, preserve our past as eef eet will endure for ever; times must change. Your world ees more complicated than when you left so long ago and we have to recognise what has happened and bend under changing winds.'

Eric's father nodded thoughtfully as if engrossed in the significance of his words. 'And then there ees this place, which you now call home and is beyond my understanding yes, quite beyond.'

Watery mist on the hills drifted lower and ripples on the inlet shrank away. The further side of the headland was so remote it could have been a foreign land.

Behind them a woman, with a brush of palm fibres, backed out of the temple and sent the collection of her efforts, a blackened banana, dead insects and dust, scattering to one side of the open doorway. She took no notice of the two men.

Stirred from his reverie, Feliciano shook his head gently.

'Does she know we are here? Does she mind eef we intrude into her holy place?' he asked.

'Actually, she doesn't care.'

'Ah! In Spain we would have been given a *buenas dias* at the very least, or maybe offered a glass to warm us on such a day. But here,' he shrugged. 'Perhaps that is the difference?'

'We are strangers; what do we matter? She doesn't need to get along with anyone outside her circle. That's why she appears rude to those with different values. But it's not really rudeness; it's just that she doesn't really see us.'

'What eef I fell down sick on the pavement?'

'If you are lucky, someone might call an ambulance. But people here don't understand being alone. You'd be someone's responsibility, so no one else will want to interfere.'

Feliciano threw the loose end of his raincoat over his son's saturated feet and watched rain dropping nosily from the roof into the hollows of its plastic surface. The two sightless lions stared out at the drab bay, and cushion-toed lizards moved silently in the rafters overhead.

'And then there are all these troublesome little rules. You see that one there?' he indicated a red-and-yellow notice on the side of the plinth supporting one of the ceremonial lions. 'Eet will be something like "No Spitting"; as eef people need telling not to spit in church. Ees no one trusted to behave well?'

'Well, as a matter of fact, no, they are not. Society is organised by doing what is beneficial to the family and a sense of Chineseness. There is no concept of universal rights, so the only way to keep people in place is by making regulations, usually of the sort saying what can't be done. Our laws are based on Christian ethics, whether we are Christian or not, but theirs on an unwavering autocracy of three thousand years. We can't expect to think alike.'

The temple custodian's brush shook around shelves and an overhead lintel and a decayed orange, half eaten up by green-and-white mould, rolled out across the sand.

'Shouldn't there be a rule for tossing your rubbish about?'

'Not if no one has thought about it, which leaves people to do exactly as they like. That's why this beach is such a god-awful mess; no one sees it as theirs, except a few environmentalists like me and, as we've seen, our voice isn't heard. It's like wind in the trees or a dog whistle; unless you have the sensitivity for the sound, it doesn't exist.'

The rotten orange received a confused stab from Feliciano's umbrella point.

'So what ees this fruit thing where it ees stuck in the wall even een busy streets? Ees eet an offering to God?'

'Oh, hell no! There is no one god in traditional Chinese culture; that's all folk-law stuff; ghosts and goblins that sort of thing ... a bit like mistletoe and Christmas trees.'

'I don't under ...'

'Of course not, but they've both crept over the sill and into places like this and Spain, that most Catholic of all countries.'

'You seem to understand many things. Are these new traditions ones you share? Have you become absorbed by China?'

The questions trembled on the old man's tongue as if he feared to hear the answer.

'I'm more or less comfortable with who I am, if not always with my circumstances, which is something you could probably say of most people, although I've seen a few others, so jaded by what they'd come from, or so enamoured by what they'd found, that complete absorption seemed to be the only solution. Yes, things might get a bit rough round the edges when Vernon get's into one of his scrapes, or money's tight, but that's life, and even if I was one of those who wanted assimilation the Chinese wouldn't let it happen. There is no integration here; no outsiders are ever admitted however knowledgeable they were of how things are. We float on the surface just like all that litter you see out there on the water. No one cares, or gives a damn.'

'So you live here, but don't live here? Then what is the reason to stay?'

'Because now there's nowhere else to go. All my real experience, as weak as it is, belongs here and besides, I've got Vernon, who was born just down the road and Sigrid. But why are we having this conversation? You know it's not realistic to think about going anywhere else.'

'Yes, yes, I do. Put eet down to a father's wish to see his son more often and to know he ees content.'

Their independent thoughts glided silently back down the decades to a distant point where they had once met and shared the beauty of things.

'When were you last on horseback?'

'Ah! you are thinking of Andalucía in sixty-two, no? That was the first time we were een the same saddle,' he laughed through his nose, 'Only seven, but when the Atlantic sunset shone een your eyes, I knew you were lost to your father in the same way Magellan and Pizarro were lost to theirs. The sea has brought Spain great glory, but the price has been paid in sons that never returned.'

'After that ride with you and Alamar I dreamt of travel. Not to stay in any one particular place, but just to go and see.'

Yes, I knew later when I found you looking at maps instead of doing school work and drawing circles round places with fascinating names that eet would not be long.'

'But the horses; weren't they beautiful?'

'They too were exiled sons. The Moors brought them and changed the face of Spain just as we have changed the Andes and the Pampas.'

'What happened to Alamar and his farm?'

'He's dead long ago. But the farm ees still there; owned by cousins living een Cordoba. A tenant works the land and sells something he calls boutique wine; not the Oloroso of the old days. I haven't visited since Mares died, but we hear news now and again.'

'And riding?'

'In Madrid it ees not possible on a pension, so we stay at home most of the time and visit with our friends.'

'Once you were active in politics. What happened?'

'When you were young only a generation had passed since the Civil War; every family had lost someone and still felt pain. But now no one remembers and, on rare occasions when I am asked we seem like history books; nothing remains for today when we are all good Europeans.'

'You are too full of regrets.'

'No, I would not say so, but there comes a time when you move slower and the world rushes by. You are left knowing what you know. Eighty years does not count to a person of twenty, but to the great Captain who has seen our duty eet will matter as much as anything written this morning.'

'Then if not regrets then sadness, to which I have contributed more than I should?'

'Eet ees like this, every father, and mother too, wants happiness and friendship for their children, but none of us live lives searching for such things. We are by nature discontent, which ees why we are never still and eef we are restless how then can we be happy? Eet ees a conundrum; we are impossible creatures who find no peace on earth, which ees why we should not try to make eet more difficult than eet already ees.'

The custodian shuffled from the temple's interior carrying a plastic shopping bag from a local grocery store and with great difficulty subsided to her knees. She took out several items of fruit and arranged them haphazardly on a dish at the foot of a guardian lion. New incense sticks were forced through the skin of an apple and orange and lit by a fifty-cent lighter. Not wanting to waste the flame she inserted a yellow cigarette in her mouth and inhaled deeply. Sharp smoke scoured through her lungs and provoked a purple-faced coughing fit into her clenched fist.

Feliciano jumped from his upturned ceramic pot.

'Oh, my dear, she ees going to choke ... ,' he began.

'Hang on a minute; she will wonder what's going on if you grab hold of her.'

'But we can't just leave her; go inside and see eef you can find some water.'

Before Eric reappeared from the temple's interior the woman's attack had passed and, with the help of the lion's head she rose unsteadily to her feet, hawked deep inside her rattling chest and spat noisily. The lighter was returned to her plastic bag and her mouth wiped on her jacket. As Eric returned with a half-full cola bottle containing cloudy rainwater the custodian left about her own business, limping rheumatically away in the direction of Sai Kung and clusters of makeshift housing lining the opposite end of the inlet.

'Doesn't look like she needed help after all,' Eric observed and splashed the contents of the bottle over the ground.

'No, but that was not so pretty and maybe the notice said not to spit ...?'

'You speculate; there's no way for us to know what it said. And even if you're right, spitting doesn't matter, because, the way she sees it, there's no one here to notice. If it's any help you could view it as a statement, not of scorn, but of our thorough irrelevance. It happens all the time and you have to live here to understand.'

'I can say this visit has shown me many things. One is that only now do I appreciate some of what eet means to be een a foreign country. Before, I had no idea; your mother, even less. But, more importantly, I see your experience has been entirely different and, whatever doubts you have about your achievements, you can teach this old man many things; just as many, perhaps, as I was able to teach you when you were a boy. For that I am gratified; you are in every sense a man.'

Uninhibited by mothers and wives, old Feliciano threw his arms round the younger man's neck and cried into the greasy ponytail.

'Come on, Dad, or you'll have me getting sentimental, too, and I'm not used to that.'

'I know, I know, but I am your father and cannot apologise for holding you een my heart.'

'Look, let me hold the umbrella and we can walk back. There's something I want to show you at home ... some drawings from an old pupil ... one in particular ... said it was of a football coach or something. He knows I'm interested in such things ... That's why I'm helping out at the festival and why I've got caught up with Sigrid's dad, although it's a lot more complicated than that. But I won't weary you with details. Anyhow, there are these sketches and I'm thinking of using them for advertising and want an intelligent opinion without any weird biases and you're the best bloke around.'

'My day would be made eef my advice ees still valuable to you.'

Along the beach's negligible slope the receded waters had exposed flats on which previously floating rubbish now lay strewn. Steady rain overtook the early-morning drizzle and further away the temple's caretaker swayed erratically from side to side, like a giant panda shambling over unfamiliar ground. On a roof on the far side of Si Kung the white back of a busy woman bobbed between straggling wet plants.

21

When Mrs Tung returned from her outing, the ugly button of her mouth was more tightly compressed than ever. Wai Pang and Budiwati read the sign and said nothing. The schnauzer, having learned the folly of inattention to change, sheltered under the kitchen sink and waited to be called.

When the door crashed open and the mistress hurtled into the apartment, all three sat up. Stressed hinges groaned and a screw pinged clear of its corroded hole to bounce and roll under the shelves supporting the flatulent lucky-Buddha and meagre book collection.

Subjected to the intensity of his mother's withering stares, Wai Pang wondered whether there would ever be a convenient, never mind a good, time to share the news of his portrait's success. Would she, could she, take pride in his accomplishment and praise him for his drawing of Isidor Nash, which was now destined for display up and down the territory?

When his selection of sketches had been sent to Eric Manley he hoped for nothing more than some thoughtful and possibly educated views on whether they were any good and, if they were, suggestions for developing the talent on which he'd set so much hope. Although enthusiasm, he accepted, was not a substitute for being any good, hearing what others had to say would shed light on whether his eye and hands held the future he felt so necessary.

There was none among his relations, least of all his mother, who would be prepared to sanction a career in art, even if his ability was extraordinary, so how could he gain worthwhile guidance from any of them? Other than his old schoolmaster, who could he trust to give an objective opinion? The others would simply throw a fit and tell him to stop daydreaming and get on with studying subjects that would help him discharge his family obligations and support his coming adulthood.

'You and your father are two of a kind; neither of you can concentrate on real work, or what a proper job takes,' he could almost hear his mother saying.

The only other possibility was Isidor, who had opened windows and let in astounding surprises, but who, Wai Pang knew, had nothing else to commend him, whatever he might have said. Only a goat would believe a herdsman's blandishments, when the flock was being driven towards the milking shed.

In his careful process of elimination and without any awareness of Eric's involvement in the Arts Festival, Wai Pang had sought help and was later astonished to hear that Eric had proposed one of his sketches as the marketing image for the posters and fliers for the approaching Hong Kong Arts Festival. In the coming months, his drawing of Isidor Nash would hang from every Kowloon and Hong Kong Island lamppost and land in hundreds of family post boxes across the territory.

Astonished, however, was a gross misstatement of how he felt following Eric's call. He was, more accurately, stunned, elated and walking on air. Nothing he had ever experienced, not even the first crazy night with Isidor, had thrilled him so absolutely and, in the middle of his bus ride to school the following day, he suddenly cried out with joy and slapped his knee, while other commuters wondered whether he was someone they should sit near.

Was this it, then? Was this going to be the real thing? And if it was, what had violin and extra maths lessons got to do with anything now?

But, although he had steeled himself to make the confession, no, not confession, revelation, tonight, the time to tell his mother never seemed exactly right.

In anticipation, he had done everything possible including, rehearsing what to say on Budiwati, but her mind was on her cooking and preparation of the evening meal and a distracted home help was a poor substitute for a precariously balanced parent, so his wish for the faint praise that is every child's right passed unsatisfied.

'Yes; hmm ... that's nice,' Budiwati had said absent-mindedly. 'But you look as if you're running a temperature. Should I make some vegetable soup? Easier to digest than the meat balls I've got in the pan.'

'No, no, I'm fine, really I am,' he had said despairingly. 'And not just OK; the fact is, I've never felt better, although just a little put out that there's no one to talk to here, that's all.'

If Wai Pang had been better acquainted with the causes of his mother's swinging moods, he might well have concluded she deserved his understanding when their situations had, at one level, something, or someone, in common, although, deeper down, their inspirations sprang from differing roots and they were as unlike as any strangers on opposite sides of town.

Unknown to Mrs Tung's family, which, for purposes of the Shatin flat, included only her son and pet schnauzer, she had, that morning, taken yet another day's leave to share covert moments with Isidor, for whom employment was as confining as sexual discrimination once was. In the latter part of the afternoon they left the shabby precincts of the Nice Hotel and strolled arm in arm towards the Kowloon waterfront, which, because it had brought them together, held a special place in her memory, if not his.

'Remember how we met?' she asked, as if the question required prodigious efforts of recall from distant periods of time, when, in fact, the event in question had taken place no more than four months previously. But, not to be denied her sentimental vision others would label a joke, she continued.

'You strode round; very intense. Thinking of your mother and father, or your job? Oh, I don't know – whatever men think about when alone. Then sat down next to me, smiled and immediately I knew you were special, so special.'

Although his conquest of this woman was a unique occurrence, Isidor was not about to lose his head and glorify it as anything other than another bucking yarn of the sort attracting snorts of laughter from blokes around the bar.

'Really? Could have fooled me; I thought I was just sniffin' abaht.'

'Very handsome in puffed lace shirt and violet trousers ... best-looking man on promenade.'

'Yeah, you're right on the money there, my dear, even if I ses so myself. 'Cept the tra'sers have gawn for a near bleedin' Burton and' – here he touched at the long wounds still furrowing his gaunt cheeks – 'my face ain't as creamy smooth as it used to be.'

Over the muffled surging of waves in the piles beneath the Kowloon pier, streamers on a twisting line of masts snapped and flapped furiously.

'Would you take me to theatre?' Carol Tung asked brightly, as if her suggestion was as natural as breathing.

'Yer what?' he said, startled out of his venal wits.

'A concert; not Chinese music. Understand if you don't like. But have all sorts this time of year.'

'Any rock and roll perchance?' he asked facetiously.

Her face showed no sign that the jest had been appreciated, so inevitably her reply was matter-of-fact.

'Not at Festival; all quite serious. See poster up there ... from a play perhaps and being used to ... to ...'

Her sentence ran out of words and she starred at the wind-tossed banner before starting again.

'... Clothes different, but picture looks like ...?'

Her vacuous prattle went unheard by Isidor while his eyes wandered unrestrainedly over young women, students and domestic helpers on errands and other business outings. Now that he had a woman in tow, even one as unappetising as

Carol Tung, his confidence and conceit bound optimistically ahead.

'What else yer got in mind, bit o' rappin' or sunnink?' he teased again.

'That picture, looks like ...'

Amid its bold lines a crooked man's portrait hinted at an equally crooked spirit. Such colour as had inhabited Isidor's bleak features drained away completely and his grip on Mrs Tung's fingers tightened until her knuckles cracked like New Year fireworks, just as his had done during their first meeting.

'Fer fuck's sake, that cupcake's got me hangin' up all over the frigin' pier. When I get 'old of 'im, the little sod, 'e'll get 'is pencils shoved right up 'is bleedin' arse!'

'Then ... it is you?' Carol Tung wailed. 'But why up there and why so ugly?'

Isidor curled a forefinger over the end of his sweating nose and squeezed, as if the action would add to his ability to concoct a plausible explanation. But, finding none, he decided expressions of ignorance would best help him wriggle out of a dodgy state of affairs.

'Frankly, I'm buggered if I know.'

'But I don't understand!'

'Me neither darlin'.'

'What will you do?'

'Er ... dunno, but 'ow about I get you on your way and enquire what's goin' on?'

An investigation of any sort was the last thing Isidor planned. His priority instead was just to get rid of this bit of fluff that had suddenly become a burr.

Why was it, he wondered, birds have so many questions, when all a lad wants is a bit of fuckin' around wivout any complications?

'Look,' he continued, 'off you go now and leave this to me an', if it'll please you, I'll make a couple of phone calls.'

Not for the first time, or because of a single emotion, Carol Tung's pricking eyes brimmed with tears.

'It's not fair; who could have done this without you knowing. You'll do something? Promise?'

'Yeah, yeah, as soon as you are on the road I'll set abaht it ... Sure I will. Now for fuck's sake, get goin', will yer?'

Excepting the violent termination of their first encounter every farewell had followed a similar course. Amidst her expressions of enduring love she clung to his arms and neck, while he, all bristles, buzz and bravado, was the boar in the mud that had had his way with a sow in season. On those occasions, after her fingers had been unwound from his hair and clothes, and her gross, last-second intimacy of squeezing blackheads from his cheeks with a handkerchief smelling of mildew had been brushed aside, he patted her on the backside and steered her towards the start of her halting journey to her other life in Shatin.

On the road, with each passing mile, she dropped in painful degrees from the shock of the Festival poster, to despondency and fretfulness, until, disembarking at the depot, her head spun in horror at the awful certainty she had become a whore. Her commissions were cruel enough, but when compounded by the ignorant gazes thrown at her, by her son and domestic employee, she fell into a well of despair almost beyond endurance.

'Sheesh, bleedin' 'ell!' Isidor muttered at the forlorn wave from the lower deck of the cross-harbour bus. 'Don't they drone on when all that's goin' down is just a bit of slap and tickle? ... After all that, I think I've earned a jar or three.'

Before all the passengers were seated and Carol Tung's vehicle pulled away he had left the waterfront to merge inexorably into the teeming millions moving through the byways where Chatham Road drops off into an unregulated maze of hairdressers', bars, brothels and shops selling all manner of fake and pirated goods, from cameras to high fashion. As he set briskly about the rest of his day, she reeled from the mind-numbing wrench of separation, as if she had been a limpet prised unwillingly from a rock by a fisherman's callous knife, and the dreadful thoughts of what she had become.

On this one afternoon, with puffs of indignation confronting the amazed countenances of Wai Pang and Budiwati, she flounced, with better than usual diction, into the centre of the living room.

'What is it, I'd like to know,' she boomed histrionically, 'that allows a good man's reputation to be hijacked and mocked, yes, mocked in public for the sake of entertainment?'

Her son and the domestic helper floundered, knowing from long experience that unsatisfactory, or no, answers often led to more rounds of chastisement. But, before retreating into the security of her domain to delay, or avoid, the falling cudgel, Budiwati attempted to curry favour.

'The new pilot is in the heater; you'll be able to take as many hot showers as you like and for tonight I've done vegetable soup, meat balls and noodles, as I thought you'd like something to keep your strength up what with all your running about and him not feeling well and ...'

A mass murder's glazed eye fell on the hapless cook, consigning her to immediate and irrevocable quiet, but not before the home help considered the possible option of running screaming from the house before a meat cleaver hissed though her hair. Mindful, however, of the monthly remittances that sent nephews and nieces to school in far Indonesia, she smothered the remains of her recitation and stepped backwards over the pet schnauzer into her tiny kitchen.

'Couldn't he sue for slander or libel?' volunteered Wai Pang as if he had been researching an answer in a volume of legal precedent, when all along his preference had been to say nothing and join the domestic in a recess behind the refrigerator.

Mrs Tung's enraged stare swivelled round to her impertinent son, while she pondered on the merits of another fulsome whipping.

'Stupid boy!' she exclaimed and dealt the table on which his elbows rested a harsh blow. 'And serve the meat balls in my room at seven thirty precisely. Do you hear me?' she roared towards the hidden cook.

Following his mother's verbal cannonade and the banging of her bedroom door, from under his exercise books littering the table Wai Pang pulled out a copy of his Arts Festival poster and a letter Budiwati had given him when he had returned from school that afternoon.

He had desperately wanted to share the poster with his mother; the one achievement, excepting his brief moment of glory on the football field, from so many unexceptional days in an endless and purposeless schooling. He was glad still to be in contact with his old English tutor who alone knew of drawing's attraction and had opened the way for this single work to be used to such rewarding effect. But, apart from Eric Manley and some of the remoter people working at the Festival, there was no one who had the least inkling of who Wai Pang was and what he could do. A mother really ought to share her child's success even in activities for which she had no liking. Wasn't the fact that he was her child enough? Shouldn't he and what he was be sufficient, and shouldn't she love him just for his own sake and not for when his interests coincided with hers and his behaviour was as she liked?

But the letter was different and not something he wanted to share, although, knowing Budiwati, she had probably worked out what the contents were long before passing them along. And, like her, Wai Pang had also looked at the back and front of the plain white envelope in the way people do, as if suspense and guessing the origin were an essential part of receiving an unidentifiable communication.

'She was Chinese, but not from Hong Kong … It was the way she dressed and spoke … When you've grown up on a farm you know how country people are … although she wasn't brown like at home … just had very red cheeks … looking like a doll …

From the mainland I'd guess … somewhere miles from anywhere. But fairly tall and slender … good looking, some would say. Most particular to make sure I knew you … The old man selling sweet potatoes and things by the bus depot pointed me out to her … Could be from someone your father works with, perhaps?'

The envelope bearing Wai Pang's name and nothing else was so flimsy it could have been empty. The boy had taken off his glasses and used an earpiece to open the cover, which fell apart rather than tore, as if it had been held for a long time in a perspiring hand.

With the crash of his mother's bedroom door still ringing in the overhead light fittings and metal pots suspended on kitchen nails, Wai Pang made up his mind about something and he shoved everything on the table, other than the white envelope, back into his school bag.

'I suppose Mama won't want to talk much tonight, so I'll slip out for a while. If she does ask, say I've gone to buy some … er … pencils and will be back soon. OK?'

'She'll want to know why I wasn't sent,' Budiwati remarked, pointing to the essential flaw in Wai Pang's stratagem.

'Urm … say these are, well, special pencils used in … er … geometry, that's it, geometry, and you wouldn't know what they were.'

The home help put her head on one side.

'Geometry … I see. Then would you want me to get rid of that letter in case she finds it in your pocket later and thinks you went out to meet someone instead of buying pencils?'

'Oh! Do you think she'll …?' he stuttered.

'You'll know your mother better than me, but if I were you …'

'No,' Wai Pang decided, after overcoming the fear of embarking on yet another unendorsed excursion. 'No, I'll need it for now … Later, maybe, you can … Tell you when I come back.'

Instead of calling the lift to the thirty-fifth floor where its protestations would clang and shake across the flat like a battlefield tank, he sped down numerous flights of fire stairs to emerge several floors below, where his mother's weakened state would not be put to greater stress than it had already endured. Once encased in tarnished chromium, Wai Pang read the message a second time.

'Bringing you Father's news. Please to meet on Friday or Saturday at Poon Woon Tea House, Yau Ma Tei side. There all days. Best meeting alone.'

When Budiwati had first given him the envelope and watched his lips mouthing the few words it contained, she knew intuitively they concerned Man Kit, who had not been seen at the Shatin flat for well over eighteen months. Why else would an unknown Mainland Chinese woman of only slightly fewer years than his mother want to contact the boy? And now, with his abrupt resolve to leave in spite of the late hour and hastening night, she nodded to herself in quiet certainty.

Although unknown to Wai Pang, the Poon Woon Tea House was not difficult to find in the few square kilometres of the warren of Yau Ma Tei, where another energetic sector of Hong Kong's untaxed economy thrived. Enquiries, directed at the half-clothed men on whose unscheduled labour local prosperity depended, pointed past a Cantonese restaurant, a butcher's and a mechanic's shop. Tables and chairs crowded with bowls of soup and loud customers, racks of bloodily dripping pork pieces bathed in appealing pink light, and parts garnered from a hundred different motor wrecks intermingled on the pavement.

Wai Pang wound through the frantic industry, over a recently dismantled automobile engine and gear box and the straggling roots of leafless trees, which clung permissively to a stone wall, so that neither risked collapsing into the thoroughfare. On a sign nailed to a lower branch he read 'Poon Woon Tea House'.

A cat, following close behind Wai Pang on fussy, tiptoeing paws, fled in panic at the sudden crash of broken glass, although the noise was not noticeably louder than most of the others in the street's colossal hullabaloo.

'*Mo ah!*' the tea house's plump owner complained, before he unhooked a hose and sprayed the bits into the gutter.

Ricocheting droplets from the rough jet fell over Wai Pang's school shoes and he wondered what Budiwati would make of the markings next morning.

'Sorry, sorry,' the man with the hose said.

Wai Pang looked up at the round countenance and two tiny points of light hidden in its fleshy folds. Local folklore was full of such smiling faces and the good luck they were supposed to bring, although the one kept on his mother shelves had not noticeably enhanced her family's fortune.

'Aahah! ... you Man Kit boy?'

'Yes, how ... ?'

'Expecting.'

The hose was returned to its hook on the wall's flaking masonry and a soiled rag whisked across the surface from where the glass had fallen.

'Then you know who I am here to see?'

'Yes, sure, my sister; she know you come.'

'Is she in?'

By way of an answer the host called out.

'Ah Ko! Ah Ko! He come ... Man Kit boy come.'

None of the labourers sipping tea and spitting leaves from the tips of their tongues looked up or stopped their chatter, but somewhere in the shop's interior a hush fell as if curtains had been drawn to muffle traffic sounds from someone with a headache.

From out of heaped plywood chests and tea-making apparatus a woman emerged, pushing her hair into an elastic band. A year ago Wai Pang might have said she was pretty, but these days he was not quite sure what he was to make of any girl.

'I've come about this,' he said, holding out the note given by Budiwati.

'Yes,' she relied simply. 'Come to back.'

He followed her through the narrow length of the tea house and up a flight of open stairs through which he could see the lights, but not hear the noises, from the outside street. In a room combining the functions of an office, storeroom and bedroom more cartons, marked with Chinese lettering and holes made by loading hooks, lined the walls. One, with several pads of receipts and clipped vouchers on its sagging surface, served as a makeshift desk. A folded divan with a yellowing sheet stuck in its folds was thrust into a gap between two towering stacks as if the tiny space had been designed for just such a purpose. Subtle aromas of tea struggled for recognition through the harsher odour of dried fish. The smells were not only in the air, but radiated from the packing cases, the walls and the woman's hair and faded denim clothes.

'You have news from my father.'

'Your father good man and ... and he miss you much ...'

The declaration seemed to affect the woman more than the boy and, while he blinked impassively, her voice broke off and she reached inside her pocket for a tissue.

'Will he be coming home soon?'

Unable to contain herself, the woman turned away and leant against the wooden wall to weep in muted heaves. Wai Pang had grown up surrounded by uncontrolled emotion and had come to regard it as the way families were, but this overwhelming grief was something new. He wanted to comfort Ah Ko, but was not sure whether he had that sort of consent until, stepping closer, he detected through the reek of fish and tea a gentler scent that carried with it hints of a woman who had once known love.

She was almost exactly his height and at eye level he could see downy threads of black hair on her neck that were too short to be caught up in the elastic band. He raised a hand to stroke them together, but just as he was about to touch her he paused and wondered if he was overstepping some hidden mark. Before the answer was clear, she spun round and threw her arms round him.

'He good man … Must never forget,' Ah Ko blurted out.

The suggestion that a father could at any time be forgotten was outrageous. But he knew instantly she had a greater story to tell.

'Forget? Why should I forget? Has he done something terrible?'

'Terrible yes, and beautiful, but now gone.'

'Where to? Is he in jail?'

'Jail?' Ah Ko snorted. 'I in jail; he gone for ever.'

'You mean he's … ?'

All of existence should be an unbroken circle and have no end. Death in a distant place beyond the reach of family was inconceivable and too final. Wai Pang's body grew limp and cold in the woman's embrace and only her firm grasp kept him from falling to the floor.

'He loved you much … same as little brother.'

There are limits on how much information an unexpectedly shocked mind can absorb and the news that he had a brother made no initial impression. Ah Ko took Wai Pang's lack of response as readiness to hear the tale she wanted to relate.

'Man Kit came Hubei, not happy. Many problems … factory losing money … workers steal, no right working … Came our restaurant, first weekly, then daily, then morning and night, too … Sat thinking, not talking, watching street, cyclists, walkers, people from countryside. Long time say nothing … took food, tea … paid, kept coming … never look up … never smile. Later, many weeks after, ask name … told Ah Ko … he nodded. Next time asked about family … met brother … same one downstairs. Walk by river … me just poor girl … heard about Hong Kong wife … but liked … came little emperor … your brother … seven years old now … look same you … same Man Kit. Then bad heart thing … in arms when happen … no doctor … no help … Took from neck this … said must give Wai Pang.'

She opened a hand and held it in front of the boy's ashen face and tight-shut eyes.

'I can't, can't ...' he stammered.

'But must ... see ... he want for you.'

The woman pulled herself free and helped Wai Pang to sit down on the improvised desk and its assorted paperwork and with the end of her blouse wiped the boy's dry forehead.

'Man Kit last word ... give Wai Pang ... give Wai Pang,' she repeated.

She lifted his clenched fist from where it pressed down hard on his knees and lowered it gently into her own open palm until the white knuckles touched a thin black neck-cord and a silver ring inlaid with chips of blue and red stone.

The fist crept slowly open before closing again over Ah Ko's slender fingers. Wai Pang unfolded from the agony in which he had been plunged and a faint tinge of colour, like the arrival of a winter sun in the highest latitudes, crept imperceptibly back into his lips and the compacted furrows around his eyes.

'I thought ... I thought this was lost long ago. It was a game we played, you know, when I was small. He used to leave it with me when he went away and said I was to be the man of the house until he returned and then I'd have to give it back.'

'Perhaps he say, when footsteps stop you continue.'

'It was on his neck when ... when ... he died?'

'Yes, wore all time. When little emperor came I said take off. He said no ... not now, only at right time.'

Wai Pang stood up and, taking Ah Ko's head in his hands, kissed her hair. The smells of the tea house seemed to have disappeared and only the odours of a woman were left.

'Thank you ... thank you for bringing the ring back and for giving me news of my father. I'd like, if we can meet again, to see my brother. Will you tell me when both of you are here?'

'Are sure you want?'

'Oh, yes ... I'm quite sure.'

Their two hands were still clasped over the ring, but now, with her mission complete, Ah Ko withdrew hers and backed away several paces to a more considerate distance. Taking the cord from her, he lowered it into place round his own young neck and, after lifting up and inspecting the ring, he touched it to his mouth before dropping it from sight inside his shirt.

'Will stay … drink tea?'

'That would be nice, but I should go.'

Instead of making straight for the mass transit railway station at Yau Ma Tei and a rapid return to Shatin, Wai Pang wanted time to think about what he had sometimes suspected, but had only now confirmed.

The troubles Ah Ko described had weighed heavily on his father. Yes, there were the difficulties of his job in Hubei with undisciplined labour, but there was more, much more, including an unsatisfactory family, or more precisely an unsatisfactory wife who had been abandoned in Hong Kong. To compensate for what he had been unable to find with her he had spent the years rebuilding a kind of parallel life, but in all the faithlessness and confusion the one strand that had not broken had held him fast to Wai Pang.

For that the boy would forgive his father anything, including the absences, the lack of provision and the bitterness left to a rejected woman that finally engulfed everyone who remained in the Shatin apartment. Wai Pang put his hand to his chest and rubbed the ring through his shirt as if it contained a wish waiting to be granted.

Without having consciously chosen any direction after leaving the tea house, or worrying about how late the hour, he realised he had made his way along exactly the same route to the Kowloon waterfront as the one he took from his Sunday morning violin lesson. Across the water of Victoria Harbour, the lights along the north shore of Hong Kong Island glittered like coloured gems on an eastern potentate's encrusted turban; on this side fashionable crowds, disgorging in groups from each arriving ferry, made their way past the clock tower and under wind-stretched flags towards the theatre and concert halls of the annual Arts Festival, while, in between, the unchecked sea stirred.

The snap of metal on a hollow pole stirred Wai Pang from his thoughts. He looked up at a banner and saw his drawing of an angst-ridden Isidor Nash repeated many times along the entire waterfront.

'If only Papa was here,' he thought. 'He would have been proud of me.'

22

'I suppose you are enjoying this?'

Dagmar gestured at the rush of well-groomed theatregoers swarming from the auditorium towards the interval bar and the restorative benefits of house wine and cellophane-wrapped sandwiches, but her disapproval, while superficially applying to what was visible, incorporated the entire theatrical event and, for good measure, everything remotely theatrical.

'Oh God! Here we go again,' complained Sigrid.

'If a thing hurts too much, my approach would be to stop doing it,' Eric Manley observed to anyone who required a point of view.

Inside the glass-fronted private room opening-night celebrity guests were meeting members of the Arts Festival Organising Committee. The principal sponsor, his wife and daughter and his son-in-law, acting in multifarious capacities of clan hanger-on, liaison officer and JBO's sleuth, progressed, with a PR lady's assiduous help, along a line of obsequious organisers keen to demonstrate the right level of gratitude for a key donor owning an important commercial enterprise.

Not content with the bit part assigned to her, the professionally well-versed, but otherwise sadly out-of-touch, PR lady thrust herself into the greasy *mélange*. Preserved in expensively acquired and lavishly applied perfume, she was not as appealing as she fancied, as the wrinkled noses round her affirmed.

'Air, I need air,' Dagmar moaned to her husband, as the PR lady breezed by gushing extravagantly and Claude Halt wrung her wilting hand.

'Wasn't that just out of this world?' enthused the Committee Chairman as he yanked Mrs Odergaard towards confidential conversation. 'And the leading actress ... divine ... My head spins, literally spins.'

The remark, confided as incontrovertible fact brooking no discussion, fell on perplexed ears.

'Is he OK?' JBO asked Eric, standing a little way to the rear. 'I know he's annoying, but he usually makes some sense and, in God's name, what has happened to his hair?'

The VIP, normally disinterested in matters of human comportment outside job performance, was not alone in detecting his employee's bizarre behaviour. Lesser members of the committee, who had not supported the Provo International Theater Company's return, had begun asking questions about procedural correctness and the proper authority to support decisions taken on the Festival's behalf. In their indirect and behind-the-scenes way they had started to wonder if their chief representative was playing a self-serving game unconnected to the well-being of one of the city's showpiece events.

'Yeah,' Eric agreed, 'he had an attack of some sort at the first rehearsal and hasn't got over it yet. It's like he thought the actors were real and not just up on the stage reading lines. Weird for a bloke you'd expect to be a bloodless reptile. He hasn't been around much since, but, whenever he does come over, he looks half off his head.'

'So you're saying I've got a lunatic managing my money? But tell me this,' said JBO, drawing Eric away from the assembly of fawning well-wishers, 'how's he getting on with that Plumpkin woman?'

'Seems to me she's part of his problem,' the liaison officer began, before being interrupted by Dagmar's off-stage complaining.

'I really wasn't taking that much notice,' she said.

'But surely you saw how ...'

'Claude! Let go of my wife, will you? She's stressed enough without you adding to it.'

'I am not in the least bit stressed and wish you would stop acting as if I can't answer for myself.'

Dagmar's mood was once again tottering on the cliff edge and in danger of falling on everyone in the vicinity.

'I was merely remarking to your good lady here that there is no knowing about talent until it's put to the test. Believing in it is never enough. Who would have thought, for instance, that I, with my head full of accruals and provisions, had an eye, a really good eye I might say, for acting potential?'

'You get my point,' Eric whispered to his father-in-law. 'As far as Mandy Plumpkin goes, I haven't seen him so much as talk to her, but you can see he thinks she's pretty marvellous and takes all the credit for what she's doing.'

'And,' JBO said, turning to Claude, 'if you'd had a career farming ostriches in South Africa, who would have discovered you could balance books? Look, I don't expect there'll be any surprises in what's left of this thing so, unless you intend dropping a chandelier on the stalls, or setting fire to the boxes, we'll be heading off. Let's catch up on Monday and assess where we are and draw a line under all this support nonsense. We don't want to get involved in another one of these things; it just eats up cash and keeps you away from what I pay you to do.'

'But ... you can't ... not halfway through ... when ... after all ... she'll get ... I can assure you ...'

'I don't understand a word. Can anyone tell me what he's saying?' JBO's voice rose to include bewildered members of the committee, caught juggling iced drinks and keeping opinions to themselves. In the loaded hush the guest of honour, assuming he was not going to be enlightened, concluded his perfunctory speech with an unapologetic 'In that case we're out of here.'

'Were Mr and Madam Odergaard not entirely satisfied with the production?' the PR lady whispered at Eric's side.

'Let's put it this way,' he explained, noticing the growing trickle of theatregoers returning to their seats, 'both have so many things to take care of that doing all of them justice needs more hours than the days actually contain. That's why people like me are brought in to see things through, you see? And while I think about it I should really check on Mr Halt, who seems to have sloped off somewhere, so if you'll excuse me?'

As he reversed away from the scented canopy she lifted a glass of sparkling mineral water in appreciation of the shared confidence. Co-conspirator in her profession was a much appreciated status.

The Arts Festival Organising Committee Chairman had found refuge from his mental agony in a corner of the glass-fronted reception room, where he mumbled to himself, like an oppressed infant counting the red vehicles passing his window, to assuage unspecified feelings of guilt. Behind the concentric circles of spectacles that were his windows on to computerised spreadsheets and financial, rather than personal, health, his eyes were wide and wild and on their periphery jagged red lines, of the sort cartoonists draw, pulsated ominously.

'I can't understand why, when we are witnessing a performance of such class, why … that man, with all his … all his … can be so needlessly offensive and … and …'

'Let's not get carried away here,' advised Eric. 'You've known him a lot longer than I have and must realise what he's like. He comes on a bit strong sometimes and isn't into literature and all that, especially something of this … niche variety, which, if you'd have asked me yesterday, I wouldn't have expected to strike much of a chord with anyone around here, although I'll concede it's going down better than expected and likely to find favour in tomorrow's papers. So let's see how things work out … if you get what I mean.'

'But just look at those faces out there … absolutely rapt … Never seen anything like it … and nothing … nothing like … her.'

Claude turned his frantic gaze from the knots of people streaming back into the auditorium and grasped at Eric Manley's linen jacket.

'Hey, mate, not so rough! ... I've only got one of these.'

'But you're a teacher, aren't you, and more appreciative than a block like Odergaard? What do you say about her performance? Have you ever seen anything remotely comparable?'

'You're talking about the actress ... Mandy Plumpkin, is that it? I realised there was an interest, but not ...'

'Of course it's not the play; the play's nothing; an abnormality at best; a mere provincialism. I don't know how we got landed with it. All alcoholism, violence, filial disrespect, broken families – who in Asia would warm to such tripe? But even poor material can blossom in the hands of the truly accomplished?'

'Are you by any chance managing her career in your spare time?'

A bell rang overhead and a voice, first in Cantonese and then in English, announced the resumption of the play. Laggards on the far side of the glass tossed back what remained of their drinks and made their silent way back into the auditorium. In her dressing room behind the stage, Mandy Plumpkin fastened her beautiful hair into two loose braids and pinned a white flower on her bosom. She looked in the mirror at her archly gleaming face and, leaning forward, pouted to herself.

'It'll take a lot to keep you down, my girl; make no mistake. You just needed ...'

'Curtain up in five minutes, Miss.'

She stood up on the squat heels of a field girl on a date and shook loose her part's Sunday-best, blue-black dress and petticoat. Her eyes, with only a little artificial help, sparkled.

'... some patience and ... to work on the right people and ... *voilà*!'

Geoffrey Keso was standing in the wings and grunted affably as she passed.

'Fine jarb; fine jarb.'

If a cat in a bone-dry attic had found the blind progeny of an absentee rodent mother and had the means to smile, it would have been of the same sort as the one worn by Mandy Plumpkin tonight, as she settled with her knees spread wide on the steps of a broken farmhouse.

She placed her palms firmly on the rough material covering her thighs, which, just as several other parts of her beautiful body, had been her only assets until the fateful meeting with Geoffrey Keso, and prepared to sow seeds of delight. Tonight, in her belief that she was no longer a supplicant at the altar of thespian fame, she had found the power to bend a thousand people to her will and turn them left and right; make them gasp and weep and frighten their wooden hearts into beating faster than they had ever known.

Alone on the stage and, inhaling for the first time the odours of living theatre, of the warm crowd, of her own make-up and the hot lights, of the boards and of a varied travelling wardrobe, she was transformed.

The tasselled curtain whooshed into the ceiling. On the far side of the stage perimeter's floodlights her audience sat, as far as Mandy was concerned, quiet and expectant. She gave no thought to whether the play was right and leapt the cultural divide; those finer points of distinction were outside her ability to reason. All she knew was that in front of row upon row of people poised to receive her words she was queen. The flush of her debut was on her and in its rosy hues she claimed, with some legitimacy, that her former aspiring actress's persona was a creature of the past.

'Five past eleven and he said he'd be here around nine,' she sobbed.

Her farm-heeled shoes were kicked fiercely away and tumbled in drumbeats over the stage boards. In a burst of humiliated anger she tore the white flower from her chest and cast it to the ground.

'To hell with you, Jim Tyrone!' she yelled and stamped on the plastic blossom.

'No, no!' someone cried out near the back of the stalls.

A middle-aged woman in a tweed jacket, who would have

passed unnoticed on the moors of North Yorkshire, shushed between her teeth. Heads twisted and necks craned towards the disturbance. With the audience's gasp and unspoken blessing Mandy Plumpkin swept on, although an unamused usherette with a torch and a preference for order spoke firmly to the man she suspected of causing the interruption.

An actor entered the stage from the left. He wasn't the almost youthful person Claude Halt had seen holding Mandy's hand at the first rehearsal, but an older, grizzled man with the appearance of one who drank too much.

'Be Jaysus,' the new arrival roared, 'I'll take you over my knee and spank your tail. If you were as big as a cow!'

In the middle stalls a pre-teenage schoolgirl looked quizzically at her mother and received a subdued explanation. A dozen rows behind, the man who had caused the earlier disturbance again called out, this time unintelligible.

'Ooo-oo-ah!'

'Will you be quiet,' snapped the tweed-coated fell walker.

'Take that then,' howled Mandy, striking the drunken intruder with what appeared to be the end of a broom handle.

'Again, again!' urged the distraught spectator.

The usherette, who was not of a literary disposition, or especially sympathetic to emotional engagement by those attending public performances, disliked infringements of her rule book and bore down on the nuisance with a uniformed security guard following close behind. The source of her annoyance was lit by accusing torchlight for as long as two strong Nepalese hands needed to reach over and pluck it from the cushioned seats of the third most expensive section in the house and hustle it protesting to the exit. The former Gurkha may have lacked inches, but nothing in his résumé hinted at an incapacity to overpower badly mannered theatregoers.

'I have no patience left, so get up from that chair, and go in your room, and go to bed, or I'll take you by the scruff of the neck and the seat of your pants and throw you in and lock the door on you! I mean it now! I've had all I can bear this night ...' Mandy scolded close to angry tears and before being cut short by the flapping auditorium exit.

'Put me down this instant, or I'll call the ... the ... Do you realise who I am, goddamnit?!'

'Outside is it, Mem?' the security officer asked the usherette, still holding Odergaard's CFO suspended in mid-air.

'Are you insane? I am the ... the Chairman of the Hong Kong Arts Festival Organising Committee and will have you both fired, just as soon as I ... I ...'

Throughout the years of a distinguished military career the guard had followed instructions to the letter, and now, if he had been told to cast this troublemaker into the street, or cut off his ears with a razor-sharp kukri, he would have done so without a second's thought. And, up to this moment, the usherette, who in some simplistic ways was the ex-Gurkha's soulmate, had owned similar confidence in the extent of her power, but the words 'Chairman' and 'Arts Festival Committee' sent a shudder of doubt through her no longer quite so tyrannical frame.

'Put down,' she said.

'Here? Right here?' the guard queried respectfully, not wishing to misinterpret an imprecise instruction.

'Yes, now. Put down.'

The guard was not a man to look for objectivity in a command; his job extended no further than seeing it properly carried out and like the soldier he had always been. He lowered Claude Halt gently to the uncarpeted floor and stepped back smartly as if preparing to stamp a polished boot and salute the regiment's colour.

'Now, if you'll get out of the way, I'll see the rest of the play and then put you two into the hottest water of your pathetic little lives.'

Claude's attempt to sidestep the ex-Gurkha was met by an opposing manoeuvre to protect the entrance to the auditorium. The removal of a noisy disturbance from the stalls, irrespective of who had made it, had been a clear directive and nothing since had persuaded its executor to amend his action – of that the guard was perfectly sure and he felt entitled to stand at the ready with feet apart and hands clasped behind his back and block anyone's path if they planned bolting into off-limits quarters.

'What is this? Are you adding insolence to idiocy? Get out of the way, man; get out of the way at once!'

The Committee Chairman grasped the shorter man's shoulders, intending to heave the impediment to one side by superior force, but the solid muscle under his weak and effeminate hands failed to move a fraction of a millimetre.

'You are mad, quite mad! All of you!' Claude Halt wailed and beat his clenched fists on the immoveable chest in front of him.

'If you are repeating that, Saar, I will be restraining you.'

The prospect of a biff on the chin brought the affronted Chairman to his senses as sharply as a cut in Odergaard's annual performance bonus payment.

Even as a schoolboy released from daily lessons he had found animalistic playground jousting full of dread and, instead of joining in and cuffing with the best, he slunk away to quieter places to cultivate the sly and manipulative character that, more than anything else, had elevated him to his present office.

Not that he had been a squeamish child. Hadn't he inflicted more torture on captive frogs dredged from his mother's ornamental pond and on trespassing garden felines as readily as any of the louts from the nearby housing estates? Hadn't he subjected a younger sister to the pain of pinched and twisted flesh that covered her pale freckles in welts? But the thought of damage to his own skin or his blood being spilt, or, horror of horrors, bones broken, reduced him to abject, bowel-emptying funk.

'You and that … that … she-dragon over there have a lot to answer for and you can rest assured you won't forget the time you crossed Claude Halt.'

Foam-flecked accusation left the former Gurkha unmoved. As

his record of facing down insurgents in more than one steaming jungle and flushing frozen conscripts out of their icy foxholes in the South Atlantic could testify, he was made of strong stuff. So, what terror could even the rowdiest Saturday-night reveller hold for him?

Claude reeled back from the Nepali's iron inflexibility with pins and needles induced by a brawnier hand impeding a dignified exit.

'Just you wait! There is not a single artist among you,' he yelled irrelevantly and hobbled away as if a pebble had stuck in the heel of his modestly expensive patent-leather shoe.

From the theatre's almost deserted front-of-house corridors to the chaotic bustling behind the proscenium arch was, in a direct line, only a matter of metres, but, so round-about and interspersed with fire doors and restricted access, Claude took almost an hour to find his way to the cast's dressing rooms.

As he circled the encapsulated auditorium he thought he caught the stifled rush of appreciative applause and, running through it, the rhythms of stage voices. The clapping, if that was what he heard, came too frequently for a truly knowledgeable audience and he pompously imagined the actors' frustration at having to battle through so much unwarranted disruption.

From out of the centre of one rolling sound wave he thought he detected, like a seagull's call over the roar of breakers, the rise of a plaintive cry. Wasn't that a woman calling, ravaged Persephone, perhaps, carried protesting across the Styx into the bowels of hell and damnation?

Claude hurried forward, swatting aside a barely obstructive ashtray stand placed for the convenience of stagehands relaxing between scene changes. Chrome-plated dish and support parted company and clanged in a shower of ash and filthy butt ends into yet another closed door. Entrance though this one, however, required not just an infuriated push, but a swipe card. In a lather of escalating frenzy he dispensed with a search of his pockets and kicked out until the hard metal barrier rattled in its frame and a face appeared at its tiny glass and wire observation hatch.

'Wassup?'

'Will … you … open … this … goddamned … door … or … will … I … have … to … knock … it … down … on … t … t … top … of … you?' shrieked Claude in a paroxysm of demented fury.

'Oh, I doubt if you could do that, mate. These things can stop a charging bull,' the unhelpful voice replied through the door's thick filter.

To the amazement of the onlooker and without further elaboration, Claude assailed the door with fists and feet flying and raised a commotion that echoed up and down the length of the corridor and into the street beyond.

'Ai, cut that out, will yer, or I'll have to call security.'

Another interview with the cruel mechanics of the building's administrative departments was not an event Claude wished to contemplate and, with the palms of his hands on either side of the window and head stooped, he subsided into a more conciliatory approach.

'Look, whatever your name is, I am Claude Halt, the Chairman of the Hong Kong Art's Festival Organising Committee and I wish … , no, not wish, I *demand* and have a duty to enter. There are things … important things you wouldn't understand that I need to attend to, so will you please, for the last time, open this door and allow me to go about my official duty?'

'I don't know nothin' about no organising committee, so you'll just have to wait while I check with my boss. Waddya say your name was?'

'Halt, Claude Halt. Yes, right, you do that, but don't take too long. This is not an inconsequential matter.'

With a parting look that could have been interpreted as 'You could have fooled me' the face disappeared from the window.

In the enforced delay, Claude's self-possession, which, in the three hours since dressing, had ranged through the whole compass of possibility, again began to wane. His wait at the door dragged from five to ten minutes and, as there was still no answer to his plea, he resorted, as he often had done, when similarly blocked in his purpose, to walking up and down and in this case back along the direction he had come. First, he measured out twenty deliberate paces, while assuring himself with each stride that by the time he returned the door would be open and he could set about his undertaking to openly discuss, yes, openly discuss with Mandy Plumpkin all their silly little misunderstandings and, after they were cleared away, to take undisputed possession of this remarkable woman.

If twenty strides failed to work the magic he knew should be his, he would try thirty or forty, whatever was needed to reignite the flame of his project, but, for now and being back where he began, he stopped short of the not quite deserted entrance from the auditorium.

'This time, this time,' he pleaded inwardly, as he reversed direction and turned into the last bend before the so far impenetrable barrier.

But, true to form, the steel door remained stubbornly closed. From the wreckage of the cigarette ash stand he took a furious lunge at the scattered parts and hoisted the chrome dish aloft.

Milliseconds before the missile and reinforced window met, Eric Manley's visage swam into view and, as quickly, ducked from sight.

'Holy shit!'

The launch of random projectiles at his head had become a feature of several recent encounters. First, that crazed woman in the municipal park had thrown her shoe at him, after being caught in a weird ritual other people might reserve for the privacy of their bathrooms, and now, turning an isolated incident into a trend, a headcase behind the fire door, who, according to the best information available, was trying to force his way into prohibited areas behind the stage, set about his skull with similarly spontaneous passion. For a man who liked to keep to himself out of other people's affairs, Eric's recently acquired knack of intruding at the wrong moment was becoming a habit.

When the long-drawn-out rattle of whatever it was dribbled away along the corridor's hard floor, Eric edged carefully up from his knees and took a second glance through the hatch.

'Told you 'e was a nutter,' the stagehand offered from a safe distance.

The appearance of a new, albeit partial, face in the window gave Claude a sudden surge of hope.

'Please assist me here,' he said in a manner lying uncomfortably between official and ingratiating, 'I've been attempting to convey to an imbecile in the theatre's employ that I am Chairman of the Hong Kong Arts Festival and demand to ...'

'Claude? Is that you,' Eric was stunned. 'I was told there was a maniac trying to batter down the security door. What on earth are you doing in there?'

'Manley, ah, my dear fellow, thank God it's you with your imperturbable reliability. Look, there has been a mistake; in fact, I would go so far as to say a hideous misconstruction. I have mislaid my card and have been trying to get access to back-of-stage, to talk to the players you understand, and some hired hand, puzzlingly oblivious of my role in this event, is being difficult. Now if you'll just unlock this ... this obstruction I can get about my business.'

'Yeah, yeah, sure; just hold on a tick.'

'I have to tell you further delay will not work in anyone's favour here. I am a very busy man and have been greatly inconvenienced and ...'

'Keep your hair on. Harry, open the bloody door, will yer?'

'After what I've been say ...?'

'Shut up and open it for Chrissake!'

'OK, OK! Bloody hell! You're almost as bad as he is.'

Propelled by Claude Halt's ferment, the metal fire door flew back and left a black indentation four inches long where it collided with the spotlessly cream plaster wall.

'Hey! What's the rush?'

'No time to explain ... matter of extreme importance ... further procrastination inexcusable,' the Chairman threw back before scampering along the corridor.

Over the previous two seasons this part of the theatre had become as familiar to Claude as the executive offices and loading bays at Odergaard Holdings. If asked, he could have recited from memory the various routes connecting one end of the theatre to the other. Anyone who had been involved in the festival for any length of time would have recognised him instantly, except maybe for those arriving late in the day with individual programmes, or the recently hired cretins from security, who, in addition to being totally uninformed, were a lot more trouble than they were worth.

'Procastin-what?' asked Harry of the departing figure.

But Claude was a man on a mission and, once clear of the hindrances that pulled at his arms and clothes like thorns from a gorse thicket, he set about its resolution with dogged ferocity.

There were two routes to the dressing rooms, one by the single staircase winding up from the far side of the stage, which, on performance days, resembled Hong Kong's busy shopping malls and their milling window-gazing crowds, and the aluminium escape ladder rising vertically to the next floor.

Throwing his leg over a sign cautioning use 'only in emergencies', Claude chose the perpendicular path and mounted narrow rungs two at a time. But, such had been his excitement since first watching the incomparable Mandy Plumpkin amble forward into middle-stage in her pigtails and with hands thrust so deep into the pockets of her cut-off-at-the-knees farmhouse denims that his heart could not have thumped any faster, even if he had run full tilt to the summit of a mountain top.

His head and shoulders emerged into a passageway containing several rooms used for production personnel's theatrical tackle and by players preparing for their performances. Although Mandy Plumpkin was the nearest thing the Provo International Theater Company had ever had to a star, she had not been accorded the distinction of a private dressing room. She, Doug Plat and the three other *Moon* cast members had 'mucked in', as Geoffrey Keso was fond of saying in another phrase he had picked up while travelling, in a manner Claude felt unbecoming for an actress of her standing.

With unusually heightened sensitivity Claude detected the sounds of padding feet and soft voices at the far end of the floor as part of tonight's crew descended the further stairs in the felt shoes and hushed tones experienced show operators found indispensable. Claude waited while the buzz faded away to reassure himself there was no need to get involved in yet another distracting conversation, before hoisting out of the ladder's aperture and into the dull sheen of subdued backstage lighting.

All of the rooms, except two, were in darkness, which, he guessed, was because they had been allocated to performers and performances from earlier in the week. He leant on each door as he passed and found several still open. One, containing instruments and bouquets, must have been used by last night's straitlaced South Korean chamber orchestra.

Without being sure of what he intended, Claude eased his way inside into the warmth and sweet-and-sour smells of decaying blossoms and the musicians' much perspired-in black evening jackets. The corridor's pale glow momentarily lit a polished cello's wood surface, several differently shaped black leather cases and a huge bunch of flowers lying on top of a large trunk, before the door glided back into place behind him.

'No woman,' he thought, 'could resist a tribute of that size.'

Groping and fumbling forward, until his knees rustled on dry stalks, he caught hold of the array in two arms and then commenced a reverse shuffle into the passageway with all his limbs supporting a mostly successful attempt at preventing yesterday's compliments from being crushed in today's unforgiving woodwork. A quick look to left and right confirmed he had not been observed and that his way was clear to the next entrance, where he discovered in the small font of a computer-generated notice, an announcement revealing this was the dressing room of 'Geoffrey Keso and the Provo Players – Performing *A Moon for the Misbegotten* – 2–4 February.'

'Huh! So why is Keso's name up there when all he is … is … a facilitator. He should be down in the offices. He has no place with performers, for goodness' sake.'

Mirrors and make-up tables surrounded the small room; outdoor clothes and costume changes were draped over hangers and stands or thrown on the backs of chairs; boots and shoes cluttered the floor; cosmetics, brushes and combs, nail files, scissors, hair-curlers, plasters and a variety of other implements and consumables, the use of which Claude had only the haziest of understanding, littered every surface. He was not at all sure that he liked the thespian intimacy that permeated the atmosphere.

What were these people thinking? It's as if the parts they played seeped into every corner of their lives. Hadn't he seen at the first rehearsal how Mandy had held hands with that uncouth oaf Plat? Getting into the part, Manley had called it. Where, Claude would like to have known, did confected feelings end and real ones begin?'

Claude felt the claustrophobic room's uncirculated air weigh upon him and he looked for somewhere to set down his cumbersome load. Next to one of the make-up tables was a clothes rack and on it he saw a yellow coat, the one he had bought Mandy during that madcap afternoon when they had chased all over Hong Kong and he, quite uncharacteristically, had spent more on her than he had ever done on any other single person.

The array of tubs and tubes on the table top were pushed

back and he lowered the enormous bouquet into the cleared space so that it blocked a good half of his reflection. From above the fading greenery and limp blossoms his tormented face looked out. His hair was not as carefully parted as usual and taking up a woman's comb with widely spaced teeth he drew his lank thatch into straight furrows reminiscent of the loamy hillocks in a potato field. He leant closer to study his appearance and wondered why his chin was so dark.

'Oh, good heavens; I haven't shaved today! What will she think?'

The question went unanswered for an hour, while Claude paced about in another froth of nervous energy, until Mandy Plumpkin, with Geoffrey Keso and Doug Plat on either side and a coterie of supporters, erupted into the room.

'Weren't we just too incredible? And the audience ... Ah ... they hung on every word! We were conjurors casting spells for children to build castles in the sky.'

'You were unbelievable, mah dear,' Geoffrey encouraged.

'Never have we had such a success, in all mah years,' Doug agreed. 'It is unbelievable, guys! And to think Ah had mah doubts. Ah take them back, Ah truly do.'

'And tomorrow, who knows?'

'Of course Mandy was good ... What would any of you expect?'

Claude had been at the extreme end of one of his pensive perambulations when the party burst through the door and, until he butted in, unnoticed by anyone.

'Oh, darling, is that you hiding over there in a corner?' Mandy said in tones of theatrical surprise that raised chuckles from her several escorts.

'Why on earth weren't you watching from front-of-house?' she continued. 'You really are a bad boy and I shan't forgive you.'

The joke was so good that Geoffrey and Doug and the gaggle of associates rocked in mirth.

'I saw every minute,' Claude protested. 'You were simply marvellous, just as I always said you would be. No one, especially me, could take their eyes off you until ... until ...' His concentration disappeared into resentful reflections of the manhandling he had received at the officious whims of security.

'But look,' he said, brightening a little and pointing to the lifeless bouquet pilfered from the Koreans' room, 'I brought you these.'

'Oh, that's nice, so kind. You really are a sweetie, but ...' Mandy paused. 'Were you charged a lot?'

Her pigtails fell back and she laughed and the sounds tinkled like bells in a snow shower, until buried beneath the blizzard of Geoffrey's and Doug's hearty baritones.

'You don't like them?' Claude was despondent.

'Of course I do, pet, but men are not as observant as they ought to be.'

The Festival Chairman in his desperation to please had become a bore to all except the Chairman himself.

'Time y'all to celebrate like Tyrone knows how,' Doug shouted over the top of the competing conversation. 'Let's find a place where there's whiskey and women who'll make us sleep till noon and leave no memory after. Where's it gonna be, folks?'

'Steady up just a minute. Mahself, Ah was thinkin' we should be eatin' dinner and goin' to bed before the cock crows. We have a long ways to go and don't want distractions before we are done.'

Directors of touring companies, especially ones from the Mormon heartlands had duties to uphold, to faith, family and community, and bald suggestions that these standards could be relaxed when no one was watching was something a God-fearing lay preacher and husband to Roth Keso could not let pass without comment.

'Ah speak in jest, dear sir,' Doug assured him. 'And had no more in mah mind than an evenin' of wholesome fun that none of us would be ashamed to relate to our wives and chilun when we get back home. But some small celebration must surely be due?'

'Then mah apologies for misunderstandin' your purpose. Ah was not aware you were still performin' in character.'

'What is the matter with you people? Do any of you know what you are talking about? You should be looking at your lines, not stuffing yourself with food and wine at midnight.' Claude's patience had snapped.

But if he thought his outburst would influence the conversation he was mistaken.

'Claude!' Mandy scolded from the seat she had taken in front of a mirror. 'You are being tiresome.'

'But I'm here to help you and support your career. What do you want me to do?'

'Look, I'm going out now with these splendid people, because I want to and because it's time you left me alone. My opinion is we should no longer spend time together. I am at liberty, you know, to go with whom I wish, when I wish. Do you understand what I'm saying?'

Mandy returned to the careful removal of her stage make-up and its replacement with shades fit for a night of subdued festivity.

Peremptory dismissal and the hardly disguised suggestion that other more important people dwelt in her life left Claude gasping and open-mouthed.

In time, he would realise that Joe Wong's inexpensive warnings should not have been brushed under the carpet with so much self-deceiving dexterity. His false hope had kept the embers burning bright right up to this last minute when all had been laid bare. Now, there was no place for sidestepping, because even he could see he had been duped, set aside, cut loose, thrown overboard, defenestrated, dumped. His mortification and despair were complete and he became incapable of coherent thought and action.

Geoffrey Keso had never really liked Claude Halt and, even

while striving to suppress uncharitable thoughts, he could not but feel Mandy's decision was quite justified, if expressed a little clumsily.

'But,' he urged himself, 'Ah still have next year's sponsorship to think of and the possibility of a record-breaking third visit to bear in mind, and after tonight's celebrity reception that's gonna need a mighty careful approach as Ah cannot rightly guarantee interesting offers would come from other directions to the Provo International Theater's doors.'

While Geoffrey wrestled manfully with his conscience and earthly ambition, Doug Plat had no such qualms. He knew what he thought of the Festival Committee Chairman and being a dutiful Mormon was not going to get in the way of enjoying a scoundrel's discomfiture.

'Wh'al, then, Ah guess we'll be on our way and mah suggestion is we take ourselves down to that there Oi Soll Mayo for some good food and local hospitality?' he said.

He took Mandy's yellow coat from the clothes stand and held it for her to slip over her golden shoulders.

As she moved from her make-up table the Korean flowers rolled forward and fell to the floor. No one took any notice and no one seemed to care.

'Then now or never it shall be,' she cried triumphantly, as if stepping forward to the footlights to receive another burst of tumultuous applause.

23

At the head of a line of crawling traffic, threading between illegally parked vehicles on one side and a high concrete road-divider on the other, a red taxi disgorged two crimson-lipped and thigh-booted guest relations personnel towards one of the many bars lining Lockhart Road. Freed of his load, and more interested in finding a new customer willing to pay above the metered rate than in facilitating unobstructed passage for vehicles at his rear, the driver inched forward at walking pace. Oblivious to honks and discombobulated catcalls from the acrid blue haze, he stopped to negotiate a cross-harbour price with a man in a Chicago Bulls T-shirt.

A route through the congestion, although posing some risk to Isidor Nash's thin shins as he sidled between a van and a minibus, saved him the nuisance of walking as far as the next intersection's traffic lights to cross and circle back to his favourite watering hole on the far side of the street.

'Where from, pretty boy?' asked a young woman with starkly contrasting black eyeshadow and white face.

'If you worked here regular, dearie,' he replied, as he swung towards The Cat's Meow club, 'you wouldn't be askin' daft questions.'

Without lifting her shoulder from the building's brickwork, she tapped ash from the tip of a cigarette until it glowed orange like one more sharp-pointed nail on the end of a serpentine finger.

'You live Hong Kong?' the girl asked, looking him up and down while knowing well enough the difference between visiting tourists and the unmoneyed flotsam hanging around Wanchai's bars with little more than the cost of several beers in its pockets.

'An' what if I do?

'Then maybe you not man for me,' she said with the sort of stare that could slice through lead.

'P'raps some of us don't need to pay,' he countered.

An unhurried draw on the thin cigarette sucked down and held for a while somewhere near the bottom of her ribcage replaced the conversation as a subject of interest.

'No more to say,' she said and turned to survey the passing streams of people.

'Bitch!' he muttered under his breath before pushing into the club's dim light.

'*Is love goin' out of fashion?*' a booming voice and thumping beat asked from somewhere in the gloom.

He waited for figures round the bar to take on a recognisable form, before searching for the familiar hulk of Anil Patel.

'*Who said it should be this way-ay? Ooh ah!*' the song demanded insistently.

'Food or drink?'

In the slow-dispelling half-light he couldn't tell who was asking.

'Huh? Oh, just here for a couple with my mate,' he replied. 'He'll be over there somewhere. I'm OK, darlin'.'

The face was becoming an outline and a perfect set of teeth smiled back.

'*Yeah! Love's not the same as passion.*'

The boom of sound reverberated round the room and glasses held by their stems over the bar tinkled as they touched one another.

Anil was leaning forward on two legs of a stool and swaying backwards and forwards in time to the music. A slap on his back stopped him in mid-movement and the stool subsided to the floor and his elbows to the bar.

''Ey! Wotcha! What's goin' on?'

'*Done with him and on my way-ay. Whoo wah!*' the singer yelled.

'Oh, hi! Nothin' much. Where've you been? Haven't seen you around?'

'Bloody hell, Stevie,' Isidor called to the barman who was busy tapping the optics on a line of inverted spirit bottles, 'we all like music, but I can't hear myself think in 'ere. Turn it down a notch, will yer?'

'Popular number this one, you should be knowin',' Stevie replied while parroting snatches of the words belted out by the canned songstress.

'*Leavin' the game to kids and clowns. That's my way-ay!*'

'Stuff me with the butt end of a ragman's trumpet! Do us a favour!'

'OK, OK, sweet Jaysus!'

The music faded down to below disco level, but not as far as a shopping mall's.

'If he keeps that up, we'll have to change our pub, uh? Christ a'mighty!'

'Sort of liked it myself,' Anil observed, before throwing back a last half-inch of whisky and banging his glass on the counter. 'Another one, Stevie.'

'You all right? Isidor asked. 'You look as if you've been havin' an early session. It ain't even dark outside yet and 'oo's that bloke leanin' on you; is 'e with you? Looks as though 'e started tossin' it down this mornin'. Hey! My old blossom; I'll have a lager ... an' make it a cold one with a decent 'ead, not like the usual muck you serve in 'ere.'

Anil shoved the inert figure on the next bar stool off his arm.

'Not really; came in right after me an' we were talkin' about leavin' HK and then 'e dropped off for a bit of a nap.'

'Leavin''? Your jokin''? You've got it good here, mate. Why you wanna leave?'

'Couple of things really; Dad's sick and my sis thinks I should go 'ome. You know, be with 'im in case 'e don't pull through and then, there's another thing. I don't 'ave anything to keep me around anymore.'

'What you talkin' about, then? Thought you'd got something good goin' with that bird your boss brought over?'

'Thought so, too, but she just fired me.'

'What! You been dumped? The great Anil Patel who's always tellin' me 'ow to get in there? Weren't you getting your end away whenever you wanted?'

'Thht!' Anil clicked his tongue. 'Want to 'ear a real sob story? Even worse than 'is,' he said, indicating the sleeping figure on the nearby bar stool.

Isidor took a long swig of larger that left a cream moustache along his upper lip and breathed in satisfaction.

'Ahh! First one today. Yeah! What's goin' on, then?'

'It's like this, see. You know I've been knockin' on 'er door over at the 'arbour 'otel? Got into 'er room by playin' a neat trick; said I was an electrician come to check the wirin'. You remember? It worked just fine and we started meetin' regular. But then somethin' 'appened. Sounds really stoopid, but what's a guy supposed to do?'

'You mean? Don't tell me you fell in love? Oh my gawd! Old Casanova Patel got stuck on the bird he thought he was pluckin'. Hah! Then what?'

'Shut up, will yer? It ain't no laughin' matter.'

'No, I'm sure it ain't. In fact, now that I can see a bit better in 'ere, you do look kinda peaky. Do you stay awake thinkin' about her; can't eat; forget to wash; all that stuff. You're a real loon and 'ere I am playin' the field just like you said I ought and goin' dippin' in everything comin' around. 'Ave you ever tried … nah! Shan't talk about it to a guy 'oo's gawn soft … might 'urt his feelin's. Aaahh! Ha!'

'Do you want to 'ear this or do you want to fuck off?' Anil was getting cross.

Caught between hoots of ridicule and another draught of

larger, Isidor choked and fizzy gobbets of froth spurted from his pockmarked nose onto the bar counter.

'Now come on, guys,' Stevie complained. 'This is an orderly house and, if you're gonna puke, get off your frigin' stool and do it in the gents, if you please. Are you understanding me at all?'

'That's not puke, it's ...' Isidor began.

'Be Jaysus, I don't give a fart what it is; it's not belonging on my counter. Now shape up or piss off, the pair of yous.'

Throughout the fractious exchange between Isidor and the barman, Anil had prodded a lemon slice at the bottom of his empty glass. He could not remember having felt so completely drained of gusto. In the space of just a few short months he had transformed from the careless, fun-loving waster taking pleasure where he could and with no regard for those contributing to his amusement, to an irrational sentimentalist whose day, once shining with light, had sunk into premature gloom at the whim of a woman who was once just a sensation but had ended up being a fixation.

Not that he regretted any of the bald lies told to finagle his way into room 2018 at the Harbour Hotel, or any of the subsequent unbelievable nights, but, now that he couldn't get her out of his thoughts and she had scorned his declarations, he could neither go back to what he had been, nor have hope for what might follow.

Mandy Plumpkin had been out and back into Hong Kong once since Anil first met her, something to do with a career-enhancing opportunity she had said. But when she returned interruptions to their relationship seemed to multiply.

During the first night, after Anil had arrived to assess the lighting, he had scaled unimaginable heights. Not once in any of his previous entanglements had he experienced such a tempestuous conquest, even while wondering who exactly had conquered whom. The crashing, shrieking and roaring as they tumbled together from bed to floor to the shower cubicle and back over the settee and table, left him dizzy and rapturous from her invention and, in the next morning's gliding lift, he sagged with the pleasure of treading the snows of what must surely be the ultimate peak.

From the second of entering room 2018's dangerous interior he was a lost man. When he was with her he was enthralled and when he was not he both daydreamed and night-dreamed about her. He stopped calling at Baby Loon's and on Anna Talaba and her friends almost immediately and the Inn on the Park lost all its former appeal. Only unscheduled visit's to The Cat's Meow and an often solitary drink saw him in his former habitat.

'Think I'll be on my way,' Anil said.

'Yer can't, not yet … I've only just got 'ere,' complained Isidor. 'At least you owe me a bit of an explanation before you bugger off! What 'appened? I thought you were goin' great guns?'

'Yeah, I was until … until … Yer see it was this part she was given that started the rot.'

Every second, since Anil's first visit to Mandy, had cut and seared its way through his mind. He could recount the expressions she wore on her face four months ago; he could relate every detail of the patterns and colours of her clothes; he could describe the way she held her fork and peeled an orange, when they had eaten together in her room, the way she crossed her unstocking legs; he knew her laughter better than he knew his own; he could repeat every word he had heard her speak and, if he had had the vocabulary, he would have been able to describe the texture of her skin and hair and the musky scents in the nape of her slender neck and between her perfectly formed breasts.

And yes, he had been in heaven until she flew off for several weeks and returned to the company of a bunch of out-of-town actors in preparation for the major gig Claude Halt had found for her, which she said would need all her concentration and take her out of circulation for a while. Several times she repeated its importance and he said he understood, but he still had trouble accepting how much she wanted to rest in the evenings.

Once, after he had heard nothing from her for several days, he had left a badly written letter at the Harbour Hotel desk, but received no reply. At first he thought the concierge, who was a disagreeable bloke at the best of times, had trashed it. But later he found a bellhop with the name Joe, although that wasn't written on his name tag, who said he'd pushed the note under the door of 2018. Anil had spent a lot of effort on the letter and he was glad all that hard work hadn't gone completely to waste.

The next thing he knew, because messengers have a way of picking up news, was that the play she was acting in was opening that very night, and congratulating her right after the performance was, in his view of their very close, call it intimate, relationship, a natural thing to do.

His conviction wavered only very slightly when he learned from a night watchman at the nearly deserted stage door that the cast, including Mandy, had left and gone to eat at a place called O Sole Mio at the back of Lang Kwai Fung. In the run-up to the production's staging he had accepted she needed to fully focus, but, now that the show was safely launched, wouldn't celebrating alone with him have been the way any woman would want to conclude such a wearing time? Creeping uncertainties started to undermine his confidence and he decided to follow her and set his disquiet to rest.

Anil leant his motorbike against a parking meter and walked into the restaurant with the savoir-faire indispensable to his trade.

'Courier for Ms Mandy Plumpkin,' he announced without slowing his pace or looking to either side.

The theatre party had been given a private room and, as Anil walked in, six glasses filled with champagne clinked in unison over a red-and-white checked tablecloth.

'To the Moon and beyond,' a voice shouted.

'The play's the thing,' called another.

'And to the Provo–Plumpkin partnership,' cried a visibly gratified Geoffrey Keso, through a cascade of extravagant laughter. 'Long may it flourish.'

'Hey! Mandy,' Anil called from the doorway. 'Can I speak with you for a sec?'

None of the diners heard him at first, although Geoffrey, who was seated directly opposite the entrance, had a clear sight of the visitor.

'Is thar something you want here, young man,' he asked above the clamour.

'Yeah, there is ... Mandy, it's me ... Can I have a few ...?'

Mandy Plumpkin leant her beautiful head to one side and asked, 'Who is asking for me?'

The messenger felt compelled to clarify his connection, if not to Mandy, at least for the benefit of those gathered around her.

'It's Anil. I wanna talk to you. Can you come out?'

Mandy's brilliant smile flickered.

'A fan wantin' an autograph Ah'll be bound,' Doug Platt suggested and passed her a menu card. 'Here, sign on this, mah dear and Ah'll give it to him.'

'I don't wanna signature; I wanna talk for Crissake,' Anil replied. 'Are you comin' out or not?'

'Mah, good man, that is no way to talk to a star and a lady,' protested Doug.

With the timing of the accomplished performer she had become, Mandy raised her hand to hush the conversation and turned to Anil.

'Then in that case I don't believe we have business together; please leave, so we can return to our meal.'

Conversation round the table stumbled and then recovered momentarily, until being abruptly extinguished, as a thumb and forefinger puts out a candle, in a final beseeching request from a young man at the end of his tether.

'I want you to marry me. Don't you get it?'

The dinner guests turned as one person and, while ready to

laugh, suspended judgement long enough for Mandy Plumpkin to take the lead.

'Oh! I say,' she said and once again the tinkling bells carried over the frosty ground between them. 'Is that where stardom takes one. Then we should be very careful about who we invite to share our performances.'

Wild laughter reverberated through the hall and the table rocked. Another cork popped and foaming wine ran over Doug Platt's hand and shirt cuff as he refilled everyone's glass.

'Wha'll thart must be the definitive declaration from a fan, mah deah. Ah doubt y'all will find one to say more. Let us drink to a new light in the firmament.'

'A new light,' they roared.

'And, if Ah may say so, to the fan who has followed us here tonight under Mandy's bewitchin' spell and who has confirmed what we all knew.'

'The fan bewitched by Mandy,' they cried with drinks raised on high and turned to the entrance from where Anil had bared his soul and since departed.

In the night and day since then Anil had not slept. After leaving O Sole Mio he had spent hours tramping the streets between rows of seemingly never-closing shops, until going home to his rough flat to watch endless television, but not to see one show from start to finish. Neither purposeless walking, nor midnight programming, however, cleared Mandy from his churning mind.

If he had not developed a thirst, the compressed easy chair might have supported his spent body deep into a second night. But realising nothing had found its way into his stomach for a day and a half he dragged upright in search of a cup. On the other side of curtainless windows the afternoon had begun its descent into evening and shadows from the hills were inching upward on the tower block across the street.

Three cups of warm tapwater and wet hands run over his face and dense black hair were not enough to restore his sparky insouciance, but enough to persuade him he was a little bit hungry. The table-top refrigerator provided by his landlord contained an apple and a half-consumed packet of processed-cheese slices. He took a bite out of the apple, but it was soft and springy and not at all appetising for a man who had unwittingly missed at least five meals.

From the dilapidated tenements of Western to Wanchai, where The Cat's Meow was open for business, took about thirty minutes. But Anil was not in a hurry and whether he looked with dull eyes out of a bus window, or at the rows of spirit bottles behind the bar, was of no real importance. An unrelenting ache under any circumstances, he decided, remained an unrelenting ache.

He hadn't been at the bar for more than a few minutes when Vernon Manley walked in and sat next to him. They had silently and morosely downed several drinks and, while Vernon had gone through a range of cocktails, Anil had stuck to whisky.

'Got somethin' to eat?' Anil asked Stevie, when the strong liquor began warming his face and giving his hands a puffy feeling.

'Chef's not in yet, but there could be some sandwiches left over from lunchtime if you're really starvin'.'

Contents of the midday remains revealed a number of colours, but Stevie was noncommittal when asked how they had started life. A dry bat's wing curl containing light brown paste might have been tuna, but the true nature of its origins, right down to the last hard mouthful, remained stubbornly unidentifiable. Not that Anil was going to be fussy; all he needed was food and whether it was fresh, or stale, recognisable or not, made no difference.

'Gotta get out, that's the only answer,' Vernon said suddenly, but with no apparent listener to agree or disagree.

Anil, distracted from the task of getting his teeth to meet through a particularly tough crust, glanced sideways. The detached announcement had come from a man of about his own age, who had been at his elbow all afternoon and slid from a more or less upright position into a despondent slouch not dissimilar to his own.

'Ay? Talkin' to me, then?' Anil asked for no other reason than that there was no one else near by.

'Huh? Sorry, no ... just thinking out loud ... things on my mind ... that's all.'

'You and me both.'

Whether out of desperation, or being so far gone in his cups he no longer cared, Vernon launched into a peroration Anil was in no real mood to hear.

'It's this girl, see,' Vernon began without waiting for consent, or to hear Anil concede that all men's troubles start that way. The entire story of Jintana and her extended family; the request for money to buy a plot of land for chickens and planting rice; the money borrowed precipitously from a shark in the alleyways of Mong Kok; the pressure exerted by Man Fat's thugs; the narrow escape from a serious beating and, in spite of his father's efforts to find funds to pay off the loan, there being no way out except to jump on a plane and write letters from abroad.

'What an unbelievable cods-up!' he finished.

'Yeah! Not exactly my problem, but near enough, so I know what you mean; doors slammin' all around ... a real pain in the arse.'

Before Vernon fell asleep on the counter and Isidor walked in, the shared hurt had produced a kind of bonding and the two distressed young men sank another round of drinks and had written each other's telephone number on the palm of their hands with a pen borrowed from Stevie.

'What a sorry lot,' Isidor crowed. 'Now, want to hear my story? Gonna make your gills as green as bleedin' grass ... You see if it don't!'

24

The Provo International Theater Company may not have flown back to Hong Kong on the wings of public acclaim, but, following the *Moon for the Misbegotten*'s final curtain call, there was no denying that this time, with a work of uncertain appeal, it had achieved extraordinary and somewhat puzzling success. If the ill-informed's tendency to over-applaud anything it could not understand was excused, what could have warranted so rousing a reception?

At first, and up to the moment of Claude Halt's summary dismissal by Ms Plumpkin, he had been ready to believe the entire event had depended on her and her alone, with his own shrewd and secretive 'bringing together', as he put it, of disparate and recalcitrant interests ensuring the final outcome. Most of the time, he was convinced, her exquisite shoulders, with his support, had lifted this rural players' job-lot to the alpine meadows where they most certainly never belonged. And, if she could achieve so much, clothed all the while in a farm girl's denim boiler suit, wasn't that just further tribute to her amazing ability?

'Beauty,' he confided to his inner self, 'is in the gift only of those naturally accustomed to the element.'

But, after the thunderbolt of peremptory discharge torched his wilfully misguided conceit, he searched for an alternative point of view to legitimise consigning her to the dunghill of forgotten performers. Wouldn't any moderately sophisticated student of modern theatre, he was now ready to argue, recognise her extreme limitations? Why, just take a look at her threadbare record of trivial involvement in the totally forgettable Cantonese film and a few boot and ski-mitten commercials, at an age when the cognoscenti would certainly question whether declining attributes could sustain her any longer.

Claude found himself wishing the play's performance had been torn to shreds by the weekend critics and hooted from the stage by fans outraged at its vile crudity. But yet, but yet, the evidence of his own eyes and those of attendant hacks and the sinecures on the Organising Committee, who basked in reflected credit and clamour, yes, the clamour that resounded in every ear, compelled him to accept his estimate was egregiously flawed.

But if anyone, in this entire lamentable business, deserved credit, it was he; yes, he who had shown the way and made the Festival possible; had created sponsorship for this most improbable company; had discovered the players and produced the leading lady, while the rest of the organisers drank champagne, bowed heads and shook hands and gave back nothing of any worth. The injustice was unendurable.

On the evening of the end-of-festival sponsors' cocktail party, when all the actors, dancers and musicians had left and gone home to their widely flung countries, Claude Halt was in an unsettled frame of mind. His housekeeper had laid out a freshly ironed white shirt to go with his eveningwear, but inexplicably he left an hour late in a yellow check suitable for a Sunday afternoon walk in Victoria Park, or a lumber expedition on the hills of Oregon and, lethally, no jacket.

Hong Kong may ignore poor timekeeping, but it does not forgive incorrect attire and when the Committee Chairman entered the Harbour Hotel banqueting hall in agitated haste and questionable clothes knots of invitees, clutching glasses and balancing plates of canapés, parted like the Red Sea before the wrath of God and hoped he was searching for someone in Canaan, or, at least, at the furthest end of the room.

Last year and before the illusion of winning Mandy Plumpkin had raised his happiness to scatter-brained heights, this same event had been Claude's greatest moment of glory. *Peer Gynt* was behind him without being a disaster and the various attending dignitaries and luminaries had gathered around offering congratulations on the completion of yet another splendid Arts Festival. The entries, they said, had produced almost full houses and continued to bring credit to the city. Claude's chest had swelled with pride as he rubbed shoulders with the arty, the influential and the well-to-do. But tonight, there were too many things on his mind for him to be at ease or to dress with due care.

After travelling the length of the hall he stopped with no one left between him and a mirrored wall, except for a gentleman and lady, clinging nervously to each other as if to caution important and unfamiliar people against expecting too much from those of no significance.

Between the reflections of the couple's heads Claude saw his own appearing as a stranger and not at all like the person who inhabited his bathroom, or the fellow with the unshaven chin who loomed above the decaying blooms in the Provo Players' dressing room. He rubbed his jaw and wondered how he had acquired exactly that expression and why his eyes had become so large, or his hair so rutted on his scalp. He leaned forward to get a better view and the nearby couple flinched.

'Pleased to meet; Mr Wu, K.C. Wu and Mrs Wu,' the gentleman said, pointing to the name tag on his lapel and then to the woman standing next to him. 'You no have label?'

'What?... Who?'

The frightened guest had hoped Claude Halt would be a gentleman and moderate the stress inseparable from a daunting social experience. But, alas, Odergaard's CFO was nothing of the sort and his detached monosyllables convinced Mr Wu that, to avoid complete shame, he should grab his wife's arm and hustle away to a distant and less terrifying corner of the living crowd where they could avoid speaking to anyone and get lost in reassuring obscurity.

As the two Wus disappeared into the mass of humanity the Arts Festival Organising Committee was simultaneously disgorged in a phalanx of stern disapproval not unlike a prison parole board or the Soviet politburo standing atop the Kremlin wall. Why, the unspoken question ran, was their honoured Chairman behaving so unsoundly?

The decision to bring him to book had not been taken easily. Direct questioning of a head of anything, let alone one in quasi-public office, was plainly a breach of every known convention. But, because matters were so far gone, they had collectively decided to act. Up until this eleventh hour they would gladly have passed word along through a succession of well-placed intermediaries until a relative or trusted colleague, perhaps, put a quiet word into the delinquent's ear

JBO would have been the ideal intermediary, but to the committee's enormous loss of face neither he nor his esteemed consort, Mrs Odergaard, had turned up and the task had fallen back upon them.

The absence of a key sponsor, from the Festival's final set-piece event, was disturbing, although, on an entirely personal level for several members of the Committee, an occasion to heave huge sighs of relief that the forbidding duty of conversation with the famously inconsiderate founder of Odergaard Holdings had not, so far, been necessary. So, until he arrived, they continued to circulate, mouthing pleasantries and tipping glasses and listening expectantly through the backs of their heads for the rumbles of commotion rattling round the entrance, should their most important private donor arrive.

But Claude Halt's behaviour, because in some ways he was one of them, created an altogether different dilemma.

His selection, for the not simply ceremonial position, had emerged after consultation with appropriate government bodies eager for Hong Kong's enhancement of its already enviable regional reputation, both as a premier tourist destination and cultural hub. Fiscal and management responsibility, connections to business, prior involvement with the Festival and even some knowledge of the world's arts scene had been evident in his credentials and promoted Mr Halt as a first-class choice. But no one had thought to dig into the man's character until it was too late and after his painful shortcomings had become a source of immeasurable regret.

'We ...,' the Vice Chair, whose bounteous jet-black hair argued bottled application and weekly visits to a hairdresser, not to mention crass vanity, began from the centre of a supportive assembly of dark-suited and sober-tied fellow committee members, before adding for clarity and, to emphasise the authorised nature of their joint communiqué, which he, as senior representative had the unfortunate duty to deliver: 'We, the Hong Kong Arts Festival Organising and Steering Committee ...'

In grave unison, the joint members nodded.

'We,' the Vice Chair repeated tensely, as if astride a horse confronting a fence higher than any previously cleared, 'wish to request, *must* request that ... arhumph!' He cleared imaginary obstructions from his throat and rushed at the hurdle intending to jump clear or perish in the attempt. '...You spare some time, only a few minutes, ten at an absolute maximum,' he hedged, 'with the estimable, yes estimable, Ms Fang from our public relations department who will share her views on correct forms of social comportment.'

From behind the Committee's terracotta-warrior immobility the Vice Chair called forth a heavily scented woman carrying a typed list of names in the crook of her arm.

'Ms Fang, you will know, of course, our Chairman, who we feel could benefit from your professional advice as it relates to right forms of personal ... ah ... presentation, yes *presentation*, at this sort of event. We are aware that tonight you will be extremely busy, but hope you will spare a few minutes, ten at most we said, I think, to provide some useful pointers ... hem ... yes? And if that is acceptable we will leave you for a while to get together and discuss. We will check later in the evening to be sure we have concurrence.'

With his responsibility wordily discharged and the residual tidying-up shoved into the hands of the PR department, the Vice Chair was anxious to return to his preferred task of meeting and greeting the city's rich and flashy. But before he completed his last sentence and took a step back into the enveloping warmth of the Committee's ranks, Claude Halt, whose mind had been roaming over other things and hadn't heard a word of the disapproving lecture, burst out.

'I've got it. Don't know why I took so long, but it's obvious … Just listen for a second, we can flesh it out later … Why don't we begin an exchange programme? In return for events like this … this *Moon* thingy, we can send Cantonese opera to Utah? If we can drum up big audiences here, what's possible over there where the population is greater, if not as concentrated, and artistic perceptions, while weak, are at least trainable?'

The prospect of taking a cultural offering, so impenetrable that it had become the preserve of a dwindling band of aging admirers, to the plain-speaking farmers and church people of Provo and its hinterland, was so unlikely that the Committee members collectively gawked.

Undeterred, Claude Halt warmed to his theme.

'We could even bring in, after a bit of orientation, I admit, one of their candidates for a lead part here, the same as happened at this festival.'

If the concept of a successful run of Cantonese opera in pastoral America had failed to ignite excitement, the suggestion that anyone outside a very tight group of steeped-in-the-medium devotees could simply 'mug up' on esoteric material was comic.

Inside her tent of drenching perfume the PR woman sniffed and sneezed.

'And carry pitch-forks perhaps?' the Vice Chair remarked unhelpfully, before regretting his frivolity.

'Huh?' Claude Halt jerked out of his meditative silliness in exactly the place where he had fallen in, 'That's just the problem with you people; never thinking outside the dots,' before adding in a worthless aside, 'No one runs by standing still.'

If the Committee, in all its splendid discipline and unity, had ever held faith in their Chairman's footing they could now unequivocally agree, without any consultation whatever, that he had indeed gone completely and irretrievably off his bean-counter's chump.

This was the moment when they should have huddled together and deputised the PR woman or a concerned and pliable relative, to take Claude by the hand and usher him into a pre-paid taxi charged with taking him home, where he could be held until such time as professional help was called to pass a verdict.

But, while a desire not to rock the boat prevailed, the Committee members allowed Claude to lurch from just-about-sanity to expounding aloud on loopy theories of cultural interconnectedness. The paralysis was complete until a waiter with a tray bearing a visiting card hurried up and murmured to the Vice Chair, who was more than ready to find refuge from his superior's absurd behaviour.

'Hmm, yes, I see,' he said and, after inspecting the card, added: 'Please take me to him.'

Adrift without their anchor, the Committee suits and PR woman spun helplessly, like disabled boats on a torrent flowing towards booming rapids. Belatedly, they clung together in the safe harbour of group thought, where no one would be held accountable, or have a searchlight shone on individual deficiencies.

'Creativity knows no bounds,' Claude was saying to astonished listeners as he slid back into the slough of madness. 'We will bring *Misbegotten* back next year and set it in Imperial Jeyjiang in period costume. Any artistic undertaking, if seriously undertaken, is legitimate and I ask, nay demand, that from tomorrow, we will put a new foot forward and cross the frontiers of ...'

Unobserved, the Vice Chair returned from his errand to meet the visiting card's owner. Abundant hair once so neatly piled into a black helmet now tumbled about his ears in confusion and, for reasons not immediately clear, his collar appeared to be having the same effect on his breathing as a garrotte.

'Gentlemen; Ms,' he croaked and summoned vacillating Committee members and the perfume-pickled PR woman to his side.

Glad for the restoration of order and a sense that someone was back in charge after the moments of incipient chaos, the group, liberated from the weight of responsibility, pressed together.

After minutes of attentive listening, the cluster broke apart, exhaled the PR woman, now shorn of her usual premeditated charm, and closed again, like a clam recovering from the ejection of a particle of foreign grit.

Ms Fang dithered, while the clam drifted on a tide to calmer waters, and found she had been cast up, marooned on rocks too proximate to the ranting Claude Halt. A pleading glance to the Committee as it floated away was of no avail, when, to a man, the suits turned their attention to other matters.

Edging forward, Ms Fang whispered words of desperation.

'Mr Halt, Sir. Would you care to sit down?'

'We will write our own rules, set new standards, break free from our chains, smite the Gordian knot, steal the Hesperidian apple, slay the Nemean li ... What! Who are you?'

'I'm ... ahem ... Ms Fang, you know.'

'Huh! Oh, yes. Make an appointment with my secretary.'

'But please, this is very important for you and the Festival.'

'When, now? I haven't got time; can't you see I'm busy?'

'But I must tell you; it can't wait.'

Her voice died away to no more than a stifled sigh.

'Well, if you must, but you are straining my patience. Go on then, what is it, what is it?'

'Better if you sit, before I say, because ...'

'Damn you, woman; don't keep sitting me. I'm perfectly fine on my two legs. Just get on with what you have to say.'

'Mmm ... OK, but please take care ... It's about Mr Odergaard, he, he's ...'

'Not here that's what. And after I have slaved for him for thirty years and brought him the best recognition in town, he does this to me and ...'

In a moment of suspicion Claude wondered if an announcement had gone out from Odergaard's headquarters about future sponsorships that cut the ground from under his feet and forestalled a discussion.

'Why? What's he done?'

'He's dead.'

'He what?'

'Dead,' she replied, but then believing her message deserved some further elucidation, began explaining the circumstances, in spite of her preference not to dwell on the indecency of passage to the hereafter.

'Last night ... heart attack ... at home ... family out ... no one with him ... found by assistant this morning ... too sad ... poor man ... much missed ... sorry, sorry.'

The entirely unforeseen news fell over Claude Halt like a shaft of celestial fire that burnt away the dried and shrivelled remains of an old order and left the ground fertile and ready for him to grow and flourish. He leant back and beat at the air like a boxer celebrating the unexpected overthrow of a taller and heavier opponent. With his painstakingly accumulated stockholding and corporate position, he was the kingdom's undoubted heir. No one could beat that and tomorrow, after the remnants of JBO's reign had been swept aside, the crown would be his.

Dagmar, although wedded to the benefits bestowed by her significant stake in a profitable company, loathed the dirty business of keeping it running and any lingering interest in the organisation that Sigrid might have held had been effectively expunged under the terms of JBO's will that Claude and the lawyers had put together years ago when she had first been in a mind to put flowers in her hair and eat plain yoghurt.

'Aha! Yahoo! Yes, sir! You can't beat that one, you old bugger. And now I'm on top and we'll do what I say. No more playing those tired old tunes. From here on I'll call the shots; bam, wham, biff, bonk, pow!'

He swung a right hook at the space in front of Ms Fang's goggling face and yelled, 'Zonk! And down he goes zoom, boom, bang, wallop and yes, he can't beat the bell, it's all over and the crowd greets a new champion, ta-di-dah!'

A tide lapped back across the cavernous hall and returned the wandering clam to Claude's feet. Incredulous members peered out through narrowed eyes as if the light was too much to bear. Ms Fang looked ready to bolt but was prevented from doing so by the delirious CFO, who caught her by the waist and slapped her on the backside.

'Ohho!' she cried, in a giddy mixture of indignation and pleasure.

'That's what you get for being the first PR lady to bring good news. But are you sure? Who told you? Is it reliable? Quick out with it; we are not talking trifles here.'

'I ... I ... it was the Committee Vice Chair. He can confirm if you wish?'

The huddled Committee swayed away as he approached, like kelp forests before an arctic current.

'Vice Chair Leung, talk to me; what do you know of Odergaard's decease? Is it true? Is it?' he demanded and aimed a gentle blow at the official's round midriff.

'Truly shocking; I understand the morning papers have the news. By seven everyone will know; a very disturbing note on which to end the Festival.'

'Yes, yes, I guessed all that, but possibilities here, my dear Leung, if you play your cards right. I'm talking about sponsorship for a third year in a row if I have anything to do with it and ... hah!... of course I will, silly me. In fact, I'll have everything to do with it, so what do you make of that?'

'Ms Fang has given you details, yes?' Vice Chair Leung enquired, 'Cardiac arrest; entirely alone poor man, so regrettable.'

'True, true. Look, I'm going to have to leave you. Company, investors and so on, people need to hear.'

'We understand,' Leung acknowledged graciously and with considerable relief, 'Expect our support.'

'Tch! But now you mention it, I could do worse than borrow your good Ms Fang here for some of that advice you say she keeps so carefully tucked away.'

'Certainly, certainly; we are only too happy if she can ... please.'

Claude transferred his grip from the PR woman's waist to her bicep and, taking her agreement for granted, bundled her across the banqueting hall and into the Harbour Hotel's foyer. Her discomfort became so intense she rose onto her toes and, while this lessened the pain, she achieved the appearance of someone enduring ligament damage.

'This place over here is OK,' he said, hustling her past a bellboy and rustling palms into the lobby lounge.

'Need help with this one? Joe can do,' the bellboy proposed *sotto voce* as his path crossed the Odergaard executive's. 'She smell good, no?'

'Go to hell,' Claude Halt replied to the offer of renewed freelance services.

Joe Wong shrugged, pulled his white gloves a little higher, but, not wanting to lose an opportunity to supplement his official wages for the want of effort, continued: 'Suit self. But still got number if need?'

Without fanfare Ms Fang was dropped into an armchair.

'You can help me here,' Claude began, drawing his thin lips apart in an approximation of a friendly smile.

A shade bruised, but with enough professional poise to spare, Ms Fang said, 'Crème de menthe, if you please.'

'Huh? What? We haven't got time for that, so if you'll just ...'

'Was my advice something you wanted? Then a crème de menthe will relax me while we discuss.'

'Dammit, woman, do you think I'm here for ... Oh, if you must,' he decided and raised a crooked finger at a waitress in a frilly cap and apron.

Once her drink was consumed and the ice cubes rested at the bottom of her glass in a green film she sat back and said, 'Well, so what can I do for the man on whom so much will rest at Odergaard Holdings?'

The turbulence of recent days, culminating in the stunning news of Jakob's death, had left Claude Halt trembling, and in an effort to steady his hands and mind he called the waitress back again to order a whisky and soda.

'And I'll have another crème,' Ms Fang said.

'Another!? Do you make a habit of ... never mind; let's move on.'

The possibilities of his situation were becoming ever more appealing.

'No, skip that,' he informed the capped and aproned waitress. 'Make it a double malt without soda.'

'And a crème de menthe,' Ms Fang clarified.

'Uh? Oh, yes, and a ... er ... crème de ... you know,' he said before turning to Ms Fang and continuing, 'Yes, I think it's safe to say I am on a satisfactory trajectory here where I will have at my disposal multiple opportunities for those who ... ah ... facilitate and support my endeavours. Do I make myself clear?'

'Not entirely, but I see a trend.'

'You see it is like this. Jakob Odergaard, or JBO as he was known in my organisation, had a reputation for – how shall I say? – indelicate conduct. Now, I believe, my dear Ms Fang, I can be frank with you. He was a man with unbecoming appetites for a leader in whom many people placed their total trust. A libertine, I am sorry to relate, who chaffed under what he saw as the yoke of respectability. Why, even this hotel here has housed his paramours – I use the plural advisedly – to the detriment of health, family and business. May I share an honest thought with you? I regret to say that the world and Odergaard Holdings are better places for his passing. Are you shocked to hear as much from a loyal and dedicated servant of thirty years?'

Ms Fang was not an ingénue; she had, in a manner of speaking, seen a thing or two and knew how business was done. She leant forward and fingered the neck of her blouse with painted nails.

'And why,' she cooed, having recovered from the shock of her recent manhandling and got into the stride of a clever woman ready and willing to bring opposite ends together for a price, 'would Mr Claude Halt, former CFO of Odergaard Holdings, share such secrets with me?'

'Simply because, Ms Fang, I detect huge possibility in you, which one day may perhaps, even in the very near future, light the joint paths of my company and your personal career – I mean, my dear, your ability to steer our corporate communications and take a seat on our board. I can't be more explicit than that now, can I?'

'That is a very generous offer and yes, I understand, but, apart from the generalities of my obvious flair and professional skill, what exactly do you require from me?'

'I have seen you operate and recognise the contacts you have in politics, the civil service, the media, most especially the media, and would have it put out, perhaps in tomorrow's first newspaper editions, that Jakob Odergaard was a scandal who brought disrepute to the organisation he led. You can add, although I do not presume to say how the press release should be composed, that with his death comes the once-in-a-lifetime chance, if you will forgive the unintended irony, for a man of integrity and upright character – I speak modestly of my own slight accomplishments in maintaining the company's financial position – to lead the corporation into the future. And I strongly anticipate that the forward-looking press reports, which I describe, will have a supportive effect on Odergaard's stock price and, incidentally, the benefits of board-status employees enjoying access to options, hmm? Do I make myself clear?'

'Thank you for your confidence. I will speak to my media contacts before leaving the hotel tonight and make some small suggestions for the morning copy, which, I'm sure, will be happily taken on board. I am a personal friend of editors in both the English and Chinese dailies and, as you have noted, benefit from some sway. And, after you have read them, I will look forward to our discussions continuing on how we may be of value to one another.'

Not only had Claude Halt and Ms Fang achieved common understanding they had begun to speak and sound like one another. She had not become like him, or indeed he like her, but they had intuitively found a setting in which they fused and created a distinctive argot that they and people of the same circumstance instantly recognise as exclusively theirs, in the same way as nuns in a convent or, more exactly, Corsican brigands bent on pillage and havoc.

Claude stood up, shook Ms Fang's hand and escorted her through the lounge entrance, under the distant but watchful eye of Joe Wong, and returned to savour sips of his double malt whisky. The morning, he thought, will indeed be the start of a new day. Who, in all the dust and confusion of just twelve hours ago, would have anticipated such an outcome, and who would have expected his star, which had once fallen so low, to thus be in such ascendancy?

As the last lingering amber drops touched his throat, he began mentally composing his message to staff, expressing sorrow while at the same time giving reassurance that the ship of commerce and everyone aboard remained safe in a competent captain's hands.

'Let me see now; how about if I begin: "Dear Colleagues, I write to you today with a heart made heavy by the death of our beloved Chairman, Mr Jakob B. Odergaard…"? Yes, not bad for a start and then …'

25

The finished note rather pleased Claude; in his judgement, it combined regret and sincerity in believable proportions, but left no doubt whose hand was on the tiller. There would, of course be others fancying their chances who would start jockeying for position, but they were gadflies, mere nuisances, who could be ignored or, in worst cases, slapped down under the commendable weight of the twenty-first edition of *Who's Who in Hong Kong*. Only he could offer the necessary reserves of experience, financial astuteness and insider knowledge together with, he added mentally with a smirk, share ownership. He was a shoo-in and the predictability of his appointment, communicated in the rapid announcement to staff, would, if the admirable Ms Fang played her part, amount to a coronation.

Claude's housekeeper, however, was not as sanguine about what lay over the horizon. She had known him for a long time and recognised every aspect of his flawed character; his obsession with detail, which showed in the degree of browning he demanded on his breakfast toast; the setting out of his toothbrush and paste on the right side of the wash basin at nine o'clock in the evening; his socks folded and lined across his top drawer in order of black, blue, brown and tan; his shirts hung with buttons pointing to the left; his cutlery arranged just as his mother had prescribed in lines according to the required number of courses, no matter how casual the meal or time of day; the daily newspaper placed directly in front of him at breakfast, but sufficiently far off for the headlines to be read without getting spattered by food; his shouts of laughter when someone he disliked got hurt; his bullying of those in no position to answer back or defend themselves; his frequent silences and his gleeful meanness and spitefulness for no apparent reason.

She recognised and disapproved of every one of his flaws, but, because they were unsurprising, she had learned to live and deal with the consequences.

'Better the devil you know,' she often repeated.

But, in the last few months, something had changed. He had become impulsive, volatile and, in her attempts to respond to the person she thought she knew, a lot was starting to go wrong.

On any other occasion she would have been severely scolded if his white dress shirt had not been ironed and ready for him to don the moment he stepped from his bath. Why on earth, then, had her assiduousness been ignored and why had he walked out to the Arts Festival cocktail party as if he was about to mow a lawn? Simply put, this was not what she expected Mr Halt to do. He was, she saw, in danger of becoming a laughing stock.

Before the change his face had been close set, with thin, compressed lips, narrow eyes and nostrils that breathed air as if it cost money he was unwilling to spend. But now all that had gone; his upper lip was pulled back from a row of off-white teeth; his eyes were as wide as if he had sat on something sharp and was determined not to flinch, and, although she had never heard the word 'dilated', his nostrils sucked in and expelled great lungfuls of superheated air as if he was a dragon released from a hillside dungeon and a thousand years of captivity.

She almost wished the man with the consistently bad attitude would come back. At least then she would know with whom she was dealing, but now she was coping with a person who, one day, was recognisable as his old dreadful self and who, the next – she was quite convinced – was not all there.

On the morning after the Arts Festival cocktail party, as she saw him through the door and handed him the same leather briefcase he had used when she first came into his employ decades ago, and a salami and lettuce sandwich, cut diagonally as he preferred, she could tell he hadn't slept well; nor, she thought, sniffing at the traces of last night's celebration, had he bathed as he ought to have done.

'What's that?' he demanded brusquely, as she held out the wrapped square.

'It's a snack, Sir, in case you are kept late at the office. I've put in rocket and cut off the stalks.'

'On a day like today? Preposterous thought. From here on I shall be dining on caviar and champagne, if not ambrosia and nectar; what would I do with common salad and, moreover, with working late ... hmm?'

The bewildered housekeeper took the statement at face value and wondered where such commodities would be found. In all her years of marketing for Mr Halt she could not, in truth, remember seeing any of them.

'In that case I'll have to ask you to write it down on a piece of paper, Sir, so I can show it to the shopkeepers.'

'Another time, another time; I have bigger fish to fry and can't be concerned with issues of household maintenance when Mount Olympus beckons. Away with your prattle, woman.'

On the ground floor Claude Halt patted the morning newspaper under his arm and decided that, from this afternoon, he would commandeer JBO's limousine and have one of Johnny Lau's drivers briefed to collect him daily, but for this one last time he'd have to be content with riding the city tram.

His habit of starting early to avoid the press of stinking construction and wet market workers in assorted hard hats, rubber aprons and boots ensured possession of a front seat on the upper deck and a place to unfold the *Morning Post*, which today contained the news he'd first read over breakfast.

'Ah! There it was again, right on the front page; I must commend Ms Fang for her efficiency, a little low down perhaps and only a few sentences, but world crises were always going on and getting in the way of more vital subjects.'

'Jakob B. Odergaard, founder of Odergaard Holdings, found

dead,' he read over a byline saying, 'Chequered history ends mysteriously.'

'Good, good, nice touch,' Claude thought, before reading on.

Jakob B. Odergaard, founder of Odergaard Holdings and an occasional art sponsor, was found dead yesterday morning by a member of his household staff. Unconfirmed reports suggest Mr Odergaard died of a heart attack following an evening spent with an unknown acquaintance.

Mr Odergaard came to Hong Kong thirty years ago and established the manufacturing and distribution business bearing his name. He was a reclusive figure, keeping out of the public eye while amassing a fortune producing modular furniture in subcontracted factories in Hong Kong and, more recently, China. While he maintained a low profile, his company contributed to the arts through sponsorship of two entries at the Hong Kong Arts Festival, the latest being as recent as this month. As Jakob Odergaard stood back from prominence, his deputy and able lieutenant, Claude Halt, the CFO of Odergaard Holdings, provided much of the organisation's business's direction and public face.

Mr Odergaard's reputation, throughout his career in Hong Kong, was dogged by allegations of personal impropriety, often assumed to be the reason for his rare presence in celebrity circles. In purely commercial terms, however, his legacy as a business leader remains secure in the hands of his presumptive successor, Mr Halt.

Mr Odergaard is survived by his widow, Dagmar, and an estranged daughter, both of whom are believed resident in Hong Kong.

The tram clanged to a stop several hundred metres from the Odergaard warehouse and passers-by stepped back as Claude Halt, after depositing a dollar coin in the fare collection box, sprang jubilantly from the front step.

'Yes, yes,' he hollered, 'game, set and match, bar the cheering, as an ace goes down the line and ... whap! It's over and the cup will be presented to ... your star player of the tournament, the one and only ... Claude the Magnificent, Claude the Great, boom boom Halt.'

The morning crowds first averted their gaze from the cavorting display until, unable to avoid it altogether, they stepped into the gutter and in so doing risked the only slightly more unpleasant flattening by speeding minibuses.

Once above the warehouse only Claude Halt was out of step with the collective mood of despondency.

'Cheer up,' he called to his weeping secretary as he marched past into his soon-to-be vacated CFO's room, 'It's not as if the share price has plummeted. And look, do this for me when you've got over ... you know ... that; call an executive meeting to be held here, in my office, in fifteen minutes and include all the top brass.'

The best approach, Claude decided, was to behave as if his confirmation was self-evident, indisputable. He'd get the lawyers and auditors, who made up the tame management board, to rubber-stamp the decision later, but for now getting the support of those actually running the company was the only material hurdle. And so it proved.

Throughout the company's history JBO had rarely hired ambition, contenting himself rather with those happy to do what they were given, for year after repetitive year, as long as he provided the occasional low-interest loan and paid salaries on the same day every month. His CFO was supposed to be of the same stamp, but, because he was the nearest thing to indispensability, his aggravating shortcomings – among them, independent thinking and uncommunicated absences – were allowed just a little more latitude.

The meeting with the beleaguered crew was everything Claude hoped, with participants overjoyed to find there was someone still manning the pumps and giving orders, when, for a few dreadful hours, they had all felt the ship's holds had become catastrophically flooded.

'So that's about it,' he had said, in conclusion of the emergency conference. 'With unanimous agreement I will take the role of acting CEO, for as long as the Board take to sign off my permanent appointment, and then we'll carry on pretty much as before – maybe a few changes here and there, but nothing that's going to alarm anyone. A press release will go out later in the afternoon; I've engaged an outside party to help with the wording as this is new territory for everyone. We will of course organise those little get-togethers to confirm key employee loyalty, as I mentioned in my staff announcement this morning, just as soon as the dust has settled. But with that it's back to our desks and ... ah ... keep up the good work – OK?'

Once the management team had filed out and gone about their daily chores the soon-to-be CEO called in his secretary.

'I've been thinking about your career development and with today's change I believe something has opened up, if you are willing to consider advancement. We really have to look at some of the dead wood in this organisation and that Carol Tung down in Admin is a classic case of stagnation. I really don't know how she spends her time, or has lasted so long.'

A close relationship with all who got things done was a basic requirement for any CEO and, for reasons he was never able to determine, the Tung woman had never seemed as amenable as he would wish and, besides, often seemed perversely attached to the late JBO. This, then, was a perfect moment to get her out of the way and replaced by a more manageable person. And then, in the interest of keeping his vessel ship-shape, he could get on with pushing a few more disobliging mariners over the side.

'Thank you, Sir,' the timid secretary bobbed, glad to be offered a less exposed position below the executive deck. 'Very much appreciate. Will you want Mrs Tung's file, to see how much notice required? Expect it will be one week, but should be sure.'

'Right, yes, thanks; good idea. I can see you will be very

helpful in the new job I've arranged for you, but a couple of things while they are in my mind. Give Mrs Chou a call and tell her I'll move into JBO's office by the end of the day. You can get my stuff moved over there and his can go in a box in the basement until I sort through what's needed. Then tell Johnny Lau I'll be using the limousine from tonight and one last thing … I need some lunch and, given the developments, maybe you should include a bottle of something? Krug, I hear, is good.'

His day was working out exactly as planned; he'd bulldozed his way through the vapid management team and made himself the inevitable first officer; Ms Fang was handling public communications; staff members were falling in line; what else was there to do to ensure his succession? He sat on the throne for sure and the sceptre was in his hand, but had he secured the kingdom? Well, not quite. He'd got the job, a sizeable chunk of stock was already his and he could afford to draw almost any salary he cared to name, now that the old man's costs were saved. But still, still he was not wholly satisfied.

The putative Administration Manager knocked and put her head around the door.

'Excuse me, Sir. Expecting you are very busy, but a gentleman is here to see you; says it's important. Wouldn't have disturbed you, but believe he is a relative of Mr Odergaard's, I mean … the late … Mr … Odergaard. Name he gave was Eric Manley.'

Claude had his feet on his desk, but snatched them off quickly and sat up when he heard the name.

'Manley? Oh! Yes, capital, send him in.'

Eric Manley had been standing a metre from the secretary's back and felt no need to be shown the way in.

'Sorry to burst in on you like this. Sure you must be up to your neck with JBO pegging out last night and all that, but I've got a bit of a situation you can help me with.'

'You need my help?' Claude couldn't believe his luck.

'Yeah, but only because Jakob's not around to sort it out. If it hadn't been for him keeling over, there'd be no need.'

'Then possibly we can be of mutual assistance?'

'Can't think of anything I could do for you with what you have going here; guess you're the next CEO and Chairman, too, probably?'

'One doesn't like to count chickens before they are hatched; conceivably my name would be on the candidate list. But in public companies, you appreciate, there has to be a process, for finding the best person that is,' Claude soothed.

'Forgone conclusion I'd have thought, but that's how much I know about business.'

Eric looked around the room and continued: 'And you'll get a better office; more space and furniture and not the sort of kit you guys make. His is real classy. Met him down the corridor a few times to give him the ... ah ... reports he asked me to help out with and that's more or less why I'm here. But do you want to tell me what I can do for you?'

'Later, later; there's no hurry. You go first, please.'

'Uh ... er ... OK. So it's like this, JBO was, you'll possibly remember, my father-in-law. To be plain, I didn't like the bloke much, but, so far as the family goes, he was in a position you don't get elected for, and after I got fired from one of my freelance teaching jobs and my lad, Vernon – don't think you've met him – got into a spot of trouble, JBO helped me out with a bit of work. There was no contract or anything, but the work has been done and I haven't been paid.'

'Oh, I see; a simple matter of cash. How much does our organisation owe you?'

Claude pulled open a drawer and took out a chequebook.

'Not sure it's Odergaard Holding's job to pick up the tab, but I suppose there is a connection. It's fifty thousand dollars.'

'That does not seem to be a great sum of money; I assume you are referring to Hong Kong currency?'

'Actually, no; it's US.'

The chequebook was returned to its drawer.

'Really! Then that would be a considerable amount. What,

can I ask, were you required to do in exchange for this … this … substantial payment?'

'Liaise mostly with your Festival folk from Provo and keep them out of trouble in Asia and generally keep an eye on Odergaard's interests … you know … that sort of thing.'

Eric found the necessity to wipe his flushed face and extracted a brightly coloured handkerchief.

'Sorry,' he said through muffling folds.

The acting CEO wondered what exactly Odergaard's Arts Festival interests were, other than the obvious one of signing off sponsorship funds and how they may be defined. Would espionage be part of the assignment and would members, or more particularly a member, of the company involved with Provo's troupe be the subject of scrutiny?

'Hmm, I see,' he said.

'And there were some other things the old man and I were hoping to work on.'

'Oh, yes? And can you describe them in as much detail as will facilitate my full understanding, being the company CFO and, as you have observed, your father-in-law's most likely successor?'

'Yeah, sure. It was like this, there's a guy called Lam Qi Fat; runs a film set up over in Mong Kok called Starburst and JBO was going to finance something he produced,' Eric lied before going on, 'And Mandy Plumpkin, you remember her? She was in one of Lam's films a year ago, before she got involved with …'

Hearing Mandy's name provoked a convulsion in Claude Halt's lower limbs and his knee came into violent contact with the underside of the heavy, wooden desk.

'Yeop!' he cried and clutched a throbbing leg. 'Thsss … stop, wait, you've lost me. What was your role here? Were you spying on Ms Plumpkin?'

'Spying? On Mandy? Good lord, no; what for? I was going to be the liaison bloke again, I suppose, and look after Jakob's money.'

'That, actually, is what I do, have been doing, for thirty undervalued years and, if you don't min ...'

Claude caught himself in mid-sentence. The entire story was beyond him, but instead of letting it and his emotions get out of control he had to realise Mandy and JBO were history and now he had to look to the future and the security of his realm.

'This man Fat, he may be useful to me. I plan taking Cantonese opera to Utah and, if he is willing, a film version could be made and distributed to a wider audience. But put that aside for one moment and let me come to the crux of what I have to say.'

He raised his chin and ruminatingly stroked the neck beneath. Several minutes ticked by and still Claude held back.

'Er ... where was I? Ah! yes; to step into Jakob's shoes in part is not enough. I wish to inherit all that he called his own.'

'Uhuh and what do you mean by that?'

'I have his job, I have his company. Tomorrow I will have his car, office and secretary and the day after I want the affections once bestowed on him. Do I make myself clear?'

'Huh! Affections? Meaning who, what? No one loved him that I know of; he had no friends, except maybe a couple of quiet admirers somewhere in the woodwork or in his not-so-quiet family, which, for the most part, actually hated him more than anyone could realise. Although Dagmar was a symbiotic necessity who's going to be in a lot of trouble in ... do ... are ... you saying you have an interest in that quarter? No, sorry, I shouldn't have suggested such a bizarre thing.'

Eric was embarrassed by the unexpected and hideous direction of the conversation and, if he hadn't had so much depending on the outcome, he would have apologised for the lapse and left.

'Ah! but Mr Manley, may I call you Eric? Eric, you have hit the nail on the head and if you want your fifty thousand United States of America dollars I require that you prepare Dagmar for my approach. I don't expect you to guarantee the result; that will be up to me to conclude, but I do expect you to massage her, metaphorically speaking, and open the way to my advances, so that when we next meet – we are already somewhat acquainted – she will be ready to respond favourably. Do we have a deal?'

'Jesus Christ almighty, what on earth are you asking?'

'I believe I have been quite precise in my request. Please let me know if there is any misunderstanding; any ambiguity; any *t*s uncrossed; any *i*s undotted.'

'Well, I guess not. If that's your price … I suppose I'll do it, but hellfire it's …'

'And one last thing before you go, do me the favour of a telephone call to confirm the ground is ready and that I may plot my course. At the same time, you may wish to provide me, or Mrs Chou, my new personal assistant, with details of your bank account? And if we are done, I shall say good day.'

Claude stood up and extended his hand. Eric looked at the pale, almost translucent fingers and wasn't at all sure he wanted to touch them, but a vision of Vernon being beaten senseless by Mong Kok thugs flashed on his mind's eye and, taking courage, he accepted what was offered.

26

So little thought had Jakob B. Odergaard given to the certainty of death that the subject was omitted from his will altogether and, following the omission and because the lawyers and Claude had concentrated only on financial matters, his body's disposal was left to the discretion of his widow. If Sigrid had been asked, which she wasn't, she would probably have said the unloved cadaver should be tossed into Victoria Harbour along with unserviceable refrigerators, dead cats and the detritus of an unsentimental city, but Dagmar, despite the turbulence of her relationship with Jakob, took the subject of his passage to oblivion and earthly disposal seriously.

Cremation would have been the simplest choice; a puff of smoke, a box of ashes thrown into a typhoon, and the period put to a bad life, leaving those that remained unfettered and ready to move on. Dagmar, however, wanted to know where he was in the same way as she had done throughout their marriage, whether in her bed or not.

When he was alive she took the view that, while conjugal fidelity was preferred, it was not expected, because it denied his nature. She was therefore willing to let him seek out the temporary palliatives he found necessary and to swallow them in squalid doorways and with whatever pitiably disposable women he found convenient. A casket under a slab of concrete held, for her, the greatest certainty.

In the past, when he had wandered, there had been only one condition: that, when he was done, he would come back, back to the person who had fought with him through the worst of storms and in the blackest of nights when the skies themselves were split by thunder. So, today, interment in the damp, worm-riddled Hong Kong sod was the perfect answer, where he would be waiting, impatiently maybe, but waiting all the same, until she joined him in the bickering and boisterous dark.

But until it was her turn to go, how would she live without him and with whom? There had to be someone, because of all people Dagmar could not be alone. She fed on conflict as others ate bread and meat and someone of comparable metal had to be near by to sustain her. If any prospect filled her with dread, it was not the loss of a companion spirit, but the absence of the outright warfare he had given her and which made their bloods boil with adrenalin.

With wealth at her disposal, finding a vacant plot in the crowded cemeteries of Hong Kong Island at short notice was not especially difficult. A facilitation payment here and a promise of preferment to a son or daughter seeking employment or educational support there opened doors a failure to plan should have closed.

The Catholic cemetery offered an especially attractive position high on the western slopes and above the sea and Lamma's shipping lanes. Johnny Lau, who could be depended on to carry out any instruction from the Odergaard clan however obscure, messy or unrelated to running the business, was dispatched to oversee preparations at the site and Carol Tung, another loyal retainer apparently, of whom Dagmar had not previously heard, was deputed to arrange flowers, guest lists and the family's post-internment reception without the slightest idea that she was just days away from severed employment. The new CEO, Claude Halt, could have interfered if he had wished, but he was completely indifferent – with the blessing of biddable company managers, seconded personnel carried out their tasks as if on JBO's personal instruction.

Only one consideration fell outside the control of the organisers and that was the weather. Late March in Hong Kong was an uncertain time between winter and summer when temperatures are as apt to be high as low and no one could determine much in advance whether to wrap up to ward off the cold or to throw off anything capable of blocking air circulation. Mandy Plumpkin solved the problem by dressing lightly and having Geoffrey Keso, who had delayed his return to Provo to attend the funeral and represent his departed players, carry over his arm her coat with the lining carefully folded outermost to protect its beautiful exterior from the burial ground's mud and propinquity of vulgar onlookers.

Geoffrey enjoyed escorting Ms Plumpkin. Her vivacity and attention to him since the *Moon for the Misbegotten*'s final night made him feel a fantastical twenty years younger than the stuffy father of five had any right to be and he was going to make the most of it before returning to the staid, but real, latter-day world of Provo.

Only the Odergaard family, household staff and senior company officers joined the cortège for the slow ride round the island's central granite peaks to the overpopulated public cemetery. In the first car Jakob's coffin, surrounded by imported flowers, travelled with professional, black-gloved undertakers. Immediately behind came a tearless and angry Dagmar, angry because of her husband's thoughtlessness at dying on his own without an argument on his lips, and Sigrid and Eric Manley driven by Anil in a stiff, rented suit that squeezed uncomfortably the frame and muscles used to freedoms of outsized T-shirts and jeans.

To the rear and in close succession came Claude Halt, who could scarcely refrain from rubbing his hands with glee, and others of his management team, followed by as many of the household staff as could be crammed into one stretched vehicle.

The cook had insisted her seniority carried the right to a seat without having to battle her way in, but, once inside, her generous proportions excluded, much to their dismay, two of her slighter, junior colleagues, who, not wishing to be left out of the occasion's romp, headed quickly towards the number 47 bus stop.

Along the narrow roads taxis, double-deckers and minibuses, delivery vans and sundry barrows and saloon cars jostled for room with the slow, sober procession. At one intersection, changing traffic lights separated the hearse from mourners and its driver was forced to pull tight against the pavement under a pizzeria's awning. A ponytailed waitress of about eighteen nodded genially through the shopfront.

'Could do with a slice of Hawaiian and a cola,' the assistant said.

'No time,' the driver replied, as he caught sight over his shoulder of the straggling motorcade rounding a bend.

If anything, the road circumnavigating the cemetery was narrower than those already negotiated and fraught with the complications of parking on a public highway.

'Pull over more!' the unsympathetic operator of a tractor and trailer called from his lofty cab to the hearse that was already squeezed against a flight of stone steps leading down to the hillside's cascading graves and the recently acquired burial plot.

Inconvenience to the undertakers was nothing out of the ordinary; this was, after all, how they earned their daily soup. Anil, although an averagely competent messenger, was not as experienced.

'Bleedin' bedlam,' he observed with some feeling and a consistent point of view.

With the dexterity born of long practice in tight places, the undertakers spirited Jakob Odergaard's mortal remains down a hundred stairs and onto a plinth parallel to a gaping hole in the earthy sward.

The graveyard, sloping precariously to the sea and, congested with tombs and memorials, offered scant standing room for the mob of spectators. Dagmar and her party and a few others who thought they should have a place of prominence threaded between the crush and gathered around the coffin and expectant grave. Above, behind a rail running along the road, clusters of people in curious and party mood looked on.

Two groups of domestic helpers from nearby apartment blocks chattered noisily and pointed fingers. A flock of myna birds, adding to the general commotion, landed and clattered over the corrugated-iron roof of a flower stall.

High above on the road Wai Pang and Budiwati, who together had brought the grief-stricken Carol Tung from Shatin on a cross-harbour bus, walked among the flower sellers and pedestrians.

Why his mother was so distraught was beyond Wai Pang's understanding. When the news of his father's death had reached him his heart and hands had turned to ice, but he hadn't fallen in a heap. Jakob Odergaard may have been his mother's boss for a long while, but was he that important and wasn't her reaction just a little too excessive? He was reminded of those incomprehensible demonstrations on television when North Korean leaders died and everyone tried to outdo each other in sorrow. But, other than a few superficial similarities, there was a lot of difference between Pyongyang and Odergaard's; if one collapsed, there was nowhere to go and probably nothing to eat, but if the other went the same way there were a thousand jobs available, especially for the sort of unexceptional work his mother performed.

So why all the fuss?

He put his arms on the rail and looked over.

A voice next to him asked, 'Ay? Aren't you that funny kid with all the questions over on the Kowloon waterfront?'

'Oh, hello. Yes, it's me, Wai Pang; what are you doing here? And why are you dressed like that? Are you another one overwhelmed by unhappiness?'

'See what I mean? There you go again. But if you want to know I'm 'ere on official dooty, not out of attachment to the dear departed, even though I worked for the old bastard and, for a while, shared some of his … ah … interests. But I just brought Mrs O 'ere because trundling people about is 'ow I earn my keep.'

'Mrs O? Odergaard? You work for Odergaard's? Wah! Really? What a coincidence, so does my mother.'

'Your mother? Good god, who the hell is she then?'

'Tung Lei Wei, you'd know her as Carol.'

'Carol Tung! Mrs Tung! Well, stuff me … what a bleedin' … She's my boss, well, not exactly; I do odd jobs for 'er now an' again. But I 'ave to share a secret; she and I don't get on too well.'

'You wouldn't be the only one; she does have difficult moods.'

'That, my lad, must be the understatement of the century. She's what some of us would call a regular old trout. But,' Anil sighed, 'she won't be troubling me for long 'cos I'm soon gonna be out of 'ere.'

'Why? Where are you going?'

Anil's reply was drowned out in the stuttering notes of a hymn sung over Jakob's coffin.

'*Thou wilt keep him in perfect peace, whose mind is stayed on Thee.*'

Dagmar kept her mouth shut and scowled ferociously at the faltering attempts to sing unfamiliar words correctly and at the ceremony's meaningless hokum. The whole business was ridiculous, but if Jakob was to be buried in Hong Kong some concessions had to be made. And who had chosen this absurd song and invited all these parasites?

'Sigrid, damned Sigrid, that's who it must have been. Just wait until all this stupid nonsense is over and then I'll …'

'*The darkness and the light to Thee are both alike … for ever more.*'

The widow could hardly contain herself; Jakob was hers and hers alone. None of these people had any claim on him whatsoever, except the obligation to thank him for putting daily bread in their whining mouths.

Some faces and names in the crowd were half familiar, but others were beyond her. There was Halt, of course, everyone knew him and his insidious habits; the infuriating Sigrid who never lost an opportunity to dig a knife into her parents' ribs; that ludicrous husband of hers who had never done a stroke of productive work in all his fifty years and his half-witted dolt of a son, Vernon; there was the woman from the warehouse, with a name that could have been anything among Wong, Weng, Wing, Ting, Tong or Tung, who had lost control of her body and was propped up by an extraordinary creature with a battered face and patchy violet trousers, as if he was attending a down-at-heel drag queens' convention and not a funeral; another person, of the same shape, height and gender as the one who couldn't stand erect, stood to the side of Halt and appeared to be making notes with her thumb on some type of mobile device, while giving off the most atrocious aroma, and then there was a couple – surely a couple from the way she leant heavily on his proffered arm and despite dissimilarity of appearance and age, he being old and as rumpled as a carpet slipper chewed and laid upon by a pet Labrador. But the woman, yes, the woman would have done justice to a duke at a society ball, or a football player receiving an international award. She had the most wonderful blonde hair, blonder even than Dagmar's or any Scandinavian beauty that Dagmar could envisage and a full, firm body encased in a black dress cut off at the knees that emphasised rather than disguised her shape. That was a woman to send any man mad and Dagmar disliked her immediately.

A creak and rattle from a hoisting device yanked Dagmar's attention from her bitter judgements to the coffin as it left the ground and swung clumsily over the yawning fissure.

'Grant this mercy ...' bawled a surpliced priest, the fingers of his left hand raised on high.

'Oh God,' thought Dagmar, 'let something happen to bring this pantomime to an end.'

The coffin jerked lower, and over its swaying rim Claude

Halt, with that strange grin of his, which seemed to advertise newly acquired upper dentures, swam into sight. Dagmar stared back with the composure and warmth of an image hacked from glacial ice.

'... O Lord, we beseech Thee,' the priest wailed, 'to Thy servant departed, that he may not receive in punishment the requital of his deeds who in desire did keep Thy will, and as the true faith here united him to company of the faithful, so may Thy mercy unite him above to the choirs of angels.'

'May he earn the justice of his misdeeds and burn in hell's everlasting fires,' thought Claude to himself, before leaning across the unsteady coffin to grab Dagmar's surprised hand.

'And, if you will permit my humble suit, I can help you to a better place.'

'What are you doing? This is not the time,' she bristled.

'Sir,' complained the priest, 'you are out of order and disturb our prayers for the departed.'

'Silence beggar,' scolded the acting CEO.

The poor priest was so startled he fell back and the crowd closed around him.

'Stop mocking me and the man who made you what you are,' Dagmar fumed.

'Divine, perfection of a woman, let me acquit myself of such a baseless accusation.'

From somewhere in the direction the priest had taken a voice cried out, 'Through Jesus Christ our lord, Amen.'

With a lurch, the coffin resumed its downward journey and crashed to a halt among the water and gravel at the pit's bottom. Cemetery attendants rushed forward, released supporting chains, hauled them free and spooned large cakes of mud into the hole. The priest, also free of his constraints, burst back into view with his prayer book.

'May his soul and the souls of all the faithful departed through the mercy of God rest in peace,' he said rapidly. 'The service is at an end. May each of you also go in peace.'

With his responsibilities complete, he raced up the several scores of steps ahead of the mourners, jumped on a parked motorcycle and departed at speed for the cloisters and tranquillity of Saint Joseph's Cathedral.

'Ah have been to any number of church services, baptisms, marriages and burials too, but cannot recall any quite like today's. Ah have to repeat mah dear things are done very differently here in Hong Kong; not at all like Utah, no, not at all, not bah any stretch,' Geoffrey Keso opined to Mandy, as he escorted her towards the road and her hotel. 'But with that sad occasion behind us perhaps when we get back we can take time to discuss your further involvement with the Provo Players, as Ah have some ideas that may appeal to you.'

A cold gust of late-winter wind turned the Lama Channel into troubled patches of broken light and surged up the hill slope and through the cemetery's tombstones. Trees and bushes bobbed in the unexpected blast.

'I'd like that, Geoffrey,' Mandy agreed gently, as she cuddled closer to his arm. 'But let me have my coat, dear; the sun is hiding and there's a nip in the breeze.'

She laughed as Geoffrey struggled to wrap the flapping yellow coat around her.

'You are a wonder to behold, you really are; the coat, black dress and hair of a goddess. Mah word, you really are.'

'Oh! Geoffrey, you mustn't get carried away. Your pretty little wife in Oota would never forgive you saying such things.'

'Hardly pretty, mah dear, and, after five children, hardly little.

Geoffrey's comfortable sides shook soundlessly.

The cemetery crowd had begun slipping away on foot and by bus and taxi, but Jakob's family and near associates hung around the grave to watch the last layer of mud patted down. As Dagmar turned away, she saw the wildly fluttering yellow coat and appeared to search for a connection.

The squint she had directed at the amused actress circled round to Claude Halt.

'Are you familiar with that garment?' she demanded.

Claude followed the direction indicated by her outstretched index finger.

'Hmm ... I don't recollect straight away,' he equivocated. 'Let me think now.'

'Don't bother,' Dagmar announced in a moment of unerring female intuition, 'I'll tell you. You, you were in that boutique. I heard you, I didn't see you, but I heard you at the back and you damn well bought it for her from right under my nose. Well, this is your reward ...'

The right hooks practised by Claude Halt at the Harbour Hotel banqueting hall and on the tramway were mere shadows, wisps, powder-puffs compared to the blow that landed on his ear and shook his wits until tiny blue dots darted over his vision like unseasonal snowflakes.

'There now, make of that what you will,' she stormed before stumping off towards her waiting car.

'Angel!' drooled Claude, 'was ever there such a woman as that one? I will lie with her or die for her.'

Behind him Eric and Vernon exchanged glances. Claude's penchant for theatrical drama had got completely out of hand.

Suspecting the moment was as propitious as it was ever likely to be and that time from here on could only take his project downhill, Eric stepped forward.

'I'm glad you feel you are making progress in the little matter we've discussed, so if it's all right by you and I wouldn't be seen as being too forward on the wrong occasion, can I call on you, say, tomorrow, to pick up the small fee we agreed?'

'Call my secretary Chou in the morning,' Claude said, still clutching his scarlet ear. 'Tomorrow I shall be in the vein. I promise you, I shall be in the vein. What's the time?'

Eric pulled back his cuff. 'Somewhat after eleven, why?'

'Then I must be gone,' Claude replied and limped off up the hill.

'Mr Halt, Mr Halt,' the lady with the mobile device called,

running after the acting CEO and stumbling on her high heels. 'I'd like to check my notes with you for the papers before you leave … Mr Halt, Mr Halt.'

'There must be something in the air-conditioning at that warehouse that sends everyone stark starring cuckoo,' Sigrid observed drily. 'Ah, well, while genuine people exist out there I know what I should be doing.'

The last few mourners were making their way to the railings on the perimeter road. Sigrid held back for a woman, who appeared to be in great distress, and her partner. As the couple passed the woman looked up and Sigrid recognised her.

'Is that you … Carol? Remember me; we met at Pak Tam Au. I'm Sigrid; in different clothes, but still Sigrid. How are you? You look awfully stressed. Were you a friend of my father's?'

'Ah, yes, sorry. Not feeling well. Your father, Jakob? Had no idea; such a good man.'

Whatever the helter-skelter ordeals and charms of the last few months had been, Mr Odergaard – JBO, Jakob – went to his grave not just with Carol Tung's heart somewhere about him, but also a sizeable part of her soul. And now there was not so much as a smile on a faded photograph for her to remember him by.

'Perhaps you weren't that close; he was not always as good as we'd like. Is this your husband … I never imagined him to be quite so … so …?'

'So young? So 'andsome? An' what would your name be, sweet'eart?' Isidor asked impertinently.

'That's not quite what I had in mind, but let it pass. But you had a son, I remember; is he here, too?'

A hand holding a wet tissue gestured at the railing and a teenage boy waved back. Isidor strained to make out the figure.

'I dunno about 'er, but I ain't got no son and him there … especially that one, ain't my son. In fact, look kiddo somethin' just came up and I'm goin' to 'ave to leave you 'ere with this fine upstanding young lady an' go an' see a man about a dog, if you don't mind.'

Without further embellishment Isidor skipped over the graves, knocking flower holders and incense tapers aside as he ran and made off through an exit at the bottom of the hill. Renewed weeping engulfed Carol Tung's quivering frame and Sigrid threw an arm round the shaking shoulders to guide her to the place where the boy had been waving.

From their vantage point on the railings Anil and Wai Pang had seen the strange disorders at the graveside: Dagmar's infuriated progression up the steps into the unwanted presence of a coterie of wealthy businessmen – if the quality of their shoe leather and watches was anything to go by – who were eager to convey the usual homilies near strangers offer in moments of other people's tragic loss; Mandy's golden departure in the arms of Geoffrey Keso and, finally, the precipitous flight of Isidor Nash through a distant gate in his sadly mutilated, but still unmistakable, violet trousers.

At intervals Anil drew his hands over his face in disbelief.

'Do you know many of these people?' Wai Pang asked.

'You would be amazed just how many have crossed my path and left a big dent in my head, and that's just why I'm goin' to leave and, if you take my advice, young man, you'll take this opportunity to do a bit of travellin' yourself and come with me and see the world. This is the right time of life, when you 'ave no responsibilities.'

'My mother wouldn't like it, I'm afraid.

'If you want to know what I think, I'd say your ma was in no position to pass any sort of opinion seein' how she's lost her rag over the bloke in the box down there and is hangin' out with the biggest scumbag this side of Putney Town Hall.'

'Isidor is not so bad; he taught me a thing or two.'

'Oh, is that so? I dread to think what you picked up from 'im that can be discussed in a public place.'

'He said nice things about my drawings, when he was coaching football.'

'He said what? Take my word for it, Isidor Nash is one of

nature's wankers and ... and he don't know nothin' about football.'

'What's a wanker?'

'Bleedin' Christ almighty, I don't believe it.'

Down below in the cemetery the discourse drew to a close and Dagmar renewed her fiery passage up the steps, to be hindered at the exit by the slow movement of Carol Tung and Sigrid.

'Come on!' she barked. 'I haven't got all day.'

'Mother! That's quite unnecessary; just wait a minute, will you? We are almost there.'

'For the love of Jesus, this has to be my worst day ever.'

'I expect it is; your husband has just been buried, remember?'

'Any more quips from you, my girl, and I'll ... I'll ...'

'What? Cut me out of your will? I thought you'd done that a dozen times already.'

From the knot of noisy domestic helpers Budiwati, who had discovered some common ground and the chance to gossip about employers, or, more precisely, about her employer and the conditions that beset her, hurried up with some red-hot news that needed instant revelation.

'Guess what,' she called before she was within conversational distance. 'Guess who I've just met? Ligaya! I thought I'd seen her before, but of course I had no idea who she was until this minute.'

Anil and Wai Pang looked back without registering any knowledge of whom, or what, Ligaya might be.

'Tch, your mum might know. Ligaya works over there in Sai Kung – nice place that is – for Mr Odergaard's daughter and her husband; I've seen him around too.'

'That's me, I'm the daughter,' said Sigrid as she stepped onto the pavement. 'And right behind me is ... "Mum". I'd ask her if she knows, but I don't think she's up to it right now. Can you get her home?'

Treading on Sigrid and Carol Tung's heels, Dagmar exploded into view.

'Driver!' she bellowed.

'And that's me; I'm on my way,' said Anil, running to open the car door. 'And if you want to take me up on that idea, young fella, give me a call. There're plenty of design schools around London. Could be the place to make your name.'

Like fallen leaves blown by winter's chill winds the last few people, except two, scattered and disappeared. On the pavement in front of the flower stalls a vendor kicked a few crushed leaves into the gutter and chased away a dog preparing to raise its leg on the tarpaulins covering his stacked planters and bits of broken masonry used for patching pathways between the burial plots. Another funeral had come and gone, but there'd be another one tomorrow.

On the steps lower down in the cemetery Eric and Vernon sat and watched container ships passing through the Lamma Channel on their way to and from the port on Kowloon Peninsula.

'Glad that's over,' remarked Eric.

'Yeah, good job people don't die all the time.'

'Yeah, that'd be a real pain.'

Below, an inbound ship swung away to its left and slowed to a stop on the rippling waters. A flurry of smaller boats, lighters and derricks put off from the shore and, like hungry piglets around a sow, took from her what she had to give.

'What happens now?'

'Dunno … but I fancy a beer.'

'Yeah, me too.'

A shadow passed over their heads and a hoarse call sounded from among the jumble of tombstones.

'Ark! Ark!'

'What's that?' Vernon asked.

'Dunno, magpie or a jackdaw maybe.'

'Only one?'

'There's another, look – a magpie and his mate.'

'Well, that's OK then.'

The wind dropped again and the sun's rays, reflected from the stone hills behind, were now hot on their backs.

'What're you going to do about Jintana?'

'Been thinking about that. Depends ... Reckon Claude's going to cough up?'

'Yeah, I reckon.'

'Then I'll pay off Qi Fat and go and live with her in Thailand.'

'Is that what she wants?'

'She'd rather get married, but I want to see how things are first. Might not enjoy the country, extended family, you know, all that sort of stuff.'

'Yeah, I know.'

'Wanna get that beer, then?'

'Yeah.'

A taxi pulled up as they left the cemetery and the driver wound down a window.

'Where go?' he called.

'Lockhart Road,' Eric replied. 'And then we can take it from there.'

Acknowledgements

There is little achieved entirely alone, even something as solitary as book authorship, which at a minimum requires the patience and encouragement of family and friends. My dear wife Del provided the environment; Judy Trusdell and Kate Williamson contributed their readings and whoops of delight; my sister Nan, who knows a comma from a semi-colon, kept the grammar more or less straight and my son Andrew, my fiercest critic of all, stopped me from falling off the rails. And at Book Guild, Joanna Bentley, Robert Anderson, Kieran Hood and Janet Wrench pulled everything together. My grateful thanks to all.